PRAISE FOR FERRETT STEINMETZ

"Do you like magic? Do you like drugs? Donut-based psychological theories? Video games? Do you like *paperwork*!? Read this book!"
Ann Leckie, author of Ancillary Justice *and winner of the Hugo, Nebula and Arthur C Clarke Awards*

"*The Flux* is the best kind of sequel: bigger, deeper, scarier, funner. The emotional journey it takes the reader on is just as thrilling as the jaw-dropping wonders of videogamemancy and bureaucramancy. With the 'Mancer series, Ferrett Steinmetz has achieved something rare in contemporary fantasy: a world that feels both truer and more magical than our own."
Ken Liu, winner of the Nebula, Hugo, and World Fantasy Awards

"*Flex* is a real gem – sharp, weird, and wildly innovative. It zigs when you think it'll zag, then tricks you into screaming when you're ready to laugh out loud. So drop everything and settle in for the night – because once you open this one, you're not going anywhere."
Cherie Priest, award-winning author of Maplecroft

"Big ideas, epic thrills, and an unlikely paper-pushing hero you'll never forget. Just when you think you know what's next, the book levels up spectacularly."
John Scott Tynes, author of Delta Green: Strange Authorities

"Amazing. I have literally never read a book like this. Read this NOW, if only to be forced to turn the page wondering what the hell Steinmetz is going to come up with next."
Mur Lafferty, award-winning author of The Shambling Guide to New York

"*Flex* is hot, inventive, and exciting. A real joyride of a story … a whole new kind of magic and a whole new ballgame. Totally recommended."
Seanan McGuire, winner of the John W Campbell Award and Hugo-nominated auth

FERRETT STEINMETZ

Fix

ANGRY
ROBOT

ANGRY ROBOT
An imprint of Watkins Media Ltd

Lace Market House,
54-56 High Pavement,
Nottingham,
NG1 1HW
UK

angryrobotbooks.com
twitter.com/angryrobotbooks
Donuts

An Angry Robot paperback original 2016
1

A catalogue record for this book is available from the British Library.

ISBN 978 0 85766 572 0
EBook ISBN 978 0 85766 574 4

Set in Meridien by Epub Services.
Printed and bound in the UK by 4edge Limited.

*To Erin, my beautifully
bold trailblazer*

*And to Amy, my entertainingly
excellent experimenter*

*I'd like to tell you girls that parenting
isn't quite this hard*

But it is

PART I

Dressing up in Costumes,
Playing Silly Games

ONE

Warriors, Come Out to Play

The Morehead Youth Soccer League met outside the local Wendy's before heading to the first scrimmage of the season, so the kids could load up on Frosties while their parents scrawled out their kids' league applications. The coach sat regally in her red vinyl booth, the parents lining up to place their forms before her; she scrutinized the waivers to ensure the kids' emergency contacts were duly filled in.

Statistically speaking, Paul thought, Morehead was the safest place in America for Aliyah to pretend to be a normal child.

She'd begged him: *I can keep my magic under control, Dad. I don't even* want *to do magic, I swear! I know your political rallies are important, they're making the world safe for us 'mancers, but... nobody takes their kids to a speech that ends in tear gas and SMASH squadrons. We're always on the run, so I hardly ever meet anyone my own age – and when I do, they never see me, just my magic.*

Can't I play soccer? In disguise? So I can have a social life somewhere?

He'd remind her how badly the government wanted to capture her, to capture *all* of them, and that the pro-'mancer rallies were only safe because he and his Project Mayhem allies planned them out months in advance. Showing up in hostile territory, among families who hadn't been vetted, with only a handful of bodyguards to protect them? That could get them captured and brainwashed. And Aliyah would go quiet and say she understood, but...

9

Late at night, he'd see her holed up under the covers with an iPad, watching video blogs of teenaged girls' manicure tutorials. She'd trace her fingertips across the screen, whispering their words back to them fondly, as if speaking *like* them created a connection that substituted for being *with* them.

On Aliyah's thirteenth birthday, Paul and Imani had agreed to let her try out for a soccer league.

She'd hugged him for an hour.

Still, Paul had used his bureaucromancy to triangulate the neighborhoods located furthest away from SMASH garrisons; he broke into government registries to find the cities with the lowest numbers of registered anti-'mancer weaponholders, comparing his population density charts against anti-'mancer polls.

Ultimately, he had narrowed his choice down to one of seven cities where Aliyah was least likely to be kidnapped if her magic showed. He then spent another three weeks mired in deep analysis before Valentine had finally thrown a dart at his map and picked the closest safe town.

Morehead, Kentucky, it was.

Still, as his wife Imani pushed him in through the door of the Wendy's, he felt uneasy leaving Aliyah in front with the other girls. She'd used her videogamemancy to reskin herself, hiding her burn scars to look like any other exuberant young black teenaged girl, but had refused to change her wild tangled curls.

"Those curls are *me*, Dad," she'd told him. "I'll hide my magic – but I won't change my skin color or my hair. The girls there have to see some of who I *really* am – or we might as well not be friends at all, right?"

She *was* right. But those curls were routinely plastered on the *New York Times*, her picture placed next to every op-ed asking whether 'mancy should be regulated instead of simply making 'mancers illegal. Aliyah was the youngest 'mancer in what remained of the world – and though he'd tried hard to convince America that he and his daughter were human beings, worthy of the Bill of Rights, he'd barely budged the needle away from "brainwash them all."

One of the girls stopped bouncing a soccer ball and moved to talk to Aliyah. Paul froze: maybe this kid had recognized Aliyah's hair. Maybe Aliyah would forget to introduce herself by her fake name. Maybe a parent would...

"Did we really need the wheelchair?" Imani whispered, as she pushed Paul through the entryway.

As expected, people turned to stare when the handicapped person showed up; Paul tugged his hat down, hiding from their pity.

"You *can* walk, you know," Imani told him pointedly.

"I can limp." Paul wiggled his artificial foot, hidden beneath layers of videogame pseudo-skin; the disguise not only covered his bladelike titanium foot with a spongy sneaker, but it masked his normal Greek swarthiness beneath a dark African-American skin tone that matched Aliyah's natural look. "If they see a girl with *those* infamous curls, accompanied by a father with *that* infamous limp, they'll know who we are."

Imani removed his hat to ruffle his hair. "This is a small town. They won't expect the world's most dangerous 'mancers to show up here. Even if they did, you're now disguised as black instead of Greek – and though I remain gloriously black, these itchy wrinkles you have festooned me with make me look a decade older. All that'll give Aliyah away today is a father who's so tensed for incoming SMASH squadrons he'll set everyone else on edge... so may I suggest you lighten the hell up?"

He smiled. Imani always cleaved through his bullshit. So did Valentine.

That was why, he supposed, Imani was his wife and Valentine was his best friend.

"I'll try," he promised. She steered him closer to the coach, who spoke animatedly with a mother who she obviously knew from previous seasons.

"You made your best plans. Now pack away that paranoia! Look, we're getting in line to file paperwork! What better way could you spend a day?" She turned to Valentine. "Speaking of enjoying the day, will you *ever* look up from your phone?"

Unlike Paul's complete makeover, Valentine hadn't disguised

herself overmuch – she'd pointedly reskinned her *Super Mario* tattoos with gratuitous Confederate flags and Dixie guns, and exchanged her usual darkly gothic cleavage-baring dresses for cut-off Daisy Dukes and a low-cut Charlie Daniels T-shirt, but she was still a curvy, hefty brunette. The local fathers snuck guilty glances as she swivel-hipped by.

Though it was a little weird seeing her without her boyfriend Robert at her side.

Valentine walked up to them, playing videogames on her phone, navigating through the Wendy's crowd without looking up. Her expression, however, was concealed behind wraparound sunglasses. A SMASH team had shot out Valentine's left eye, and all her videogame reskinning couldn't restore her lost vision.

"What, pray tell, am I missing by keeping my nose in a game?" Valentine asked, thumbs tapping away. "The rampant excitement of parents changing diapers? The ebullient *joie de vivre* of young boys playing punch buggy?"

"I hope," Imani said, dropping her voice low, "that you'll stop playing games once Aliyah gets onto the field."

For a woman in her early thirties, Paul thought, Valentine did the disgusted *Gawd* huff better than any teenager. She lowered her sunglasses to peer over them at Imani, cocking her head as though she couldn't quite fathom how she and Imani *still* failed to understand each other despite five years on the run together.

"Have you ever played a game of *PlayStation FIFA Soccer*?"

"You know I haven't." Imani didn't play videogames except to teach Aliyah; she'd considered them a waste of time before her daughter had become a videogamemancer. Imani had never quite understood how her daughter, who she'd envisioned becoming a Yale corporate lawyer like her dear old mom, had become so obsessively entangled with *Super Mario* that her videogame love punched holes through physics.

"Well, the reason Aliyah chose soccer is because *FIFA* is the most tedious fucking game in the entire universe. There are no fiery trails streaking behind the ball, no fireworks bursting overhead when someone scores a goal – nothing to spark

Aliyah's fertile imagination into magical outbursts. *FIFA* is a perfectly ordinary replication of a perfectly ordinary game made for perfectly ordinary people, and as such *I* will only survive this impending tedium by defeating all comers at *Infinity Blade*."

Imani blinked, disappointed. "Aliyah seemed so excited to play soccer."

"She's excited to fit in with someone who's not us." Valentine directed Imani's gaze through the front window. A group of kids had gathered around Aliyah as she told some crazy story; the girls smothered giggles with their hands. Yet whereas every other girl clutched a soccer ball, Aliyah's sat on the ground. "She'll tolerate the soccer."

"Then why'd *you* come?"

"Two reasons." Valentine ticked them off on her fingers. "First, Uncle Robert can't make it, because he's prepping a local safehouse. He'd been doing soccer drills with her. So she needed at least *one* of us here."

Depending on who you talked to, Robert was either Valentine's boyfriend (as he described it) or her lover (as she described it) – a former Fight-Club-o-'mancer who'd outgrown his Tyler Durden persona to become the thoroughly non-magical, hyper-competent security chief of Paul's organization.

"And the second reason?" Imani asked.

"Because Paul's paperwork magic won't stop an angry redneck's bullet. If Aliyah shits the bed, you guys are gonna need me."

Imani nodded. Though she'd never understood what bonded Paul and Valentine, she respected their friendship – and respected Valentine's hyper-violent *Grand Theft Auto*-inspired mayhem more.

Valentine's New York City sneer was far too dismissive of the small-town life for Paul's taste – but she'd been the one who'd handed her Nintendo DS to a burned girl trapped in a hospital, thus passing on her videogamemancy to Aliyah. "Besides, I've told Aliyah I'll elbow Valentine whenever she makes a good play. Watch."

He nudged Valentine in the ribs. She flung up her arms

reflexively and yelled, "GO OUR TEAM!"

"See?" Paul said brightly. "I've got her trained."

Imani snorted, hiding her bemusement behind one manicured hand. Even in her aged pseudoskin, masquerading as a soccer mom, she looked as elegant as the day he'd fallen in love with her.

The last parents finished talking to the coach. Imani pushed Paul into position. The coach, an elderly woman wearing a Wildcats baseball cap, plucked a fresh application off a stack of blank forms.

"Well, aren't *you* a feisty bunch?" She fished a pen from her pocket. "Welcome aboard. We'll just need a–"

But Paul had already placed the paperwork on the table – every field filled out in legible block lettering, the forms stacked in the order they'd been presented on the website, the $35.00 check paperclipped to the left corner.

"Huh," the coach said pleasantly, flipping through to double-check Paul's work. "*You* came prepared."

Imani gave their cover story about how they were homeschoolers, and all too used to government paperwork–

–but all Paul noticed was the sloppy stack of forms by the coach's elbow, and the big blank space on the top waiver where someone's "Emergency Contact" information should be.

That empty space is no big deal, he told himself. *This is a small town; everyone knows everyone.*

Yet to Paul, that unfilled data felt like a dead child. It was *unlikely* the coach would be out sick when a kid got hurt. Yet Paul envisioned worst-case scenarios: a kid breaking her neck on the field, nobody knowing who to call, a disastrous medical decision made because nobody could contact Mom in time.

Unlikely, but... bad things happened.

Paperwork kept records for when good people needed them, he thought. And as he envisioned the empty paperwork, tuning out Imani and the coach, he thought how good it would be for that information to be there, and...

The name on the form correlated to seven babies born at Morehead hospital, but only one of those kids was old enough for the Soccer

League. The date of birth matched this child up to one mother, name of Leslie Hornor, who lived in Lakeview Heights...

An audible noise, like pencils scribbling.

The blank emergency contact field filled itself in.

The stack of forms straightened itself into a neat pile.

Imani coughed – *she* knew what 'mancy felt like – but the coach turned around, perplexed.

"Did you feel something move?" the coach asked.

"Must be a gust of wind," Imani said.

Paul gripped his wheelchair, looking away from the forms. That spontaneous magic was why it was so hard to control 'mancers, yet so wrong to imprison them. Few set out to become 'mancers: magic stemmed from relentless obsession. If you believed with a diamond-hard conviction the universe *should* act a certain way, sometimes it *did*. You didn't mean to make it do anything, it just... shuffled out of the way.

The universe moved because the world was better off for the changes you wanted to make. Having all the emergency contact fields in that stack filled out was a minor change, but Paul felt better knowing that all the kids here were as safe as he could make them.

Yet it was also why today's game would be a test for Aliyah. Like most 'mancers, Paul had been an ordinary man for almost forty years before his bureaucromancy blossomed – the result of one too many nights working for Samaritan Mutual. Valentine was considered an exceptionally talented 'mancer for sparking in her late twenties. Both had lived as mundanes, internalizing the "normal" way the world worked.

Aliyah, however, had been made into a 'mancer at six years old. Physics had always scurried out of her way. And she kept forgetting the world wasn't supposed to have rainbow roads and showers of gold coins.

Her 'mancy was beautiful, of course, her digitized pixels popping out of mid-air to form what, in a better world, would be considered art... But ever since the European Broach, the world had been all too willing to murder 'mancers, or brainwash them.

"Thanks for being patient while I checked your work," the coach said. "You have no idea how important paperwork is around here."

"It's what binds the universe together," Paul said. And for him? It did. That's why he'd accidentally done 'mancy.

Today, he'd see whether Aliyah loved friendship more than videogames.

TWO

An American Girl, Raised on Promises

When Aliyah was six, she'd killed a magical terrorist by summoning the power of Fire Mario.

When Aliyah was eight, she'd channeled the God of War to battle her way into a drug dealer's compound.

And when Aliyah had turned eleven, her father had finally trusted her to guard his political speeches, so she'd suited up in BioShock's Big Daddies to ward off SMASH's endless abduction attempts.

Yet Aliyah had just turned thirteen – and nothing, *nothing*, had scared her more than the three teenaged girls kicking a soccer ball outside the Wendy's.

Aliyah had clutched her freshly-purchased soccer ball to her chest like a shield, wondering why she was so afraid. She'd begged her father to set aside his pro-'mancer rallies, to find a place she could play with girls her own age.

In all the world, there were no 'mancers her age. She'd have to make do with normal girls.

Normal girls scared the *fuck* out of her.

She'd sized her fellow soccer players up for threats: too many years on the front lines of Daddy's speeches had trained her to hunt for the gun-bulges in clothing, for the hard military stance of trained SMASH members, for the jittery look in every Unimancer's eyes as they communicated with others of their kind.

These girls had looked *nice*.

A tall redhead had pulled open her cheeseburger, peeling off her pickles to hand them to a smiling Asian girl – a ritual exchange that spoke of friendship. The girls had shouted cheery greetings at the other soccer players as they pulled into the parking lot: everyone knew each other.

When they'd noticed Aliyah, they'd cocked their heads: *Wanna come over?*

Aliyah had almost summoned a Portal gun and teleported away.

This is playing the game on expert, she'd told herself. *Mom, Dad, Aunt Valentine: they're obligated to love you, because they're your family. These kids don't have to like you.*

Her burn scars itched underneath her videogame reskinning. Would they still wave her over if they saw the shiny keloid markings on her cheeks?

She straightened her shoulders. Like Aunt Valentine said, everyone saw the "Game Over" screen sooner or later.

She'd walked over without looking too dorky. They'd bobbed their heads, muttering hellos – and Aliyah had realized they were as shy as she was around new people. Aliyah and the three girls had shuffled their feet, trying to remember what came after "Hello," the silence swelling like a cancer.

Aliyah had imagined dialogue prompts from roleplaying games, offering one of three options to choose from:

Hey, I'm Aliyah Rachel, the new kid in town, and I'm here to be your friend!

Name's Aliyah Rachel. What's yours?

Name's Aliyah Rachel. But you'll never forget my name after you see how badly I'll whip your asses.

She blinked the dialogue suggestions away. As a videogamemancer, if she'd chosen an option, her 'mancy would have made these girls react appropriately to the Bioware standard nice/neutral/jerk conversational gambit she'd picked – and she didn't want to influence their actions. She wanted them to like her for being *her*.

How did you *do* that?

Then the red-headed girl had gasped and seized her hand. Aliyah hadn't broken the girl's wrist; instead, she'd trusted this lanky redhead.

"Your *nails*." Her eyes had gleamed as she'd held Aliyah's hand up to show off Aliyah's nail art to her friends. "Did *you* do those?"

Aliyah's nails were painted glittering-gold flames. *I can't show them my burn scars*, Aliyah had thought as she'd painted them last night, *but I can put fire on my fingers*.

"I looked up techniques on YouTube." She'd repressed the urge to shove her hands into her pockets.

Which had downplayed the hours she'd spent perfecting her nail techniques – she couldn't always play videogames when they were hiding from SMASH, but she got nervous when she wasn't learning.

"That's *amazing*." The red-headed girl had realized she was still gripping Aliyah's wrist, then made a face when she realized how rude she was. "Can you teach us? After practice?"

Aliyah had stared, too shocked to say anything.

The girls had backed away – coltish and awkward after asking a stranger for a favor. They blushed, wondering how to extricate themselves.

"I'm sorry," the red-headed girl had said. "I shouldn't–"

Aliyah had grinned.

You didn't treat me like a hand grenade, she'd thought. *You didn't try to teach me how to master my powers. All you see is a kid who paints cool nails, and…*

Oh God.

That's all she'd ever needed.

Aliyah had faked a sneeze to cover her tears. She'd unlocked the greatest videogame achievement ever:

Ordinary girl.

"I would *love* to paint your nails," she told them.

The redhead's name was Savannah. By the time Aliyah and Savannah finished a spirited debate on whether *Steven Universe* would have been better if it had been a girl-led show called

Yvette Universe – Savannah liked Steven's pluck, whereas Aliyah planted herself firmly in the "moar girl power" camp – Savannah had asked Aliyah if she wanted to ride with her family down to the field.

Aliyah had leapt at the offer – though she fretted at how worried Daddy looked as Savannah's family drove away. Daddy's fears were silly; if trouble popped up, Aliyah would Scorpion-teleport to safety.

She felt guilty at how *free* she felt, riding in a car without her parents – especially when Savannah's dad put on gospel music and they all sung along. They never sung gospel music at home.

Her freedom soured into disappointment when they pulled onto the soccer field. It had no bleachers, no changing rooms, no concession stands; it was a patch of grass down by the park, the goals made from PVC piping and fishing nets. The parents set up folding chairs around the spraypainted white touchlines, handing out Capri Suns, the mothers smearing suntan lotion on the brothers who'd come along to watch.

It seemed… disorganized. When her daddy gave a rally, hundreds showed up – he'd draw thousands if his speeches weren't illegal – and he made sure things were set up professionally: first-aid stations stocked with anti-tear-gas eyewash stations, Wi-Fi signals strong enough to punch through Army jamming signals, escape routes marked with signs…

"It's not much, is it?" Savannah asked.

Aliyah realized what a jerk she must look like, her face scrunched up with disgust.

"N- No!" she lied. "It's great! It's just–"

"It's OK," Savannah assured her, grunting as she hauled her equipment out of the trunk. "See, if you've got any talent, Mrs McBrayer will put you up *there*." She gestured up to a distant hill, where other kids were already practicing fiercely. "That's Gold Field – the field where the kids who'll make varsity play. They've got *real* equipment. Silver Field's on the other side. Bronze Field's by the lake, which means you get mosquito-bitten, so at least we don't have to deal with *that*."

"And this?"

Savannah swept her hand across the muddied grass. "Welcome to Washout Field. Where Morehead's weakest players wash up."

"But don't call it Washout Field in front of Mrs McBrayer," said Bennie, the Asian girl, bending over to lace up her sneakers.

Latisha, one of Savannah's other friends, puffed herself up in a creditable Mrs McBrayer imitation. "Not unless you want a big lecture on how *sportsmanship* is the gold standard we play to here, missy."

Aliyah made a time-out gesture. "Whoa, whoa – you're *OK* with being last?"

Savannah, Latisha, and Bennie frowned, baffled. They consulted each other – should *we be upset?* – then looked out over the soccer field, as if the answer could be found out on the grass.

The answer *was* out there, in a way – there was no scoreboard to be found.

"It's just a game," Savannah shrugged, tying her hair back in a ponytail.

"The best part's the pizza afterwards," said Bennie.

"You're gonna come out for pizza, right?" Latisha asked.

Just a *game*?

Was this what normal kids *did*?

Aliyah tried to think of a game she'd played and hadn't beaten. *Rock Band* had taken her a while, but that's because her fingers had been too small to hold the plastic guitar neck – and eventually she'd gold-starred "Green Grass and High Tides." She'd found every star in the last *Mario* game. She hadn't Platinum-trophied *Bloodborne* yet, but that game was ridiculous.

How could her new friends be OK with losing?

The soccer drills were *not* led by Mrs McBrayer, who shouted orders up on Gold Hill, but were instead overseen by Mr Sheltowee, a stoop-shouldered black man with a drooping mustache. The coaches kept exhorting her, no matter how minor an effort she made: "*Good try, good try, good hustle!*"

Were they afraid she'd get disheartened if she failed?

The first step towards being excellent was sucking. You

sucked at every game when you started. Then you died a hundred times, learning from each failure.

Though judging from Savannah's frowns whenever she missed a pass, some kids *did* need the support. Bennie missed shots she could have stopped if she'd dived for the ball. And the coaches *rewarded* them for this unfulfilling exertion, wrapped it in a smothering wad of "good sportsmanship."

When she played *Destiny* with Aunt Valentine, they traded high-fives for making an excellent kill – even when, especially when, they shot each other. SMASH showed no mercy, so neither would they.

How would Savannah and Bennie and Latisha cope when they competed with people who *cared*?

"Excellent footwork, kid!" Mr Sheltowee told her. Aliyah beamed with pride: she'd practiced drills with Uncle Robert all winter. "A little work on reading the other players, Rachel, and you'll be top-notch."

She'd known teamwork would be her weakness. She'd memorized every play in *FIFA PlayStation*. But mapping out approaches from an overhead camera was different from peering through twenty players to see who was open.

She looked at Savannah and Bennie, who sang some weird YouTube song instead of playing defense.

Her new friends didn't know what winning felt like.

Aliyah could get to Gold Hill. Yet without Savannah and company, that'd be a different kind of loneliness.

No, Aliyah vowed. She would train them. Once they saw what a winner looked like, they'd realize they didn't belong in Washout Field. She'd forge a team of friends – they'd go home, flush with battle triumph, to a sleepover at Savannah's house, where she'd paint Bennie's nails...

As the coaches split everyone off for the practice game, she looked back at the sidelines. Aunt Valentine was crushing competitors on *Infinity Blade* – but she randomly thrust up a fist to yell "SPORTSBALL!" Mommy laughed as she offered donuts to the other families – she'd always loved playing hostess.

Even now, Aliyah ached, wondering what life she might

have led if Anathema hadn't inflicted magical powers upon her.

But Daddy…

Daddy sat glumly in his wheelchair, baseball cap pulled down over his head, scoping the other parents as though they might produce shotguns from their butts.

Though he meant well, his concern made Aliyah feel like a dumb kid.

She blew Daddy a kiss, a secret message: *It's gonna be all right*.

Daddy, looking frail beneath the videogame old-man reskinning, blew her a kiss back: *I hope so, little firebrand*.

Then Mr Sheltowee blew the whistle.

Game on.

Aliyah was lucky – her team had both Savannah and Bennie on it, though judging from the way the other team cringed when Latisha shuffled over, maybe they were better off without Latisha.

You can't think that! Aliyah chastised herself. *Latisha's your friend!*

They chased the ball, Mr Sheltowee barking out suggestions. Aliyah panted – in videogames, the hardest physical labor was replenishing her stamina bar, so being soaked in sweat felt grittily wonderful.

Though Aliyah drove the ball down the center, Savannah and Bennie missed her cues. She kept getting swarmed with nowhere to pass to. Despite Latisha's lackluster play on the opposition, soon they were down 1-2.

Savannah gave an ill-at-ease *whatcha gonna do?* hands-in-the-air gesture after her failure to intercept put them down 1-3. Then Bennie yelled, "I'm ready for pizza!"

And.

Savannah.

Cheered.

For *pizza*.

The next play, Aliyah snagged the ball and charged down the field like a winner damned well should. She noticed the opposition cringing back as she corkscrewed a path towards the end goal.

The crowd called her name, a thunderous roar rumbling over the lake: *Aliy-ah! Aliy-ah! Aliy-ah!* The goalie froze in terror, begging her to stop–

Aliyah backflipped, kicking the ball straight at the goal. The ball boomed as it broke the sound barrier, going so fast it caught flame from the wind resistance, a supersonic comet hitting the net and bursting into purple fireworks that spelled out GOAL.

Then Aliyah remembered: *They don't know my real name.*

Then, in slow horror: *I did 'mancy.*

The net was on fire, the plastic burning. The goalie shrieked "'Mancer!" and fled, the other kids running with her.

The flux squeezed in around Aliyah, the low pressure of an incoming stormfront. Even if you didn't mean to do 'mancy, the universe *hated* it when you broke its rules. It inflicted surges of bad luck upon you to even out the odds.

Aliyah dimly heard parents calling 911, grabbing their children, flinging open the trunk to get their shotguns. But all Aliyah could think about was K-Dash and Quaysean – her friends who'd burned to death because she'd loved them when the flux hit. The flux hit you in all the places you feared most, and it would chew your friends to pieces to make you miserable.

She'd fallen in love with Morehead.

Her love endangered them.

But it was OK. She reached into her pocket for the Contract – one of the unique magics Daddy had mastered to disperse bad luck safely. Once she called upon the Contract's power, she'd–

"What... What did you do?" Savannah stared at Aliyah as if she couldn't quite process this. "Did you just try to–"

Aliyah backed away as Savannah stepped towards her, hands held out, begging Aliyah to tell her the truth:

"–did you just try to kill that girl?" Savannah finished.

Aliyah hadn't. The ball would have bounced off; the goalie had been sheathed in a protective aura of videogame physics. Yet she realized that soccer ball had looked like cannon fire to everyone else...

As Aliyah flinched from Savannah's fear, her flux squirmed away before she signed the Contract, bad luck seeking the worst possible consequence–

"*Savannah!*" someone bellowed – Savannah's dad, who'd looked over his shoulder fondly at her in the back seat as he'd sung *God Is In The House* loud enough for Aliyah to read the lyrics off his lips.

Except now Savannah's dad grabbed Savannah by her shoulder, yelling "*Get behind me!*" as he aimed a revolver at Aliyah.

Aliyah prepped a videogame shield, knowing this wasn't even the bad luck. Savannah's dad wanting to murder her was just what she got for losing control.

The flux would, somehow, make this worse.

THREE
3-2-1 Contract

Paul had planned for Imani to push him around so he could chat with the other parents – but he'd picked up a small flux-load from magically altering Mrs McBrayer's paperwork. Rather than risk having it squirm off higgledy-piggledy, he'd had his wheelchair jam. So Imani had played socialite while Paul sat sidelined.

He dug through the cooler they'd brought: she got headaches in bright sun, so he'd packed Advil and suntan lotion, and he'd tucked away a special supply of donuts so they could play the Donut Game with Uncle Kit on the way home...

The only thing he couldn't get her was friends. But she seemed to be making those on the field.

He smiled, proud.

Valentine sat next to him, clutching a concealed margarita one of the mothers had snuck her. "Whoo!" She flopped down. "I am *so* not used to getting drinks from people who aren't trying to get in my pants."

Paul arched his eyebrows. "Making friends with the locals?"

"Wasted effort, Paul. I'm a kinky bitch, and I'd lay dollars to delicious donuts there's not a kink club within a hundred miles. I could never connect with these adorable vanilla confections."

Yet Paul noticed Valentine had discreetly swapped her Confederate flag tattoos out for some less confrontational Garth Brooks ink.

Then Valentine's head snapped up as she felt the surge of videogamemancy.

"Oh God," Paul muttered. "Is she...?"

"She's shit the bed," Valentine pointed at Aliyah; her fellow players backed away as a black arrow shimmered into existence above her head, pointing down at her. "She's *selected* herself. As the active player."

The parents elbowed each other, looking for confirmation they weren't hallucinating.

"*Aliyah!*" he yelled, trying to get her attention before she went too far – better to have them know her real name than for people to see 'mancy. But Aliyah's magic twisted his cry, turned it into a thunderous roar of approval, a thousand people chanting *Aliy-ah! Aliy-ah! Aliy-ah!*

It could have been a beautiful moment of approval, except for the furious parents charging out onto the field to tackle Aliyah. Some – too many – reached underneath their shirts for concealed carry holsters–

"Get me targets, Paul," Valentine said, leaping to her feet.

Paul sucked in a deep breath and dove into the records. He focused on the man sharing an ice-cold lemonade with Imani, the glass dropping from his hand as he squinted at Aliyah:

Braxton Tolliver: his Google history indicates many posts on anti-'mancer blogs, as well as repeated visits to the Magiquell website, a corporation that manufactures injectable nerve-gas cocktails designed to impede a 'mancer's concentration. Failed the certification exam to purchase Magiquell last October.

Paul scanned Tolliver's posts – *I'm not saying I hate 'mancers, but they did destroy Europe* – and marked him as a bright orange THREAT LEVEL: HIGH before breaking into Tolliver's bank histories to list recent purchases. He sorted through endless Sam's Club and SafeWay receipts, scanning for dangerous expenditures: tasers, guns, pepper sprays.

No weapon purchases. Nothing to elevate Braxton Tolliver to a red THREAT LEVEL: SEVERE.

By the time Paul snapped into an analysis of Eliza Tolliver, Braxton's wife, the lemonade glass was hitting the ground. He devoured her Internet history, her phone records, her email, compiling a comprehensive profile that would have made the FBI's best work look shoddy. He flashed his attention to the coach, to Savannah's parents, to Bennie's mother and the–

"Speed it up, Paul," Valentine said. Aliyah had detonated a blazing ball into the net, which had bought her a couple of moments as people dove for cover. "I'm glad for a little action – *finally* – but I can't fight them all!"

Paul suppressed a flare of irritation. *Or you could just, you know, teleport us all out to safety.*

That was unfair, he knew: Valentine's magic ran according to the videogame rules she had devised, and Valentine would never play a game that allowed her to teleport away from a battle. She couldn't retreat any more than Paul could magically drop millions into a bank account – the universe only bent to their will because they believed in an alternative system, one with different unbending rules. Paul believed paperwork made the world safer; he couldn't conjure up money, or embezzle it.

Likewise, scrappy Valentine needed to face down her opponents one by one.

"Come on, Paul." She bounced from foot to foot, anxious to mix it up. "Less planning, more punching."

He finished profiling. "Ready for download."

They touched fingertips. Their 'mancies intertwined; Paul shivered as his bureaucratic dossiers were converted into a game mod. As a videogamemancer, Valentine could gamify just about anything.

"Disable, don't destroy," Paul reminded her. "Remember, we brought this to them."

"*Arkham Knight* it is."

A bat-winged cape fluttered down from Valentine's neck; she flicked her fingers out, covering them in leather gauntlets. She wasn't quite Batman – she'd kept her thick figure, still pudgy and womanly beneath the cowl – but cloaked in shadow, she looked deadlier than anything else on the Morehead soccer field.

She leapt out towards Braxton Tolliver, grabbing him by the

shoulders and burying her knee in his gut, before launching off him to leap into Mrs Darby as she fumbled out a Magiquell hypodermic from her purse. Valentine bounced around the soccer field like a pinball, her batcape flapping behind her, each successful attack adding numbers to the combo meter above her head.

Paul winced. Valentine's takedown should have shattered Mr Sheltowee's spine, but the videogame rules turned him into a bruiseable videogame villain. He staggered to his feet, little birds circling above his head, to rush at Valentine with a club he'd pulled from nowhere.

"You're him," a southern-accented voice said: Mrs Tolliver, cradling her husband's unconscious body. "You're that terrorist the President hates."

"Please disperse – we'll contain the situa–"

The flux smashed in around him, crippling migraine pressure. The universe knew the difference between information he could have dug out with a couple of Freedom of Information requests, and the sneaky hacking he'd done to ferret out private citizens' records. This flux was the universe's fury at being violated, wanting to rebalance the magic with gouts of bad luck–

"You hurt my husband." She was numb with shock.

"I'm sorry." Paul held up his hand in a mixture of apology and forbiddance. "'Mancy is a delicate operation, and–"

The flux hammered in at him: *It's a delicate operation? What could go wrong, pray tell? Let us turn your worst nightmares into reality.* Paul kept his mind blank; if he worried about Mrs Tolliver's mental health, the flux would find a way to drive her insane–

He reached into his breast pocket, pulling out the only thing that could safely disperse this flux:

The Contract With America.

The Contract was handkerchief-sized, made of rich vellum, inscribed in impossibly tiny yet calligraphically-perfect lettering. His tension eased as he ran his fingers along the Contract's sewn edges: he would never have dared put Morehead's population *near* 'mancy without his generous volunteers to reduce the danger.

Paul snapped the Contract open, unfurling it to the size of a kite. On it were the names of 32,503 people who supported pro-'mancy legislation – supported it so thoroughly they'd signed the paperwork that allowed Paul to assign his bad luck to them.

Paul had learned the trick from an old enemy. Yet unlike Mr Payne, who'd buried his flux-dumping in the thousand paragraphs of a EULA agreement, Paul had open-sourced his legalese. He allowed people to refuse or accept the bad luck at will, ensuring no one person would ever be assigned fatal misfortune.

Even with all those safeguards, being caught signing a magical contract would get you a lifetime prison sentence. The fact that thousands risked imprisonment for Paul humbled him.

Those thousands allowed him to keep giving speeches despite SMASH's best efforts – he could enact great acts of 'mancy to keep bystanders safe whenever SMASH turned peaceable rallies into war zones.

Once again, Paul closed his eyes and offered thanks.

Then he poured the flux into the Contract, assigning tiny inconveniences. With this many people, he could chop this deadly flux-load into a thousand stubbed toes–

"You're trying to destroy Morehead – like those 'mancers destroyed Europe!"

Mrs Tolliver aimed a taser at him – but there was no record of a taser purchase anywhere in the Tollivers' finances. How could Paul have missed that on their threat-check?

Paul cursed himself: not everyone bought their weapons legally.

"Mrs Tolliver," Paul said. "I'm not trying to destroy Morehead. I just… I just wanted to let my little girl play soccer."

The flux struggled to escape the Contract. It didn't want to be broken down to be dispersed among strangers locking their keys inside their cars – it burned to wreck Paul's life personally–

"Your girl kicked flaming death at my daughter," Mrs Tolliver murmured. In the background, Valentine kicked the guns out of three men's hands, oblivious to Mrs Tolliver's threat. "Your fat friend broke my husband's arm. The President's right – someone needs to stop you obsessed murderers–"

Years of training stopped Paul from imagining what could go wrong. Any fear would be a lightning rod for the flux to course down.

And he *did* fear destroying Morehead. All it would take was one sharp jab at the thin barriers that separated this world from the demon dimensions, and deadly buzzsects would come pouring through, the buzzsects that had devoured Germany, devoured France–

Devour Morehead! the flux roared. It took all Paul's skill to blank his fears.

A gun cocked.

"Mrs Tolliver." Imani evinced more compassion than you could reasonably expect from a woman aiming a gun at someone's chest. "I brought you donuts. We're not here to hurt you."

"Then why did you hurt my husband?"

Paul wished he had a better answer than *Because your husband said mean things about 'mancers.*

Who was he, to profile people?

"Because, Lizzie," Imani said calmly, "he would have shot Paul with his stun gun."

Oh. Right, Paul thought.

"I know things look bad, Lizzie," Imani continued, emphasizing Mrs Tolliver's first name. "But believe me: things will get worse if you fire that weapon. Give Paul a moment to clean up the flux, and we will leave. We will leave and never come back."

Mrs Tolliver slowly raised the stun gun.

Imani chewed her lip, trying to work up the gumption to pull the trigger. Robert had trained her personally, giving her paramilitary lessons since they'd gone on the run from the government. She could punch tight clusters of shots through any paper target.

Mrs Tolliver endangered everyone here – yet that was because she'd bought into the news' anti-'mancer propaganda. Imani and Mrs Tolliver had been exchanging donut recipes a few minutes ago; switching from that to inflicting a sucking chest wound was a transformation Imani could not quite complete.

Most days, Paul would have taken pride in her hesitation.

"A broach is imminent, Mrs Tolliver." Her sudden formality was not lost upon Mrs Tolliver, nor was her finger tightening on the trigger. "If you don't stop, I'll have to fire. Please." Her voice hitched. "Do *not* make me."

Mrs Tolliver's lips moved as she tried to tally up the facts. Her husband laid next to her – unconscious, not dead. Imani could have shot her.

Then the soccer coach's limp body flew past Mrs Tolliver as Valentine kicked him into a Chevy truck.

"*No more tricks!*" Mrs Tolliver said, and fired.

Paul felt a sickly squirm of flux. His? No:

Aliyah's.

As Paul watched in horror, the taser's barbs embedded themselves into the Contract's fragile paper, the electricity triggering prematurely to disintegrate this complex magical structure into a maelstrom of loose 'mancy–

Creating a sharp jab at those vital barriers that separated Morehead from the hellish otherworlds.

"*No!*" Paul cried.

As he was flung away, Paul heard that infernal buzzing. Swarms of buzzsects poured through a rift, each a color no human could comprehend, ready to gobble down the color of grass, the speed of light, the beat of time.

Paul fought to stay awake, knowing he was the only person within a hundred miles who could contain a broach.

The concussion hammered him into unconsciousness.

FOUR
All the Good Things in the Universe Burn

"*Daddy, no!*" Savannah screamed.

The gun didn't worry Aliyah: no single bullet ever killed a player in the games she played. Headshots merely chipped away at your health bar. Savannah's father couldn't bring himself to pull the trigger, but if he had shot, then Aliyah's videogame confidence would have transformed his .45 gunshots into flesh wounds.

Aliyah was more concerned about Savannah's daddy's safety.

"*Valentine, no!*" Aliyah yelled, as Valentine dove and rolled towards Savannah's father, her Batman-cape fluttering behind as she came up in a quick snapkick aimed at his neck.

Aliyah hooked into Aunt Valentine's game and swelled into the Joker, intercepting Valentine's attack with a double-block of crossed arms. Then she shrank back into a girl wearing a mud-stained soccer uniform.

The gun slipped from Savannah's father's fingers. As he hyperventilated, Aliyah read the emotions on his face: his need to protect his daughter, his self-loathing that he'd pointed a loaded gun at a girl he'd sung gospel songs with an hour ago, his confusion about why Aliyah would protect him after she'd tried to kill the goalie with a soccer ball...

"He's *scared*," Aliyah said, blocking Valentine as she swung again.

"Scared enough he's practically shitting bullets in your *face*!"

Valentine roared, her voice Batman-guttural. "Why *shouldn't* I take him out?"

"Because friends don't punch each other!" Aliyah remembered how scared *she'd* been the first time she saw magic. "And we're friends. Aren't we... aren't we friends, Savannah?"

Savannah shivered, taking in the unconscious bodies lying around the soccer field, the black smoke rising from the burning soccer goal.

She squinted at Aliyah. "Have you..." Savannah swallowed, glancing uneasily at the curvy Valentine-Batman hybrid as it cracked its knuckles. "Do you kill people with your 'mancy?"

Aliyah shook her head. "I don't–"

– *"I said* burn*!" Aliyah shrieked, raining down fireballs on Anathema as she begged for mercy. "'Mancers burn! Bad people burn! All the bad things in the universe burn!"* –

– *A fire poured in through the doorway as K-Dash and Quaysean drew their guns to protect Aliyah, the two lovers struggling to hold hands as their fingers blistered to the bone* –

"Not anymore," Aliyah pled.

"Not any*more*?" Savannah echoed.

"I didn't ask to be this!" Aliyah yelled. "It just happened, Savannah! 'Mancy's *hard* to control! And nobody–"

There was a wet noise, like the skin being pulled off a man's back.

Aliyah whirled around, the hair on the back of her neck horripilating. That shredding sounded like it'd come from behind – but no, everyone still standing on the soccer field was turning in circles, trying to locate that horrid sound's origin. The noise had disobeyed the laws of acoustics.

Then she heard the low buzz of hundreds of insects boiling out – and *that* noise swelled until they clasped their hands over their ears, hundreds ramping to thousands, thousands multiplying into millions.

The sun darkened as something sucked the tint from the sky.

Aliyah looked back towards Daddy. The space above his empty wheelchair had burst open like a blister, revealing an eye-watering glimpse of alien worlds beyond as the buzzsects chewed their way out with chelicerated jaws.

The air around the rip stretched sickeningly, sagged like too much garbage tossed into a bag, burst open to birth more buzzsects.

"Aunt Valentine," Aliyah whispered, unable to look away. "Is that a broach?"

Valentine didn't answer.

Her silence terrified Aliyah. Aunt Valentine had walked straight into a serial killer pyromancer's lair to save Aliyah, had charged head-first into SMASH teams to buy them time to escape. *Nothing* scared Aunt Valentine, except maybe commitment.

Yet Valentine had taken off her sunglasses to stare straight into the abyss. Her remaining eye was filled with despair.

Aliyah remembered something Daddy had told her once: *If there's a broach, get me. You can't seal a broach. No 'mancer can. The only people who've ever done it are me, or Unimancers – everyone else has died.*

Then she realized: the broach had opened above Daddy's wheelchair.

Daddy might be dead.

She reached out to the Contract, checking for signal, got a blank line.

Daddy *was* dead.

You killed him with your flux you killed everyone now no one can stop the broach

Panic flooded through her; she squashed it. Aliyah had too much experience in combat to let fear jumble her thoughts. She contemplated a retreat; if she called in the Unimancers, they might – might – arrive before the incursion swelled to obliterate Kentucky. If Daddy was dead – and some screaming part of her was already weeping at Daddy's funeral – then her best bet for survival was flight.

"What *is* that?" Savannah shrieked. Her father crouched down to press her face into his shoulder, shielding her as best he could.

The buzzsects surged out from over the wheelchair; the

grass wilted purple as they flowed across it, chewing the photosynthesis from the plants and excreting their own universe's rules. They chewed the wave-forms from the sunlight's photons, leaving strange radiations sizzling in their wake.

They expanded outwards, headed for the people.

"I love you, princess." Savannah's dad shut his eyes. The buzzsects flowed towards the unconscious bodies on the field, ready to consume the rules that kept humans' hearts beating.

"Ha-*douken*!"

The *Street Fighter* fireball surged out of Aliyah's palms before she'd even thought it through. Yet as the blue flame sailed towards the broach, she felt the correctness: she could not leave these people to die. She'd brought this upon them.

Who's to say she couldn't seal the broach?

The buzzing noise dropped in pitch as they sensed Aliyah's 'mancy. They swirled around in great arcs, converging on Aliyah's fireball–

And snapped it up like the fireball was the most delicious morsel ever, poured back down the trail back to Aliyah, homing in on the source of this delicious 'mancy.

Well, at least I distracted them, Aliyah thought, running backwards to draw the buzzsects away from Savannah and her father. Savannah's father looked baffled as Aliyah pulled the buzzsects away, squinting as if he couldn't quite understand why she'd rescued him.

She pulled up a menu in mid-air, white text against blue; the world paused helpfully while she flicked the cursor down the available options. The soccer players' mouths hung petrified in mid-shriek, the smoke from the burning soccer net freezing in place like a snapshot. The buzzsects cruised to a stop, caught like flies in amber.

If anyone's left standing after your best shot, Aliyah thought, *then find a bigger gun.*

She flicked through her selections:

Attack

Magic

Summon

Item

Aliyah selected "Summon," then browsed the submenu:

Anima

Zodiark

Eden

Nova

"When in doubt, go with the classics," she muttered, moving the pointer down to "Nova." But as she made her choice, she realized in horror:

The buzzsects had started moving.

The rest of the world had paused, but the buzzsects ignored her 'mancy.

Above her, the dim sky turned midnight-black, the now-bright stars sweeping overhead as the heavens glimmered with mathematical formulae. A distant star glimmered into existence, swelled, producing blinding explosions as it smashed through meteors and small moons alike, hurtling inexorably across the solar system.

The buzzsects moved in counterpoint to the impending destruction, sluggishly headed towards Aliyah.

Come on, come on, Aliyah thought, trapped in the animation cycle. She'd chosen the most powerful effect at her disposal, a videogame finisher so overwhelming it took almost two minutes for it to land – but in the game she'd stolen the Nova Summon from, everyone waited patiently for their next turn.

The buzzsects slowly woke from torpor, chewing Aliyah's 'mancy, growing faster.

Her blazing star zoomed past Saturn, obliterated the asteroid belt, swept the atmosphere off Mars. She stood, trapped by her own rules, as the buzzsects split into flanking curves to surround her–

"*Run!*" Valentine screamed, yanking Aliyah out of her animation with a surge of counter-'mancy.

Aliyah stumbled backwards as the Nova Summon went off.

Aliyah's 'mancy roared down from the sky like a nuclear missile, the clouds parting to make way for the star Aliyah had

38   FIX

ripped from a distant galaxy and flung at the Earth.

It hit the buzzsects' center mass dead on, sending Aliyah flying. The ground buckled around them, rocks hurtling into the air–

The buzzsects soared up in merry clouds to devour the rocks.

They gulped down the shockwave, shuddered, swelled, burst into fresh swarms.

Her 'mancy was *aiding* the buzzsects. They erased the laws of physics, and so did she – fighting a broach with magic was like fighting fires with gasoline.

Flux clogged her sinuses–

"I tried that once!" Valentine cried, hiking her shirt up to showcase the angry red buzzsect scars crisscrossing her flabby belly. *"We can't beat them."*

"Then *how*?"

"Valentine! Aliyah!"

Her mother's voice rang across the battlefield like a gunshot – assured, confident. Despite the mayhem as the buzzsects wheeled around towards her, Aliyah felt at peace.

She knew her family: Dad had a vision. Mom had a plan. And Aunt Valentine had the firepower.

"Mom!" Aliyah squinted through the teeming madness, glad the buzzsects were so busy devouring her 'mancy they hadn't wolfed down the laws of sound. *"What do we do?"*

"Get your father!"

"Is he–"

"He's out cold!" Mom yelled, pointing beyond the wheelchair – Daddy must have been thrown to safety. Valentine hugged Aliyah hard. *"I can't revive him. But* you *can!"*

"Dunno if you've noticed, Missus T," Valentine yelled, *"but we've got an aerosolized Cthulhu standing between us and Paul, and right now they're Aliyah-seeking missiles! What's your plan?"*

"She made noise – you make more! Go over the top with bigger 'mancy and lead them off!"

"You mean–" A dreamy smile floated across Valentine's face. "You're *finally* authorizing me to go full super saiyan?"

"Yes!"

Valentine cracked her knuckles, turning to face a sky teeming with hungry invaders. "Years of 'Play it safe, Valentine. We'll bring you out when we need you, Valentine.' I haven't had a good scrap in *ages*!"

"Aunt Valentine! You…" Aliyah almost warned Valentine to be careful, realized she was still bloated with flux. She clamped down, blanking her mind before her flux made her worst Valentine-fears come true.

Valentine looked down at Aliyah with love. "No worries, kid. It feels good to be needed. Now link into my game."

She put a finger over Aliyah's lips, never looking away from the buzzsect hordes fighting to get at this cluster of 'mancy. Then she spread her arms wide, embracing the incoming chaos.

"If it takes the apocalypse to let your parents take the reins off, then I say '*Good Morning, Gotterdammerung!*'"

She snapped her fingers. A large red "S" with fluttering angel-wings dropped from the sky, bounced on the grass to land next to her. She stomped on it; the "S" shattered into gray metal shards that leapt up to swirl around her, knitting weaponry around her torso, fashioning a ludicrously large machine-cannon with three barrels pointing in different directions. It was so cumbersome the gun had to be strapped to her body – but she bore its weight proudly, sliding her finger through the trigger-guard as though touching a lover for the first time.

She let loose a disbelieving cackle as the buzzsects raced towards her.

"*Contra spread-gun, motherfuckers! Anyone who's not an extradimensional roach? Run for cover!*"

Aliyah tore off in a long, looping end run as Valentine opened fire.

She couldn't resist looking back. Magic was terrifying, a constant chaos.

But when Aunt Valentine went full-nuclear on someone, it was a work of art.

Howitzers boomed across the soccer field, flexing Aliyah's eardrums. The three cannons unleashed a steady stream of bright orange grenades, each exploding into the clouds of buzzsects with a fiery thunderclap, sending them spinning away. She was a one-woman battleship, filling the air with obliteration.

The buzzsects split apart, confused – some battened upon the explosions, others gnawed at the 'mancy until they gave birth to shiny new ruptures spilling free with buzzsects, others fell upon their wounded compatriots to shred them alive. The rest homed in on Valentine. They came in such numbers, no way Aunt Valentine could dodge that many of them–

Valentine backflipped out of their grasp.

"*I beat Gradius!*" she cried. "*R-Type! The greatest shoot-'em-ups in videogame history! You think you fuckers can overwhelm me?*"

"*Aliyah!*" Mom cried. Aliyah looked away, clamping down on her fear that Aunt Valentine was making a last stand.

"*I hope one of you fuckers is YouTubing this!*" Valentine cried to the crowd, her gun strobing devastation, laughing as though blasting alien invaders to pixellated smithereens was the greatest pleasure anyone could have.

Still, Valentine hadn't drawn all the buzzsects away, so Aliyah mentally hit the "Player 2" button, connecting with Aunt Valentine's game.

She'd never played *Contra*, but videogames were made to be shared.

The gun dropped into her hands – a humming power glowing warm in her palms. She took high, arcing jumps over the Morehead soccer players, yelping with surprise from the joy of it, looking down in admiration.

The Gold, Silver, and Bronze fields had commandeered pickup trucks, driven them into the teeth of the swarm to rescue their own. Which, given their FOX News-inspired terror of magic, was a bravery Aliyah could not imagine. Aliyah blasted buzzsects away, protecting them, her heart boiling with conflicting emotions: pride in this town, despair she'd brought this mayhem upon them, anger at the overreaction that had caused the broach...

Mom looked grim. She cradled Daddy's head; Daddy's cheeks were a mottled red from where she'd tried to slap him back to consciousness. He was sprawled out on the grass, the bladelike sweep of his artificial foot poking through the tattered remnants of Aunt Valentine's videogame pseudoflesh.

Aliyah flattened her hands against Daddy's chest, relieved at the thump of his heartbeat, trying to remember what game mechanics revived an unconscious player.

What if we bring him back and he's too brain-damaged to help? she thought.

That'll do, said the flux, pouring down her arms, threading through the soft veins in Daddy's brain.

No! Aliyah thought, pulling back. *His ribs are broken!* She focused the flux like a weapon, replacing her vague fears with firmer terrors it found irresistible. The flux raced down Daddy's jugular, disappearing into his chest: there was a dull crack, as some hairline fractures sprung open.

Worse, that hadn't drained her flux. If she panicked again, she'd–

She blanked the thought angrily before the flux had another channel to flow through.

Why was her flux so overwhelming now? She hadn't shit the bed like this since she was eight. She hated how she could never predict how much flux she'd get – that's why it was *called* flux. Aunt Valentine had gamed the system seven ways to Sunday and had resigned herself to the randomness. Whereas Daddy said the best way to reduce flux was faith – if you truly believed the world was better off for doing your magic, then the world would agree with you and the bad luck would slide away.

Problem was, you couldn't bullshit the universe. She tried to tell herself soccer was more exciting with videogame flourishes, that she'd done crazier 'mancy with Aunt Valentine – but the universe knew how guilty Aliyah felt about inflicting a magically-flaming soccer ball on an unsuspecting crowd.

She tried to tell herself that Aunt Valentine burst buzzsects all day with her *Contra*-gun, and *she* barely had any flux, and so Aliyah should be flux-free. But Aunt Valentine destroyed the hordes with the conviction that she was meant to stare straight into the demon dimensions and give them the finger – and whenever Aliyah had pulled the *Contra*-gun's trigger, she'd felt out of her depth.

Daddy said no one truly understood flux. Yet Aliyah sometimes thought 'mancers understood that flux measured faith – they just couldn't acknowledge the secret conflicts stashed deep in their heart.

Right now, though she saw buzzsects, all Aliyah could remember was Rainbird, pyromaniac Rainbird. When she'd been eight, she'd accidentally sent Rainbird on a fiery murder spree through the Institute. He'd made her watch as he'd roasted her friends.

Once she'd put Savannah and Latisha and Mr Sheltowee in danger, her old guilts had condensed into a flux big enough to rip a broach open…

"Breathe, Aliyah." Mom was always calm, no matter how bad things got. "Remember the exercises. Remember our *lists*. What videogames can help a downed agent?"

Aliyah resented her mother for a second – such a baby question – until she realized Mom was trying to distract her from her flux.

Mom treated their lives like their existence was a test she intended to ace, burying Aliyah underneath lists, notes, cheat sheets. Daddy planned a lot, but trusted Aliyah to an extent that terrified her. Aliyah had learned from Valentine, but not in any organized way, just by bullshitting with her on the couch.

Mom had no 'mancy, but they'd have fallen apart without her.

"Medpacks for critical injury," Aliyah recited.

Mom raised a finger. "Medpacks are for temporary healing. They'll break open as soon as the level ends. And your father's not…" She grimaced. "*Wasn't* hurt. So what else?"

"Phoenix Down potions if someone's unconscious."

"Is your father…?"

"*Yes!*" Aliyah was furious Mom was making a lesson out of this. Aliyah pulled up a menu, scrolling past Attack/Magic/Summon to Item, and selected "Phoenix Down."

A feather coalesced onto Aliyah's outstretched palm, lifted into the air to trace glimmering circles around her father's unconscious body – and helping her father was exactly what she was meant to do, so her flux manifested as a mild set of hiccups.

The 'mancy hoisted Daddy up like a puppet; he blinked owlishly as the Phoenix Down potion set him back on his feet.

"Aliyah?" he asked. "Imani? What's–"

lynchpin, the buzzsects roared, millions of insectile wings uniting into one eardrum-puncturing voice. *devour him. now.*

"*Hey!*" Valentine yelled, as the buzzsects peeled away from her. She fired heat-seeking missiles, chewing up their flanks – but every buzzsect headed straight for Paul. They lifted into the air, chewing up sunlight as they rose into the sky, a tsunami wave of extradimensional nightmares.

And Daddy...

...looked *peeved*.

It was the same look he'd given Aliyah when she'd spilled milk on Daddy's new phone: irritation, inconvenience, a cost they didn't want to incur, but salvageable.

He pulled out a handkerchief to dab the sweat off his forehead as the buzzsects smashed down upon him.

"All right," Daddy muttered. "I can fix this."

FIVE
Repairs and Despairs

Back in the days before Paul had fallen hopelessly in love with Imani, he would find himself seized by shameful urges in his dates' apartments. His dates would urge him to sit down next to her on her messy bed, the college dorms so cramped they were practically spooning; Paul laced his fingers together to avoid temptation.

His dates always smiled when they noticed his discomfort. "Whatcha thinking?" they'd ask.

"Can I..."

"Yes?" They'd tilt their chins, all but begging to be kissed.

"Can I rearrange your bookshelves? They're out of alphabetical order."

The dates ended shortly after that.

But even on the occasions he'd suppressed his organizational desires for carnal ones, he'd glimpse those books over his date's shoulder while they kissed – and those jumbled shelves would offend him.

It's not that Paul didn't want to kiss beautiful girls... but any disorder felt *wrong*. He couldn't work until his files had been catalogued. He was drawn to forms because of how easy it was to bring order to blank space – write the address in that field, check that box, until everything that needed to be filled in *was* filled in. Allowing books to sit in random disarray when the A-Z system was at hand struck him as being...

Well, a disorganized shelf struck him like a wound that needed mending.

(Whereas Imani had countered that if one was to rearrange books, why not use the Dewey Decimal System instead? By the time they'd debated the overkill of utilizing such a large classification system for such a small sample size, Paul was rapturously in love.)

So when Paul saw the buzzsects chewing up the sky as they arced towards him, he barely noticed the buzzsects.

The chaotic physics they left in their wake maddened him.

The buzzsects ate the speed of light. Paul had no technical education in physics, but he'd spent his life living in a universe where the fastest that something could go was 186,000 miles per second. He felt that top speed instinctively, every molecule in his body functioning thanks to natural laws that cascaded inexorably down from that single axiom. Standing beneath this canopy of mangled constants, where the buzzsects had snipped speed from the universe, he felt the offense of theft.

A few inches away/a thousand miles away, a buzzsect gulped down the concept of linear space and landed on his left arm.

"No," he repeated, mesmerized by how much there was to *do*. "I'm sorry, but *no*."

He flicked the buzzsect away absently. "*You* are not aerodynamic."

The buzzsect's wings beat against the air, reminded of the impossibility of its flight – and the universe flowed through Paul's certainty, reinforcing the necessity of air resistance, of the Bernoulli principle, of Newton's laws of action and reaction.

"*None* of you can fly," Paul snapped, and they dropped from the air in a hailstorm of nightmares.

The act *satisfied*. It was proper. There was an order to things, and Paul was reasserting that order. Gravity attracted other objects according to its mass. Atoms intertwined with each other according to established principles. Those principles gave birth to astrophysics, chemistry, biology, self-awareness...

This was not 'mancy; he wasn't altering physics, but reestablishing them. He replaced these invasive, extradimensional rules with the tried-and-true concepts this universe had run on since its beginning.

And who was more qualified to enforce rules than a bureaucromancer?

He mended the broach, the buzzsects flopping on the ground as he undid the alien laws they excreted. They disintegrated in microbursts of compressed quantum forces as he squeezed them within Earth-standard physics.

As an encore, Paul sewed up the broach with Fermat's Principle.

"Daddy!" Aliyah clapped her hands, jumping up and down. "You *did* it!"

"Almost," he muttered, turning his attention to the smear of lightless sky above.

That broach was a messy tangle where the swarm had consumed the speed of light – thousands of wavering lines crisscrossing where the individual buzzsects had chewed our physics away. It reminded Paul of ants digging tunnels into the earth, individual crawlways of darkness opening up into excavated gaps where nothing moved.

He'd never *let* a broach get this far out of control before.

He reached out, probing at the violation's edges – and recoiled.

It was worse than he'd thought. The speed of light was the universe's speed limit – but these extruded alien dimensions held no concept of speed. Which made no sense: the buzzsects had managed to move through there, yet their idea of motion held only superficial similarities to how anyone in *this* universe viewed it. They got from one place to another utilizing principles that gave Paul an instant migraine.

It made no sense. Worse, he had no time to comprehend these mind-warping physics. Someone here must have called SMASH by now. They had thirty-five minutes before the Unimancers arrived – he'd chosen Morehead because of its distance from SMASH response centers – but the local cops would arrive much sooner.

Still, regardless of the pressure, Paul felt a tingle of pleasurable anticipation. It was like looking at Valentine's apartment, strewn with dirty clothing and old Burger King wrappers; he didn't necessarily want to do the work, but it was going to feel *so good* to relax once he'd put everything back into order.

He traced the gap's outlines, then reached out to the Earth dimensions – the clean ones that allowed biological life – to knead the idea of "speed" back into the violated area.

It resisted.

No, Paul thought, horrified – a broach had never resisted him. This violation *defied* him, having existed long enough to gain a dim sentience. It struggled to retain its own integrity, another universe jammed deep within ours.

It wanted to grow.

Panicked, Paul assaulted the broach with Bragg's Law of X-rays, greasing the path with the slower velocities of Cherenkov radiation, dropping the crushing weight of the laws of relativity on it.

Still the violation refused to budge. It contracted, pulling in its strength–

Wave-particle duality Casimir effect Maxwell's equations the Constancy Principle

Paul didn't know the names of the physical laws he used to crush this violation – he understood them instinctively, a man who had mastered grammar not through studying language but through having read a thousand books. He bludgeoned the violation, making inchoate noises of terror, until–

Something gave.

He squeezed in through that opening, introducing the concept of "motion" back into that alien space like a virus.

Yet introducing earthly motion into this alien space broke it, somehow; it held its own alien replacement for movement, a flicker-stutter dimensional shifting that would have sliced human bodies into cross-sections. Paul tried to override the broach's alternative rules with his concept of speed, but the flicker-stutter was too ingrained. The best he could do was to inject clauses that *also* allowed for Earth-standard movement – but the two styles conflicted in a boil of contradictory physics.

The broach deepened.

Paul chipped away at the alien space, shoving in the Earth-needed concept of speed until it was the *dominant* motion.

The best Paul could do was to make the speed of light twenty miles an hour.

The few stragglers on Washout Field watched in awe as the darkness overhead writhed. A wavering rainbow light limned its edges as the photons overhead smashed into the violation and were slowed enough to be pulled apart into refractive indexes. Stale ozone wafts drifted down as the near-immobile gas molecules inside were pushed out by the pressure of light.

The broach hissed as the excess energy of the light impacting the top of the violation was converted into bursts of infrared, radio waves, radiation.

This place isn't safe, Paul thought. *The radiation will make it uninhabitable.*

Worse, it wasn't stable. He'd tried to excise the flicker-stutter movement, but had only dampened it. A slow war for supremacy raged inside this zone, one where eventually the flicker-stutter would claw its way back out to cause another broach.

"I can *fix* this," Paul muttered, gritting his teeth – if he kept at it, he'd double that speed to forty miles an hour, then do it again, until the old hurts were erased–

"Paul," Valentine said. "We gotta go."

"I have to *fix* this!"

She jerked her thumb over her shoulder, drawing Paul's attention to the distant sirens. "The cops will shoot you on sight. And I can't protect you."

She was right. The slightest whisper of 'mancy would provide that flicker-stutter the energy to grow again – and would trigger a hideous broach, worse than the last.

Paul stared, aghast, at the messy jumble churning above him. The conflicting systems felt like a needle in his eye.

He had to fix this.

"Daddy." Aliyah tugged at his sleeve. "We gotta *go*."

He looked down at his daughter, then up at the broach. This

was no jumbled bookshelf; this was burning the Library of Alexandria to the ground. He could recreate the documents, given time – he'd healed a broach in Long Island, he'd sealed the broach in Payne's office so thoroughly people still debated whether anything *had* broached–

The distant flash of cop cars told him his time was up. They had no choice but to flee – and when they returned, Unimancers would guard this space. And the Unimancers had never healed a broach this far gone – all they'd done was slow the progression. Leaving would condemn America to a slow-growing cancer that would eat up Kentucky.

Except *he could fix it.*

"*Paul.* We have to go!" Imani said.

They'd never leave without him. Staying would get him shot, condemn his wife to a lifetime in prison, get his daughter and his best friend brainwashed. Even then, SMASH would be more interested in torturing Paul than letting him repair his errors...

Nothing he could do would save Morehead. They wouldn't *let* him.

Paul let his wife pull him away.

SIX
Fellowship of Nothing

Aliyah had never seen Daddy this distraught before. He stumbled back from the broach, his face so gaunt Aliyah worried maybe she *had* given him an aneurysm.

The flux tried to latch onto that thought. She clamped it down.

"Mrs T," Valentine said.

"This isn't your fault, Paul." Mommy had to guide Daddy to the car because Daddy refused to take his gaze off that horrible blotch. "The locals, they got scared. They stopped you when they shouldn't have…"

"Mrs T!"

Mommy eased Daddy inside the van, kissed his forehead – and then slammed the door shut hard enough to make Aliyah flinch. As Mommy whirled on Valentine, Aliyah realized just how furious Mom was – at the townsfolk, at the 'mancy, at everything.

"First off, it's *Ms Dawson*." She ticked off the things Valentine did wrong. "Not 'Mrs T.' Second, Paul is traumatized, so if you'd keep your voice down–"

Valentine squeezed her eye shut, breathing in through her nose. Aliyah had never seen Aunt Valentine *avoid* a fight with Mommy before. "The van's broken."

"What?"

"Check the tires."

The van sagged sideways, the four tires flattened. Mommy catalogued the damage, squeezing her fists into balls. "How did *that* happen?"

"I bled off some flux."

"By crippling our *getaway vehicle*?"

"I thought I'd go *Grand Theft Auto* and hijack us a new car!" Valentine yelled, finally losing control. "How was *I* supposed to know I'd wind up in a no-'mancy zone?"

"...In a *what*?" Mommy was so competent, everyone forgot she had no 'mancy – how could she have known what the blotch overhead meant? She couldn't feel the slimy softness that threatened to rip open into another broach.

"You mean you can't do any 'mancy at *all*?" Mommy spluttered, jabbing her fingers towards the sirens.

"*Ixnay on the ancy-may-ot-at-all-nay*," Valentine hissed. But Savannah and her father stood behind them – Savannah's face smeared with mud, her daddy clutching the gun.

He could shoot them all, and none of them could do a damn thing about it.

What worried Aliyah was Savannah. She looked as traumatized as Daddy – and why not? Nobody in Morehead had seen 'mancy before. Now they'd witnessed the worst nightmares magic could summon.

Her gaze demanded answers Aliyah could not provide.

Mommy stepped forward, ready to play the host – and then hesitated. She settled for discreetly placing herself between Aliyah and the gun.

But Savannah's father worked his mouth as if trying to make introductions. Eventually, he nudged Savannah, who nodded as though she'd expected this.

"Daddy says you can have our car. To escape. For saving us." She looked up at the broach. "Or trying to."

Savannah's father crept forward to drop an Ale-8-One Ginger Ale keychain into Aliyah's palm.

"That's–"

"It's generous." Mommy stepped in front of Valentine before she said anything stupid. "Is there any way we can repay you?"

"Yeah." Savannah glared at Aliyah. "Show me your face."

Aliyah was looking right at Savannah. What could she–

"Your *real* face," Savannah clarified.

Oh.

Under normal circumstances, Aliyah would have ducked into the van and changed out of her pseudoskin. Yet even that trivial 'mancy would rip open another broach here.

She reached up with her fire-painted nails and peeled off her artificial skin.

She uncovered the ragged widow's peak above her forehead where the fire had melted her scalp to the bone.

She revealed her cheeks, which had been reconstructed, but her left lip still tugged to one side where the flesh had puckered.

She bared the glossy keloid scars on her neck.

I'm not a burn, she had told Aunt Valentine long ago. And in truth, her scars were barely noticeable at a distance. Nothing, her father had told her, could dampen her radiant smile.

Savannah traced Aliyah's deformities with a combination of glacial fury and bottomless pity, examining Aliyah as if trying to understand her.

Aliyah did not cry. Not in front of people.

But when she ripped the pseudoflesh from her eyelids, tears spattered.

She met Savannah's gaze, refusing to be ashamed, yet refusing to pretend she was normal anymore. Which hurt most of all; seeing Savannah scrutinize all the ways they were not alike, after having cherished all the things they had in common back at the Wendy's.

She closed her eyes, listing what they had in common: *You love nail art. You love Steven Universe. You love YouTube karaoke, and*–

"You didn't choose to be a 'mancer." Savannah gestured towards the smoking soccer goal and the murky smear overhead. "This isn't your fault."

Aliyah sagged in relief. Savannah understood. Her daddy understood. Maybe *Morehead* understood. If they could find a way to–

"But you can't ever come back." Savannah turned away.

Aliyah did not cry. Not when Savannah's father whispered in her ear to "Go with God, child." Not when Mommy turned on the car and gospel music blasted from the speakers. Not when she looked out the rear window to see Savannah standing beneath that glimmering blotch as the cop cars screeched into the soccer field.

Aliyah did not cry. She peeled away the remaining strips of pseudoflesh, feeling the rashes grow as she ripped them off like Band-Aids, relishing the pain as she uncovered herself inch by inch.

She bled until she felt nothing at all.

SEVEN
Smiling Weapons

Imani was a patient woman. She had tolerated a decade of Paul's withdrawn silence before filing for divorce. (All it had taken was Paul's death, Aliyah's enslavement, and a war that imploded several skyscrapers to get them married again.) She had endured three years of Aliyah's inexplicable outbursts before Paul had let her in on the deadly secret that their daughter was a videogamemancer. Imani, in fact, prided herself on her forbearance: her mother had taught her to be ladylike above all things.

But if Valentine planned to play "I Spy" for the next two hours, she was going to strangle that bitch.

"I spy, with my little eye," Valentine said – and here, she always tapped her right cheekbone merrily to accentuate the fact she had one eye – "Sooooomething beginning with 'R'."

Nobody answered. Nobody *had* answered, ever since they'd fled Morehead an hour ago. Paul sat stricken in the SUV's passenger seat, wheezing and clutching his broken ribs. Aliyah slumped against the window, hugging a soccer ball to her chest.

Imani cruised down the freeway, glad Valentine had stolen a trick from *Grand Theft Auto* and pulled their stolen car into an empty garage, then backed out an instant later with a different paint job, tinted windows, and a magical field that shielded them from cops.

That stabilized their situation as they headed for a safehouse in the Appalachians. She'd memorized the route to the closest 'mancer-friendly harbor before heading to Morehead – a decision that seemed positively prescient after they'd channeled away Paul's excess flux by shorting out the GPS. She'd get them somewhere to plan their next move.

But Paul and Aliyah were imploding here, in this stolen SUV, and Imani didn't know how to help them.

The back roads here wound around mountains; some of the signs had been shot off their posts. Still, she kept glancing at Aliyah in the rear view mirror: Aliyah never lifted her eyes from the car's floor, examining dried McDonald's French fries with dull disinterest.

She squeezed Paul's hand; he returned Imani's affection reflexively, but his other hand drew on an imaginary whiteboard, trying to map out what had gone wrong at Morehead.

This would have been easier if they weren't 'mancers, Imani thought.

Paul and Aliyah had always held this bizarre delusion that perfect efforts equaled perfect results. God forbid Aliyah lost, as she'd scour the replays of her videogames, hunting for the frame where she'd input the wrong command.

Imani had worked in corporate law for too long to hold onto such fragile illusions. Sometimes, you laid out a perfect case, and your company panicked and settled out of court. Sometimes your star expert had a fatal heart attack. Sometimes your legal documentation was flawless, but the opposition found a sneaky way to buy the judge a vacation villa.

Sometimes, no matter how smart you were, you lost.

Yet Paul and Aliyah's 'mancy ran on certainty. Imani found videogames so distasteful simply because they promised consistent results: play long enough, and eventually you'd beat the big boss.

And yet... her daughter's delusions fueled potent magic.

Aliyah's 'mancy allowed her to face down armies *because* she could not comprehend losing. Just as Paul could not comprehend a world where filing legal documents would not produce justice. Their 'mancy was, in a weird way, a magical incarnation of the American Dream: hard work guaranteed rewards.

Now Aliyah had lost her friend despite her best efforts, and she was crumpling inside. Just as Paul was freaking out because there was a Broach he wasn't allowed to heal, and–

"...No?" Valentine peered around eagerly, as though anyone had answered. "Well, just so you know, the answer was 'road.' And why, yes," she said, straightening with magnanimous pride, "I *did* give you an easy one." She thumped the seat. "But this next 'I Spy' will *test your vocabulary to its limits*!"

Valentine had no phone to play games on, Imani knew; she and Aliyah had shorted their handheld devices to pay down their flux loads.

Still, Imani wondered whether Valentine could fit a dead cell phone into her mouth.

They were headed for safer territory... or so Imani hoped. Without cell phones, they couldn't be sure the Appalachian safehouse hadn't been busted. SMASH had contributed to ripping open a broach during a battle with Paul – and that error had been so unforgiveable, New York had barred them from operating within state boundaries for two years.

That was what they did to *good* guys who ripped open a broach that had been healed. Whereas the four of them had scurried away, leaving a wavering tear in reality, hovering ominously over a beautiful Kentucky lake.

Imani shuddered, thinking how that must look on the news.

She squeezed his hand again; no answer. He looked over at Aliyah, trying to coax a smile out of her. Except the grim expression he bore would never produce any cheer.

Ordinarily, he'd haul out the stuff he'd packed to cheer her up – a fresh box of Dunkin' Donuts to check in with Uncle Kit, a new videogame. But they'd lost everything back at Morehead.

Valentine harrumphed, then craned her neck around, looking for the next target.

"*Got it!* I spy, with my little eye, something beginning with 'B'."

Valentine paused before arcing her index finger up, then

planting it firmly on Aliyah's head.

"'Burned Kid,'" Valentine said. "I see a burned kid."

Had she fucking said that?

Imani's head snapped up, ready to chew Valentine's face off. Paul whipped around then groaned in anguish, clutching his ribs.

Yet Valentine held their gaze coolly in the rear view mirror – an arch look that said *Trust me, I know what I'm doing.*

The thing of it was, Imani did trust Valentine – even if she hated her for *needing* that trust. Paul had often remarked how Valentine and Aliyah spoke their own language; part of it was they were both videogamemancers, of course.

But Aliyah had always been wilder than Imani had meant her to be. And so was Valentine.

Aliyah's eyes narrowed. "*What* did you call me?"

"I spied something beginning with 'B,'" Valentine shot back. "*You* did not answer. So *I* saw a Burned Kid."

"I am *not* a burned kid! And you have *never* made fun of my scars–"

"Then what do *you* see when you look at you?"

"I see a badass who's gonna kick your ass in–"

"–*language*–" Imani said.

"I," Aliyah said stiffly, "am a *badass*. Which is... It's not a bad word, Mom, they use it in *Borderlands*. It means a big boss."

"Then why not say 'Big Boss', Aliyah?"

"Because it's... it's not as *badass*."

Imani decided the moral lesson wasn't worth the energy of arguing. "Fine. Badass."

Aliyah jabbed her finger into Valentine's belly. "I see a badass who will *shred* you if you ever – *ever* – make fun of me that way again."

"Fine," Valentine said. "Your turn."

Aliyah scowled, sensing a trick – but she still wanted to know what happened next. "Fine. I spy, with my *two* little eyes–" and here, she poked her fingers underneath both of them "– something beginning with 'I'."

Valentine spread her fingers across her cleavage in a dainty motion. "'Ignoramus'? 'Imbecile'? 'Idiot'?"

A sly grin crept across Aliyah's face. "I was thinking more 'Irritating Player of I-Spy.' That game's for six year-olds."

"Fine. What do you want to play next?"

"I don't want to play anyt... Ooh! *Punch buggy*!"

Valentine grabbed her injured bicep. "There was no buggy! You just wanted to punch me!"

"It was *super* fast. I guess you didn't see it out of your right eye... oh, sorry, your *only* eye."

"My single eye sees just fine when it whips your ass at *Destiny*, kid."

Aliyah bopped her with a soccer ball. Imani would have guessed they were about to brawl, if it wasn't for Aliyah's goofy grin.

"*You kids play careful! I* will *pull over the car!*" Imani barely got the words out through her laughter. She shot a grin over at Paul, hoping the tickle fight in the back seat would draw him out of his funk...

Paul had fished out a pair of earphones from underneath his seat, and had plugged them into the car's headphone jack.

"Turn on the radio," he whispered.

Imani knew Paul could have turned on the radio by himself. He was seeking permission – like an injured junkie asking someone he trusted whether it was OK to take this Oxycontin.

"Paul, you can't listen to the news *now*," she whispered. "Give yourself a while to heal before you pour that poison into your ear."

"I gave myself precisely one hour to bathe in self-hatred." Though he wore an old-fashioned clockwork Timex, he showed her the watch face as though his self-inflicted deadline was engraved on its surface. "Now we need information to keep Aliyah protected while we're on the run."

He wouldn't be running anywhere, Imani thought. Paul had unbuttoned his shirt and removed his tie – a look that, for her dignified husband, was nearly naked. He peeled his shirt's sweat-soaked fabric away from his bruise-blackened ribs.

"She doesn't need to hear this." Paul jerked his head back

towards Aliyah. "Let me find out so she doesn't have to know."

Imani nodded.

He snapped on the radio.

– the first unsealable broach on American soil, almost certainly a terrorist act –

Valentine and Aliyah froze as the announcer's voice boomed through the car. Paul scrabbled at the headphone jack, which was apparently broken–

– or had it been working when they got the car, and this was someone's stray flux coming home to roost? Imani never could tell a genuine bad break from flux, which always unnerved her. After a while, it felt like the entire universe was out to get you.

"Sorry." Paul flailed at the radio in an attempt to shut it off, accidentally switched the channel.

– I repeat, the President will be making a speech in a few minutes. In the meantime, she has called upon America to remain calm, stressing the need for stronger anti-'mancer laws to "conscript and retrain those who would do us harm" –

Imani smoothed her dress so she wouldn't punch the window. Under normal circumstances, turning on the radio would have blasted music – but even the pop stations were interrupting the latest boy band's hit to explain that buzzsects were spilling out from the Morehead broach.

"Sorry," Paul repeated, cranking the volume down. "Sorry."

"No." Aliyah leaned forward in her seat, the soccer ball slipping from her fingers. "It's OK."

Valentine pressed the ball back into Aliyah's hands. "Come on, kid. It's just gonna be *blah blah blah* more funding for SMASH *blah blah blah* do we want to go the way of Europe *blah blah blah* 'mancers aren't people. And that's... not something you wanna listen to right now."

"You're people, baby." Imani reached back to clutch her daughter's hand.

Valentine gave her a curt nod of approval, which worried Imani. Valentine's and Imani's goals for Aliyah generally overlapped for brief periods, like an eclipse – and like an eclipse, those periods presaged dark times.

Aliyah shrugged off her mother's touch. "I did this to Savannah. We should... we should hear what I did."

– no statement from Paul Tsabo, who is rumored to have triggered at least two broaches before –

"I'd make a statement, if I could get to a *phone*," Paul muttered.

Yet Imani had sat through enough PR meetings to realize what was happening. Paul had sealed broaches ripped open by the Unimancers – and yet he'd been fighting to protect his daughter, and so the press had gone easy on him.

Not anymore.

– the broach that consumed Europe at the climax of World War II continues to spread across the continent despite the efforts of a global squadron of Unimancers. Instabilities on the Belgium border last winter caused the broach to expand twenty miles closer to the Atlantic ocean, prompting fears of what might happen if the broach crosses the coast to expand into deep sea areas –

Valentine drew a finger across her throat. "Ix-nay on the otal destruction-tay oadcast-bray," she whispered, glancing towards Aliyah, who hid behind her soccer ball.

A soccer ball with Savannah's name written upon it.

She wanted to tell Aliyah this wasn't her fault. But Aliyah had lost control on the soccer field. Not for the first time, Imani wished there was a place to get Aliyah's power under control – but the last school they'd taken her to had turned Aliyah into an assassin.

"Sssh," Paul said. "The President's coming on."

They hushed. As Imani passed a gas station, she noticed the parking lot filled with people who had pulled over to listen.

Good afternoon, the President said, her voice somber. *A few hours ago, our country – our very dimension – came under attack thanks to a broach triggered in the sleepy town of Morehead, Kentucky.*

Paul Tsabo ripped open this broach – Paul Tsabo, the criminal leader of a pro-'mancer political movement called, worryingly, "Project Mayhem."

Already, Tsabo's defenders have claimed the act was in self-defense, that he was simply attempting to allow his daughter to play soccer, that he intended to bring no harm to the people of Kentucky.

Yet "intent" cannot be our standard. A drunk driver does not intend to harm people, yet by their own blinkered judgement they kill children. And every 'mancer's judgement is impaired by a psychosis so encompassing that it weakens the fundamental principles of the universe. They are simply not competent to make decisions about safety – particularly when Europe has already been lost to 'mancers' mistakes.

This administration's stance is, and has always been, that 'mancers are not human – they are smiling weapons, waiting to go off.

Valentine checked off an imaginary square on a bingo card.

Yet because they look like us – even used to be us, the President continued, *we have been lenient in allowing ordinary citizens to campaign for anti-'mancer laws. Yet Paul Tsabo – a fugitive criminal – has acknowledged his organization trains 'mancers, runs 'mancer safehouses, hides 'mancers from SMASH's helpful rehabilitation.*

Valentine wrapped her hand around an imaginary cock and jerked it off. "That's not rehabilitation, it's brainwashing…"

In the past, some people have been sympathetic to these goals – but in the wake of the Morehead broach, America is united. With Congress's full approval, I have just declared Project Mayhem a terrorist organization. Anyone aiding or abetting Project Mayhem from this moment on – whether a 'mancer or an ordinary citizen – will have their assets seized, and face jail time.

"What?" Imani catapulted from her seat.

"Can they *do* that?"

"They can," Paul whispered.

However, we offer amnesty. Any former Project Mayhem members who wish to provide us with information and *avoid prosecution can do so toll-free by calling 1-800-SMASHEM…*

Paul grabbed for his cell phone before realizing it was broken. "I need to make a statement. Pull over, Imani, we'll find a phone – the Unimancers have never sealed a broach in their lives, only patched them over! Maybe we can broker an agreement to let me back in before the broach rips open further–"

"Stop, Paul. Just stop."

– in addition to additional emergency funding for SMASH, I have

called for our best magical expert from Europe, General Saagar Anil Kanakia, to help stabilize the Morehead broach –

"No, Imani!" Paul shook with anger. "They haven't heard our side!"

She punched his arm.

"That. Does. Not. *Matter*!" Imani hated to see that puppydog terror he always got when she yelled at him – but she had to get through to him *now*. "They're telling America that we almost disappeared down the same interdimensional sinkhole that ate Europe – and they're not wrong, Paul. You didn't seal it up like last time."

Paul objected. Imani rolled right over him.

"And it doesn't matter anymore, Paul, because they won't give you the chance. They're going to rain hell down on us. People will barrage Capitol Hill with angry letters until the politicians parade you around America as a nicely tamed Unimancer. I know you want to tell them how this never would have happened if Morehead hadn't panicked. You want to tell them you could fix it. Maybe that's even *true*. But... what we did today is exactly what they've been telling people *all* 'mancers do.

"We just lost the argument, Paul. Now the hammer will fall."

Paul's face went pale. He gulped, looking back towards Valentine, who nodded in acknowledgment. Aliyah did her best to sink into the back seat; Valentine reached over, pulled her into a tight embrace, as though she feared this might be the last time.

"I just wanted friends," Aliyah whispered. "This isn't fair."

The President had moved onto promising that America would be safe, their Unimancers would guard this broach to keep it from swelling further–

Paul shut off the radio.

"OK," Paul murmured, his chin sagging to his chest. "OK. I guess our next step is... we have to get to the safehouse."

She pressed down on the accelerator, wondering whether the Appalachian safehouse was still there – wondering how long it would shelter them before SMASH's forces rained down on them.

EIGHT
'Til the Landslide Brought Me Down

The final road to the safehouse was a muddy ditch threaded around a mountain. Paul tried not to pay attention to their surroundings as Imani wrestled the wheel; to their left was a crumbling rock face, to the right a steep wooded slope. One slip and their car would tumble into a hundred-foot drop.

"How much longer is it?" Aliyah asked.

"I didn't memorize distances, sweetie, only directions." Imani's voice was remarkably even. "It's at the end of this road, wherever that is."

Aliyah pushed her way across Valentine to peer out the passenger side window, shaking her head. "The seclusion is good, but what's our exit strategy? If SMASH corners us on this mountaintop, we've got no retreat capacity."

Paul frowned. A thirteen year-old girl shouldn't have to worry about such things.

"Hey," Valentine chided. "Uncle Robert set this safehouse up. I'm sure it's got a few tricks."

But was Robert still in charge there? As the road twisted in towards a thick forest canopy, Paul tried not to consider the possibility that someone working for the camp had betrayed them to SMASH, and now instead of a haven they'd find armed men with Magiquell darts...

They rounded a curve to find the road blocked by a huge golem of teetering rock.

"What the–"

Imani slammed on the brakes – but as they slid to a halt, Paul took in the monster straddling the road. It stood higher than the trees, thousands of moss-covered rocks stacked roughly into a man shape, its clumsy hands reaching out to grab two tree limbs as it bent over the road protectively. The sunlight glimmered through the chinks in a torso formed of fist-sized crystalline rock and shale slates.

Yet what stood out most was the grizzled old man standing on a ladder next to this faceless rock brute, reaching up to tend to his creation with deft care. His bushy eyebrows lifted high in surprise at their approach.

He tapped the beast's side, as if to get its attention.

The great rock beast made an angry clattering nose as it dove for their car, breaking apart into an avalanche, banging on the windshield as the rocks flowed over their SUV, rolling beneath the wheels, trapping them.

Valentine tried to open the door; it was stuck fast. Then she leaned forward to tap the windshield, which was miraculously uncracked, though covered with rocks with a jigsaw puzzle's precision – allowing them absolutely no view outside.

"Well," she said, "I think we have our answer as to whether 'mancers still live at the safehouse."

"*Oh, shit!*" they heard from outside – muffled, but at great volume. "That's Paul! Dammit, Yoder, I told you to stop anyone *suspicious*!"

Whoever responded spoke in a low, slow, subsonic drawl, like an earthquake that chose to speak. The words were lost through the layers of rock and an impenetrable accent, but the gist was clear: *Hold on, now, how was I to know these were your friends?*

"Look, Yoder, when SMASH comes, they're gonna be arriving in tanks, not a soccer mom special... oh, never mind. How long will it take to dig them out?"

"But a touch," the rumbly voice said, trudging closer. His steps were well-paced, as if no fuss could make him move faster. "All I must do is pop this rock out, and–"

There was a sharp *pop* as he yanked one stone free – and the rocks cascaded away from the car like water, rolling off obligingly to reveal Robert Paulson striding towards the car door.

Paul had never gotten used to the new Robert, though he understood the new look was a side effect of his security chief giving up his *Fight Club*-inspired 'mancy. When Paul had first met Robert, Robert had called himself Tyler Durden, and his magic had shaped his bruised body into a carbon copy of Brad Pitt. But after he'd met Valentine, his need to be Tyler Durden had dwindled – and he'd slowly mutated into a beefy six-foot-five man who looked like an aging nightclub bouncer, complete with a lurking air of ominous violence, a battered leather jacket, and a sagging paunch.

Yet anyone who knew Robert thought of him as a teddy bear. And he looked like a teddy bear, crouching down with his arms open, grinning like a polecat as he shouted, "*Rock star*!"

Valentine burst out of the car to leap into his arms, wrapping her legs around his waist, grabbing his face by both cheeks.

"You should have *seen* what I did, baby!" Her face was flushed with excitement. "*Full super-saiyan!* I made it *rain*, and what I rained was *destruction*!"

"I *did* see it!" He held up his smartphone, matching her giddiness. "Somebody posted it on YouTube!"

She twirled around to curl up in his arms, and they watched Valentine's magical battle with the cooing fondness that other couples might use to watch baby pictures. Robert squeezed her tight every time an explosion went off – he still had a *Fight Club*-mancer's appreciation of his girlfriend's devastation.

When it was over, they had the faint flush of a couple who'd watched a particularly satisfying porno. "Whew," Robert said. "When was the last time you teed off on anything like that?"

Valentine stepped gracefully out of his arms, like a woman regretfully bowing out from a dance. "It's been a while."

"...has it?"

She stiffened.

Paul knew Valentine's inactivity had been a source of tension.

She stayed by Robert's side, which was handy because Robert generally stayed by Paul's side – but between Robert's brute competence and Paul's extensive planning, there hadn't been much need for violence. Even the rallies had grown efficient enough that Valentine's magic was used mostly for crowd control. And since Valentine's videogame magic couldn't create anything lasting, she'd sat by the sidelines as Robert had built safehouses or delegated Project Mayhem duties or just took Krav Maga classes.

He shrugged apologetically. "Sorry, love. Your 'mancy remains a glorious supernova to behold. It's just, you know... things have been going *right* lately."

She waved him off. He took her hand, holding it tight and long – a little too tight and a little *too* long, Paul judged. And if Paul noticed Valentine's discomfort then it must be blatantly apparent to everyone else.

Then Robert glanced over Paul's shoulder.

"How's she doing?"

Paul realized Aliyah had yet to get out of the car.

Valentine shook her head: *not good.* Robert hunched down, stuck his head in through the window.

"We're safe, kid," he assured her. "I've set up tons of safehouses and I assure you – this will be the last to fall." He gestured back towards a distant set of rustic cabins, where a small militia tended to gardens, unpacked crates, toted water buckets. "I handpicked every man and woman for loyalty. And the feds are distinctly not welcome here in the Smokeys. More importantly, we've got some real unique 'mancers in our stockpile. Wanna see 'em?"

It was a good gambit: Aliyah loved naming new 'mancies – and given 'mancy could spring from any obsession, the endless varieties of magics that flourished in their safehouses were a delight. Seriously, how often did you get to be embraced by a stone golem? Put that lumbering statue in a museum and art critics would have praised its rough-hewn beauty. This 'mancer had taken a thousand rocks no one would have looked at twice, seen a secret magnificence within them, and labored until he joined simple stone into a geologic clockwork.

Aliyah stared at the heaps of stone as if all she saw was an avalanche.

She reluctantly allowed Robert to lift her from the vehicle. She looked back towards Paul.

"You're coming along, right, Dad?"

Paul was so filled with gratitude that he leaned down to enfold Aliyah in a hug before his broken ribs made him recoil in pain. Like most teenagers, Aliyah ran hot and cold – she couldn't have abandoned him fast enough back at the Morehead Wendy's.

But going to visit the new 'mancers? That was their ritual.

"Come on, kid," Robert said. "You've been marinating in your own misery for hours now, get out and walk it off. It'll do ya good."

"…except for that blazing ball of death overhead scarring my fine pale skin…" Valentine muttered darkly.

"Got you covered. Literally." He tossed her a travel-sized sunscreen bottle. She snatched it out of the air before slathering it on her skin with exaggerated "yuck" noises, and for a moment Paul marveled at how the two of them functioned like a single organism.

"Who'll drive the car back? Will he do it?" Aliyah asked, pointing at Yoder, who had ignored the conversation to pick up rocks. This was, sadly, something Paul had come to expect; most 'mancers were so obsessed with their craft, their social skills had atrophied into indifference.

"Clip-clop, clip-clop, clip-clop, *bang bang*, clip-clop, clip-clop, clip-clop," Robert said rhythmically.

"…what?" Aliyah squinted, suspicious. Valentine stifled a laugh with her hand.

"Yoder doesn't drive," Robert explained. "He's Amish. All he knows are horse-drawn buggies."

"So what was that noise?"

"An Amish drive-by," Valentine explained, and both Robert and Valentine dissolved into childish giggles while Aliyah stood stiffly, not getting the joke.

Paul wondered how the Amish treated 'mancers in their reclusive communities, then decided a selfish devotion to a hobby didn't go over well with a community that shunned computers because they felt possessions detracted from brotherly love.

"Does his 'mancy have a name?" Aliyah asked.

Some 'mancers were so into their passion they'd forgotten their names, let alone the names of their magic – but Aliyah needed to catalogue things, a trait she'd inherited from Paul. *Her room is messy but her mind is tidy*, he thought.

Robert shrugged. "He's a… rock… balancer… -'mancer. We spend enough time sweeping up rocks that we haven't had time for better nomenclature."

"So what do they call his hobby? I mean, in scientific circles?"

"They call it 'rock balancing.' It's… a pretty weird hobby, even by hobby standards. And the guys who do it tend not to *really* get out much."

"You mean they don't get *in* much," Valentine interjected.

He shot her twin fingerguns as payment for her zinger.

Aliyah brightened – enough for Paul to feel they could get through this. "So *I* get to name it?"

"Yoder, you care?"

Yoder weighed two different rocks in his hands, having already rebuilt a stack of schist up to waist height. He chewed a piece of straw as he eased one of the two rocks onto the teetering pile, serene as a meditating monk.

"…Yoder doesn't care. It's yours."

They headed towards the camp, leaving Yoder and his pile behind. Aliyah bounced along at Paul's side, trying out various names and discarding them. Up ahead, there was the distant sound of men chopping lumber, an old woman rocking on a chair. The wind rustled through the trees, a rich chlorophyll scent – out here, he could pretend America wasn't mobilizing to capture them.

"So," Paul said. "You told Aliyah this would be the last safehouse to fall."

"Yup." Robert was sober, but confident.

"Which implies others *have* fallen."

"Hammer's fallen, *mon capitaine*. Five of our safehouses have gone dark in the last four hours."

Imani arched an eyebrow. "Out of how many...?"

Robert chuckled. Though he'd discarded Tyler Durden's swagger, he'd never quite lost the *Fight Club* black humor. "Now, Ms Dawson. You know you're not allowed to know that. Not when you sleep in the same bed as Number One."

The Unimancers had forced them to adopt distributed tactics: once you were inducted into the Unimancy squadrons, everything you knew got absorbed into their collective hivemind. That was why the government had been so desperate to capture Paul; they thought if they got him, they'd have total access to Project Mayhem.

But Paul had ensured no one person's defection could bring down Project Mayhem. There were overlapping areas of expertise, so the removal of one person wouldn't erase vital institutional memory – Paul had constructed a complex chain of responsibilities to ensure everyone had exactly what they needed to know to accomplish their mission, and no more.

Yet Imani had always chafed at being left out. She was too used to being the CEO's right hand.

"I think," she said politely, "that given how many of our safehouses are going dark, it might be time to reevaluate who knows what."

"We've planned for contingencies like this, Ms Dawson. Suffice it to say that it's a significant percentage of our sheltering operations."

"In four *hours*?" Paul asked.

Robert smacked his lips. "Yeah."

"SMASH can't have gotten that efficient in the last four hours... Can they?"

Robert made a *comme ci, comme ça* gesture. "Can't say for sure, Paul. They're *dark*. But if I had to guess... no, SMASH isn't more efficient. It's everything else that's changed."

Valentine nudged him in the ribs. "Hey, not everyone needs to hear this." Aliyah sucked air between her teeth.

"I'm not a *child*, Valentine," she hissed. "I've fought just as hard to protect us as *you* have. You *know* what happens if you try to cut me out of the loop, so don't start *that* shit again."

"–language–" Imani chided absently. They remembered when Paul had tried to shield her from his operations – frustrated, she'd used her 'mancy to warp into his operations, with disastrous results.

"*You* don't always know what's right for you," Valentine shot back. Paul cringed. Valentine had let loose a high sniper's shot that implied if Aliyah had avoided the soccer league, none of this would have happened.

"*Enough!*" Imani snapped. "So why are our safehouses falling apart, Robert?"

Robert shrugged. "Part of it's the Morehead broach sending folks into a panic. Lotta people have tolerated their crazy neighbors for years. Now the President's convinced everyone y'all are walkin' nukes, they're putting two and two together."

"And the other part?"

"...Mr Olizewski mentioned something about the Contract going on the fritz?"

Paul slumped against a tree, overwhelmed, feeling the pain from his grinding ribs.

Of *course* the Contract's destruction would affect more than him. The Contract had been a way for wayward 'mancers nationwide to disperse their flux.

That was why SMASH was so good at hunting 'mancers. They didn't have to be supernaturally efficient – though they were – all they had to do was force 'mancers to use enough magic to generate a tide of bad luck, and their prey would drown in their own backlash.

And the 'mancers in the safehouses, mostly awkward asocials like Yoder – nobody would have told them the Contract had imploded. They would have done 'mancy same as always, then found their bad luck boomeranging back on them.

Imani rubbed his back while Paul tried to get himself under control. He tried not to think of innocent 'mancers hauled off to the Refactor, men and women with quiet hobbies like cryptography or glassblowing or stamp collecting – tortured until they lost their minds, then reprogrammed into government-friendly drones.

"We're going to lose more, aren't we?" he asked. "Before the day is over?"

"Lots," Robert said.

Aliyah gasped; Imani buried her daughter's face in her shoulder.

"Aliyah Rebecca Tsabo-Dawson," Paul said sternly, using the Parent Voice every dad used to command his child's attention. "Look at me."

Aliyah turned, reluctantly.

"I won't lie, Aliyah. Your flux caused this broach. But your bravery stopped the broach from ripping Kentucky apart. If you hadn't been clever and bold, Savannah and her father would be dead. We'd *all* be dead."

Her chest hitched. She'd always hated showing weakness. "I should have kept my flux under control."

"It would have been better, yes. And you'll *do* better. And... we'll adapt."

Robert cleared his throat. "Step one would be rebuilding the Contract."

Paul sighed. "That'll take time. People have to sign it in person. And there'll be a lot less people willing to sign up now that we're officially terrorists..."

"You've got thirteen Project Mayhem folks here who'll take the hit. Start there." He waved over at three college-aged kids troubleshooting a generator–

– instead, an elderly black woman came running over towards them, flailing her arms. She stopped, hands on knees, catching her breath, then gasped: "The broach, sir – news says – it's expanding – they're evacuating Morehead–"

"Have you got a desk ready?" Paul asked. "Five fresh Bic pens, a stack of legal pads?"

"Sir," Robert said proudly, "in the highly likely event that you are captured, I cannot divulge the number of American safehouses to you. But I *can* tell you each Project Mayhem safehouse comes prepared with a fresh set of bureaucromantic scrying tools."

The crisp metal desk looked absurd in the rundown shack. A handful of the Project Mayhem acolytes – there really was no better word for people who'd chosen to abandon their lives to tend to 'mancers in the Appalachian foothills – swept the dirt floor as Paul walked in.

"This'll do," Paul said.

They straightened with pride. Then they flattened themselves against the walls, silently requesting permission to watch him work.

He still found that a pleasant change. When he'd started, the only mundanes who'd *wanted* to watch him work had been K-Dash and Quaysean. 'Mancy terrified most ordinary people, and they no sooner wanted to be in its presence than they wanted to hang around a toxic waste dump.

Paul crossed himself: he wasn't religious, but he missed K-Dash and Quaysean, and had no better way to mark their passing. And, on his more cynical days, he thought maybe their deaths had proved the ordinary people's point: hanging around 'mancy had led them to a horrible end.

After the Morehead broach, Paul wanted no distractions. He shook their hands and politely escorted them out.

Paul sat down at the desk. It seemed ridiculous, to be so calm when broaches were tearing open – but a righteous bureaucrat gathered information first.

He closed his eyes. Robert set up the desk just the way he liked it; his fingers closed around a box of Bic pens. He ripped the shrink wrap off the legal pad, feeling delightful blankness underneath his fingertips.

He clicked the pen. And wrote the mantra every form began with:

First name. Last name. Address. Address 2. City, Street, Zip...

The key, Paul thought, was the Unimancers' records of the Morehead broach. They'd need to commit the data somewhere, to compare the broach's energy outputs to how it had looked an hour ago – and they'd need to send that data to other scientists, to make requests for comparisons to the European broach's data, to compile summaries to send to their superiors.

Someone had to have access to those records.

Bureaucracy was about getting proper access.

Paul could recreate a Freedom of Information Request without blinking, had committed to memory all the forms private investigators used to get information on recalcitrant clients, knew the FBI's clearance levels by heart.

This wasn't hacking, oh no; hacking would have had Paul hunting for weaknesses in the system.

Paul was attempting to convince the system he needed proper access. And who needed to know what was happening at the Morehead broach than a man who could seal broaches singlehandedly?

Once he'd gotten the information, he'd demonstrate his expertise, then broker a peace long enough to band together to solve the problem. Because bureaucracy triumphed when petty politics failed.

The legal pad expanded outwards, the edges sagging off the desk, Paul's fussy handwriting condensing into neat Helvetica fonts as the legal pads folded themselves into stacks. He bootstrapped up the info, using the most arcane methods – reaching forward into the future to file Freedom of Information Acts from two decades from now, certifying himself as a scientist with the proper credentials, using layers of forged identities to ensure no one could track him back to this address in Kentucky.

He chipped away the government's record-keeping layers, skirting their alarm systems. The more secure facilities had opals that cracked in the presence of 'mancy – a precaution that couldn't keep a 'mancer out, but would alert the authorities when someone had rifled through their files. Yet Paul's 'mancy was no louder than a paper dropped into a file. Only the most expensive opals might track his presence, and those would have shattered near the Morehead broach.

Most 'mancy was a vulgar assault on reality, like Valentine's summoned guns: Paul's 'mancy was what an insanely determined man with infinite time could have accomplished.

Paul's pen stopped writing in flowing lines, started hammering spots into the legal pad in even rows: the stuttering recreation of an old-fashioned dot-matrix printer, spooling off sheets of classified data.

Paul held up the two accounts, comparing them: the Morehead broach's readings when the SMASH emergency intercept team had set up their first equipment at 12:17 pm today, and the latest readings filed fifteen minutes ago.

He squinted.

Paul ran his thumb down the numbers. He was no scientist, but the readings didn't appear to fluctuate wildly. He triggered a search, requesting comparisons: the broach's size, its radiation emanations, snapshots.

All identical except for minor variations.

So why would they claim the broach was expanding? Yes, that would make Project Mayhem look even worse, but it would throw America into a panic. Yet America was already *in* a panic. The President was getting everything she'd wanted.

What could the government accomplish by lying about an expanding broach that they couldn't do with a stable one?

– they're evacuating Morehead –

"Daddy says you can have our car."

Paul dropped his pen.

There'd been at least two hundred people on those soccer fields, and SMASH would debrief every last one to see what they knew about Paul and Aliyah. SMASH must have known the broach precluded 'mancy – and thus, some mundane local had assisted their escape.

This could be their way of spiriting away people for more brutal interrogations.

Yet even black-ops agencies had to track their prisoners. Paul shifted gears – he had long ago passed the bar in every state he needed to, had a terrifyingly comprehensive understanding of how to pressure the legal system. Finding secret prisoners would be trickier, as he'd have to escalate up the chain, but–

The data plopped obligingly into his hands, addressed to him.

Paul hesitated, the paper greasy to the touch. He wondered if this was a magical trap. But no, the trade-off of turning a 'mancer's unique passion into the gray slurry of Unimancy was they couldn't do anything other than share data across the hivemind.

Yet the names of the people allowed to access this file were clear: the President, her cabinet, some high-ranking United Nations members... and Mr Paulos Costa Tsabo, leader of Project Mayhem.

He read it.

After preliminary interviews where it was confirmed that Aliyah Tsabo-Dawson, also known as [PROJECT HOTPLATE], was attempting to befriend several of the girls on the field, our conclusion is that the Morehead broach was no accident. [PROJECT HOTPLATE] is the youngest known 'mancer to evince powers, and the generally accepted version of events is that she was accelerated into premature 'mancy by the terrorist acts of [PROJECT BLACKBURN].

We believe this broach was not in fact intended to be a broach, but in fact was a clumsy attempt to accelerate the creation of 'mancers of [PROJECT HOTPLATE]'s age. Psychological profiles indicate that [PROJECT HOTPLATE] is undergoing adolescent trauma caused by a lack of age-appropriate socialization.

"No," Paul whispered. "That's ridiculous, we never would have–"

As such, we have been authorized to a) incarcerate the eighty-four potential 'mancers who were present on or near the field at the time of the broach, along with their custodians, b) remove them to a secure facility, and c) monitor them for an unspecified time period until such a time as we can ensure no one there will threaten American interests.

Unfortunately, as it is well known that [PROJECT MONGOOSE], [PROJECT HOTPLATE]'s father, has the ability to access secure records of any sort, General Saagar Anil Kanakia has requested that no records be kept in any form as to who is being relocated, or as to where they are located, or as to the former residents of Morehead's current conditions.

The President has authorized this request.

We acknowledge this regrettable lack of record-keeping means it is possible we may lose track of who was incarcerated, or when. Without access to medical records, we will not know which of them have conditions that may prove to be fatal in captivity. Furthermore, with no ability to delegate responsibility, we acknowledge this lack of institutional memory may lose sight of these poor souls, condemning them to a lifetime of imprisonment for reasons no one guarding them can remember.

The only way to ensure these people get the proper treatment they deserve is for the only man who can stop this security breach to turn himself in to SMASH forces immediately.

Your move, Paul.

Sincerely,

General Saagar Anil Kanakia, Commander, United Nations Broach Suppressions Unit

NINE
Sturdy Bookshelves

The green kite hung high in the blue sky, darting back and forth like a combatant. Birds flew nervously past it.

Aliyah couldn't see the kite's owner yet, though a quivering taut string led down to what Uncle Robert explained was the glade where Hamir practiced. Uncle Robert kept up a steady stream of talk to distract her, telling her how difficult it'd been convincing Hamir to switch to a camouflaged kite so his 'mancy wouldn't show up on aerial surveillance.

Sadly, only Daddy could keep her memories at bay.

She was vaguely curious to see this new 'mancer's kite-magic. But without Daddy to hold her hand, she kept thinking back to poor Idena, who'd shyly folded paper until her creations unfurled into beautiful origamimancy blossoms. She remembered Mrs Vinere, the masqueromancer, who'd fitted ceramic masks to your face that let you roar like a lion. She remembered Wayne the plushiemancer and his hammock of pink kitten dolls.

She remembered the comfort she'd felt back at the Institute, where Mrs Vinere and Wayne and Idena had lived. She remembered the triumph as she'd raised her sword and called out to the sixteen 'mancers who lived in Mr Payne's luxury apartments: *"My name is Aliyah! I am almost nine years old! Who wants to play with me?"*

She'd thought happiness would keep them safe.

The birds squawked as they circled around the kite. A hawk high above darted down, sensing easy prey, a reddish-brown blur thrumming from above–

The kite thrashed once, twice, three times.

Its string trisected the hawk – first lopping off one wing, then mercifully slicing through the torso in a piñata of gore.

Now that Aliyah looked closer, the string glinted in the sun, covered in ground glass.

"He's a sweetheart, he really is," Uncle Robert assured her. "But I'm the best kite flyer in the camp, and I make Charlie Brown look like Ray Bethell."

Like Aunt Valentine, Uncle Robert made a lot of references that nobody quite got. You learned to skip past these little ignorances, like thumbing past a cutscene.

"Anyway, Hamir needs to compete. It took me weeks to convince him the locals hunted birds, so he could too."

She heard the *smack* as the hawk's body hit a rock. It sounded like Rainbird slapping her.

You killed once, in self-defense, Rainbird had told her. *Now it's time you murdered*. And *that* memory cascaded into flashbacks of Rainbird slaughtering everyone at the Institute to cover up their trail. Aliyah had done too much 'mancy, Rainbird had said, and he had to guarantee SMASH wouldn't track them down.

She remembered how Rainbird had burned Wayne's stuffed animal friends as they'd waddled in to rescue him. He'd cried the whole time, and then Rainbird had pushed him into the pyre. She remembered Idena, wrapped in her own origami and set alight…

"…Uncle Robert?"

"Yeah?"

"I don't want to see 'mancers."

That was the nice thing about Uncle Robert; Mom, Daddy, Aunt Valentine, none of them knew how to relax. Robert understood the need for downtime.

"We got a guest cabin you can kip out in, if you need to stare at the walls a while," he offered.

"That'd be good."

He led her back to the main area. She trailed behind, wishing she could hold Dad's hand and not feel quite so lonely.

Dad hated what Rainbird had done – but when he spoke of the incident, it was with pride: Rainbird, he told people, had proven Aliyah wasn't a killer. And... yeah. After watching what killing had done to Rainbird, what Rainbird had wanted to do with *her*, Aliyah had vowed never to kill anyone ever again.

That wasn't what Rainbird had taught her, though.

They walked up to the cabins – which weren't cabins. They were raised off the ground on white oak boxes, which was weird–

– but what was even weirder was the cabins' outward-facing walls were *shelves*.

In fact, now that she paid attention, the cabins had been assembled from identical, waist-high bookcases mortared together. Each bookcase had two shelves, glued into slots in the side, with a flat board on the top and bottom. Each seemed competently made, but not flashy.

The boxes on the bottom of the cabin, Aliyah realized, were bookshelves facing downwards, their backs pointed up. The walls were yard-high bookcases pushed together, stacked on 2x4s to separate them, and then the gaps plugged up with clay to keep the wind out.

Even the roof was bookcases slanted at an angle, the shelves facing downwards into the room so the rain wouldn't catch in them, stacked onto beams and strapped in with nylon tie-downs.

"That's... a lot of effort to build a cabin," Aliyah said.

"Oh. Yeah." Robert did a brief double-take, as if this bizarre sight had become so ordinary it had ceased to register. "Thaaaaat'd be Mr Oliszewski's handiwork. He's... Well, it's a matter of debate around the camp what his 'mancy is. You could ask him yourself, if you don't need responses. Quiet man. Like a walking marshmallow."

She stepped up into the bookcase-cabin, squeezing through an entryway that was precisely the width of one narrow bookcase. The floor sunk under her weight. There was no door, aside from a heavy plywood sheet to slide in front of the entry gap. They'd put a wobbly rocking chair in there.

"Did he make the rocking chair?" Aliyah asked.

Robert snorted. "Oh, no. No, no, no. At 8:15 every morning, Mr Oliszewski rises. He bathes, dresses, at 9:25 he makes himself an egg-white omelet with low-fat Swiss cheese – he is *very* particular about his brand of Swiss cheese – and at 10:15, he starts cutting the boards for the day's bookcase. At 11:10, he begins sanding. At 12:30, lunch – a ham sandwich with salad. At 1:15, he routs the dadoes for the shelves before dry-fitting the carcase at 2:05–"

"–I get the point–"

"–and come 4:30, he has glued together a bookcase. A very *sturdy* bookcase. Mr Oliszewski has been doing this ever since his retirement eighteen years ago. The exact same bookcase. Every time."

"So why not tear them apart?"

Robert gave her a knowing grin. "You could *try*. We did. We have the reverse-Excalibur challenge – we bought an industrial-grade axe, and whoever makes a dent in one of Mr Oliszewski's bookshelves gets to be King of Appalachia. Thus far? Not a *scratch*. Fire doesn't touch 'em, we've thrown 'em at bears, dropped them off cliffs–"

Aliyah repressed a giggle. This was what her father loved about 'mancy – its unpredictability. Who would have guessed some reclusive hermit would produce unbreakable bookshelves?

She wanted to share this with him. He was so good at making magic seem like some marvelous gift. That's why she always took him to see the 'mancers – Daddy would have found some way to make that dead hawk seem beautiful.

"So you built cabins out of them?"

"Mr Oliszewski makes one a day, rain or shine. They had them stacked into a pile we used to call Bookshelf Mountain, but that got to be visible from the air. So... they made cabins." He thumped the side affectionately. "One day we'll find a libriomancer and these guys will get on like a *house* on fire."

She laughed – and then remembered what happened the last time she'd made friends with 'mancers, Rainbird had murdered them.

"Get out."

Uncle Robert bowed and backed away respectfully.

She shouldered the heavy plywood in to block the entryway. The darkness felt good. Laughter was an addiction she needed to purge herself of.

Instead, she sat in a musty room, acclimating herself to the taste of no one.

Dad thought Rainbird had taught her not to kill. What Rainbird had *actually* taught her was that her friendship was a curse. She'd spent months telling herself she'd trained in 'mancy, it was safe to hang around people, she wouldn't rain down unfathomable catastrophes on anyone she called a friend.

Aliyah bit her fingernails, felt the paint chip in her mouth.

She opened her backpack, set out the nail files and sponges she'd rescued from Morehead field. She scraped the old polish off, decided she was bored with these colors, mixed her own hues until she was satisfied. She sponged on a quick fade – a gradient from dark green at the cuticles, shading to pale white at the tips.

Boring. She'd *done* fade ombres before.

Frowning, she got out the cat-tail brush, deciding what to put on her nails. She threaded black throughout before realizing these were *Minecraft* colors, so she drew tiny creepers in the woods and diamond swords and pixelated Steve faces...

The creepers on her thumbs moved.

The diamond swords on her pinkies gleamed.

Aliyah screamed, snapping the brush in half.

She put her head in her hands, realizing yesterday's nails had popped into flame when she'd concentrated on them. She just hadn't thought anything unusual about it at the time.

It wasn't videogamemancy she'd done, but fingernailmancy. *Anything* she focused on enough would spark magic.

Kid, you're a 'mancer, Aunt Valentine had told her once. *Your dreams bleed out of your head and turn into reality. That means you will spend your life alone.*

Even if she'd gotten her nail party with Savannah, she would have ruined it. She'd have gotten bored doing French manicures and tried something crazy, and concentrating on a new nail art would have sparked magic.

She flung the nail bottles at the wall, shrieking as they shattered. She clawed at the paint–

She'd destroyed a town full of good people for something that *wouldn't have even made her happy*.

Worse, even with all that, she knew she'd try again. After a couple of years of loneliness, she'd get desperate enough to risk someone else's life.

She hugged her knees, curling up in a corner. If she only had the strength to live alone. But family wasn't the same as friendship, she was starved for friendship–

The plywood entryway splintered into pieces.

Aliyah screamed. Had SMASH found them at last? She felt relief – her struggles were over, someone would punish her–

Aunt Valentine stepped inside with smoking hands, biting her lip with embarrassment. "Sorry," she apologized. "I panicked when I heard you yell. But your father – he's summoning a War Table."

"This is the most secure location you have?" Dad clutched a manila file folder to his chest as they approached a log cabin.

"It's so secure you'll need special glasses to visit Mawmaw," Uncle Robert assured him, handing out black plastic horn-rimmed glasses. "Mawmaw's sweet as sugar, but do *not* take these visors off or it's *Petrificus totalus* time."

They were prescription lenses that turned Aliyah's vision into painful blurs. Valentine squinted out of one eye, fumbling her way ahead with outstretched hands towards the cabin, which seemed covered in dilapidated spiderwebs.

A pair of white-tailed deer stood before the cabin, staring mindlessly at the walls. They didn't move as Imani crept towards them; the deers' attention was focused entirely upon the fluttering white webs tacked to the cabin's side.

"Sometimes I pretend this is a really good movie they came to watch," Robert said. "You know, like one where Bambi goes on a roaring rampage of revenge against all the hunters."

Uncle Robert slapped the deer on the flank – they looked startled, then fled.

"The cabin catches rabbits, raccoons, squirrels – they even found a bear hypnotized out here once. Waking Miss Grizzly up was some good times, I'm told."

"Is this some *Kiss of the Spider-Woman* bullshit?" Valentine asked. "You *know* I'm not good with spiders. The best part of any dungeon crawl is reducing those chitinous fuckers to stains."

Robert rubbed her shoulders affectionately, like a ringman readying a boxer. "Mawmaw wouldn't hurt a fly. Come on, you'll love her sweet tea."

Mawmaw, as it turned out, was a sweet sun-wrinkled grandmother who apologized for not having more ice for her sweet tea, the electricity kept going out here, but all the boys and girls were absolutely lovely. She was far too old to walk around, these fine people had taken her from the nursing home, but they'd put her up in this *lovely* well-kept cabin and have you seen my doilies? Goodness, I couldn't get by without my lace. The boys, they put them up on the walls for me.

Mawmaw sat in her rocking chair, surrounded by wafting lace circles, a ball of thread sitting by her gnarled feet, her knitting needles never ceasing as she leaned forward to ask Aliyah how old she was.

Aliyah tried her best to answer, but the elaborate lace patterns on the doilies distracted her. They spiraled into tight Mandelbrot loops, impossibly complex patterns that kept revealing more patterns. Following their corkscrew arches with her eyes had the pleasure of chasing a man down a busy street – she trailed a thin thread through a complex intersection, then navigated her way to the anchor-point of the next knot.

Mawmaw had been talking for minutes. Aliyah couldn't tell you what she'd said.

She reached up to take off these damned glasses to get a better look...

"Hang on, kid," Robert warned her, grabbing Aliyah's shoulder. "She's almost asleep..."

Sure enough, Mawmaw slid into slumber. Yet even though she snored like a frail spinster, her knitting needles clicked on in her sleep.

Aliyah felt light-headed, despite the monstrous headache shooting through her temples from the glasses. She needed to follow the patterns to the center...

Valentine rapped her knuckles on Aliyah's scalp. "Not the time to see the sailboat in the Magic Eye, kid," she whispered.

Aliyah had long determined she'd never get all of Aunt Valentine's references.

"They *are* pretty," Mom sighed, looking around. "It's not the worst thing to lose your mind in, I suppose. She doesn't even know she's a 'mancer, does she?"

Robert shook his head. "No. But she almost took out her nursing home. The nurses went into her room to look at her craftsmanship. They stayed for days..."

Aliyah felt a tremendous sympathy welling up for this old, frail woman. Like Aliyah, she'd set off a process she hadn't fully understood – Mawmaw had meant to make pretty doilies.

She wished she could still see things the way she had back at the Institute, back when she'd been intoxicated with masqueromancers and plushiemancers. That old Aliyah would have admired the cunning knotwork, gushed to her daddy how Mawmaw had made patterns so artful that they were, literally, mesmerizing.

Yet all Aliyah could think of was that roomful of starving, hypnotized nurses.

Now Mawmaw had nodded off, the only sound in the cabin was the *click-click-click* of her needles.

Dad flipped nervously through the folder he'd brought, frowning down at it.

Mom sat between them, wearing too much makeup – never a good sign. Mom was usually super-stylish, but when she got stressed she scrubbed her face clean, then repainted it with sharp edges that made her look catlike. She sat stiffly, looking haggardly at Dad like she was committing his face to memory.

Aunt Valentine and Uncle Robert, well… They held hands lovingly, thirsty for each other's skin contact as always, except Aunt Valentine was squinting at the doilies as though they were a puzzle to be solved and Uncle Robert was sweating as he fumbled in his pocket.

It's a ring, Aliyah realized. *He's working up the courage to give her a ring.*

Aunt Valentine and Uncle Robert had dated for five years, and even though Aunt Valentine had made it clear she retained the ability to date whoever she goddamned well pleased, she'd never so much as looked at another man since they'd almost snapped the Institute in half with their disgusting magical kinky sex.

They kept everyone up at night, slapping and grunting and slamming each other against walls, which everyone pretended not to hear. And Aunt Valentine always glowed with cryptic smiles the next morning…

But then she'd trail behind Uncle Robert as he went about his day, thumbing her Nintendo DS while Robert oversaw the creation of another safehouse or did another security walkthrough for Daddy's next speech or disappeared for a day or two as he made secret Project Mayhem plans that Aunt Valentine couldn't know about in case SMASH pried open her brains.

And Aunt Valentine stayed glued to her screen, coruscating with banked magical potential, charting increasingly elaborate speed runs on the toughest games as she prepared for the day when Uncle Robert would need her to go super saiyan.

Except Uncle Robert was so good at what he did, he needed super saiyan Valentine less and less.

But Aliyah knew what Uncle Robert was thinking. He'd almost lost Aunt Valentine to the Morehead broach. The government was coming for them. Shouldn't he propose before something went wrong?

Aliyah tolerated their squicky sex because they were still ridiculously schmoopy despite their bruisetastic ways. She could see Uncle Robert debating whether proposing now would be romantic enough, then deciding the War Table would be too much of a distraction.

She should have been disappointed. But proposing to someone like Aunt Valentine was like tipping over a Coke machine – you couldn't do it in one push. You had to work your way up to it.

She wondered what kickass dress she'd get to wear at the wedding.

Daddy cleared his throat. "All right. I, uh… This is too big for one man's decision. So I'll take your vote."

He passed out copies of a memo – official-looking paperwork, brandished with a government seal, signed with a flourish by some general with a *ridiculously* swoopy signature.

It was hard reading it through the warped glasses. Aliyah had just gotten to the terrible part when Valentine ripped her copy in half.

"This guy has balls the size of Rhode Island, if he thinks we're gonna let you turn yourself in," she spat, keeping her voice low so as not to wake Mawmaw. "And I'm gonna remove his swollen balls, plop 'em on a fuckin' hibachi, and chop 'em into testicle sashimi so I can force-feed him balls till his stomach bursts."

Daddy sagged in relief.

She realized: *He thought we'd ask him to turn himself in.* She realized Daddy had been willing to sacrifice himself a hundred times over to save Aliyah, so of *course* he'd sacrifice himself to save the people of Morehead.

All that held him back was his loyalty to his family.

She thought *she* felt guilty about Morehead.

"You can't turn yourself in," she said. "But… we have to rescue them."

"We will not." Mom's voice was taut as piano wire. "We don't know where they are. We don't have the Contract anymore. With the government out to get us, we *cannot* afford to take risks."

"Actually…" Dad ignored the way Mom's head snapped around. "I think I know where they are."

"They're off the books! They are *invisible* to you!"

"They are, yes. But… troop logistics always leave ripples. Morehead-Rowan airport has been closed to the public until 12:00 noon tomorrow. There's been emergency jet fuel supplies diverted there. It's possible that's to handle the broach, but…"

Valentine nodded. "…driving two hundred native prisoners of war across the country risks seriously bad PR. They're gonna fly 'em out."

"If this operation is off the books, their organization has to be for shit," Robert said. "They don't know *we* know where the prisoners are. They won't expect us to come at them – especially given we've never rescued mundanes before. Given that it's been–" he checked his cell phone "–a little over six hours since everything hit the fan, they probably won't be expecting us to go on the offensive.

"This could work." Uncle Robert tapped his fingers against his teeth. "This could actually work."

Mom gripped the rocking chair's armrests hard enough to yank one of them straight off the frame. "That's too many ifs to risk a family on. Driving back into a hornet's nest of Unimancers when they're *already* on high alert is suicide! What will we do when they capture you, Paul?"

Daddy swallowed. "We've kept me separated from the day-to-day business, so they won't get much. And with the Contract destroyed, they can't get access to the people who signed up for–"

"I don't *give* a shit about *Project Mayhem*!" Mom leapt to her feet, ignoring the way Mawmaw came to. "I'm not asking you 'How do we function politically?', Paul! I'm asking you how *this family* will function when they scrub your brain and turn you into a smiling Judas! How will Aliyah react when her turncoat father comes to kidnap her?!"

Mom flexed her hands like she wanted to punch something.

Everyone turned to look at Aliyah.

"I think…"

And if Aliyah thought Daddy would judge her for what she was about to say, she'd never have spoken. But she thought of her friends who'd burned at the Institute. She thought of K-Dash and Quaysean hugging as the flames consumed them.

She thought about Savannah and her daddy huddled next to each other for warmth in a barbed-wire prison, singing gospel songs to keep their spirits up.

"...I think," she said, "I'd live with that a lot better than I would knowing a hundred innocent people were rotting in prison because of me."

Mommy slumped to her knees, sobbing so fiercely even Mawmaw clambered out of her rocking chair to comfort her. Daddy, Valentine, Robert – soon everyone in the room touched her, stroked her, lent her strength.

"I can't," she said, through gritted teeth. "Dammit, Paul – you'll sacrifice everything for her, won't you? You'll kill yourself so she doesn't feel guilty..."

"Mommy. Look at me." She pried her mother's hands from her cheeks, feeling this strange responsibility: *I have to carry you now*.

Maybe that's what growing older was.

"I don't want Daddy to die," Aliyah told her. "But Savannah and Latisha and Bennie... they can't be punished for *my* sins.

"And... I know it's scary, Mom. But this plan won't work unless you help. We have to do this tonight, because maybe they're carting them away as we speak. We have to work fast. So... can you help us plan? Because..."

She hesitated. It was a low blow, hitting her mother in her weakest point. But it would get Mom functioning again.

"...we work best as a family."

Mom grabbed Aliyah and Dad by the backs of their necks, pressed their foreheads against hers. "Goddammit," she muttered. "She got this overinflated sense of duty from you, Paul."

Dad laughed – then realized she hadn't meant to be funny. "Would you have it any other way?"

She sniffled back tears. "No. No, I would not. I am proud of the daughter we have raised." He looked happy for a moment, until she added, "But some days, Paul, I wish you'd never met that goddamned illustromancer."

Aliyah knew what Mommy meant: *I wish you'd never fucked us up with your 'mancy.*

Aliyah felt that way too. But it would kill Daddy if she ever said that out loud.

Imani helped Mawmaw back to her rocking chair, then straightened her dress.

"All right. The quicker we go in, the better our chances. I want a full list of all the resources we have available."

Valentine smirked. "Oh, what I wouldn't give for a holocaust cloak."

Mom whirled around on Valentine so fiercely that Mawmaw dropped her needles. *"What the fuck is a holocaust cloak?"*

"Hey, hey." Dad massaged her shoulders. "It's just Valentine riffing." Imani allowed Daddy's touch as though it was yet another trial she would endure.

Aliyah wished she felt guilty. But she'd left her friends behind once too often.

It would kill her to do it again.

TEN
Metal Gear Solidified

Valentine swept the binoculars across Morehead-Rowan airport again, wondering why Robert was down there instead of her.

This airport was dinky – a single, mile-long runway sitting disconsolately next to a dozen tin-roofed hangars and a small lodge for private pilots to cool their heels.

And as sunset approached, it still held that sleepy feel – even with several military aircraft refueling on the tarmac. But even the soldiers seemed relaxed, walking into the lodge to get a bite, checking in on the hooded prisoners who'd been herded into an electrically-fenced area beneath one of the hangars.

Nobody seemed tense except for the coffin-sized surveillance drones that swooped across the field like oversized bumblebees. And why should they? Judging from the small number of prisoners – they were down to fifteen – Morehead's most dangerous child soccer players had been airlifted out.

Robert had crawled into the waist-high grass that surrounded the airport, claiming he needed to disable the anti-'mancer sensors before she could do her spectacular work, and she hadn't seen him since. Maybe someone had spotted him. Maybe they'd dragged Robert into the lodge for questioning, had him tied to a chair, were beating him senseless.

But though she tried to muster concern, she couldn't cough up any real worry for her sweetie. Robert had taught himself the arts of stealth so well that even Valentine couldn't catch him unless she used 'mancy. And when she tried to fret about strangers tying Robert up to a chair and beating him, well, she remembered doing that to him last Thursday.

It was remarkably hard to torture a former *Fight Club*-mancer-turned-masochist.

"We have to get them out," Aliyah repeated for the tenth time, bouncing up and down. Valentine pushed her back further into the woods that surrounded the airport.

"Stop creeping closer to them, kid. Remember, if one of those goddamned Unizombies catches sight of you, *all* of them will know we're here – and they've got super-fast helicopters with response squads in the air."

"But our plan is to get the prisoners before they refuel–"

"*My* plan is to get to the prisoners. *Your* plan is to stay put, kid. The only reason we brought you with us is because leaving you alone at the safehouse left you totally open to a SMASH attack…"

"But if the planes fly off with the last of the prisoners, then they're lost *forever*!"

"Yeah, well, maybe Uncle Robert will save them singlehandedly."

She refocused the binoculars, furious at how *clumsy* these damned things were. Robert had tried to train her how to use them, but she kept twisting the knobs to focus, squinting until her eyes ached. And she couldn't use her left hand, for fear of loosening what was taped to her palm…

Real binoculars zoomed in automatically on their target. You never had this problem in stealth games.

The lenses flexed, and–

She quashed the helpful flare of videogamemancy that wanted to adjust the binoculars to her preferred reality. Robert had told her they couldn't afford any 'mancy here until Paul had disabled the black opal sensors around the compound – one of SMASH's aggravating upgrades. They'd embedded expensive (and sensitive) microchips of opal inside electronic fracture detectors. The slightest whisper of 'mancy would crack the opals, and the fracture would trigger alarms, and the place would be overrun with Unimancers in their signature black helicopters.

Paul couldn't disable them until he had the detectors' serial numbers. Which required Robert to sneak in to an armed base, which should be *her* goddamned job instead of hanging out *babysitting*…

She heaved the binoculars into a tree.

"Aunt Valentine!"

"It made me *feel* better, OK?"

She turned before the kid yelled at her – and why was the kid in the line of danger, anyway? OK, fine, leaving her behind at a safehouse with no exits, shitty reception, and a handful of college volunteers to stave off a SMASH invasion was probably not wise, either. But that wasn't really why they'd brought her.

Truth was, if things hit the shit here, there was a good chance either she'd get Unimanced or Paul would. And if that happened, Aliyah should know as soon as possible that her favorite aunt would come hunting her.

Yet as she peered into the fading light looking for her goddamned… well, "boyfriend" had been applied to their relationship inelegantly for years, so it would do today, she resented the fact that there weren't *four* 'mancers at the airport.

Back when he was Tyler Durden and topped off with crazy, they'd have romped on down there together to knock down soldiers like bowling pins. And while she'd thought it was adorable when his *Fight Club*-mancy had faded, she'd been sure he'd pick up some other obsession, and…

He hadn't. Instead, he'd gotten really good at things. She'd watched him pick up lockpicking, and rappelling, and camouflage. He'd tried to teach her Krav Maga, and looked disappointed when she'd surpassed his Israeli karate in a burst of *Call of Duty*-'mancy.

You can master this stuff too, you know, he'd told her.

She'd brandished the Xbox controller at him. *I* did.

He flitted from talent to talent like some cut-rate Batman. Everyone else loved what he was doing, oh, he was *so good* at running Project Mayhem, he always had the right connections to find a friendly face at the worst time, he could find rogue 'mancers the safehouse they needed.

She should love it. She was proud of her boyfriend, she was. He and Paul had polished Project Mayhem until it ran like a fine watch. But here she was again, thumb up her ass like she was some proctologist Little Jack Horner, waiting for Robert to finish his work, and why the hell was she here?

She'd tried helping Project Mayhem. She'd *Sims*-ed together a house to hold the refugee 'mancers, but her pixelated creations fell apart in an hour. She'd fit wooden beams together like Tetris blocks, creating frames Robert and his men could hang sidings on, but when she got four beams in a row they'd blink into nothingness.

All she was really good at was violence, and there was less and less of a need for that all the time.

She thought of leaving, sometimes. Going somewhere she could kick ass and take names. Then she imagined going to bed alone, never seeing that wicked grin when she grabbed his wrist to slam him against the bed and he wrestled back, knowing she'd achieve a wet victory after covering him in bruises and semen…

"Miss me?"

She whirled around to chuck the binoculars at the sudden noise, then realized she'd already thrown them. And it was Robert, fucking *Robert*, dangling a black opal detector off the end of his finger.

He knelt as he offered the detector to her.

"Sorry the opening act took so long." Her anger was swept away by the manifest adoration in his eyes. "Took me a while to find a security breach big enough for me to jimmy out a lock. But the stage is now set for the star of tonight's show."

Valentine could not say why his words itched like another herpes breakout.

She squeezed him tight, burying her face between his beautifully soft man-tits.

"Sorry," he said. "I worked as fast as I could–"

She stepped away. "No apologies. Just call in the sensors' model number."

"I already did," he said. She turned away, trying not to get too invested in his boo-boo faces. "Paul's disabling them right now."

That was the unnerving thing about Paul. When Aliyah went off, she could sense the kid's 'mancy from miles away. When Tyler – Robert – had been in his prime, she'd homed in on him from across the state.

But Paul was a ghost. She knew he was pulling up the factory records of the places these expensive government sensors had been built at, quietly rejigging their quality control routines so that each sensor was a dud, had always *been* duds. He wove a tremendous magical effort, reaching into the past to backdate errors, a magic threading its way through every sensor installed across two square miles of airport – and Paul, who'd never felt comfortable using paperwork for destruction, would be swimming with so much flux he'd be useless for the rest of the night.

Despite the huge upswell of 'mancy Paul generated, Valentine couldn't feel a damn thing.

For a nebbish amputee who hugged like a praying mantis, Paul could be one scary-ass dude.

The encrypted walkie-talkie squawked. "OK." Paul spoke with all the tension of a man who'd shooed a moth out of the house. "You're safe to go. As safe as we get here, anyway."

"Remember, your flux is a limited resource," Imani said. "Treat your 'mancy as if it's a potion: save it for the bosses."

Valentine touched her palm to ensure Imani's secret weapon hadn't fallen off. "I gotta burn some to get in close. I'm not, you know, fuckin' Jason Bourne like *some* people here."

Robert winced. "Not every situation calls for 'mancy–"

"Can we agree that some situations *do?*" She shrugged off Robert's sad brown eyes, took Aliyah by the shoulders. "OK, kid, who's the cavalry here?"

The kid registered her resentment by looking past Valentine, towards the hooded prisoners huddled miserably underneath the hangar. "Mom is."

"That's right. Things aren't gonna go wrong–" One of the

coffin-drones buzzed overhead, turning her swagger into stammer. "But if we wanna get your friends out of the Gimp Suit, we're gonna need your 'mancy to hijack the plane and fly 'em away safely. Unless Uncle Robert's taken a correspondence course in flight I'm unaware of..."

He crossed his arms, aggrieved. "I'm not certified, no. Just online simulations."

She rolled her eye. "Anyway, Aliyah – save your flux for airlifting the civvies." She grabbed Aliyah's face, forced her into eye contact. "Because remember, kid – you got them into this, but your flux can still make it a *lot* worse for them."

If Paul was here, he would have referred to this conversation as their "Good cop, bad cop" routine – he provided the love, Valentine doled out the guilt. But Valentine didn't do it to ping-pong the kid into some cheap affection. She did it because Aliyah was as hard-headed as her goddamned father, and sometimes that kid needed to be shocked right the fuck out of her fantasies.

Aliyah's gaze drifted towards the horizon: they couldn't see the broach from here, but by God it loomed large in Aliyah's mind.

She hugged Aliyah, gave a hesitant wave to Robert. He fumbled in his pocket for that damned ring, like he'd done for weeks. She hated poking at him with the Jason Bourne crack, but she'd been tightrope-walking that wire for weeks – enough kindness and he'd feel comfortable enough to pop the question.

She didn't want to look at his engagement ring until she was sure what her answer would be.

Valentine pushed her thoughts away to stare at the field of uncut grass. The soldiers paced back and forth, shooting the shit, lighting up cigarettes.

She watched for the pattern.

There was always a pattern to the way guards moved.

Sure enough, she began to mark the guards' pathways. That little runty one paced in circles around the jeep. The drones had a complicated figure-eight pattern overhead, leaving gaps a skilled infiltrator could slip through. The guards went into the

lodge to get water, rested for forty-five seconds, slipped off to
doze–

This wasn't magic. This was the way a just world *worked*.
She shouldn't get out of breath climbing the stairs – she should
run for miles. She wasn't some housewife wannabe cooling her
heels while her lover brought home the bacon – she was the
star of the show. She wasn't a klutz with bruised knees from
tripping over tree roots – she was a predator, vanishing into
the grass.

She wasn't waiting helplessly for a relationship to implode.
She was a badass, about to *kick* ass. She made the world into
her own videogame, a luscious art that trimmed away all the
world's drab redundancy to transform a military compound
into a playground.

Valentine made her way towards the hangar bay, feeling her
flux building. Not a lot. This was who she *should* be – she was
just giving the universe's image of herself a little boost.

A drone swooped overhead; she hunkered down instinctively.
And that, she thought, was her greatest failure in raising Aliyah:
the kid wouldn't have ducked, she'd have fought. Which was
Valentine's fault for letting the kid choose her own games. She
hadn't realized she *could* pick games for Aliyah until Imani had
come to them with a list and said, "These games have tactically
useful mechanics. Can you learn them?"

The experiment hadn't been *entirely* successful. Some of
those games had sucked. But what had become very clear was
that Aliyah loved modern RPGs and her action games, where
the proper response to every challenge was either to battle it
head-on, or to level up until you *could* battle it head-on.

Whereas Valentine's affinity was for old-school games,
stealth games, fighting games – games that punished unwise
choices with permanent game overs. She understood that you
couldn't fix some mistakes with a simple "Restart from last
checkpoint," but Aliyah had the headstrong magic of someone
who didn't understand finesse.

Given that SMASH had R&D divisions devoted to neutralizing
'mancy, Valentine did not want to discover what those hefty

black-box drones did when triggered. Even the helicopter refueling on the runway made her nervous. And she'd *fought* helicopters.

She inched closer to the guards by the barbed wire, scooching past a marine with reluctance. Oof. You could have bounced a quarter off that one's ass. He stopped, making conversation with his friend:

"Know who these mooks are?"

"Got orders from on high to guard 'em. They haven't made a peep all day."

"Maybe they're drugged."

Valentine paused, palms touching the sun-warmed tarmac, to see if they'd spill any other information:

"Know who these mooks are?"

"Got orders from on high to guard 'em. They haven't made a peep all day."

"Maybe they're drugged."

They'd given all the exposition they had, the poor little pinheads. But they stood before the barbed-wire fence penning in the Morehead prisoners. So she grabbed Guard #1 around the neck when Guard #2 turned around, dragged Guard #1 around a corner. She snatched the keycard off his unconscious body, feeling her flux swell – her only indication that he hadn't *had* a keycard before she'd gone looking for it.

She knocked out the other guard, used her keycard to open the prison gate, walked in.

The fifteen prisoners dangled like sacks of meat from a beam someone had spot-welded across the hangar – each of them clad in hi-tech, black leather straightjackets with glowing monitors studded over their hearts, over their arms, on their thighs. Black sacks had been tugged down over their faces, their feet twitching in mid-air like dogs, dreaming.

Jesus, what Frankenstein experiments were these fuckers running?

Yet if the prisoners were being monitored, then someone might be alerted when she freed them.

"Get ready," Valentine muttered into her walkie-talkie.

"We're about to tumble into Tartarus."

She padded up to the first person sagging at the end of the line – a tiny body Valentine could have bench-pressed. She leaned in, getting as close to the hood as possible so as not to trigger any hidden microphones. "I'm here to get you out."

The thing under the hood twitched. "Heeeelllppp... mee..."

"First step is getting off your hood." Valentine hesitated. She knew how this went in games: remove the hood, their skin would be ripped off their faces, or they'd have been transformed into Borg, or *something*.

She yanked off the hood, bracing herself.

Yet the face underneath was perfectly normal. The prisoner wore a helmet underneath her hood, but the faceguard was clear plastic. The person underneath was not one she recognized from the soccer field – a generically middle-aged white housewife.

The housewife's face broke into a Tom Cruise-crazy grin.

A hand closed around her wrist. A sharp pain: needles. Electronically-assisted needles, seeking out her veins, injecting something fast acting.

Valentine pulled away, but the woman was as strong as a soldier.

The hooks above released with a series of hisses, fifteen leather-clad people dropping to the ground in perfect unison, removing their hoods with dance recital precision.

"Ms Valentine DiGriz," the woman capturing her said – but the Unimancer spoke with a reverberating male voice and clipped Indian tones. He spoke merrily, as though inviting her to his vacation villa.

"General Kanakia, I presume?"

"Please don't run. We're here to help you."

The hangar slid to the left – no, whatever they'd injected her with did that. She lurched to one side, but the Unimancer held tight with a wrestler's grip. As long as one of them was a trained wrestler, *all* of them were.

They surrounded her in a perfect circle, arms raised, ready to intercept her.

"Where is Paul?" their commander asked through the young woman's face. His voice was filled with concern, her face with disgust. "We know he's here. The psychological profiles guaranteed this op would hit all his buttons..."

"You *planned* this?" Valentine tried to uncurl her left hand – her fingers tingled–

The woman bowed demurely. "Improvised. America's long sent its best SMASH agents overseas to deal with the real crisis in Europe. Today, they decided dismantling Project Mayhem was worth risking a broach expansion. Now you're dealing with the *real* professionals."

"Real professionals?" Valentine huffed. "What's your health care package? I need my Valtrex topped off..."

She clawed weakly at the Unimancer's face. The Unimancer's expression was a merging of two expressions – the commander speaking through her was sympathetic, but the woman underneath was red-cheeked furious. Which made sense: Valentine had killed a *lot* of Unimancers the first time they'd gone toe-to-toe. They'd been so furious, they'd ignored orders to let Valentine go...

"*Not gonna work, bitch.*" The Unimancers around her spoke as a chorus, their voices distinct, but speaking in measured contempt. "*She's wearing a helmmmmmmmmmm...*"

"I knuh." Crap. Her voice was slurring. What would *that* do to her one-liners? "Think *we* didn't bring... tricks?"

And as her left hand peeled away from the Unimancer's helmet, it left the spiderweb of an infinitely interesting doily.

The Unimancer's eyes crossed – if she saw the intersecting threads, *all* of them could. The remaining Unimancers surrounding Valentine leaned forward, staring in random directions, each bending the power of the hivemind to trace this fascinating set of knots to its center...

She staggered out of the hangar, pulling a green foaming bottle of antidote out of her inventory. She gulped it down – why did "antidote" always taste like NyQuil and India Pale Ale? – and felt her sobriety returning, her flux levels rising.

Floodlights snapped on.

Bullets tore up the runway, headed in her direction.

The helicopter had waited in ambush. They didn't need to fly – they just needed to fill the air with bullets. Its rotors spun up, the copter rising into the sky...

She brought up her force shield in time, a red health bar and a blue shield bar appearing above her head, the blue shield bar rapidly depleting. Her flux spiked, and she cursed a literal blue streak; if she'd been fighting cops, she could hold a force shield all day. But the networked Unimancers believed the only 'mancy should be their hivemind, and so their presence spiked flux to near-fatal levels–

They had to be rubber bullets, but with this much flux even nonlethal weapons had fatal ramifications.

Valentine pushed past the fusillades of bullets, making her way back to the hangar's shelter, hoping the Unimancers weren't back online yet. But no – they worked in conjunction like a human centipede, grabbing each other to orient themselves, finally making their way back to the housewife to pluck the doily off her faceplate.

Facing down fifteen angry, magically-fuelled soldiers?

Time for Batman.

With another shudder of flux, she felt the cape flutter across the back of her knees. Kicking ass was as instinctive as breathing to Batman. She'd fight her way past these schmucks, *Grand Theft Auto* up an escape...

She leapt at Housewife, figuring she owed that bitch a face full of Batboot. She was gratified to see Housewife bring her hands up to block the incoming Batman, and have it be useless: Housewife was, after all, a 110-pound woman, and BatValentine was 240 pounds of muscle.

Housewife went flying. Valentine rebounded off her, spinning into a kick to take out the next Unimancer, knocking a hulking black dude on his ass for a two-hit combo–

"She's utilizing the *Batman Arkham* series," the general said. "Activate countermeasures."

As one, the remaining thirteen whipped out cattle prods.

"Goddammit," Valentine yelled, furious – the game only

allowed one or two stun-prod guys in each group, they were fucking annoying but you could leap over them to kick them from behind–

She hurtled over one Unimancer, but three stepped in to press the shock-probes against her–

She tried to list the games Imani had drilled her in. But Imani hadn't quizzed her while she was shaking off whatever concussion cocktail they'd filled her full of – what might work? *Mortal Kombat*? *Robotron 2084*?

She shifted into *Robotron* mode, and got zapped again.

"Oh, come *on*!" she screamed. *"When the fuck isn't Batman enough?"*

The commander answered as though the answer was self-evident. "When you're facing troops who've faced down the *real* enemy in Europe."

Shit, she thought. *What if they* do *take me down…*

The flux slipped effortlessly down that thought, riding her fears. She tripped, falling into a cattle prod.

She passed out.

ELEVEN
Outgunned, Outmanned, Outnumbered, Outplanned

"Sir, with all due respect, no one told us this was a SMASH operation – we thought it was a straight containment and transfer..."

"Because if you had *known, you would have informed Ms DiGriz in a cutscene."* General Kanakia's voice boomed from fourteen different throats as the remaining Unimancers carried Valentine out to the field – a fireman's handoff, this complex peristaltic motion where they handed her body from one to another.

The squadron's sergeant tagged alongside the Unimancers, looking from face to face, unsure who to talk to. "Sir, we have no training in fighting 'mancers–"

"Also purposeful." One of the Unimancers, a lanky blond man with cropped hair, waved to a drone flying overhead. *"If Mr Tsabo had determined who'd been assigned to this airfield, he would have seen inexperienced troops – easy pickings to entice him in."* The sergeant jumped in surprise as one of the other Unimancers clapped him on the shoulder. *"Rest easy, sergeant, you're in good hands."*

The drone landed with a clumsy *thump* on the tarmac. It was a clunky mechanism the size of a refrigerator, and made a whirring noise as it propped itself up obligingly on hydraulic stilts. One of the Unimancers pulled the drone's door open, revealing a padded coffin interior, complete with pillow.

They placed Valentine inside, slammed the door shut. The

remaining Unimancers took position in a defensive ring around the drone, assault rifles at the ready, leaving the blond at the center to stand next to it.

They faced out in all directions, an organic omnidirectional speaker.

"*Mr Tsabo!*" they shouted, their voices blending into a reasonable approximation of the man controlling them. "*We know you can hear us! You wouldn't have left; you want to rescue Ms DiGriz. And why wouldn't you? Your loyalty is a laudable trait – I assure you, the Unimancers value no quality more than loyalty.*

"*You believe we are the enemy. Your thinking is small. Once you're a part of the collective, once you've seen what we must do, you'll understand how insignificant the rights of a few American iconoclasts are.*

"*You are a good man, Mr Tsabo. I am here to ask you to contemplate you may be on the wrong side.*"

The Unimancers scanned the horizon. Some squinted into the setting sun, others peered into the grass.

Nothing happened.

"*Paul,*" the Unimancers said. "*We know your Contract was destroyed. The witnesses didn't understand what happened on Washout Field, but we did.*

"*We also know you're brimming with flux. We've seen your 'disable the quality control' trick before – we know how badly it costs you. The black opal sensors were a decoy to disable you.*

"*We're not sure if you brought Aliyah with you. That depends on how defended your nearest safehouse is, and that we do not know. But if she is here–*" The Unimancers racked their rifles with a simultaneous *ka-klack–* "*then she'll have to fight her way past an assault helicopter* and *a trained team of Unimancers. The same team, I may add, that took down Ms DiGriz in under two minutes.*

"*Please, Paul. Do the smart thing and surrender. I guarantee you it will be the best decision of your life – no more worrying about flux, no more worrying about broaches, no more living on the run. Let us turn you into a force for good.*"

They watched the skies this time. Nothing. The blond near the drone harrumphed and hovered his palm over a big red button.

"You see this, Paul? This is our latest anti-Tsabo technology — we call it the Snow White Surprise. Whoever's put inside is fed anesthetized gas to disable them — and when I press this button, a rocket here will launch it at 250 mph towards a radio signal we've set up. There's no input settings, Paul — no records for you to alter. Just a single button — and when I push this, Valentine rockets off over the horizon. If you fiddle with the quality control off the assembly line, well... We made it finicky. If something fails, you risk gassing her to death, or the rocket explodes on takeoff."

Another dramatic pause. The Unimancers got more agitated as the sky darkened, the sun slipping away. The helicopter rotated, preparing for an assault.

"You cannot win, Paul. We have factories devoted to your destruction. The minute I send Ms DiGriz off, I will have to assume you are a hostile — and the hunt starts.

"With as much flux as you're carrying, capture attempts skew fatal. You might get hurt. Your wife might get hurt. Your daughter might get hurt. And despite what you've heard, we have no more interest in hurting civilians than you do.

"You're alone. Outnumbered. And outclassed. So please, Paul. Surrender."

The blond Unimancer's face remained expressionless. After a moment passed, there was a collective exhale, as if the general had let loose one regretful sigh.

"So be it."

The blond moved to slam the button.

A kite string bisected him.

TWELVE
The Terribly Short Triumph of Hamir Singh

It irritated Hamir when people called him a 'mancer. He wasn't.

He fought with kites. It was easier for losers to blame magic than to analyze the weaknesses in their tactics. They lost not because of some nefarious kite-shifting powers, but because they refused to put the time in.

Hamir had put the time in. He'd spend days building the perfect kite from paper and wood, had tried out hundreds of string types and pastes and glass coatings. His skin was baked almost black from standing on rooftops from sunrise until sunset, stripped down to his underwear, every hair on his body attuned to shifts in the wind.

He became such a staple of the neighborhood that crowds gathered around his rooftop vigils, a constant yelling bustle of gamblers. He'd tolerated their presence because they brought him water, fed him when he passed out.

You should get a cut, his sister had told him one day when she had found him again, washed his sores clean.

Cut what kite? he had responded.

Not to cut a kite! she'd yelled, so mad it was all he could do not to run up to the roof to escape her. *Get a cut* of the money, *you buffoon. They're flying in competitors from Brazil, from Bangladesh, from Nepal to fight you – there's real money here, Hamir.*

All I want is a challenge, he'd told her.

He couldn't remember if he'd seen her after that.

Yet the challenges had dried up. The gambling men had suggested he should lose a few fights to let his opponents feel like they had a chance. And to be fair, Hamir had tried. Yet when he lifted that razor-strung kite up into the air, he held a sword the size of the sky.

He could not withhold the perfection of his stroke.

Losers had accused him of 'mancy. The police had come. Someone had smuggled him out – who? He wished he could remember; all he remembered was seeing the airplane and wanting to tie a cable to it to make it fly. They'd smuggled him out to these mountains with these bizarre people with their doilies and their rock heaps.

Yet a beautiful thing had happened. The burly man – he had a name, Hamir was sure – had told him to battle birds. Which was ridiculous. Birds darted quicker than kites, were less predictable, were *far* more durable.

Yet the secret, Hamir had discovered, was to find the weak spots. A sharp eye could seek out the softest parts of the bird. It took skills he never would have unlocked in his homeland, that place, wherever it was.

He did feel bad for the birds, though. He made it quick for them. And buried them, yelling when the burly man suggested they might be eaten.

These are competitors! Hamir yelled. *Would you eat the losers of a race?*

OK, OK. The man held his hands up, backed away. Good. The man, he was disrespectful.

Yet the man came back later, to ask Hamir if he wished for a real challenge. Of course Hamir said yes. And they stuffed him in a crowded van where he huddled over his kite to protect the fragile thing, and told him to stand in some woods and wait, and then the man told him through a radio to walk to the runway's edge.

Those are soldiers, Hamir had said, dumbfounded.

Can you fight them? the man had asked.

No one can fight soldiers with a kite.

Can't you?

Hamir had stiffened. It was true; he had fought birds. Maybe he could fight soldiers. *Are these evil men?*

They would kidnap a child.

Then I will try, Hamir said.

That's good, Hamir, the man replied. *But remember. There is a storm coming. When you feel the pressure squeezing in around you, you must run. Things will get very bad if you stay.*

Ridiculous. Hamir's body was a weathervane. He felt no sign of storms.

He loosed the kite. It sailed up into the sky, swooping in the sunset; Hamir knew how to mask his kite in the fading rays of the sun, making it near-invisible before he twisted the line to send it dashing down.

And that soldier, the one who the voice on the radio was yelling at him to attack – he was covered in armor. But the soldier's belly was soft, and if he hit the man just right his kite would sail through the soft parts of the spine–

The kite string bisected him.

"*I did it!*" Hamir yelled, reeling his kite in, feeling an odd congestion pressing down upon his ears. And the remaining soldiers, he whipped the line through them, his kite unstoppable, his skyward-sword cleaving them neatly as an eagle–

The helicopter rose up, the wash from its rotors beating his kite down, its guns coming to bear upon him.

It was large. *So* large. It commanded the runway like a predator, swelling to fill the sky.

Get out! the man yelled over the radio. *Hamir, you've done enough, the flux will–*

Hamir's kite twitched.

Only one person would rule this airspace.

Hamir watched the rest of his life unfurl in slow motion.

The air beneath the copter was a chaos of wind currents, would have been impossible for anyone but Hamir to navigate. Things were complicated by that odd pressure numbing his fingertips – like a thousand angry sisters asking him what was wrong.

Hamir's fingers worked as delicately as a pianist's, navigating the kite up through the storm his opponent generated beneath its great rotors; his eyes skittered across the copter's black bulletproof frame, seeking the one spot a taut line might sever.

The copter's guns spat fire at him.

Hamir jerked the kite straight up through the rotors.

That was, Hamir thought, the path to victory – to use the beast's own momentum against it. The blades smashed into the frail wood, pulling the line taut, a one-in-a-million shot only Hamir could have made–

– and the kitestring hit a hairline fracture in one of the rotors, an impact at the perfect angle to have it shiver down its faultline and crack, tumbling free of the helicopter. The other blades smashed around into it, spinning free as the copter sagged sideways, and Hamir watched in glory, the world slowing to a crawl as it always did when Hamir severed his competitor's string, as if the world itself wanted him to witness every detail of victory.

"*I did it!*" Hamir cried, raising his arms. "*I–*"

That was when he saw the jagged chunk of severed rotor spinning towards him. The shattered airfoil punched through his chest, sent him tumbling in a spray of blood.

He twisted his neck back, looking above the landing strip. The copter had crashed in a fiery wreck, spilling burning fuel everywhere, turning the tarmac into a hellish blaze–

Hamir noted the remnants of his kite, inexplicably floating above the chaos, the smashed struts held together by tattered paper. It should have fallen to earth, but the inferno below lifted it up, wafted it high–

A champion.

"I did it," Hamir wheezed, and died the happiest man alive.

THIRTEEN
Flux Leads to Suffering

Paul sensed the mission was going off-kilter when the helicopter exploded.

"What the—" Imani bit off a curse as she peered out the narrow slit that remained of the windshield. They couldn't tell what caused the explosion; the SUV's impromptu customizations blocked off nine-tenths of the windshield. Imani screeched around curvy roads as she rocketed down to the airfield, the car's strapped-on armor threatening to fly away.

The fireball was blinding. Paul wondered whether the explosion had been some side effect of his flux, but no – his head still ached from that migraine-like pressure.

Carrying a near-fatal load of bad luck while charging into a war zone?

He'd had better ideas.

"What the hell was that?!" Paul yelled into the walkie-talkie. "Hamir was supposed to *distract* them!"

"That dumb fucker." Robert made the condemnation sound mournful. "I *told* him he was a 'mancer, I *told* him he needed to manage his flux. He... Aliyah, *no!*"

Aliyah leapt up to shout into the microphone. "Daddy, Aunt Valentine's coffin is in the flames! She's cooking! I'm going in!"

"Negative!" Paul shouted.

"We're inbound at fifty miles an hour," Imani snapped. "*Do not move*, princess."

"Daddy, you've got flux – I don't! I can take the–"

"Mommy's plan doesn't involve 'mancy." Paul cringed at the white lie – her rescue plan depended on Valentine's 'mancy, and who knew whether *that* was still active. "This mission's gone from a rescue to a retreat. Robert, get Aliyah and get out – we'll meet you at the safehouse."

"Daddy, you can't get captured – Project Mayhem can't function without you–"

"And I can't function without you. Do *not* come in, sweet pea. We've got this."

Imani steered the car towards the carnage's center. The remaining Unimancers and soldiers had finally noted the SUV rattling towards them, raising their rifles to fire at the inbound threat.

Paul tried not to imagine the things that could go wrong. Or they *would* go wrong.

"Paul," Imani said. "If we get out of this alive, I am going to strangle you."

He stifled a laugh. "*You* insisted on taking Robert's defensive driving course."

"I did it to protect you!"

"Come on," Paul grinned, as the soldiers knelt to get a better bead on them – and then looked startled as they took in this absurd contraption bearing down upon them. "You never had this excitement when you worked for Taft, Steinberg, and Hollander. Sure, we might die – but you're driving an invulnerable battering ram to rescue a friend from the United States' military. Isn't this a *little* cool?"

Her sour-faced look melted away into girlish excitement. She adjusted her grip on the steering wheel.

"OK," she admitted. "It is a little cool."

And as Imani shoved his head down so he wouldn't be in the line of gunfire, Paul had never been more in love.

But what he loved far more was the satisfying *chunk* of high-caliber bullets bouncing off the magically impenetrable bookcases they'd strapped to the car, followed by the sounds of government soldiers diving aside.

They plowed through the fire, scattering flaming bits of copter wreckage. Imani torqued the car sideways, muttering, "*Come on, wheels, hold together…*" The car jerked as Imani caromed the SUV into Valentine's coffin-drone, sending it skittering out from the burning pool of jet fuel in a spray of sloppy flames.

Paul couldn't breathe. The impact had flung him into the seatbelt, his broken ribs jabbing into his side like steak knives–

Imani threw the car into a side-spin, the car juddering underneath her.

The wheels, Paul thought. *They're melting from the heat–*

The SUV was – or had been – wrapped in Valentine's belief that no good videogame chase ended with popped tires. The bookcases were strapped on as sturdily as the safehouse acolytes could manage – but no way this would hold together without a good binding of videogamemancy.

And as Paul worried they might melt from the heat, the flux drained out of him and into the tires with a *bang*. The tie-downs so improbably holding the bookcases to the SUV slipped, stray bullets fraying their tension to send them clattering to the ground as Imani fought to keep the car from rolling.

They slid to a halt on the far side of the crash, putting a dimming blaze between them and the soldiers.

"Get her out," Imani yelled, ducking as bullets bounced off the remaining bookcases. Paul hated that he could distinguish between the impact of rubber bullets and live fire – the Unimancers fired rubber bullets, the panicked soldiers shot live fire.

"*Go around to the far side of the wreckage to cut off their escape!*" the remaining Unimancers ordered, their voices still saturated with the general's precise tones. "*Do not fire! Mr Tsabo is saturated with flux! We must help him before he hurts himself!*"

Paul pushed the door open, stumbled over a fallen bookcase as he made his way to Valentine's drone, choking on the stench of burning rubber and hot metal. He batted at the air, suppressing flashbacks to the apartment fire he'd crawled through to save Aliyah–

This rescue was tactically unwise, he knew. Better to let

Valentine burn; she was already unconscious. She'd die unaware, at peace.

That was a good death for a 'mancer.

But he'd already watched his daughter burned alive. He'd never sleep again if he left his best friend to roast.

He made his way to where the drone had skidded to a halt. Paul braced his artificial foot against the tarmac, wrapped his tie around his hand to protect it from the heat, and wrenched open the door.

The acrid, burning chemicals wafted out – the padding had begun to smolder. The Bowser tattoo covering Valentine's left shoulder was blistered beyond recognition. And...

He covered his mouth in horror.

She looked so *small*.

Valentine had proudly called herself "Paul's Wrecking Ball" – he aimed her at his enemies, and she'd plowed through them. But in this transport vehicle, she looked like a pudgy goth girl in her mid-thirties passed out after a night of drinking – not Valentine the legend, but Valentine so fragile it hurt to see her.

"Get her out, Paul!" Imani snapped into the "defensive fire" position Robert had taught her. *"Incoming!"*

Paul shoved his hands under Valentine's armpits, screaming as his ribs stabbed into him. She was a big girl, he was scrawny – why had Imani tasked him to carry her?

He remembered his days at the police academy: *Rookie, your body's as sturdy as a scarecrow. I should mark you a washout. But goddammit, you do* not *quit.*

He ignored his ribs, ignored the flux, ignored the coffin's piping hot foam padding.

He had a friend to save.

He yanked her towards the car–

A metal canister bounced towards him, the first of many: flashbangs, designed to stun 'mancers. The Unimancers had flashbangs, they had tear gas, they had all the goddamned advantages.

Don't work, he commanded, reaching out with his 'mancy to squash the flashbang. He snuffed the remaining flashbangs in the area, disabled the Unimancers' tasers, shut down their radios–

WHAT DID YOU DO

The flux roared in, a tsunami of bad luck, sweeping Paul off his feet–

Oh crap.

When he'd suppressed the black opal detectors in the compound, Paul had done 'mancy properly – he'd gotten the serial number, traced the trail back to the manufacturer, flipped through their production facilities, found the factory that made these detectors, pulled up lists of components, analyzed quality control routines to search for soft spots.

Everything he'd accomplished with his 'mancy until now *could* have happened. He'd justified his magic to the universe step by step, walking it through how fifty detectors could have failed simultaneously – the sequence of events was unlikely, and the universe had resented his changes, but at least he'd had a rationale.

In his panic, he'd demanded the equipment fail for no reason.

The universe, trusting his word, had allowed him to do it.

Now the flux exacted its price, and Paul had nothing to tender in exchange. Before, he'd offered the universe a glorious vision: good record-keeping tracked when the rich stole from the poor, it logged what went wrong so the wreckage could be examined for potential improvements, it created best practices that stopped dumb failures like, say, half a hundred government-sourced 'mancer-detectors from failing at once.

WHY DID THIS HAPPEN, the flux roared; the universe coalesced around Paul's guilt, gave it a throat to speak.

My best friend Valentine. Paul spasmed on the hot ground. *I... She was going to die–*

MILLIONS DIE EVERY DAY

Maybe someone else could have justified what they'd done, but Paul believed in rules. You didn't bend the rules just because someone wanted something – you still had to work through the process, fill out the forms, have your case judged by the proper authorities–

In disabling the equipment, Paul had tried to bribe the judge.

"*What's happening?!*" Imani yelled. Paul realized a black cloud swirled around him, visible to non-'mancers.

"It's the flux," the Unimancer squadron said in General Kanakia's voice, nine people pulling up to a halt as Imani aimed the gun in their direction. "We've... We don't know what that is. But we can help. Please, Ms Dawson, let us help."

She waved the gun between the nine soldiers, settled a bead on the closest. "Do you promise to let them go afterwards?"

They shook their heads like a metronome. "You know we can't promise that, Ms Dawson. He broached in Morehead, and now this – he's a danger."

She swallowed. "You will *not* brainwash him."

"It's not brainwashing." Their hands reached out to Paul like firefighters trying to haul someone out of a burning building. "We'll show him some new priorities. They'll help."

"*No!*" She put weight on the trigger. "Step back or I'll shoot."

"Ms Dawson." The lead Unimancer stepped forward sorrowfully, hands raised. "We know you're Project Mayhem's pacifist. Paul's a zealot. Ms DiGriz is a killer. But Aliyah doesn't kill because of you. We know you don't want to shoot."

Her fingers went white on the pistol, the trembling barrel fixed on the Unimancer's forehead. "*Then give me better options!*"

The lead Unimancer shook her head, wishing she had better options to give. Paul tried to say something, but the flux poured down his throat, choking him–

"That flux is a public menace." The Unimancer spoke in General Kanakia's voice, but they all nodded in syncopation as though their hivemind concurred with him. "We have to drain it away."

She stepped towards Paul.

Imani blew her head off.

Paul would forever remember the way his wife looked then. She was not stoically blasting the life from the incoming squadron, nor was she firing in panicked terror. No, Imani was crying as she shot, an ordinary woman driven to murdering someone in cold blood.

Her efficiency was an awful thing to behold. Imani swallowed back vomit as she blinked her tears away for better aim.

The Unimancers shuddered as Imani shot the next soldier, falling apart into disharmony. Paul had seen this once before, the first time he and Valentine had fought SMASH forces – the Unimancers had stumbled into a trap, and they'd been chewed up by Gunza's men. In the end, the Unimancers had hated Valentine so much they'd ignored their commander's orders and tried to capture her.

– *they all kill* –

– *you can't trust them* –

– *they'd broach the whole Earth if we let them* –

The Unimancers spread apart, rolling to dodge shots with shared expert precision, just as the soldiers tackled Imani to the ground.

I have to die before I do more damage, Paul thought. *My ribs, they're puncturing my heart.*

The flux flowed into his chest, kicking his ribs like a horse trying to break out of a stall. He convulsed on the runway, struggling for air, vision fading.

The flux stopped.

NOT GOOD ENOUGH.

Paul quivered as the Unimancers rolled him over, the flux poured into the Unimancers, guiding their hands. They ripped open his shirt to do CPR, getting his lungs working again. His heartbeat stabilized, his consciousness pinwheeling back as air, precious air, flooded down his throat–

Paul struggled to get up, but was too weak to move.

Why had the flux saved him?

"*You killed him!*" Aliyah shrieked, her voice a guttural bellow, transforming into something deep and masculine. "*You killed my* father!"

Aliyah, no, Paul thought, helpless to say anything. But he understood what had happened: Robert had ordered Aliyah's retreat. Yet thanks to the flux, she'd looked back at the perfect moment, seeing a scene that stabbed her worst fears – her mother captured, her father dying, Valentine burned.

Everyone she loved, sacrificed to her bad decision.

The perfect lure to draw her into an unwinnable conflict.

– she's in God of War mode –

– we practiced for this –

– spread out –

"Give us your weapons, fools!" the Unimancers yelled as Aliyah plowed into them. They grabbed the assault rifles, pinwheeling backwards to avoid Aliyah's swinging knives.

Paul shivered. Aliyah was channeling Kratos, the God of War, the game that summed up her most violent impulses. She hadn't summoned Kratos since that final rooftop fight with Rainbird.

Aliyah was going for the kill.

It didn't matter, though. In the game, the creatures always made a beeline for Kratos, obligingly piling up to get within range of his bloodied weapons. The Unimancers looped around Aliyah, keeping their distance, emptying their rifles into her. The health bar above her head dwindled as they beat her at her own game – one making feints to lure her into committing to attacks, the remaining Unimancers dancing away.

"It's not fair!" Aliyah shrieked, trying to clear a path towards her father. *"IT'S NOT FAIR!"*

Paul struggled to crawl to her, but the soldiers stomped on his neck. They flung Imani down next to him, handcuffing her.

The Unimancers ceased fire the instant Aliyah was knocked unconscious. They murmured among themselves:

– can't believe –

– he'd send his own daughter –

– into a warzone –

– do we even want him in with us –

– the general says we need him –

They waved a new coffin-drone down, placed Aliyah into it reverently.

They looked down at her with a newborn parent's pride.

Then they pressed the red button, and Aliyah shot off to her new life as a Unimancer.

YOU WILL LOSE YOUR DAUGHTER IN WAYS YOU

NEVER IMAGINED, the black flux roared. It clung in tendrils to the coffin-drone.

He'd never seen the flux refuse a fear before, but now he realized:

Dying was easy.

This titanic amount of flux demanded *suffering*.

"Your turn." They closed in around him.

FOURTEEN
"Your Kid Will Pull the Trigger"

Another coffin-drone landed on the runway with a heavy *thud*.

Paul barely noticed.

Aliyah's gone, he thought. And there'd be no way to get her back before she was Unimanced – this was a special flux, a *sticky* flux. He'd made an enemy of the universe, and the odds would thwart him until his daughter was a brainwashed government zombie.

He saw Robert, racing towards them in a stolen Jeep. Two Unimancers raised their rifles, ready to shoot out its tires. There would be no escape.

He went limp in the remaining Unimancers' arms as they lowered him into the coffin with synchronized reflexes.

"No!"

He tumbled into the coffin as half the Unimancers let go. Their smooth coordination collapsed into a schoolyard tussle where some arms grabbed his lapel to pull him out, others pushed him back in, while still others recoiled in horror. The movement jostled his ribs, the pain snuffing his cries of anguish–

Their unison broke apart into different voices, an argument rippling through them.

"You promised you wouldn't bring his daughter and *him into the fold!"*

That voice was young, teenaged, outraged.

– *it's not like that, Ruth* – the other voices in the collective murmured.

"Don't lie! That's *exactly* what you want to do to her – you want to squeeze them both inside the same brainspace, exactly what my mother did to me–"

– is it that bad? –

"Oh, I keep Her walled away from you. But if you wanna feel what She does to me, well, *have a taste of my memories*!"

Paul dropped into the drone, landing with a bone-jarring *thump* as the Unimancers staggered away in different directions, clutching their heads, weeping.

Was this the flux? Or something unexpected?

A Unimancer hauled him out. The body was a stocky Korean man, but it moved with an adolescent girl's gangly motion – and his late-forties face was mapped with the pissiness of a teenager in full-blown rebellion.

"Your kid's gone," the girl-in-a-Korean-body said in a clear Chicago accent. "Can't get her back. But you... well, I don't give a shit about *you*, murderer, but she'll never be free with you trapped inside the same mindspace. So get out. We'll come to consensus eventually."

Three of the Unimancers aimed rifles unsteadily at the soldiers, who stood there, confused. Paul felt sorry for them: they'd not been trained for 'mancy, they were completely unequipped to handle this.

Heck, *Paul* felt completely unequipped to handle this. Someone inside the Unimancers was rebelling – they'd broken ranks before, way back during their first encounter, disobeying their commander's orders to capture Valentine. But that disobedience had seemed like a group effort. Now one girl appeared to be overriding the hivemind.

A *young* girl. Had they found another 'mancer Aliyah's age, and absorbed her? How could one girl override the network? He'd barely understood a word she'd said.

He realized how little he understood about the Unimancers.

"Who... are you?" he asked.

"Like I'm giving you an ID to trace? Fuck off, papermancer, time's running out. You–"

They freed Imani from her handcuffs as General Kanakia's

voice emanated from the Unimancer squadron.

"Ruth." His voice was fond, but firm – an indulgent uncle. "Yes, Aliyah is in our control, but Paul's the real target. He's the one who understands broaches."

"*We* understand broaches."

"Then why haven't you–"

The Korean man punched himself in the balls, regaining control. "You telling me the President *won't* order you to bring them *both* into the hivemind?"

Another Unimancer spoke weakly for Kanakia, whose voice was fading like a distant radio station. "Set him free, and he'll cut a path to hell to find her – remember what he did to New York City?"

"I'm not living with New York City in my goddamned brain. You *know* who I'm living with. I thought you *saved* me from that."

The general's voice fell silent... but the Unimancers nodded proudly.

Robert pulled up; the Unimancers loaded Valentine into the jeep, tossed some of their rifles in, helped Paul and Imani up.

The Unimancers turned to Robert. "Step on it, asshole. Get out before the backup choppers find you." She smacked Valentine's cheek, a little too hard to be affectionate. "I even left you this deadly bitch in case you need to dodge local trouble. But after that... stop doing 'mancy. Go live a quiet life somewhere. Stop your fucking amateur hour magic; you almost killed yourself today, you almost ripped open America. Jesus fuck, you dumb sack of elephant shit, how much does it take for your bloated ego to realize how incompetent you are?"

"I am not incompetent," Paul wheezed. "You stopped me from fixing–"

She jammed a gun into his throat.

"If we see you again, I will put a bullet through your windpipe. And your kid will pull the trigger. *Do not fuck with us.*"

They waved Robert on. He peeled out.

Paul breathed shallowly, trying not to worsen his ribs. Everyone else fell into a mournful silence as they raced down back roads, only allowing themselves to hope once they'd lost themselves in Kentucky's deep woods.

Imani clutched a rifle to her chest, staring straight ahead, flecks of someone else's blood drying on her cheeks. Valentine woke sluggishly, picking open blisters on in her shoulder, wincing as she watched the last of her tattoo disintegrate into ooze.

Paul groaned as he leaned forward, dabbing the blood off Imani's face with his handkerchief. She caught his wrist in a death grip.

"We have to kill them all." Her eyes held no remorse. "We're not safe until every last Unimancer's dead."

Paul nodded.

Aliyah, he thought. *I have to stop them from brainwashing Aliyah*. That Ruth-thing, she'd been so brutal, so callous, so at ease with murder. Paul had spent his life encouraging Aliyah's independence, and now...

YOU WILL LOSE YOUR DAUGHTER IN WAYS YOU NEVER IMAGINED

Even if the whole universe fought to deny him, how could he let her go?

Valentine hugged them both – a hug that emphasized their incompleteness: an empty space stood between them, an Aliyah-shaped hole that would not heal until they had their girl back.

Robert fidgeted at the wheel, saying nothing.

PART II

Hans Plays With Lottie,
Lottie Plays With Jane

FIFTEEN
Neuropeptalks

Forty-five minutes after Aliyah was kidnapped, Paul was arguing with a Walgreens pharmacist.

The clerk, a weary middle-aged white man with horn-rimmed glasses, thumbed through the prescriptions Paul had handed him.

"Neuropeptide Y?" he asked. "5-Dehydroepian-drosterone? Mister, we're a small-town pharmacy, we don't carry anything like that here…"

"Just look in the back," Paul said. He didn't look like his normal self – Valentine had wrapped him in an octogenarian retiree's pseudoskin – but he spoke with such desperate certainty, the pharmacist shuffled off.

The pharmacist returned a few minutes later with an astonished look, clutching two small boxes. "I don't remember ordering these."

That's because they weren't there an hour ago, Paul thought. He'd rejigged the pharmacy's orders to have these very specific medications delivered to their doorstep a month ago, waiting for Paul to pick them up. He felt that delivery's flux crackling around him.

"They're anti-anxiety medications," Paul explained. "They're getting more popular all the time."

"Sure, sure." The pharmacist peered into the back room, frowning; Paul could see him thinking, *We have a thousand medicines, I don't know them all.*

Paul got away with a lot of bureaucromancy simply because magic was so rare. Who would leap to a crazy idea like *a 'mancer fiddled with my shelves* when good old forgetfulness was at hand?

The pharmacist adjusted his glasses nervously. "Now, the antibiotics, sir, not a problem. But this sheaf of pain pill prescriptions: Ativan, Valium, Oxycontin. That's a... it's a good load, for an out-of-towner."

Paul gritted his teeth. "My wife and I were on vacation. She lost her luggage in the broach evacuation."

"Sorry to hear that, sir." The pharmacist's words were courteous, unconvincing. "All the same, I'm afraid I'll have to call your physician to confirm."

YOU WILL LOSE YOUR DAUGHTER IN WAYS YOU NEVER IMAGINED

Paul clutched his head. "My daughter's in danger and my wife is on a *countdown*! I've got two hours before the trauma sets in, and–"

Paul noticed the pharmacist quietly putting his hand over the button that summoned the police – and realized the pharmacist would have pressed it already if Valentine's magic hadn't made Paul look like he was one hip fracture away from the nursing home.

This was ludicrous – he had to get Aliyah back, and that meant getting medications to suppress Imani's impending PTSD, and he needed his–

The pain in his sides made him sit down. He couldn't yell with these ribs.

"Sorry." Paul leaned heavily on his cane, sucking in shallow breaths. "Yes, of course it's correct to call the doctor to verify a suspicious prescription. It's *procedure*." He flailed his hand, feeling as old as his disguise. "Call Doctor Paulson. He'll confirm the legality."

Except, Paul realized, he had to do some emergency 'mancy. Doctor Paulson was Robert, who was sitting out in the transformed Jeep in the parking lot with Valentine and Imani.

Robert had studied medicine for two years under Paul's

tutelage before Paul would do the bureaucromancy to certify him as a nurse practitioner, legally capable of writing prescriptions. Robert had complained, asking to skip the tests, asking, *Why can't you let me prescribe whatever I want?*

But that wasn't what certifications were *for*. The point wasn't to get drugs – the point was that the certification made Robert worthy to dispense them.

His trust in certifications seemed foolish as he clutched his sides, craving painkillers. But that didn't matter. What mattered was that Robert only carried his burner phone on missions, and Paul had to reroute the "official" number of Robert Paulson, APRN to this burner phone before the pharmacist finished dialing.

The act should have been trivial. A single form, filled out. Under normal circumstances, Paul would have blinked his eyes and redirected the number.

The universe no longer trusted him.

Every act of bureaucratic magic was slower after his misstep at the Morehead airport – slower, and more dangerous. He closed his eyes to envision the Verizon Custom Redirect Service form. He filled out the first name, the last name, Robert's social security number, backdating the form to have been filed six hours ago.

He had to justify everything – and now that his family's safety was on the line, he resented it. This so-called "magic" was almost as slow as filling out a real form, and–

The flux from finishing the redirect dimmed the lights around him.

It buzzed around him like angry wasps, seeking something to go wrong. But what else could go wrong? Aliyah was off the government books, being jetted to some nameless Refactor prison. Imani was melting down. The Morehead broach was still unstable, and the Unimancers blamed *him* because they refused to let him repair it.

You want a piece of me? Paul thought angrily. *Go ahead, fuck with my insides.*

Something new snapped in his midsection. Another rib, tearing loose.

Paul didn't even realize he'd screamed until the pharmacist came over.

"Sir," the pharmacist said. "Let me call an ambulance, you're clearly–"

"I need my prescriptions."

"But you–"

"Fill them. Please."

The pharmacist hung up before Robert could answer. Apparently, getting this crazy old man his drugs before he code red-ed out in his shop was a priority.

Paul hissed air through his teeth, trying not to let the pain overwhelm him. He hadn't even needed to *do* that 'mancy.

The pharmacist shoved the pills towards Paul, who signed the usual waivers without glancing at them. He scooped them up, dropping the cane onto the tile floor, and staggered out towards the car.

Except, he realized, he was headed across the street to the Dunkin' Donuts. Aliyah always asked him to get a baker's dozen, so they could call Uncle Kit and have him read their mood through donuts.

Aliyah wasn't getting any donuts.

If he didn't find her soon, she'd forget her love of donut-based games – the government would erase her hobbies.

YOU WILL LOSE YOUR DAUGHTER IN WAYS YOU NEVER IMAGINED

No. There was still time to fight this. And he was envisioning a weapon to aim at that terrifying hivemind, but first he had to get back to the car.

The jeep was a van, now. Valentine had backed into a garage and selected a different vehicle. She rapped her fingers on the wheel as Paul clambered into the back.

"Aliyah's landed by now, let's get to her–"

Paul ignored her, shoving a water bottle into Imani's shaking hands. "Take these pills."

Imani was so far gone, she didn't even ask Paul what she was taking. Paul took the opportunity to slip her rifle away from her.

"Hey, if you're handing out the fun drugs, gimme some," Valentine said.

"Those aren't fun drugs," Paul told her. "Those are cortisol dampers. They'll blunt her body's reaction to traumatic stress. Minimize her flashbacks."

"PTSD?" Valentine's irritation flared, then vanished as she craned around to peer at Imani. "What happened?"

Paul swallowed a handful of antibiotics and Oxycontin, hoping Imani would answer. She didn't. "She shot three Unimancers in the fight. Three perfect headshots."

Valentine went pale. "But she…"

"No," Paul said. "She's the only one here who's never killed anyone."

Valentine scowled, looking at Imani with hatred. Paul didn't understand – until he realized that look was guilt, burning a hole through Valentine's heart. *I was supposed to be the wrecking ball*, that look said. *I was supposed to protect Imani.*

Imani gripped Paul's wrist. "Valentine's right. Aliyah's still in transit. We have to go–"

"I have two motel rooms reserved," Paul said. "We have to sleep."

"*No!*" Imani fumbled in her lap, looking for the rifle. "They have our *daughter*, Paul, this isn't the time to–"

"We have been up for eighteen hours, and been on the run almost the whole time. Yes, Aliyah's in transit, but if we race off again, we'll fall into their *next* trap. That's how they got us – rushing us into bad decisions. We'll make a plan – we have *never* lost when we've made a plan…"

You've never pissed off the universe the way you did back at the air base, Paul thought–

"So we *lose*?" Valentine shouted, red-faced. "I don't *lose*, Paul! May I remind you Aliyah is–"

"Aliyah is *my* daughter!" Paul yelled, and then regretted it as the pain shot through him again. He wheezed. "Don't – make – this – about – who loves her – more. It's *strategy*."

She thumped the wheel. "*Fuck* strategy! We hit 'em hard, hit 'em fast! We don't let 'em get *away* with this!"

"Valentine. Look at me." Paul tapped the underside of his right eye. "Tell me you see an ounce of retreat."

Valentine wiped her nose with the back of her hand, then bobbed her head, acclimatizing herself to a temporary retreat. "We'll fuck them up?"

"There won't be a SMASH when we're done."

Valentine closed her eyes, drawing in a breath through her nose; Paul knew how much standing down cost her. Valentine *hated* losing. Whenever she was outclassed at videogames, she'd spend days rooted by the television, honing her skills, unable to rest until she'd beaten her opponents...

"All right. One night. But we'd better kick ass, and soon."

They got to the Marriott a few blocks away. Paul reached into the glove compartment, where the keys to the rooms had materialized, his signature placed on a hotel invoice.

It should have been easy. Everyone had cancelled their trips, fleeing from the Morehead broach. But even with all those vacant rooms available, rooms he'd *pay* for, that effort buzzsawed through his ribs.

All his 'mancy hurt now.

"Paul," Imani said, as they staggered towards their room. "We don't know where she is, we don't know how the Unimancers act, we don't know *anything*–"

He sat her down on the bed, put his arms around her. "It's OK, sweetie. You've got this."

"But I–"

"Every time you think of a plan, you remember their skulls shattering."

She blinked, not comprehending what Paul had said. Then she flinched, ashamed.

"It's OK," he repeated. "That's Post Traumatic Stress Disorder. I... I went through it when I shot the illustromancer who..." He hated saying what the illustromancer had done out loud, so instead he glanced down at the titanium blade that served as his right foot. "I shot her right over her left eyebrow. She was in an alleyway, worshipping posters of Titian's artwork, and the posters peeled off the wall like mourners, staggering over to fall face-first into her blood. And... I dreamed, for months..."

Concentrate on Imani, he thought, realizing he'd drifted into his own flashback.

"Anyway, when I realized Aliyah had her own PTSD when she... hurt... Anathema during her magical awakening, I studied up on it. Just in case it happened to someone else I loved."

Imani's smile was the sun peeking out from around a storm – a promise the skies might clear again someday. "You think of everything, don't you?"

If I thought of everything, Aliyah would be safe. "Anyway. Here's how it's going to work." He reached out for the USPS packages lying on the bed; they, too, had been magically backordered. "Your goal is figuring out one thing."

She opened the packages, looked at the books quizzically. "*Honeybee Democracy*? *Ants at Work*? *Interaction Networks and Colony Behavior*? Paul, these aren't therapy books..."

"The therapy is redirecting your mind onto more productive tracks. I'll figure out how to get Aliyah; you figure out how to disable the Unimancer hivemind."

She flipped open the books, confused. "Why am I studying bees, Paul? Give me government studies, you can get those dossiers..."

Not now I can't, he thought, but now was not the time to tell her.

"I've tried to access that information before, sweetie; General Kanakia has blocked formal studies of Unimancer behavior for decades. Whatever the Refactor does to break people down, the Unimancers keep that knowledge to themselves. They can keep good records; they're a living brain.

"I want you to put a cancer in that brain," Paul continued. "To break their connection. We have to smash SMASH – to show America brainwashing 'mancers *is not a solution*."

"How?"

Paul shrugged. "You'll find a way. I'll be tracking down Aliyah; you think of ways to destroy their Unimancy. So whenever you think of those Unimancers'... wounds... you study these books."

She flipped through the table of contents. She was starting to plan; good. She only relaxed when she felt useful. But her eyelids fluttered; the cortisol dampers, doing their work.

He steered her towards one of the double beds. "We have to sleep apart for now. If you bump my ribs in the night, I'll scream. But if you wake up, come get me – I'll talk you through it. We'll figure this out."

She struggled a bit to get up. Then she pulled him down to kiss him – a gentle kiss he didn't deserve, considering Aliyah was in the hands of maniacs.

"Can I confess something?"

"Anything, sweetie."

"…it's not the three dead men I think about."

"OK. What *do* you flash back to?"

"The fourth." Her sleepy vengeance was terrible to behold. "The fifth. The ones I didn't get to shoot. Is that…" She shook herself awake. "Is that bad?"

Paul smiled. "That's… I think that's the attitude we need."

Only Valentine's lover was allowed to dress her wounds.

She found the ritual comforting, even in this antiseptic hotel room – Paul had given them a place so nice it made Valentine feel out of place.

What made her feel at home was watching Robert.

He disinfected the plastic drinks tray, then laid out his paramedic equipment – the scissors, the gauze, the antibacterials. He cut her clothing from her body, neatly avoiding the places where the fabric had fused with her skin.

She'd lost her Bowser tattoo. Her long black hair was seared down to the scalp.

She heard Aliyah joking once they got her back: *Oh, now I see a burned kid.*

But for now, she sank into Robert's brutal touch. He didn't shy away from her wounds, and she loved him for that. He didn't mutter reassurances like *this is going to hurt* – he trusted her to take whatever he dished out.

In turn, she trusted the pain he gave her was what she needed to make her strong again.

She sat still as he plucked at peeling blisters, debrided her sores, wiped stinging disinfectant across ragged cuts. She let him repair her like a machine, and when he fixed her up she *felt* like a killing machine, even if there was a part of her asking, *Weren't you supposed to be the star of the show? What happened to that production, anyway? And...*

Her eyes were wet.

"Common reaction after smoke poisoning," Robert said. He tilted her head back, dropped Visine into her eyes.

Was he making excuses? Was he disappointed?

He wasn't. His gaze held such adoration that she had to look away. If she watched him watching her, she'd start to wonder what she'd done to deserve that look, and then she'd start cataloguing what she *had* done, and...

Justifying her lover's presence would drive her crazy.

Crazier, anyway.

And when he'd trimmed away the last of her singed hair, he gave her painkillers. Valentine wished her videogame magic could heal wounds. The best she could do was produce medpacks that hid injuries until the next scene. Like videogames themselves, her magic never produced anything of lasting change.

He unbuckled his pants, removed a bright purple strap-on he'd strapped to his thigh, kneeling before holding it out in his palms for her inspection.

"What the..."

He gave her a shy grin – such a childish, beautiful grin on such a big, burly man – and retrieved a set of leather cuffs, a small paddle, a knuckle-whip.

He placed them at her feet.

"We left our shit in the car," Valentine said, stunned. "We lost it fleeing Morehead."

"Yeah," he shrugged. "But I always carry something with me for you. You need to work out stress after a bad day."

He was always so adorably embarrassed whenever his

submissive side came out – a glorious secret that only Valentine ever got to witness. He unbuttoned his shirt, turned to present his magnificent backside.

"You keep a strap-on dildo on you at all times in case I need to work off steam? You're the kinky hero that Gotham deserves," she said.

I was Batman, once, she thought. *It didn't help.*

"Look, I… appreciate what you're doing. But tonight…"

She wanted to wipe the tears away. But she let them show, to him.

"I just need you to make love to me, OK? No whips, no clawing, no punching. Just you, with me, where I can… where we can be together. Tonight, I need something…"

"…simple?"

"Yeah." Why was she so fucking tongue-tied? "Simple."

"I can do simple."

If he'd looked grim when he said it, or his eyes had welled with pity, she would have slapped him. But his face was still wreathed in that angelic halo of a smile, a smile that said he was happy to do whatever she needed him to do, and when he climbed on top of her she wondered whether that was the first time she'd ever let him on top.

Then she kissed him until she forgot herself.

SIXTEEN
Teachers Leave Them Kids Alone

Let me save my family, Aliyah had prayed to no one in particular, *and I will never ask for anything again.*

She'd charged down to the airfield, Kratos' knives falling into her sweaty palms. Yes, she'd told Mom this mission was worth the risk of losing Dad. But *Mom* was there. *Valentine* was there. Her bad decision had cost *everyone*. And she–

She'd had to fight.

She came to *still* fighting, yanking on her handcuffs, an IV pinching the back of her hand, rattling the comfortable office chair she'd been manacled to.

She stared at the upholstered leather, her gaze rolling along the deep stitches like a river flowing into a valley. The leather was a burnished dark brown –

With all due respect, Mrs President, a muffled voice snapped from beyond the walls, *Aliyah Tsabo-Dawson is not a bargaining chip. She is a burning fuse. And you are not prepared to deal with Paul Tsabo's brand of explosives.*

Aliyah's attention snapped up to the wood-paneled walls, sliding along the grain. She frowned, then closed her eyes; even though she sat perfectly still, she felt every twitch of her neck muscles as they adjusted her balance, felt the throb of the IV in her hand, the gentle breeze of air conditioning on the nape of her neck – all as distracting as taps on the shoulder.

They'd drugged her with something to hyperfocus her

attention. Which made sense. She couldn't do 'mancy if she–

Do you remember what happened the last time someone kidnapped his daughter?

The voice was faint, but her sensitized ears picked up every syllable. She heard the floor creaking under General Kanakia's boots as he strode back and forth – not *quite* screaming, but speaking with the strained tones of a man desperately trying to prevent someone he respected from being an idiot.

The last time someone kidnapped Aliyah, Mrs President, he decimated New York. *And despite the fact that we had every advantage in this operation – leading him into an ambush, fifteen of my best Unimancers, with Paul's flux-dispersing mechanisms disabled and no time to plan –* he still *neutralized two-thirds of the squad. We haven't lost nine men to an unassimilated 'mancer since – oh, wait, since the last time we lost* nineteen *Unimancers to an unassimilated 'mancer,* which was also him.

His terror felt *good.* She loved it when people thought her daddy was a badass.

Yet the drug chopped facts into tiny pieces, confusing her. She laid her thoughts down one brick at a time, assembling ideas like a Minecraft level:

She was a bargaining chip. That was one brick.

They were worried about Dad. Brick two.

That meant they *didn't* have Dad.

Tears of relief coursed down Aliyah's cheeks.

Brick three was – an absence. Something Kanakia wasn't discussing. Mom? Or Valentine. No, Mom *and* Valentine. They must have gotten away, because Kanakia would have crapped his pants if he thought Dad would be coming for the whole family.

Her father was coming for her.

Aliyah wanted to applaud, but that would have been a bad idea with the IV and the handcuffs.

Her plan fell into place: escape the Unimancer prison, or endure the Refactor torture techniques until Dad arrived. As long as she held out against their brainwashing techniques, Dad would come get her before these assholes zombified her.

These drugs were only the start, though. They'd use more insidious techniques.

She needed to escape.

Kanakia talked again – *SMASH has a limited number of Unimancers to cover the United States, Mrs President. It is irresponsible to fling them away on a local dispute. Yes, I do understand how much funding the United States provides to SMASH operations–*

She bit her cheek again, tuning him out.

They had her in a holding cell. She had to find the escape route.

She opened her eyes, got boggled by the wood grain – no. Refocus. The drug zoomed her attention in on random fragments, like a rogue camera in a videogame. She thought the room had too many windows at first, but then she realized the "windows" were all black-and-white images.

Photos. The office had framed black-and-white photos stuck to the cheap wood paneling. Pictures of buildings. One was a beautiful castle, sticking out of the top of a wooded mountain. Another was the Eiffel Tower. One was a big blocky arch, standing uselessly in the middle of a square – what was that called? The Triumphant Arch?

Was this a prison or a travel agent's office?

Then she realized: *those don't exist anymore*. The walls were hung with famous landmarks swallowed up by the broach.

And this wasn't a prison cell, but an RV office, the kind you'd find parked outside a construction site. The floor was covered with threadbare blue carpeting, the screw-together desk made of particleboard. A chalkboard with half-erased agenda notes was propped in the corner next to a sink brimming with unwashed coffee mugs.

She jerked her attention over to the door. It was an office door with a simple lock, and when she dragged her concentration over to the hinges, they were flimsy aluminum. She could kick it down easily.

If she was a high priority target, why had they stashed her in someone's trailer?

She leaned forward, searching for something to pick her handcuffs open–

The door cracked open.

A teenaged girl snuck in.

The girl was a welter of details, dazzling Aliyah's addled consciousness – sweeping strokes of long red hair, constellations of rust-colored freckles on pale skin, the gleam of sleek Unimancer leather. She shrugged slender shoulders, seemingly apologizing for jangling Aliyah's vision.

The girl moved like well-oiled machinery, gliding noiselessly as she shut the door behind her, holding a finger to her lips to shush Aliyah. Even her sliding into the chair across from Aliyah held the air of a martial arts kata – leaning forward in a formalized bow to deposit a pink-and-white box on the desk, then leaning back to go motionless as a statue.

The new girl's immobility felt like a gift.

Aliyah exhaled, realizing her first order of business had to be shutting off this drug. But she couldn't yank out her IV with this teenaged stranger in the room. So instead, she leaned forward to examine the package she'd delivered:

A box of donuts.

A box of *Dunkin'* Donuts.

Her stomach rumbled. She hadn't eaten since the Morehead Wendy's. Those donuts laid open invitingly, a standard assortment of sprinkles and Boston Kremes.

She wondered how well the Unimancers knew her family. Her Uncle Kit was thoroughly mundane, but everyone made fun of him for his "donutmancy" – he claimed he could tell your mood by your donut choice, and so whenever they were on their way back from an adventure they called up Kit in his retirement home to tell him their selection.

These donuts transformed the room from a prison into…

…well, Aliyah didn't know *what* this office was. But her concept of prison cells did not include pastry trays.

Aliyah could have taken a chocolate glazed (*a solid donut*, Uncle Kit would have said, *the sign of a sober temperament*), but instead she locked gazes with this new girl.

The girl – who couldn't have been two years older than she – peered right back, frowning as though she was sizing up all the problems that an Aliyah in her life presented.

Her hazel eyes jittered: the mark of a Unimancer, distracted by the hivemind's voices.

The good news, Aliyah thought, was that she had finally found a 'mancer her age.

The bad news was, the Unimancers had brainwashed her.

SEVENTEEN
Chekov's Orange Juice

Valentine had placed a glass carafe on the edge of Paul's desk, then taped a sign to it that read "CHEKOV'S ORANGE JUICE."

"What does that even mean?" Paul asked.

"You know I don't footnote my jokes, Paul." Valentine slouched back in her chair, playing *Arkham Asylum* on the hotel room's television. She was playing as Batman, facing down massive groups of thugs; whenever she took a hit, no matter how small, she waved her hand at the screen to rewind the game in yet another attempt at a flawless match. "But trust me, that juice just spoiled the fuck out of any playwrights in this room."

There was nobody in the hotel room except Paul, Robert, and Valentine. But Paul did not get involved in Valentine's ever-inscrutable references.

Instead, he used the orange juice to wash down another Oxycontin to dull the pain in his ribs – and returned to rewriting the Contract, paragraph by paragraph.

His sides ached. But to save Aliyah, he needed to distribute his excess flux to volunteers – especially now the universe was out to get him.

Fortunately, he'd open-sourced the Contract so anyone could suggest changes. He was glad to see the remaining Project Mayhem members had devised legal workarounds to reduce liability now that signing the Contract was a jailable offense. Paul incorporated their modifications, adding automated burn-

and-dump clauses that severed the Contract's connection in case of arrest.

He dimly remembered how this had been his escape once. There had been such satisfaction in anticipating every potential snafu and walling it off with legalese, creating a wise protector to keep everyone safe...

Yet with every revision, Aliyah slipped further away.

He did not have *time* for this.

But the Unimancers had poisoned his magic. That black flux had not only cursed Aliyah, it had broken him so the smallest infraction drowned him in bad luck. Using a new Contract to disperse his flux was his only hope of unlocking enough magical power to track down Aliyah. He doubted many would sign it – the news had become the Morehead broach channel, claiming Project Mayhem had doomed America to become the next Europe – but even a hundred signatures would give room to maneuver.

He had to write out the Contract by hand. It would have saved so much time if he could have printed out a copy and made revisions. But that wasn't how his 'mancy worked. His 'mancy required tedious detail.

His 'mancy didn't care if Aliyah wound up a weaponized zombie.

"There!" He finished the Contract with a flourish, then waved Robert over. Robert had paced back and forth in this third hotel room Paul had rented as an office, calling all his connections to see who had a lead on Aliyah. He'd cursed vociferously, discovering safehouse after safehouse had gone dark.

Normally, he and Valentine would be lovey-dovey – he'd bring her a donut, she'd reward him with a kiss on the cheek – but Valentine stared at the screen, rejecting his help. Robert talked on the phone, trying not to be rattled by her diffidence, walking in circles that paced some nebulous border at the edge of her attention.

Robert looked for all the world like a confused waiter, trying to bring someone a meal that they had once ordered but no longer wanted.

Paul sighed, spreading the Contract out across the desk. Interpersonal relationships weren't his strong point; he'd ask Valentine what was going on later.

"Got a task for you, Robert," he said.

Robert hung up. "What's up, *mon capitaine*?"

"Our new Contract." Paul handed Robert a fresh Bic pen. "Wanna be the first?"

"Why, Paul," Robert said, stifling a fake blush, "I never thought you'd ask me to be your first."

Valentine pointedly ignored his innuendo.

Robert examined the clauses. He knew most of them by heart, having gone over the signing with a thousand recruits – but like Paul, Robert took a certain satisfaction from ensuring everything was in proper working order.

He placed the pen tip against the "Sign here" at the bottom. The pen crackled with fresh magic, prickling Robert's arm hairs. Robert inhaled deeply; his own *Fight Club*-o-mancy may have faded, but he still loved watching magic.

He signed the Contract with a flourish, completing the magical circuit.

The letters bunched up in a typeset seizure, then vomited black flux over Paul's shirt.

"Did it… reject me?" Robert asked, too stunned for snarky comebacks.

Paul clawed at the bad luck crawling across his shirt, mystified – *every clause is perfect!* he thought, enraged.

Then he realized: the math didn't work out anymore.

Once, the universe trusted him enough to have him trade spare flux like a commodity – he could broker the bad luck away, because what was a bureaucrat for if not to shift blame to other departments?

Yet demanding the Unimancers' flashbangs to fail for no reason had triggered a massive tax increase in his flux-debts. The flux-cost incurred in finalizing the Contract had swollen so massive that he could no longer trade flux at a profit.

The Unimancers had stopped him from healing the broach, they'd stolen his daughter, and now they'd disabled the tool that would get her back...

YOU WILL LOSE YOUR DAUGHTER IN WAYS YOU NEVER IMAGINED

"*Fuck!*" Paul screamed, thumping the desk; the flux flowed out of him, finding the orange juice, which tipped over to wash the ink away in a bright citrus flood.

"Chekov!" Valentine shot fingerguns at the mess. "The world's most accurate shot."

"I don't even know what that *means*!"

Robert mopped up the soggy remains of the Contract with a towel. Valentine put her controller down, eyeing Paul.

"It means I don't get why we've wasted five days with you scribbling *words*, keeping Imani in another room reading *books*."

"Hearing you play videogames reminds her of Aliyah," Paul snapped. "And she's researching ways to break the Unimancers..."

"Why *bother*?" Valentine chucked the controller into the couch. "I'm ready, coach, put me in! Whip up your bureaucromancy to track down Aliyah–"

"–which led us into a trap last time–"

"–the principle applies! You can sift through the government's files at will! I mean, sure, yeah, she's off the books – but you can analyze flight records, track troop movements, snoop through internal communications! Don't fine-tune the data, Paul – get me close enough, I'll make Aliyah a quest item, I'll home in on her. But I can't start with no clues! *Get me clues!*"

Paul realized she was as frustrated playing *Arkham Asylum* as he'd been writing this stupid useless contract.

Paul put his head on the desk, which seemed like a good idea right up until he dunked his forehead in sticky paper-pulped orange.

"OK." He ran his hands through his hair, trying to regain his dignity. "I have to tell you a secret, Valentine. But you can't tell Imani."

"Why not?"

"She's overwhelmed. That's what happens when you kill someone for the first time."

Valentine ran her hands over her ash-smeared stubble, wincing as she realized she'd failed in her duty to Imani. "Don't I know it."

"She needs to focus on disrupting the Unimancer network. She can't worry about me. So I need you to... to compensate for me."

The difference between Valentine's "irritated" face and her "concerned" face was almost undetectable, but Paul knew her well enough to catch the shift. She leaned forward, as if ready to catch him...

...and then scowled at Robert with an *oh, you're still there?* look.

"I *got* this," she snapped. Robert lowered his head in embarrassment, realizing he *had* been hovering, his fingers outstretched to help Valentine if she needed it.

He slunk away, closing the door behind him.

"Alright. What's happening?" she asked.

Paul squeegeed a dribble of orange juice out of his hair. "When I saved you... back at the air base... I... *did* something. I did a 'mancy I shouldn't have, and now it's like... like I'm starting over from scratch. Before, I knew all the steps I could have taken to get that authorization and could shortcut them, but now the world is forcing me to fill out everything one step at a time. So I'm slower. And less effective. And... the flux is approaching critical."

She tapped her fingers on the desk, trying out buttons on a controller. "So you've lost your mojo. Is this something you can... heal?"

"I don't know. Maybe I'll get my speed back. But if not, I..." He took out some of the books he'd ordered in, spread them across the floor. "If I can't get my old strength back, then I have to find where the smallest changes make the biggest impact."

She tapped the covers, frowning. They were 1980s era textbooks with professorial-sounding authors: Knuth, Stroustrup, Kernighan.

"...I can't even make sense of the *names* of these books, Paul." Valentine pushed aside a cryptic tome by Schneier. "It's like a dyslexic barfed alphabet soup."

"It's the modern language of bureaucracy," Paul said. "But the point is, Imani's under strain. So I need you to compensate for my weakness. Can you cover for me?"

She exhaled through pursed lips. "...yeah. In fact, I think I might be able to fix your problem altogether. Can you gimme a second to get something for you?"

What could Valentine have to erase this flux? Paul wondered. Valentine had been a 'mancer for longer than he had; she'd taught him how to bleed off his flux. Who knew what other tricks she'd learned?

He waited patiently as Valentine left the room.

She returned with Imani.

"You can't do 'mancy anymore?" Imani didn't sound mad. She rushed to his side, brushing his sticky hair as if she could reveal the wound that had stolen his powers.

"Sorry, Paul," Valentine shrugged. "If you'd told me you were jerking off to teddy bear porn, well, maybe I woulda kept your secret. This shit could get us killed."

"You–"

Valentine batted his objection away. "Did you learn *nothing* from Payne locking away Aliyah, Paul? You keep secrets from your wife, you handicap yourself."

"You're not trying to protect me," Imani told him. "You're *ashamed*. Or you would have told Valentine right away."

"It's like 'mancer erectile dysfunction!" Valentine said.

"Not helping, Valentine. The point is, Paul, you hate looking weak. After you lost your foot, you let me divorce you before you'd admit how miserable you were. And now? Well..." Imani shrugged. "At least you're smart enough to tell a friend who'll tell me."

It was true. He was already so broken, after letting down Morehead, his head buzzing with painkillers, humiliated by SMASH – losing the only thing that had made him special was almost too much to bear.

But Valentine had been right.

He couldn't conceal this.

Paul squeezed back tears. "I'm sorry. With this much at stake, I..."

"You need to be honest about your capacity. You're strong and smart regardless of your magical potential. It's why I married your ass. But remember: I am this group's goddamned Batman–"

"–let us not tussle for the Batman position here–" Valentine interrupted.

" –and if there's a flaw I need to account for when I'm destroying the Unimancers, you need to tell me." She grabbed his cheeks. "I know you hate being weak, Paul. But whenever someone breaks you, you grow more powerful."

Paul grinned. Terrible as it felt to have his magic sabotaged, he had family to lift him up.

"I won't lie again," he promised.

Imani thumped him in the chest. "I am a lawyer. That is a *verbal contract*. The one thing you *have* to respect, my idiot husband, is contracts."

"...the *fuck?*"

Everyone turned to see Robert, his eyes bugged out in disbelief.

"So you're *forgiving* him?" Robert spluttered. "We've spent five days in a *public hotel*! May I remind you Paul set off a magical suitcase nuke? There's a hotline with thousands of bucks in rewards for anyone who wants to play the 'Let's Snitch On Paul Tsabo' game! I bribed the maids because I thought Paul's 'mancy was covering us – but if Paul's fuse is blown, I had *much* better positioned safehouses!"

Imani held up a finger. "OK. Granted, hunkering down in an insecure public space was not the wisest move Paul's made – but creating the Contract to compensate for Paul's increased flux loads was worth trying. Besides, the time it's given me to study hiveminds has... well... I think I have a way to shut the Unimancers down. But it's going to be bloody."

Valentine cracked her knuckles. "When it comes to Unimancers, the only flavor I want is 'bloody'."

"And if I know my husband's detail-obsessed brain, he

had contingency plans on the back burner. Or am I in error, sweetie?"

"I've got a backup plan," Paul admitted. "You won't like it."

Valentine arched one plucked eyebrow. "Anything that gets us closer to Aliyah will make me happy."

"Robert." Paul straightened his tie. "Policy is, you don't clue me in on Project Mayhem's details so SMASH can't get the information out of me. But... a month or so back, I heard a rumor about a huntomancer?"

Robert held his hands up in a *whoa, let's not get crazy here* gesture. "You mean the guy so obsessed with moving silently that he slit his own throat so he'd never make a sound?"

"Yeah."

"You mean the maniac we lost three good 'mancers capturing before he murdered his way to *yet another* mob hit?"

"Yeah."

"You mean the psycho we keep caged up because a) we're not quite sure how *to* kill him, and b) we don't dare let the Unimancers incorporate this maniac's tracking powers?"

Paul held Robert's gaze. "That was the rumor, yes."

Robert approached Paul with the air of a man sneaking up on a lion. "Paul. We're all worried about Aliyah. But I've got leads, *good* leads, from people working overtime to track her down. The huntomancer, he's... he's not an option I'd recommend. Especially when we're negotiating for Aliyah's release. They won't touch her until talks collapse..."

Imani spluttered. "What fresh bullshit, Robert! *We're* negotiating, and *still* calling in all our chits to break Aliyah out of prison – you think *they've* stopped torturing her because we're *negotiating*?"

"They don't know Paul's lost his power!" he snapped, waving his arms around at an imaginary Congress. "They're politicians! They have got to be scared shitless that Paul's digging through their files for embarrassing revelations! A little bureaucromancy can unleash scandals that make Watergate look like an overdue library book!"

Paul blinked. Why *hadn't* he thought to do that, back when

he'd had the power?

The answer came ringing back, sounding hollowly naïve: *because you don't use paperwork to blackmail people.*

But what if it made for a better world? Why *hadn't* he been unearthing scandals to cleanse the government of bad politicians?

"That blackmail potential is why I think they'll move *quicker* to neutralize him," Imani replied. "If they can brainwash Aliyah now, they'll have a permanent hold on him."

"Of *course* we have to hurry," Robert agreed. "But... let's explore other options before the huntomancer..."

"Other *nonmagical* options?" Valentine's cynical voice cut through the tension. "Last time I negotiated with the Unimancers, it cost me this eye and my last boyfriend."

"And unleashing a magical killer on the world is good *strategy*?"

"Oh, come *on*!" She slugged his arm, dodging around him, throwing shadow punches. "What happened to your sense of adventure? When the hell did Tyler 'You can't make an omelet without breaking a few eggs' Durden become some dickless accountant?"

Robert snatched her fist out of mid-air – and then brought it to his lips, kissed her knuckles.

"I didn't need Tyler," he whispered, "once I found what made me happy."

She flicked her hand like she was shaking off dog drool. "Oh, no. No, no, no, Robert. Don't you *dare* go there–"

"Stop," Paul said. "I know this is dangerous, Robert. But – your other safehouses with 'mancers who might help us have been captured, right?"

He hunched down, defensive. "We've still got 'mancers on tap. But the skillsets that could locate Aliyah are narrow..."

"So what's your odds on our mundane connections getting us a bead on Aliyah's location? Especially now that Project Mayhem's an illicit operation?"

"It's... possible." The way he said it didn't give Paul much hope.

"And how long does it take for the Unimancers to torture someone over to their side?"

Robert studied his shoetips. As Valentine elbowed him, Paul realized with a shock: *He didn't want me to know how bad things could get.*

"It... varies. They have to retrain them physically up to military standards. But we've seen some old allies reappear on the other side in as little as a month."

"So what do we do when someone's abducted?"

"Standard policy is to eradicate all evidence they had access to within ten days."

Paul couldn't breathe: in the worst case scenario, they had five days left to rescue her.

"Look," Robert urged. "I know it's bad. But trust to negotiation. Trust to *procedure*. Just... trust the organization you've built will find her."

YOU WILL LOSE YOUR DAUGHTER IN WAYS YOU NEVER IMAGINED

"Robert?" Paul asked.

"Yes?"

"Take me to the huntomancer."

EIGHTEEN
Welcome to the Jungle

"You should taste them," the Unimancer teenager said to Aliyah, sweeping her gloved hand across the box of donuts. "We don't have a... Dunkis out here, but we have some people who worked at Dunkins. We tried our best to recreate the donuts in our mess hall."

Aliyah got a clear vision of Unimancers working together in a kitchen – one whipping up frosting, one dropping donuts into a fryer, moving in that gymnastic synchronization so they never bumped elbows.

She shook it off. She had to escape.

Though she *was* hungry.

And not eating when she had the opportunity seemed foolish.

Especially when the opportunity was donuts.

She leaned over and almost toppled over, the drugs messing with her balance. But the teenaged Unimancer – the word RUTH was embroidered in white thread on a leather shoulder-patch – did not move to help her. Ruth studied her with the seriousness of a doctor diagnosing a patient.

Yet when Aliyah's fingers closed around the chocolate glazed, Ruth's expression softened into something Aliyah recognized – that hopeful look Aliyah had back at the Wendy's, that half-grin of someone searching for someone to smile back at her.

Well, Aliyah *had* to eat the donut now.

She took a bite. Sweet sugar glaze crackled under her teeth, her mouth filling with sticky chocolate. She crammed the rest into her mouth, wishing for a glass of milk to wash it down.

"Oh good," Ruth sighed. "I was worried we'd gone to all that trouble for nothing."

The singular pronoun shocked Aliyah. "I?"

Ruth's contented smile was whisked away as neatly as a magician whipping a tablecloth out from under a dining set. "Yeah." She thumped her chest. "*I. I* snuck in here, *I'll* get in trouble if Kanakia catches me, *I* broke consensus to see you. So yeah. *I.*"

Aliyah didn't know why she felt sorry when she'd been beaten, drugged, and hauled to a new location – but Ruth's angry reaction held the reflexive hurt of someone constantly misunderstood. Aliyah couldn't erase someone's unique identity, especially the only other teenaged 'mancer she'd ever heard of.

But she wouldn't apologize, either.

"Well, *I* don't know that," she shot back. "All *I've* ever seen is *you* guys trying to kidnap us – and you finally did. Good for you. But don't make it sound like I *should* have known you had hobbies when you're not shanghaiing defenseless doilymancers."

"*Ha!*" Ruth leaned back in her chair, impressed. "Oh, *that* polled well."

Aliyah felt she should have understood what Ruth meant, but the drugs clogged her thoughts.

"OK," Ruth whistled, impressed. "You're fearless. I can see how you survived with nothing to back you up."

"I had plenty to back me up. I had my daddy's Contract, and Valentine's expertise, and Mom's–"

Ruth waved her off. "The fact that you think that's 'plenty' tells me you don't know what we work with. By our standards, what you did was like climbing Mount Everest in a diaper."

"I suppose being a Unimancer is like flying to the top in a helicopter?"

Ruth's eyes flicked to one side, consulting with someone

else. "You'd crash. The air's too thin up there for helicopters." She stared over Aliyah's shoulder, her voice mutating into a deeper male voice's recitation. "The 2005 altitude record used a specialized copter with the weight stripped off…"

Ruth shook away the information.

"No. The Unimancers are… they're a Sherpa team. The saggiest, softest millionaire can show up at the base, and their expertise can haul anyone's ass up the mountain."

"Yeah." Aliyah yanked at the handcuff contemptuously, as though she'd break it off any moment. "That's not happening."

"No." Ruth looked pensive. "It won't."

Aliyah did a double-take, which fuzzed into a triple-take as she almost fainted from the movement. Stupid drugs.

Ruth blotted the sweat from Aliyah's forehead. "General Kanakia is furious at me for letting your father get away. He's the one we want inside the collective – well, the one the general wants, anyway."

"Why?"

"He's got some off-the-charts talents for sealing broaches – the reports from Long Island were chaotic, but eventually we concluded Paul healed a broach without Unimancer backup. Rumor is, he later purposely triggered a broach to kill his enemy Payne, then sealed it up so thoroughly we couldn't find a trace of the disruption."

Aliyah kept a poker face, neither confirming nor denying the rumors. Even though, she thought with pride, they were true.

"So you're out," Ruth said. "If we Unimance you, we can't bring Paul's talents in. We can't have a father and a daughter inside the hivemind at the same time."

Maybe she could goad Ruth into giving up intel. "Why? Because your stupid SMASH torture techniques can't break a father's love for his daughter?"

"What? There's no–"

Ruth's fingers popped open in surprise. Her eyes darted back and forth like ping-pong balls, trying to follow some internal roar of debate that Aliyah's words had generated. Aliyah watched as Ruth's face morphed into a hundred different people, each hotly arguing – some angry, others earnest, some begging for peace – Ruth's skin tones shifting up and down the pigmentation spectrum.

But those morphing facial features all held an unmistakable core of Ruth. Yet with each physiognomic transformation, Ruth's certainty wavered. Eventually, she brought her fingers into a fist over her heart – the symbol of the SMASH logo.

"Consensus," she whispered. Ruth's face held the giddy relief that Aunt Valentine had whenever she emerged mussy-haired from a motel room with Uncle Robert.

"No dissenting opinions allowed, eh?" Aliyah needled.

Ruth wasn't bothered. "No *unwise* opinions. Why should I tell you how we operate, when there's a risk of you being a chip in some hostage exchange? I'm not sending you home with new intel just because you got my goat."

Aliyah bleated.

Ruth smiled. Aliyah hated the way she *liked* that smile. She'd always fallen for people who challenged her. But Rainbird had challenged her – and Rainbird had been a psychopath murderer trying to turn her into a hired killer.

She was already thinking of Ruth as a friend, which was the most dangerous trap of all.

So when Ruth left – and Ruth *had* to leave before someone discovered her, because she'd admitted she wasn't supposed to be here – Aliyah would figure out how to get the handcuffs off. Uncle Robert had taught her how to unlock cuffs, and if she could remember how to–

Ruth closed her fingers around Aliyah's wrist.

Aliyah realized she'd been staring at the handcuffs as she pondered her escape, telegraphing her next move.

"You're gonna escape unless we get you to realize why you need to stay put," Ruth whispered. "You're not like the other 'mancers – I've seen Legomancers cry when they realized we had nothing for them to assemble. Most of the others sink into the drugs. The general thinks you'll break down without your dad – but you'll fight until you get back to him, won't you?"

Aliyah closed her eyes, refusing to give Ruth – and all the

Unimancers watching her through Ruth – an answer.

Ruth unlocked the cuffs, slipped the needle out of Aliyah's hand. Aliyah tensed – was this a psych-ops challenge, where they'd pretend to set her free to see how she reacted?

She sat in the chair, refusing to budge.

Stiff fingers jabbed into the inside of her elbow. Ruth tugged; Aliyah's body followed before Aliyah told it to stop.

Aliyah braced herself. Ruth stepped alongside, dropping into a policeman's come-along position – but when she jerked Aliyah's wrist to the breaking point, Aliyah stayed put.

"Think this hurts?" Aliyah hissed. "Try having your skin stripped off in the burn ward."

Ruth pulled her forward again, experimentally. Aliyah didn't move.

"You little…" Ruth's consternation was laced with an admiration that Aliyah drank up. "I'm trying to help."

"Help one more step, and I'll yell. How will the general react when he finds you smuggling me out?"

"Jesus Christ. You're my age."

It should have sounded like a complaint – but it was a compliment. They were both teenaged 'mancers, forced into lifestyles they'd never asked for. And though Aliyah didn't know what had happened to Ruth, they were both veterans. They should be competing on the cheerleading squad, or daydreaming about their driver's license–

Yet they both felt more comfortable in this prison than they would have on a soccer field.

"Come on." Ruth let go. "You'll hurt yourself trying to escape. You'll hurt all of us, unless I show you why you want to stay put. I know you don't want to hurt anyone."

Aliyah resisted long enough to pluck a Vanilla Kreme donut from the box before exiting. If the Unimancers *did* speak Uncle Kit's donut-language, they'd know Vanilla Kreme meant "reckless rebellion."

She stepped outside. The sky was splintered into golds and crusted reds, streaked with colors that hurt to look at. Aliyah slumped down on the three wooden steps leading up to the office – which she noted *was* on wheels – clutching her head.

"It's the drugs, mostly." Ruth caught Aliyah in one hand, rescued the donut with the other. "Once you understand why you can't escape, we'll see if we can't talk the general into lowering the dosage. Otherwise, you'll fuzz out whenever someone walks by. Eat the donut, a filled stomach will help."

Aliyah studied her shoetips. Her mission was clear: play on Ruth's sympathy, flush the drugs from her system, chip away at their security.

"I suppose you'd know all about what they do to 'mancers here…" Aliyah muttered.

"Well, *yeah*. But only because I'm linked into everybody else's memories. I took a different path into Unimancy."

"'Cause they caught you doing 'mancy before you were out of diapers?" That wasn't strategy – it slipped out. She really *did* want to know how Ruth had become a 'mancer.

"No. Because I…" Ruth blew a lock of hair out of her face. "Yes. Yes, I *know* she's working me. Just trust I'm not gonna fuck this up?"

Aliyah grinned ruefully. She knew that tone all too well.

"Unimancers?" she joked. "More like Unimommies."

Aliyah was expecting to see either Ruth's anger, or her shy grin – but instead, Ruth hugged her knees to her chest. "They're a real family, Aliyah. They protect people. Not like the selfish pack of idiots *you* call kinfolk."

"They're not selfish – Daddy would give his life for me–"

"And the lives of everyone in Morehead!"

Aliyah's skin prickled: how had that slipped her mind? Her flux had opened a broach that had triggered an emergency evacuation. Savannah and Latisha, forced to move from their homes–

She'd *forgotten*.

Maybe she *was* selfish.

But she wouldn't admit that to Ruth.

"That broach opened because they were afraid!" she spat. "Because *you* made them afraid! Your anti-'mancy propaganda, you scared them until they fought us, and–"

Ruth's cheeks flushed with rage. "You think you want your dad to rescue you. You think you wanna escape. You even have the gall to think you're the good guy. Well, stand up, little 'mancer. Time to meet the *real* world."

Ruth hauled Aliyah to her feet.

This had been a mountain town, once, a grand street winding between great gabled houses – but it had been encroached by thick forests, and unhealthy black trees had pushed massive holes through the brick walls. The survivors had strung plastic tarps between the gaps of the leaning buildings, shored up the collapsing houses with stout oaken logs, created a tiny refugee city in the hollows of what once had been a thriving town.

Aliyah saw black-uniformed Unimancers stepping from wooden barracks piled high with camouflage-green sleeping bags. Yet the city was strewn with haggard survivors: two emaciated boys staggering home underneath the weight of a dead deer. An old woman with a plastic axe, her gauze-wrapped hands bleeding from where she'd chopped wood for the incoming winter. A family working in unison to make arrows – a boy carving the shaft, his sister tying machine-tooled metal heads to the front, the father applying the fletching.

They wore bizarre mixes of deerskin boots and puffy orange winter jackets. And they worked in conjunction with the Unimancers – a Unimancer trotted in on a horse, and the locals helped the Unimancer down, rubbed her horse dry, offered to clean her rifle.

The locals ignored Aliyah. They set to their tasks with the grave singularity of people who depended on their work to survive, their necks bowed from forever staring downwards.

The Unimancers, however, strode out to stare at Aliyah with grave sadness.

Ruth shook Aliyah. "Don't look back at us. Look up. Look at what your people *did*."

Aliyah lifted her gaze up over the shanty refugee town. She looked up the steep mountainside, past the blasted slopes of dead trees–

Her scream died in her throat.

The sky was *splintered*, like a shattered pane of stained glass. It flexed dangerously, as though some immense oceanic pressure from the other side weighed down upon it – and every time it pulsed, it exhaled buzzsect swarms–

"*Look* at it!" Ruth grabbed Aliyah's hair, forced her gaze back to that shattered landscape. "*You* know what that is! *Everyone* does!"

Some of the shards had tumbled from the sky, falling out like jigsaw pieces to reveal a blank whiteness – an emptiness more terrifying than any black. And obscured behind those gaps was a striding storm of edges, a six-legged whirlwind crouching down to push itself through the gap–

"Say it." Ruth shook her like a rag doll. "Say where we are!"

"Bastogne." Aliyah wanted to sound tough – but watching this devastation, Aliyah's voice leaked out like a deflating balloon. "World War II's final battle. The broach's epicenter."

"You're in Europe now, kid," Ruth told her. "And your daddy doesn't dare come here."

NINETEEN
Wodehouse is a Very Very Very Fine House

"So who's guarding the huntomancer?" Paul asked.

As Robert fumed at the wheel, driving them to an unknown location, Paul wondered whether handing the fine details of Project Mayhem over to Robert had been a good idea. It meant the Unimancers couldn't destroy Project Mayhem if SMASH brainwashed Paul – but it also meant Paul was reliant on Robert's dwindling goodwill.

The silence lengthened, became itchy. Valentine sat in the back, arms crossed, expecting an apology. Except she seemed rattled by Robert's coldness; she'd kept stealing glances at him over her Nintendo DS, as if expecting him to reach back to take her hand.

"Robert," Paul insisted. "I recognize your concerns about this mission's exposure. But if we're going to use him to find Aliyah, I need informa–"

"The Butler is guarding the huntomancer."

Robert spoke curtly, a prisoner giving his rank, name, and serial number.

"I assume he's a 'mancer?"

"The Butler is neither a 'he' nor a 'she.' At best, they identify as 'servant.'"

Paul nodded, mentally checking off the "other" box in the male/female/other field on his internal forms.

"But yes," Robert continued. "They're a servantmancer."

Valentine coughed. "Shouldn't you get, I dunno, a guardomancer?"

Robert glared out at the road. For a moment, Paul thought Robert might ignore her. Given that Valentine was gripping her DS like a weapon, he wasn't sure how he'd keep the peace if Robert blew her off–

"Jailing people wasn't our mission," he said stiffly. "When I've *had* a choice in which 'mancers I've been able to save, I've prioritized acquiring combat and camouflage skills to keep us safe come the day."

"*What* day?" Paul asked.

"The day they outlawed us. I thought we had seven years before they dropped the RICO act on us – but whoa, Morehead yanked the hands forward on *that* Doomsday clock."

"You were planning a decade ahead?"

Robert gave a bitter laugh – reminding Paul that sunny Robert still had plenty of Tyler Durden's black nihilism floating around inside. "Ending segregation took a hundred years, Paul. Gay marriage took forty. Did you think you'd make the world safe for 'mancers in time for Aliyah's sweet sixteen party?"

Robert chuckled as he flicked off the headlights, nudged a creaking gate open with the bumper, and pulled onto a cracked road leading into an abandoned asylum.

Paul scratched his neck, feeling foolish. He'd kind of thought he *would* fix America's politics for Aliyah.

"*That's* what happened to my sense of adventure, Valentine," Robert said pointedly. "Staying ahead of the government. *Winning*. This is a guerrilla war, and you win those through smart use of forces and moral superiority on the ground. Project Mayhem was designed to *endure*. This is what we *do*."

"'You are not your job,'" Valentine quoted dully. "'This is your life, and it's ending one minute at a time.'"

Quoting *Fight Club* to Robert was like slapping him in the face. He hunkered down over the wheel, face darkened.

"As for the huntomancer," Robert said quietly, "I'll let Butler explain the sitrep to you."

Imani frowned. "You haven't called anyone since Paul made

the decision to come here."

"Butler always knows when company's coming."

He backed the car up next to a set of wide, cracked steps. The asylum had once exemplified the grand brass architecture that only really got funded in the 1940s, but its steps were now littered with water-soaked roofing tiles and broken beer bottles.

Paul quashed the itch to magically access the failed building inspection records so he'd know when the institute had been condemned – once, acquiring that information would have been trivial. But he felt the black flux pressing in, eager to punish his curiosity. From the half-collapsed roof and layers of graffiti, he guessed it'd shuttered its doors two decades back.

The overcast moon above gave them enough light to pick their way up the buckled stairs.

The chained doors rattled open.

A hooded lantern shone respectfully at their feet, offering guidance.

They had to move quickly; most of Project Mayhem's safehouses were squatter locations. Robert had tucked the car by the asylum's side, out of casual observers' sight; they didn't need the cops arriving to investigate.

Paul braced himself to see a stern Englishman in a valet outfit, holding the door for him–

Which is why he was surprised to find an old, bare-chested white man in a leather collar, vest, and cap.

Paul cruised to a halt, staring, knowing he was being rude but uncertain how to stop. He knew he was being rude by thinking of Butler as a man when the Butler identified themselves as a *they*, but...

The Butler stood at an attention so firm, any rudeness slid off their polished leather vest. Moonlight glinted off the silver chains that connected Butler's nipple rings to Butler's burnished leather pants; though their body was grizzled, Butler's face was hairless, cherubic, their cap set at a jaunty angle.

Butler held their leash in one hand, the lantern in the other, ready to offer either if needed.

"Sheeeeiiiit." Valentine's voice was low with admiration as

she joyfully turned to Robert. "So these are the kinds of secret adventures you're off having? This is top-tier magic, Robert." She saluted Butler. "High-protocol service kink turned to 'mancy? Not my style – too many rules – but respect, old bean. *Respect.*"

She held out her fist. With a glimmer of 'mancy, Butler slapped their leash over their shoulder in a crisp military salute, then reached out to meet Valentine's fist-bump, their two protocols melding seamlessly.

Butler bowed, nipple-chains jangling. "Mr and Ms Tsabo-Dawson. Mr Paulson. If you'll allow me to escort you inside, I'll do my best to answer your enquiries."

Butler led them through decaying hallways strewn with rusted gurneys and smashed-in prescription cases.

"I leave it untidy near the entryway, so casual visitors won't investigate," they said, in a voice tinged with a faint Southern drawl. "I have arranged nicer accommodations for our poor guest."

"*Poor*?" Valentine asked. "*Guest?* Didn't this huntomancer murder three 'mancers?"

"So he did," Butler agreed. "But you don't murder that many people without carving up your soul. Adding more punishment wouldn't help the poor lad. I care for him with all possible gentleness, in the hopes that kindness might resuscitate his compassion."

Paul flicked a gaze towards Robert, understanding why he'd chosen a servant to imprison the huntomancer. Butler was both detail-oriented, and devoted to the huntomancer's safety: a perfect warden.

Valentine shot him fingerguns. "Man, if I'm gonna be chained up, I want it to be you, Barney."

Imani did a double-take. "Did you call them a purple dinosaur?"

A slight grin crept across Butler's face. "No, ma'am. She's referring to Hannibal Lecter's able prison caretaker in *Silence of the Lambs*. A high compliment."

Valentine threw her hands up in triumph. "At last! Someone who gets my pop-culture references!"

"My former master was quite fond of movies involving dungeons," Butler demurred. "In any case, yes, I am Mr Steeplechase's caretaker."

"I thought…" Paul blushed, hating to ask foolish questions, but Butler's ease made every query seem reasonable. "Didn't he slit his throat?"

Butler rounded a corner, moving deeper into the asylum's interior; the lantern played over scrubbed cell doors, the cells themselves threadbare but as welcoming as hostel accommodations. "So he has, sir. I've never heard him make a sound – you could listen all day and never know he was in his cell."

"So how do you know his name?"

"His clothing had a name stitched upon the inside."

Paul frowned. "Steeplechase. The mob had a huntomancer, back when I worked on the force…"

"Same person, sir." Butler led them down a freshly-mopped stairwell, into a basement where the peeling paint had been scraped away. "We got an anonymous mob informant. Apparently, his superiors had set Mr Steeplechase on a target so monstrous it caused a crisis of conscience. They begged us to stop him before he reached his target."

"Yes, but…" Something about Steeplechase tickled Paul's memory. They'd called in the mob's huntomancer once to track down a serial killer. He hadn't been involved, but he'd heard rumors–

He wished he hadn't popped another Oxycontin before their arrival. His memories swam away like startled goldfish.

Yet as they walked down the stairs, Paul felt his cares easing away. The smell of chamomile tea filled his nostrils, and somehow tiny Butler had hauled several comfortable leather chairs into this distressing madhouse basement, giving it the semblance of home. Robert's favorite newspapers lay spread open across silver trays, and a thick chocolate milkshake sat inside a chilled ice bucket waiting for Valentine, and a pressed business suit in Imani's size was hung neatly inside a small armoire.

"Did you lay this outfit out for me?" Imani asked, plucking at the emergency clothing they'd purchased at a Target.

"I purchased them earlier," Butler demurred. "I have... instincts. Instincts that help ensure I have the proper things when people need them."

Paul scanned the area, seeing nothing he needed. "What about me?"

"Alas, sir," Butler said solemnly. "I'm afraid there's only one thing that will allow you to relax."

Butler stopped before an old-fashioned cell door: it had a slot to push food through, and a narrow opening to check in on the prisoner. Inside the cell, moonlight streamed through a barred window set high in the stained concrete.

The chipped walls had been inscribed with mysterious spiderwebbed lines.

And of course Butler was right. All Paul wanted was a lead on Aliyah.

Two lucite-encased mirrors were set high in the far corners; the protective shield surrounding the mirrors was cracked but not broken. The mirrors reflected dim starlight onto a barren mattress, an empty bucket, a tray with plates licked clean.

Through the mirrors, Paul saw the cell was empty.

Yet that blank space held a puzzling allure – Paul's eyes skipped across the shadows. *Something* lurked in there. Hairs prickled on the back of his neck; looking away seemed dangerous. He had to find where the huntomancer hid, because the alternative was that something dreadful had escaped.

He stepped forward to get a closer look–

And it *flickered*.

The thing inside the cell moved too quickly for Paul to process – it practically teleported from shadow to shadow, like a smash-cut in a movie – blink, blink, and one muscled arm thrust out between the bars to crush Paul's throat–

Butler pulled him back.

Bloodied fingers closed centimeters from Paul's tie.

Paul froze, understanding why deer went numb in the headlights.

Steeplechase thrust his arm out, quivering with exertion – but though he'd slammed his body against the steel door, the only sound echoing through the asylum was Paul's strangled cry of terror.

The huntomancer was old – older than Butler, scrawny, wiry, gray. Steeplechase had the grizzled, emaciated look of an ancient animal, something too stubborn to die. The curlicued scar around his wattled neck highlighted where his larynx had once been.

His ragged fingernails were chewed to razor-sharp points, but his bloodshot eyes were wet with tears.

Steeplechase held Paul's gaze for a moment, furious – and when Butler jerked Paul backwards, Steeplechase flickered away to the far wall, clasped his hands over his balding head, and crouched down, bobbing in mute agony.

"He's a bit of a guided missile, sir," Butler explained. "He can't think of anything but his target. He worsens daily. Which makes sense, I suppose; we *are* thwarting his obsession."

"It must be…" Paul straightened his tie – a tie that seemed like a liability now that someone had tried to strangle him with it. "It must be a chore keeping him pent up here."

"Not as much as you might think, sir," Butler demurred. "He's powerful, but terribly untrained. No capacity to hold his flux. His 'mancy rebounds on him. He's found chinks in the walls – but utilizing his magic to do violence upon those weaknesses guarantees some unfortuitous coincidence alerts me whenever he's close to freedom. If he could hold his flux, sir, he might be magnificent."

Paul imagined those sharpened nails slicing his jugular. "Not the word I'd choose to describe him."

"I don't care how you describe him." Imani stepped forward, peering fearlessly into the cell. "The question is, can he find our daughter?"

Steeplechase's head whipped around.

Another flicker, and he was once again pressed against the

cell, cocking his head like a hawk to examine Imani. His arm hung down from the cell window.

His cheeks glistened with tears.

Imani bowed her head, approached Steeplechase as though approaching a feral cat. "Her name is Aliyah. She's a fighter. They *stole* her from us, Mr Steeplechase. She's in the hands of men who will hurt her."

With serene grace, Imani stepped into range of Steeplechase's bladelike nails. Paul reached out for her – only to find Butler gripping his shoulder, one hand held up in a *let's see what happens* motion.

Imani rested her palm on Steeplechase's bloodied hand. He flinched at her touch, then froze as though afraid he might hurt her; he turned away, his tears flowing in streams.

"Please, Mr Steeplechase." She spoke with the dignity of a down-on-her-luck businesswoman asking a renowned lawyer to take on a tough case. "Help us find our daughter."

Steeplechase craned his head to look out through the barred window, out into the moonlight, clearly pondering his current target. Paul knew a 'mancer couldn't break his rules – if Steeplechase believed he couldn't give up the chase without cornering his prey first, he might not be able to switch targets.

Steeplechase's scarred throat convulsed – was he trying to say something? Crying? Barking? It was hard to–

"*Freeze!*"

Flashlights bobbed across Paul's face.

Four county cops made their way down the stairwell, guns out, screaming for everyone to get on the floor.

TWENTY
Death of a Salesmancer

In Bastogne, Aliyah remembered a funny story Mommy had told her about Frisbee-herding sheepdogs.

The dogs had not, as Aliyah had surmised, herded Frisbees. But Mom's friend *had* owned three shaggy dogs, and they ran free in a field while Mom's friends played Frisbee. As usual, athletic Mom had sent the Frisbees soaring high and far across the field towards her buddies...

...except after half an hour, Mom's friends were clustered within twenty feet of each other.

It was the damn sheepdogs, Mom had told her. *We never noticed them herding us. They'd clip your heels here, crowd you close there, and before we knew it we stood in a circle laughing.*

Theoretically the Unimancers let Aliyah wander freely, but they were sheepdogs.

If she approached the forest that covered Bastogne's far ridge, a Unimancer stepped out from behind the washing line. If Aliyah side-eyed a horse, trying to remember what she'd learned from *Red Dead Redemption*, the Unimancers would start repairs on the ramshackle stables. If Aliyah darted into the refugees' living quarters, which were mazes gouged out of the remaining buildings, a Unimancer would sit down on one of the wooden plank bridges above that connected the alcoves.

The Unimancers were ragtag – wizened Peruvian women

dressed in men's uniforms, stout African men with barrel chests, a pair of androgynous Russians who were either lovers or twins. Yet when each caught her eye, they shot her Ruth's cocky grin.

Aliyah seethed. Bad enough the Unimancers had beaten her. But to know Ruth was *taunting* her...

Well, actually, seeing Ruth made her feel better. Now she'd witnessed the Thing lurking inside the broach – the first broach, the biggest broach, *the* broach – Aliyah's gaze drifted upwards. The Thing twitched in the edges of her drugged vision like a spider, saturating her in a numb panic.

Nobody in town seemed to notice the chaos seething in their skies. They never looked up. She wanted to ask them how they lived beneath such dread mayhem, but none of the locals spoke English – and once the Unimancers had explained this strange girl's presence to them, they nodded uneasily and kept their distance.

Aliyah caught fragments of German in their vocabulary, pondering how she might talk one of them into letting her escape, but their conversations didn't sound like any German she'd ever heard; she suspected it was some pidgin dialect developed locally. Which also made sense. Aside from Unimancers arriving on horses, no visitors came.

Aside from the Unimancers, Bastogne had been isolated from civilization for over seventy years. Here was where the German Aryomancer squadrons had collected in a last-ditch attempt to break the incoming Allied forces – and the Allies had opted to make Bastogne a 'mancer-on-'mancer war, sending in the OSS Extraphysics Departments and the American Paranormal Paratroopers and the remnants of the Russian Deathless resistance to blast out the last of the German magic.

It hadn't ended well.

She looked for cars, motorcycles, any vehicle to steal – but those required roads, and it had been half a century since there'd been enough people left to lay asphalt. The paths the Unimancers took into the forest were dense trails barely wide enough to fit a horse.

Even if she escaped into the woods, where would she go? The horizon was crisscrossed with mutated physics: shimmering green fire-fields, spirals of glowing Cherenkov radiation, hazy black vortexes.

Between the obvious dangers stood empty fields. There were no trees in those cracked groves, no grass, no water. But *something* had changed in those innocuous-looking zones.

Getting lost in the woods would have been dangerous even in Kentucky. One wrong step here could transform her oxygen to radon. Using her 'mancy to guide her would rip open a new broach.

She couldn't see a way out. Not without help.

She wasn't sure *how* to guilt Ruth into helping her escape. But they *were* the only two teenaged 'mancers on the planet, as far as she knew; Ruth had been as curious to see her as Aliyah had been.

Separating Ruth from the hivemind would be her path to escape.

Still, escape seemed unsatisfying. She didn't *like* looking up at the Thing in that cracked sky, but...

The locals lived in the skeleton of a once-great town. And even though these people were generations removed from the people who'd seen the broach end World War II, she saw Morehead in them – people who'd loved their town so much, they'd refused to leave.

Walking away from Bastogne gave her that queasy feeling of abandoning Morehead all over again.

People high in the buildings pointed up eagerly – a squadron of weather balloons drifting in, supplies dangling from their bellies.

The locals waved furiously at the balloons, as if hoping to steer them–

Four balloons hit a pocket of distorted physics, crumpled into nothingness.

Aliyah winced; sure enough, those woods *were* dangerous. The supply balloons rippled as a massive turbulence rose up from below, sending some crashing into the spiky trees.

Aliyah wondered how many balloons SMASH had sent out. They couldn't have all been for Bastogne. They must have released thousands of balloons, drifting to cities across the continent, knowing a heavy percentage of supplies would never make it.

How dangerous was it, crossing Europe on horseback?

She wondered what Morehead would look like in fifty years.

Three balloons floated over the buildings; the Unimancers shot them down. Unimancers and civilians alike cheered, rushing towards the crashed food crates. Some they pawed through and recoiled from, holding their breath; somewhere along the way, something had transformed organic compounds into ammonia.

The rest scooped a broken sugar bag off the road and sifted out the dirt.

What a luxury those donuts had been. They must have contributed so many supplies...

It moved. The splintered sky shifted again.

Aliyah froze. If the Thing in the sky had raged, hammering at the interdimensional chinks, she could have relaxed. But that Thing moved nimbly, methodically, a burglar creeping up on windows to test the locks. It focused Its attention on weak spots, conducting unknowable experiments.

There was an *intellect* behind this amalgamation.

She curled up on a rooftop, trying not to think about It peering into Morehead.

Look at what your people did, Ruth had hissed.

How could Daddy have done 'mancy, knowing all this destruction was a bad spell away?

Her father would have a comforting explanation ready, she was sure. But alone, Aliyah struggled to justify her existence.

Ruth pulled herself up onto the roof with a gymnast's skill. Aliyah kept her gaze on the sky, refusing to acknowledge Ruth's presence – but Ruth pulled up hip-to-hip with her.

After a while, she asked, "Wanna get some dinner?"

The thought of eating made Aliyah sick. But company sounded good.

"I gotta top off your euclidosuppressants," Ruth apologized, fishing a hypodermic out from her belt. "The general's authorized a lower dosage – but you know what'll happen if you do 'mancy."

Ruth's prison guard demeanor galvanized her. They had *kidnapped* her. If they didn't need her to blackmail her father, she'd be in one of their torture-camps.

Her father was coming for her. Even in the most desolate place on Earth, her family would come get her – and when they rescued her, she'd gift them with dossiers of intel.

And then she'd beg her father to explain why he'd risked Morehead's safety for a soccer game.

Ruth fumbled with the needle for a moment. Then her eyes glowed and her slender fingers found Aliyah's vein with borrowed medical experience.

Aliyah respected the way Ruth didn't press her for responses.

They sat on the roof as Aliyah felt her attention contract yet again. Before, the waving of branches in the wind had waved her attention up to that Thing; now, she could keep her focus down among the pines.

"We eat down the road," Ruth told her.

Ruth helped Aliyah down. Her grip was sure and strong and more comforting than Aliyah wanted it to be.

They headed down a path through the woods – not a road, not after seventy years of overgrowth, but Aliyah picked out a trail from the buckled cobblestones embedded in the soil. Unimancers and locals plodded down the path.

Ruth stopped Aliyah near an otherwise uninteresting thicket.

"In the next five steps or so, you're gonna see a blue flash." Ruth pointed at a shimmering curtain rising into the air, a sparkling glow lost against the bobbing ferns – almost hypnotizing, in her current state.

Aliyah bit her cheek again. "In your next five words or so, you're gonna give me an explanation."

"Wish we had one. Far as we know, that's trace amounts of

the higher elements in your body disintegrating into radiation. Theory is the nuclear forces have weakened here, so anything high up in the periodic table..." She spread her fingers apart in a "poof" gesture.

"The *theory*?"

"Hey, we've got the brainpower–" she tapped her temple "–but even we can't sense radiation. Baseline, we're still human."

"You're SMASH. Shouldn't you have fancy equipment to monitor things?"

Ruth pointedly stared out into the thick woods. Aliyah blushed, trying to imagine hauling delicate scientific equipment through the forest on horseback.

"The nuclear forces calm back down in a quarter mile," Ruth continued. "But then you get to the mess hall, where mass spontaneously produces kinetic energy. At least that's why we think everything vibrates there."

"That doesn't sound safe."

Ruth snorted a bitter laugh. "Try walking into a zone where electrical resistance triples. Doesn't affect trees, but it'll stop your heart before you finish that step."

"Best not to start that step, then. How do you tell the difference?"

"Maybe we don't."

Now Aliyah snorted. "So you wander blind? After seventy years of battling broaches? No wonder you're losing."

Sure enough, Ruth rose to the bait. "We–"

Then her eyes glowed, and Ruth gave Aliyah a smile as slow as syrup, nodding in admiration.

"Alllllmost got me," she acknowledged. "But you're in the only place on Earth we can guarantee your dad can't get you. It's not in our interests to educate you."

Aliyah glowed with the compliment. This was literally the highest security prison in the world, and Ruth was correct: anything less, and she would have broken out, or Dad would have broken in.

Or maybe this whole activity was a psych op to give her Stockholm Syndrome.

"You're not my friend," she told Ruth, walking straight into the blue flash.

Families gathered around a cavernous nylon blue tent, chatting loudly and drinking booze from plastic jugs. As Ruth approached, they shot her proud salutes; Ruth returned their salutes with cocky fingerguns.

The locals laughed with approval.

"They seem... happy... to see you," Aliyah said.

"They've seen our sacrifices." Ruth hugged a small child who brought her a sprig of rosemary. "We come to town to eat because they feel safer with us around."

You can't ever come back, Savannah had said.

Out in back, Unimancers and locals cooked a huge meal over campfires, adding spices from a plastic rack. Inside, the locals sat down, glad to socialize.

Yet Aliyah focused on the sixty Unimancers, each lining up to take a pitcher of gray fluid from a chilled rack. As Ruth had promised, the liquid in the pitchers churned despite the fact that they sat on ice-filled shelves; Aliyah felt her stomach gurgling, the fluids moving on their own.

That didn't bother her. The Unimancers grabbing pitchers in synchronization, like a centipede's legs? *That* made her shiver.

It felt like a drug trip, and her hyper focused attention didn't help the matter. The Unimancers didn't look at each other; Aliyah had fought them long enough to know they didn't have to. As long as there was a critical mass of Unimancers present, they crowdsourced each other's field of vision until they created a three hundred and sixty degree shared area map.

She should have been tense, but...

The locals hugged the Unimancers, waving them over to sit down, thanking them for the day's assistance. And Aliyah was skeptical – *this is where I discover they're brainwashed to serve as the Unimancers' slaves* – but when she scrutinized the Unimancers, they looked more exhausted than the locals.

The drug also auto-focused her attention on the motion when

the Unimancers moved to massage each other's shoulders. Others hugged in groups, relishing the touch. Aliyah followed the ripples of laughter crisscrossing the room as the Unimancers shared secret jokes.

Aliyah smiled too. Then Ruth tugged her hand. "Come on!" She seemed happy Aliyah was into what she'd offered.

No more smiles. Time for reconnaissance.

This mess hall felt more like a family than a military operation. The euclidosuppressants made her lurch to conclusions, skipping over the steps that had brought her to a realization; Aliyah fought to backfill the reasons why her conscious mind felt this was a Christmas reunion.

The answer, as she scanned the Unimancers' faces, was age. Most were in their mid-forties, with a fair contingent of retirees. Some hobbled on canes.

Which made sense: it took decades for obsession to blossom into magic. Aunt Valentine was considered precocious for casting spells in her late twenties. Daddy had been pushing fifty when he sparked.

Aliyah remembered SMASH as fit military men. They must have sent the youngest Unimancers after them.

Still, the Unimancers made Aliyah feel *freakishly* young. She focused on the Unimancers' wrinkles, then Ruth's smooth ginger freckles.

Ruth brought her to a long table set with a single tureen of meaty stew; *this is the kids' table*, Aliyah thought. The stew was covered in a dark black crust, sitting atop a Sterno can, a bubbling vat of beans and sausage that quivered with this area's kinetic bleed-off.

Aliyah looked around guiltily; only she, Ruth, and the locals had stew. The other Unimancers had that unappetizing gray fluid.

"Don't worry." Ruth crumbled her rosemary into the stew. "My family will drink the fluid – it's nutritionally balanced – but when I eat this cassoulet, they'll plug into my tastebuds. You'll see. But before we eat, we hold the daily memorial service."

Ruth let that last sentence hang.

Once Ruth had determined Aliyah would give her no reaction, a heavy quiet swept over the room. The locals lowered their heads, the parents shushing their children.

"*Consensus*," the Unimancers whispered, bringing their clenched fists up over their hearts.

"Sean Patrick Kelly," they recited.

A respectful pause. Then a beautiful Californian-looking housewife said, in a gravelly Texan accent:

"Ben Franklin's truth: get a man to do you a favor, and he will like you more."

A sickly-looking Mexican woman nodded as though some ritual had been completed, then said in the same male voice:

"Consumption of coffee gives people a mental boost that makes them easier to persuade. Give free coffee in meetings when you can – but don't drink it yourself."

A butch leather dyke with a buzzcut spoke, in the same accent: "The kinesthetic internal modality of proprioception can be hijacked to lead the customer to a conclusion they were already arriving at mentally."

Aliyah tried to memorize each statement to tell Daddy later – but it became apparent they were reciting Unimancer sales tips, leavened with random facts like, "When accessing shared memories of rifle shooting, remember shoulder pressures are variable."

This didn't seem like a memorial service. More like a disjointed seminar.

Ruth leaned over to whisper into Aliyah's ear: "Sean's gone, but we can each store something he wanted us to remember."

"So you live on forever inside the…"

Aliyah wanted to say "hivemind," but maybe that term was impolite. Nor did it feel polite to note that these memories seemed impersonal, uniformly clustered around salesmanship – though she found it reassuring that people seemed to retain their own obsessions inside whatever passed for the Unimancer shared space.

"Do you live forever inside of each other's memories after… death?"

Ruth swallowed. "No. That's been… it's been done. It doesn't end well."

Aliyah still wasn't certain this ceremony wasn't a trick – but Ruth's distress seemed very real.

"I know this seems a little abstract to you," Ruth explained. "But… this is… it's a thin afterlife, I guess. Bits of you float around in us, and some of your memories become useful, and take root. But it's not you. You wouldn't want it to be you."

Ruth reached for a glass of water, but her hands shook. The Unimancer next to her picked up the glass and poured it into her mouth.

"Do you choose what memory you get?" Aliyah asked.

Ruth's face paled. "I'm stuffed with memories. I'm *overflowing* with them."

"Stuffed? How can you–"

An elderly black Unimancer with her gray hair in a bun tapped Aliyah on the shoulder, shaking her head. Ruth rubbed her temples, her lips twitching, like a crazy person arguing with themselves.

Aliyah longed to comfort her. Ruth felt like a missing piece of Aliyah's puzzle; Aliyah had been accelerated into 'mancy as part of a terrorist's botched plan, and however Ruth's magic had been called forth, it had scarred her as surely as it had Aliyah–

Sean's salesman techniques mutated into a list of folks he'd rescued from the broach. The Unimancers who spoke for him seemed especially proud of these, and Aliyah realized that yes, while Sean Patrick Kelly had started out as a salesmancer, saving lives had become his real obsession.

"Kara Owl," the Unimancers recited before sharing Kara's divination techniques, followed by her memories of rescuing a family from a broach near Bruges. "Richard Shealy," who had much to say on the chatoyancy properties of gems, and had saved three rogue 'mancers who would have overloaded on flux.

And then "Cassandra Khaw."

Silence.

"…did something go wrong?" Aliyah whispered.

Ruth mashed her face into her palms. "…some don't have a

lot to say, you know?"

"She's got to have *something*." Aliyah felt foolish – she'd never considered a Unimancer's passing as anything more significant than trimming a toenail. Now she knew Unimancers had memories, seeing one of them ignored at their funeral was worse than death. "You have to remember her."

"She's in here," the black woman assured her, answering as though Aliyah had spoken to her – which Aliyah supposed she had. "But *we* are larger than *this*. We are thousands, spread across Europe, clustered next to the worst rips and the remaining population centers. Trust us, Aliyah – we remember our dead, because no one else will."

They left a respectful gap to mark Cassandra's demise, then: "Ramez Assad," a neurochemist who'd talked a man out of suicide. "Sara Harvey," a clothier who'd made fitted tops for breast cancer survivors.

Aliyah tapped her feet nervously. With each name they spoke, she became certain the Unimancers would name "Malik 'Pee Wee' Reles."

That had to be the drugs talking. Pee Wee wasn't even a 'mancer. He'd been a small-time gangster who'd gotten in her way, and she'd smashed him through a wall. It was only after the fight that she'd realized she'd shattered his skull. She hadn't even known his name until the *Watch Dogs* game she was channeling popped up a mini-profile next to his body.

She had Daddy check in on Pee Wee periodically. He was on lifetime disability. He could walk for up to five hundred yards before he needed his motor scooter.

Rainbird had trained her to be a killer, but Pee Wee had saved her.

Why was she thinking of Pee Wee?

Then she realized: *the Unimancers.*

They had names.

She'd vowed never to kill *anyone* after what Rainbird had done to her. But the Unimancers had been goons to be swept aside, as impersonal as swatting wasps.

She closed her eyes. She didn't *want* to know them. She'd

have to fight them when she got back with Daddy.

Or was this the psych ops?

She wanted the drugs gone. Without the drugs, she could be sure whether this was some show, and this didn't *feel* like a show, but...

"How many deaths do you remember on an average day?" The words squirted out of Aliyah's mouth.

"The average is between eight and nine," a bushy-haired geriatric man volunteered. "Two die of old age, one of unrelated accidents, five dead to sealing broaches. The technical average is 8.4 per diem, 0.6 above our current replenishment rate. At this pace, combined with the broach's expansion rate, our calculations predict Europe will be critically understaffed in a decade."

"That's... good information," Aliyah stammered. Did he think they weren't brainwashing *enough* people into being Unimancers?

She thought of that mangled sky.

She'd never considered *why* they'd abducted her friends.

Ruth leaned over to whisper, "Numbers there was an actuarymancer. As you can see, *he* still finds comfort in tabulating demises."

"But..." Numbers held up one quivering finger, "the average, as always, varies. Seven memorials today. One under. Though that hardly makes up for the astounding *nineteen* Unimancer deaths we chronicled one day last week–"

Icy silence.

Numbers clapped his hands over his mouth, dismayed, the Unimancers turning to face him–

"*What happened last week?*" Aliyah demanded.

"That wasn't your fault," the old black lady said.

"He shouldn't have spoken," the Russian twins intoned, swooping in to carry him away.

"Sometimes, you catch something close to your old passion, and it makes you disregard wiser minds," Ruth said. "We apologize. The culpability isn't yours."

"No!" Aliyah grabbed Numbers, keeping him close. "He can say what he likes!" Numbers pulled back, trembling from the

Unimancers' collective displeasure. "What happened last week, Numbers?"

Numbers blinked owlishly.

"We..." He glanced over towards Ruth, who nodded. "We captured *you*."

A kite string, bisecting a blond Unimancer.

Fiery helicopter wreckage raining down.

Mom putting bullets into skulls.

"Nine dead in a single confrontation," Numbers said. "A high aberration, *high*. Capturing rogue 'mancers is a statistically safe activity – except when it comes to your father. He's killed more in one day than we normally lose on patrol in six months – a walking spike in fatality rates."

Aliyah had never thought of her daddy as a murderer. But here in the heart of the Unimancer network?

Paul Tsabo was the goddamned boogeyman.

The Unimancers escorted Numbers away. Ruth curled an arm around her.

"That has nothing to do with you." Ruth hastily spooned some cassoulet into Aliyah's bowl. "You've never taken our lives. It's why we honor you, Aliyah – despite your father's bloodlust, some innate morality has kept you pure."

"That has *everything* to do with him," Aliyah shot back. "He taught me we're not the people who kill!"

Another 'mancer stepped forward, old, scarred. "Tell that to the seven 'mancers who died when he dropped an earthquake on our headquarters. Tell that to the squadron swallowed up by the broach he ripped open in Long Island."

Aliyah's head spun; the Unimancers pressed in around her, their movements dizzying. "You came after him! You *hounded* him!"

"He was brewing magical *drugs*, Aliyah! Handing raw 'mancy to thugs!"

"He was–" Aliyah clenched her fists, trying to remember the good reasons Daddy had done that. This was like a game of *Phoenix Wright, Ace Attorney*: her best friend was on trial and she had to muster the facts to acquit him.

Except the locals rose up, concerned because the Unimancers were concerned. Their angry faces were too much to process...

"Dad was trying to save *me*!" she blurted out.

Ruth fishmouthed, shocked. "So dumping drugs into New York and tearing open broaches was worth it to save your *face*?"

This *was* a game of *Ace Attorney*. The evidence rose before her, menus displaying facts that could clear her father's name. "It was worth it because the 'mancy was *beautiful*! Because you – you're melting down these unique magics into one hivemind!"

"Beautiful," Ruth spat at Aliyah's feet. "Look out *there*, at that rift, and tell me that's beautiful. Men like your father created that."

"My father is – he's nothing like–"

"He's exactly like. We *remember*. We have memories from dead 'mancers at the Battle of the Bulge. They want us to remember those bright scientists – so organized, so certain, so convinced 'mancy was *rational*–"

"Those scientists weren't 'mancers – and my father *is*–"

"Your father's triggered three broaches. Do you think that's wise, Aliyah? You think *Morehead* thinks that's wise?"

The Unimancers murmured their approval, which made Aliyah sick – Ruth distorted the facts. She closed her eyes, trying to map out the evidence like a real ace attorney.

"Thing is, Aliyah," Ruth continued, cheeks ruddy with anger, "your father doesn't give a damn what happens to the world so long as a handful of petty iconoclasts can cast whatever pretty magic they please–"

"Ob*jec*tion!" Aliyah boomed, pointing dramatically at Ruth.

The Unimancers fell preternaturally silent, rendered mute.

Aliyah looked down. She now wore a blue suit instead of the gray prisoner's uniform she'd had on. Her black skin had faded to a pale Caucasian. She touched her hair with her non-objecting hand and discovered her curls had slicked back into an aerodynamic hairstyle, like she'd stuck her head into a wind tunnel.

Phoenix Wright. In her rage, she'd channeled the Ace Attorney.

She'd done 'mancy at the heart of the broach.

The universe split open at the tip of her index finger, unraveling in loops around the tent as the people of Bastogne began to scream.

TWENTY-ONE
An Indecent Proposal

The cops' faces contorted in confusion as they trained their guns on everyone in the asylum basement.

Paul imagined how things looked from their perspective: they'd been called into a disturbance at the old asylum, found portions of the decrepit institute repaired, then walked into the basement to see a geriatric kinkster with nipple-chains holding back a one-legged accountant, and a woman fondling a bloodied hand sticking out from a cell door.

Then he saw Steeplechase reorient his fingers, his razorlike claw-tips poking into the veins on the underside of Imani's wrist, quietly taking his wife hostage.

Paul froze: was this stray flux or honest bad luck? Maybe the cops had seen Robert pull into the asylum parking lot. Maybe this was Butler's flux seeping out after weeks of tending to Steeplechase. Or maybe

YOU WILL LOSE YOUR DAUGHTER IN WAYS YOU NEVER IMAGINED

Maybe it was that sticky black flux. That was the problem with flux – things went wrong in ways designed to punish the 'mancer who'd created it.

Between Valentine, Butler, Paul, and Steeplechase, Paul had no idea who was being punished. He couldn't tell what to brace for.

But if he yanked Imani free, he'd be punished with his wife's messy death...

Then Butler held up both hands, bent down on one knee.
Calm radiated across the room.

"Officers," Butler said – and when they spoke, the word
"officers" held the solid weight of graceful authority, noble
lieges to a great hierarchy. The cops relaxed, though they kept
their guns raised.

"I understand this situation is confusing to the untrained
eye." Butler's voice was as satisfying as warm syrup poured
over pancakes. "But if you'll join me for a drink, I assure you I
can provide a profitable explanation of events."

Butler gestured; over in the corner on a silver stand sat a
French coffee press, an electric kettle with kukicha tea, a two-
liter Dr Pepper bottle, and an ice-cold glass of milk.

Those weren't there when we came in, Paul thought. Butler's
'mancy had conjured the cops' favorite drinks into existence.
Paul felt Butler's skin flushing with new flux.

Imani tried not to scream as Steeplechase pulled her closer to
the cell, knowing anything might break Butler's tenuous spell
of politeness.

"Paul," Valentine whispered. "Check what facts they've
radioed into headquarters. We can handle the local yokels, but
inbound Unimancers…?"

Paul nodded. These were local cops, but the Morehead
broach had spooked everyone. They'd call in SMASH for
anything odd. And if they'd alerted SMASH, then this place
would be swarming with Unimancers any minute.

He could look up the dispatch records from the local station,
but…

He didn't know which department had jurisdiction here.
He needed a form to chain himself deeper into the station's
bureaucracy to procure tonight's alerts.

A badge number. He could file the right paperwork if he had
a cop's badge number.

"*Paul!*" Valentine hissed as Paul crept closer to the cops, who
allowed Butler to approach the silver stand. All the while Butler
talked, that mellifluous voice ensuring the police that of *course*
proper procedures would be carried out, but surely a spot of tea

would help settle the waters...

Paul limped, dragging his telltale artificial foot behind him, glad that Butler was so unique that for once, Paul wasn't the most interesting thing in the room. Two officers hung back in the stairwell, listening but not quite convinced. Paul leaned in as one cop hesitated, not quite willing to put down her gun to take the proffered cup of tea.

Officer A Sharpe, Badge #379.

My wife is in danger! he thought, furious at having to spend time ensuring they weren't in *more* danger.

All this slow caution might get his wife murdered.

He wanted to thrash these cops for their insolence. Butler was assuring them of *course* the law should investigate potential intruders in abandoned property – but Paul seethed with anger that these idiots had shown up at the wrong moment.

He tracked Sharpe's badge number back to employment records at the Poughkeepsie station, chained into the hiring records to locate the names of the dispatchers, checked the shift records to see who was on for tonight. And though he fought to keep the details straight through the haze of painkillers, he determined that no, the last known call was four officers investigating a plateless SUV.

No SMASH alerts triggered.

Good. But he'd wasted half a minute filling out stupid forms – now he had to disable the cops' ability to contact SMASH.

Flux smashed into Paul.

No! he thought. *I'd checked the dispatch records! That was a simple request!*

YOU WILL LOSE YOUR DAUGHTER IN WAYS YOU NEVER IMAGINED

He was weak, so weak–

And he'd unleashed a tide of bad luck into the room.

Butler tripped. The tea cup tumbled to the floor, shattering both the fine porcelain and Butler's reassuring spell.

The tea flowed across the floor, directing the officers' attention to Paul's artificial foot.

Their eyes widened. An artificial foot and 'mancy meant one man.

Four panicked officers fired at Paul.

"*Paul!*" Valentine cried, flinging up a blue videogame shield. Bullets sparked off, ricocheting around the room, trailing black streaks as Paul's flux guided them into the most disastrous targets–

Two bullets smashed into Butler's thigh. Butler toppled over, blood spurting into the tea.

Paul realized where the other bullets were headed – Imani, trapped by a maniac. An easy target for a stray gunshot.

Except she was encased in that thick blue barrier, shielded from every possible angle by Valentine – who'd realized Paul's flux endangered Imani the most. Valentine's eyes bulged as she battled Paul's bad luck to a standstill–

The bullets rebounded into the cell door's hinges, shattering them.

An inhuman, silent strength shoved the doorway open.

"*Down!*" Robert yelled, shoving Valentine and Paul to the floor as the officers whirled to fire on the gray beast erupting from the cell.

Only Officer Sharpe got off a shot.

Flicker. Steeplechase smashed his elbow into Officer Sharpe's head, her spine shattering, grabbing her gun so quickly her severed fingers bounced off the walls–

Flicker. Steeplechase rammed his forehead through another officer's skull, the cop's brains exploding like fireworks as a spray of flux erupted from Steeplechase, and–

Flicker. He stood at the top of the stairwell, flinging the two remaining officers down the stairs until they smashed like eggs against the concrete floor, and–

"Hey!" Valentine cried. "Don't you fucking leave before tracking Aliyah!"

She reached over her shoulder, grabbing a rifle from an imaginary holster – and produced a spider-like gun humming with plasma energy, so large she grimaced holding up its weight.

Flicker. Steeplechase stood framed at the bottom of the

stairwell, kneeling by the two dead policemen he'd murdered, pressing his palm against their cooling chests. He still clutched the stolen gun, but the breaths he drew in were ragged. He cried silently as he looked towards the door, gesturing as though he wanted to explain himself.

Valentine pulled the trigger.

A jagged electrical arc wrapped around Steeplechase's ankle, hoisting him into the air.

"Gravity gun?" Robert pushed Paul back towards the cell as he pulled a first-aid kit out from his trenchcoat. "Good choice."

"It's called the Zero-Point Energy Field Manipulator!" Valentine snapped. Valentine fought for fine control – even slight movements at this distance jerked Steeplechase around at neck-snapping speeds. "Now, you fucking wendigo, you'll–"

Even upside down and dangling and yanked at random, Steeplechase's aim was unerring.

Blood fountained from Valentine's forehead as two conflicting world-views collided in a magical concussion. The impact sent Paul tumbling as he scrambled to check on Imani; Valentine's gun flew from her hands. Steeplechase smashed into the stairwell.

Being shoved onto a concrete floor had crushed his ribs; only the painkillers allowed him to keep moving. Still, he cried with relief when he saw Valentine alive.

But she crawled with flux.

In Steeplechase's world, bullets are pure death, he thought dizzily. *In Valentine's endless shoot-'em-up games, bullets are an inconvenience. Their 'mancy just went head-to-head, and Valentine barely survived…*

Imani rammed the door away with her shoulder, flipping it over Valentine's body, using it as an impromptu shield.

"*Robert, get on Butler before they bleed out!*" Paul felt elated: his wife was alive and barking orders. "Paul, how's Valentine doing?"

Valentine staggered to her knees, her eyepatch blown off, blood dribbling down into her puckered eyesocket scar.

"That fucker…" She spat pink-tinged phlegm. "He's not…

he's not getting away..."

Of course Steeplechase had vanished.

She stumbled towards the exit.

"Are you OK?" Paul shook her shoulders, trying to get her attention.

She hyperventilated, blinking, unable to focus on Paul. "That fucker *shot* me. That..." She swallowed. "It hurt." She fell to her knees, clutching the door as if she intended to cram it down Steeplechase's throat. *"I'm not gonna fucking lose twice in the same week!"*

"Valentine." Robert's voice was cool, calm, a paramedic's command. "I need you here. Butler needs a medpack."

She wobbled between her lover and the escape route. Then she flicked blood off her fingers. "Sure, sure. I got a little 'mancy to spare before I give that fucker a pistol endoscopy."

She limped past Robert, headed towards another cell – and Paul almost yelled at her *get back here*, before remembering Valentine couldn't just conjure up medpacks. Like any good first-person shooter, she had to hunt for health packs.

Another cloud of flux wreathed Valentine as she silently placed medpacks, pushing her dangerously close to her limit. *She can't fight him*, he thought. *He believes in his weapon's deadliness, and whenever she stops his bullets she's taking on near-fatal levels of flux...*

Imani crossed herself as she examined the impossible ruins of each cop's body.

"This won't fix Butler," Valentine said, crouching down beneath a cart to find a glowing white box with a red cross on it. "Remember, these things last half an hour tops."

"That's fine." Robert bent over Butler with surgical scissors, grimacing as he cut off their fine leather pants. "The artery's nicked. It'll take major surgery to close it up..."

"Temporary's better than dead, sure, sure, got it." She pushed the white box into Butler's gurgling body; the wound closed shut.

She clutched her head, her flux overflowing. Seeing Valentine lose it filled him with terror – Valentine had *never* shit the bed on her flux...

A tiny box tumbled from Robert's vest pocket.

His engagement ring rolled across the concrete to land at Valentine's feet.

"Oh, no," she muttered, recoiling in horror. "Oh, no, no, no, you *didn't*..."

Robert crouched down to scoop the ring up, inadvertently kneeling before her – and Valentine tripped, falling ass-backwards. "You don't understand," he apologized. "I was going to..."

Tears mixed with her blood. "I *know* what you were going to!"

He took in her terror – then clutched his belly like he'd been punched. He rolled the ring between two fingers, squinting as if he couldn't believe what he was saying:

"Your bad luck is me *proposing*?"

"No, baby." She tensed, ready to flee. "It's more complicated than that–"

His face contorted in exquisite betrayal. "Your bad luck is me discovering how much you don't want to be with me?"

"No! Jesus, do you know how *happy* you make me, you dumb fuck? I want to be *with* you, you just... you can't *go* where I need you to–"

"I'll go anywhere."

She clawed tears away. "You *say* that, but then you won't come with me!"

He stood up, leaving the ring behind, pulling Valentine to her feet. "Where do you want me? I've always stayed a footstep behind you in case you needed me–"

"How would you know what *I* need, you asshole?" She stared down at her hands wrapped in his as though his fingers were the gentlest of handcuffs, trembling with shock and humiliation. "I just got *shot*! Maybe you should, I don't know, *paramedic* or something! Because you sure can't go *punch* that fucker, like you used–"

"*Stop it*!"

Imani's voice boomed across the room. She looked so shaken,

her weariness highlighted their argument's extravagance.

"You can…" She wiped her bloodied hands on her skirt. "You can fix your personal issues on your time. Right now, the man who can find Aliyah is *getting away*."

Robert frowned at the dead cops. "We wanna sic that on Aliyah? The living murder-tornado?"

Imani traced the claw marks on her wrist. "He… Yeah. I'm not excusing that. But he also slammed me behind a door so I wouldn't get shot once he went for them. I think he's sympathetic to our cause, he just can't…"

She massaged her forehead.

"He can't *not* hunt his next target. So Valentine. Find him now. Work out your marital issues on your own time."

Valentine nodded, conspicuously kicking the ring into Steeplechase's former cell. Robert pointedly walked away; Paul trotted in to fetch it for them for later.

Steeplechase had etched the same pattern into the wall time and time again – the same snarl of straight lines and curves, repeated up over the ceiling, across the floor…

Valentine pressed her palms together, then irised them open. A *Grand Theft Auto* radar map bloomed between her hands.

She smiled as a bright yellow dot winked into existence, showing them the path to Steeplechase. Then it flickered out. Valentine shook the map angrily like it was a Magic 8-Ball; the yellow dot faded, then disappeared.

"*Fuck!*" Valentine smashed the map against the floor; it shattered into dissolving pixels. "His stealth powers are cancelling my mission marker! I- I *want* to find him, but…"

Paul hunted through Steeplechase's cell for the ring, understanding. Valentine couldn't make Steeplechase appear on the map because to Valentine, Steeplechase was a stealth game personified – and in her heart of hearts, stealth targets *never* appeared on maps.

Valentine couldn't fake the game. Even if that meant losing Aliyah.

"OK." Imani drew in a deep breath. "So we freed a maniacal hunter, we got four small town cops killed when they crashed our murder party, we maybe killed Butler, the hunter's headed towards a target so bad even *mobsters* shuddered to think of it, and we *still* don't know where Aliyah is."

Paul frowned, looking at the cell walls. He ran his fingertip down one of the curved lines Steeplechase traced.

He's a bit of a guided missile, sir, Butler had said. *Unable to think of anything but his target.*

"Aliyah's still lost." Paul turned in slow circles, taking it all in. "But…"

He wouldn't have identified the walls as maps if he hadn't seen Valentine's. But now he realized Steeplechase had traced the same selection of streets over and over again…

"We've got Steeplechase's next target."

TWENTY-TWO
Trying to Do the Unimaginable

First you destroyed Morehead, Aliyah thought. *Now you've destroyed the world.*

Rifts roared out from Aliyah's outstretched fingertip, slicing through the air like razors across eyeballs. They cut furrows through the chilled racks of gray fluid, sending waterfalls of goo down to puddle in the dirt; they lopped the wooden mess hall tables into chunks, sending 'mancers and Bastogne locals diving for cover.

She was still trapped in an exaggerated "*objection!*" pose by her 'mancy – but the rifts vacuumed up power from Aliyah's spell, devoured it. The living rifts looked like black plows made of razors, rocketing forward in sweeping curves that brushed against the oval mess tent's nylon walls. They left incisions behind, carving away Earth physics – and the air in front of the tent walls drooped down like peeling wallpaper, revealing seething chaos beyond.

The rifts had trapped everyone inside, turning the great tent into a kill zone.

The Thing in the sky roared, a triumphant subsonic bass that flowed through Aliyah's bones. *She'd* opened the doorway for It to step through.

She'd learned nothing from Morehead.

Now she'd set off the chain reaction that would unravel the world.

Having cut off escape, the razor-rifts looped back and crisscrossed the dining hall's interior, sewing up the great space so no one could flee. The arrow-making family dove behind the black iron stewpot as a trio of rifts homed in on them; the old woman with axe-blistered hands brandished a knife at an incoming rift, holding up what was left of a chair as an impromptu shield.

And one razor-rift arced back around, leaving contrails of mangled physics as it zoomed in on Aliyah.

She watched it chew up the space between them, knowing she deserved this. She'd tried to make friends at the Peregrine Institute, and had instead led a murderer to their doorstep. She'd tried to make friends at Morehead, and had wrecked the town. If she'd turned down Ruth's invitation, this would never have happened.

The rift narrowed its blades, homing in on Aliyah's left eye.

She stared it down. She'd watch her demise, and–

Numbers stepped serenely before the incoming menace, flattening his palm against his heart.

He curled his fingers into a fist.

Consensus.

The rift imploded him at the molecular level. Alien physics reduced Numbers to a fourth-dimensional smear of tissue, splattering him like a bug against an extradimensional windshield–

With his dying breath, Numbers enfolded the rift like gift wrapping surrounding a present.

Aliyah looked around; other Unimancers lay dead in front of the Bastogne residents, having sacrificed themselves to protect the mundanes. The black woman who'd reassured her had slid apart, the friction in her body lowered until her individual cells had rolled away like marbles – but the arrow-family stood trembling, alive. The Finnish bodybuilder's veins had swollen from some unearthly pressure to the size of toy balloons, his muscles splitting open as they burst apart in gory flowers – but the old axe-woman was safe.

The rest stepped in to encircle the rifts, held their hands over their hearts, clenching their fists:

Consensus.

Aliyah felt such a blast of love that her vision blurred before she realized she was weeping.

She'd seen Daddy reknitting the universe after a broach, all fussiness: he believed the world should be orderly, and repaired the world like a watchmaker fitting parts.

But the Unimancers – their faces glowed with affection. They stared into the wrecked physics with the fondness that someone would look at a lover they found begging for change in an alleyway – with adoration, with hands outstretched in forgiveness.

Numbers' remains flowed outwards, taking root to provide a fulcrum for the remaining Unimancers to shovel in love to seal up this destruction. And as their gazes swept across the rifts, the chewed-up mess tent re-raveled itself, the peeled gaps closed, friction congealed to normality.

Aliyah sank to her knees; there were thousands of Unimancers, and each held a deep love for something on this earth so profound that their adoration had once powered magic. The physicists reminded broken atoms how their electrons *should* spin. The carpentrymancers' devotion rebuilt the shattered tables. A gardenmancer remembered the rift-eaten dirt with such intensity that withered plants grew back.

And yet, Aliyah thought, they held each other in restraint. Just as they had collectively assembled a 360-degree view of the mess hall, the Unimancers held a precise understanding of the Earth's limits. A lone culinomancer might have recreated some magical nourishment from the puddles of ruined gray fluid – but the group mind knew nutrition's limits, held the culinomancer back so she created normal food and nothing more.

They were each other's safety mechanism. Daddy's Contract rerouted flux, it didn't stop 'mancy from spiraling out of control.

They *sang* as they mended the broaches, repudiating the Thing in the sky, restoring the world to a place where the people of Bastogne could thrive. She felt the Unimancers' love

– a love so potent, they'd sacrifice themselves joyously if it meant others could live.

No *wonder* the Bastogne villagers adored them.

Then it was over. Aliyah's hair prickled; the Unimancers had rebuilt the concept of electricity incorrectly, making her eyelids twitch.

She knelt, ready for the executioner's axe–

Sobbing.

She'd vowed never to cry in front of anyone. But now? She realized why the Unimancers hated her. She realized why they wanted to jail her, torture her, expunge her – everything her father had done to keep her safe was wrong. She *deserved* to be drugged, she *deserved* brainwashing…

"Hey."

Ruth crooked her finger up underneath Aliyah's chin, forcing her gaze upwards.

Ruth peered at her with the love she'd rained down upon Bastogne.

Her compassion made Aliyah weak.

The Unimancers stood behind Ruth, united in their affection for Aliyah.

"We know," Ruth said, gesturing back at her people. "We were all scared once, too. We know you can't stop it. We know this isn't a *choice*."

Ruth grabbed Aliyah in a tight hug, holding her closer than anyone had ever held her before, holding her with the force of thousands.

"This wasn't your fault," Ruth whispered. "*Nobody* can control this alone. And you have been *so brave* for trying–"

Aliyah broke, wailing with years of exhaustion, realizing all she'd wanted to hear was some stranger admit how hard this was, feeling like some great cyst inside had popped.

The Unimancers moved in to comfort her, a reassuring hand on her shoulder, squeezing her calf, a hug from the collective.

Aliyah lost herself in their touch.

TWENTY-THREE
The Sunset Gardens Assisted Living Facility

Paul felt his sides twist painfully as he let the flux meld with his own self-hatred. Somewhere deep in his broken ribs, an infection was taking root – something good and painful.

He'd used his bureaucromancy to figure out the location of that knot of roads. Even that small act generated septicemia. Yet he'd figured where Steeplechase was headed, and the answer was terrifying:

An assisted living center for the elderly.

Paul had inspected their housing records: it was a small living center, for twenty-five seniors, booked up full – which meant when Steeplechase tore through them, he'd slaughter nurses and old people alike.

Valentine had *Grand Theft Auto*ed the cop car, racing through the highways – but Paul remembered Steeplechase's inhuman speed.

He'd unleashed that.

He'd gotten those four cops killed.

Remember, they fired first, Imani had told him as she and Robert had bundled Butler into the SUV. Robert had a medical safehouse forty minutes away, but the medpack's stabilizing 'mancy would wear off before they arrived; he needed to stay in the back to look after Butler while Imani drove. So the team had separated, but not before Imani had tried to talk him out of his guilt.

It's a tragedy, Paul, but... they shot you.

His ribs throbbed with each heartbeat. He'd been gobbling Robert's antibiotics to offset his flux-inflicted damage. There wasn't time to recover, not with Aliyah in jeopardy, and the cops were what happened when he let his flux loose on someone else.

He popped another Oxycontin.

Maybe SMASH had a point about 'mancers.

He needed to talk to Valentine about morality – or maybe to beg her for a medpack. But she skidded through traffic, nobody noticing her crazy driving thanks to her *Grand Theft Auto*mancy.

She was deep in concentration, still rattled by her argument with Robert. Paul fingered the ring in his pocket, wondering what to do with it. He didn't dare ask. She carried a heavy flux load, and distracting her would rain havoc down on them.

Normally, he took comfort in her videogamemancy. He loved to watch different 'mancies – kiteomancers and rock-balance-mancers and servimancers producing ineffable beauty.

Or they produced mangled bodies on an asylum floor.

He'd forgotten something about the huntomancer – he hadn't been on that case. But the one time the NYPD had unofficially teamed up with the mob to stop a serial killer had been the scuttlebutt of the station. There was some salient fact he couldn't dredge up from his memory – but between the panic and the painkillers, recalling facts was like trying to organize a filing cabinet in a hurricane.

He sighed in relief when Valentine skidded to a stop before the Sunset Gardens Assisted Living Facility. The hand-carved sign out front was surrounded by bright flowers blooming on a warm summer night. The facility itself was imposingly institutional, but the staff had tried to brighten it up with windowsills full of more flowers, and the windows had grandchildren's crayon drawings taped over them.

Paul knew this because the building's lights were on.

His stomach sank. You didn't turn on all the lights in an assisted living home unless something had gone terribly, terribly wrong...

As Paul and Valentine got out of the cop car, a stern Italian nurse charged out to meet them, her white uniform spattered with blood.

"*We didn't call no cops!*" she cried. "*No cops! Why are you–*"

Then she saw Valentine's eyepatch and videogame controller. She saw Paul's bloodied suit and artificial foot.

"Crap." She backed into the facility, holding up her hands in surrender –

"We're here to help," Paul assured her. "Where is he? Is he still here?"

She nodded, eyes widening, glancing around to plot escape routes.

"All right," Paul said. "We'll take care of this. We're... We're sorry..."

She bolted off, running into the humid night.

Valentine swallowed. "You braced for what's inside?"

Paul straightened his tie. He wasn't sure what they would do. She still burned with flux, and any 'mancy he could scrape up now came with titanic consequences.

But a killer was loose in this old-age home.

A killer who held their only chance at finding his daughter.

Maybe he'd surrender to SMASH. But not before he fixed this.

The hallways of the Sunset Gardens Assisted Living Center were dingy, laced with the faint scent of piss. The residents, old but not yet decrepit, had wheeled themselves out to their doors, peered out through cracks to watch them pass. The seniors' rooms were packed tight with threadbare furniture taken from the homes they'd lived in, and Paul was glad to see the tiny refuges they'd been forced to retreat to had gone untouched.

The remaining staff, three nurses and a janitorial crew, holed up in the central station, too terrified to move.

Two nurses lay sprawled dead before them, heads blown apart, guns still in their hands.

...*guns?* Paul thought.

"Don't you fucking move," Valentine ordered the remaining

staff. She knelt down to examine one of the guns. The two dead nurses looked like they'd lifted refrigerators in their spare time.

Their guns had been fired. Not that it had done them any good.

Who felt comfortable starting gunfights in a nursing home?

She peered over at the three nurses, who were older, their uniforms well-worn; to Paul, always sensitive to chains of command, they had the feel of long-time trusted staff. "Where is he?" she snapped.

"...Room 105."

"Do *not* move," she repeated.

A trail of blood, growing heavier, led down the hallway. As Paul and Valentine got nearer to Room 105, they heard a muffled sobbing. An old man, weeping behind a shut door.

Strategically, Paul knew they should kick in the door, take the people inside by surprise. But a glance showed Valentine also wanted to respect this stranger's grief.

They pushed open the door.

Compared to the other lushly-furnished rooms in the Sunset, this one was stark as a prison: no paintings, no comfortable couches, just a metal hospital bed.

The crying man was old, hair unkempt, dressed in a filthy sweatshirt; he stroked the dying Steeplechase, who slumped against his wheelchair. He wailed, tugging on his handcuffs – though they'd chained him to the wheelchair, he fought to hug Steeplechase.

Steeplechase bled out from multiple gunshots.

The handcuffs were both unimaginably cruel and completely unnecessary: Paul realized the crying man's legs had been amputated below the knee.

Steeplechase was almost too weak to move, but reached up to stroke the crying man's cheek, his mute face begging forgiveness.

"You shouldn't have come, Grayson," the crying man told him. "You shouldn't have risked it. I never wanted to..."

Steeplechase turned to see Paul and Valentine. He squinted, vision almost too dimmed to recognize them – but when he saw them standing in the doorway, his mouth curled up in a smile. He spent his final breath laughing silently, merrily patting the man in the wheelchair to get him to look at the new arrivals.

The crying man, confused, refused to look away. But Paul noted the resemblance on their faces.

The mob had two *huntomancers*, he remembered. *Twins.*

Steeplechase had been trying to rescue his brother.

TWENTY-FOUR
Love is Not Enough

Eight 'mancers were to be honored at today's memorial service: two dead of old age, one by accident, five sacrificed sealing broaches.

Everyone agreed Numbers would have been pleased to see his death take place on a statistically average day.

Aliyah hadn't wanted to go to the memorial service, but it would have felt disrespectful to stay away. She was raw after breaking down in the Unimancers' arms yesterday.

She'd always been her family's anchor. Here, she'd become someone who relied on people.

Why couldn't she rely on the people who'd raised her?

The Unimancers, for their parts, had kept a respectful distance, like waiters standing in a restaurant's corner. The people of Bastogne had taken their lead from the Unimancers, refusing to condemn her.

She longed for someone to yell at her, to give her something to fight against...

But Aliyah's only human contact had been Ruth, come to top off her euclidosuppressants. She craved that drug now. She *wanted* her 'mancy locked away.

Getting to the mess tent involved dodging messy smears where light boiled inside like tea in a kettle – the scars from yesterday's rift. The Unimancers acknowledged Aliyah with encouraging smiles. How could they? She'd killed three people.

Yet though she scoured their expressions for traces of disgust, not a one of them blamed her.

She thirsted for their forgiveness. Worse, knew they'd give it.

That opened up doors she wasn't ready to step through.

Today's ceremony was overseen by a pot-bellied, dark-skinned man in a crisp military uniform. He stood at the head of the mess tent, looking somber; his nametag, drowning in a chest full of medals, read KANAKIA.

Aliyah stared. *This* man had beaten her? With his balding fringe of gray hair and his bulbous nose, General Kanakia looked like a store clerk, not a warrior.

Yet when he turned his calm gaze upon her, she felt like a virus under a microscope. Aliyah bristled; that gaze spoke of hours studying videotapes of her, implied nothing she could do would surprise him. Occasionally he bent down to whisper a question to Ruth, and Ruth always nodded as if to confirm the truth of whatever he'd surmised.

They spoke – Ruth arguing strenuously, the general reluctant – and came to a conclusion.

Ruth thanked him and came over to get Aliyah.

"The general says Numbers' memorial service will have classified information you're not cleared for." Ruth cracked open a storage case, strapped a bow and quiver over her shoulder. "Come on, let's go for a walk."

"I killed them," Aliyah said. "I can't walk away–"

"If you truly honor them, then you won't make this memorial about you."

Aliyah couldn't have blushed faster if she'd been slapped.

"That's not fair," she protested. "You've got all those salesmancers and psychomancers and marketingmancers inside you. Are you manipulating me into doing... doing whatever you want?"

Ruth nodded. "Check my eyes, Aliyah."

Her eyes were a speckled hazel, kind enough that Aliyah wanted to trust her–

–they weren't jittering.

They hadn't jittered during this whole conversation.

Had Ruth severed herself from the collective?

"That's all..." Aliyah wasn't sure how to say it. "That's all *you*?"

The freckles on her cheeks darkened before she turned away. "It's always me, Aliyah. Just sometimes I have help."

Aliyah remembered being enfolded in the Unimancers' embrace the other day, cresting high on their love...

"Look," Ruth said. "If we were bringing you into the collective, sure, we'd use every trick to charm you. But you're off-limits. The general's made it quite clear that if I ever interfere with his attempts to capture your father again, he will have me shot. But..."

Ruth sighed, uncertain whether she should talk. "I don't have to channel salesmancers to know how you're feeling. You think you killed people. You're cringing with guilt. But we told you this wasn't your fault – and it *isn't*."

"Bullshit. I triggered the broach."

"And I triggered you." Ruth dug her fingernails into her ribs, her body curling inwards in shame. "I carry... I've got too much influence over the collective at times. They feel guilty over how I got in. They don't want to countermand me unless it's necessary. And when I picked a fight with you, they rode my anger when they should have quashed it, and I *goaded* you. Until you *broke*."

Was Ruth crying? Shit, Ruth was crying. Crying hard.

Aliyah didn't know Unimancers *could* cry.

Aliyah moved to embrace Ruth – then stopped. She didn't *know* Ruth, hugging her might have been what Aunt Valentine called a *consent violation*.

In the end, she didn't hug Ruth. Mainly because she remembered how good it had felt when Ruth had hugged her yesterday, and how much she craved those soft embraces again, and Ruth's stinging *don't make this about you* felt far too applicable.

"Did you know I could... do that?" Aliyah asked instead, feeling like she should interrupt these waterworks somehow.

"...do what?"

"Broach if you pushed me?"

Ruth laughed. "Shit, no. I thought you'd just cry. As it turns out – *Jesus*, you're strong. Smashed past a dosage that would have incapacitated anyone else."

Aliyah flashed back to Morehead: *This is playing the game on expert*, she'd thought. *These kids don't have to like you.*

Your enemy's compliment was the most addictive drug.

"I'm that good, huh?"

Ruth frowned, realizing she'd conceded a point. "Could have also been a bad dosage. There's some weird flux haloing you. Maybe from your dad, maybe from someone else."

Aliyah felt better about that, too. Any excuse to feel like she hadn't doomed mankind.

"So somebody else's bad luck fueled yesterday's raging clusterfuck?"

Ruth scrubbed her eyes with the back of her hand. The thought clearly made her feel better, too. "Maybe."

"So the world is suicidal, and it's using us as the razor to slit its wrists?"

Ruth blinked – then gave Aliyah the goofiest grin. "Who the hell *talks* like that?"

"Me," Aliyah said proudly. "Fuckin' flux."

Ruth spat on the ground. "*Mother*fuckin' flux."

Aliyah realized she hadn't braced herself for a "language" from Mom or Dad. She'd let the fucks fly freely.

She should miss her family. But it felt nice having nobody looking over her shoulder.

Somebody different looking, anyway.

"A whole flux-fucking *family!*" Aliyah said experimentally. Ruth giggled. Aliyah worried maybe she was disrupting the 'mancer memorial service – but the Unimancers had unobtrusively filed out of the mess hall.

Sheepdogs, Aliyah thought.

"Come on." Ruth jerked her thumb towards the woods. "Let's move, before the general drugs your ass into incoherency."

"You can *try*. Maybe the flux would fuck that up, too."

"Seriously? The flux wants you awake? You wanna argue

the best luck I can have today is beating you unconscious?"

Aliyah followed Ruth into the underbrush without conceding the point.

Twenty yards into the woods, Aliyah realized how easily she could get lost. The Appalachians had given her a taste of deep nature, but hikers and homeowners still wandered through there. Everything here was buried beneath decades of growth, unchecked by any serious human habitation – wildlife rustled beneath each leaf.

Ruth led them down mossy creek banks, tiptoed across the rocks. Aliyah struggled to follow.

Do not *think of this as a videogame challenge*, she thought.

"OK," Ruth said cautiously. "I think we both agree talking shit about your father is off-limits."

Aliyah's cheeks burned with anger. "Goddamned straight."

"So I'll start with a compliment: You saw how we had to work together to stave off that broach. If your dad can do that solo – *if* – then he's working some powerful juju."

Aliyah matched Ruth's politeness. "He's one of the smartest men in the world."

Ruth skipped from stone to stone, looking down as if she was far more comfortable traversing treacherous streams than she was talking to someone her own age. "I don't… OK, sure. But let's say your dad *was* the best guy in the world, you know, *my* mother, *she* was so good, and yet she…"

Ruth reached back to grab Aliyah's wrist before Aliyah toppled backwards. She pulled Aliyah up onto the far shore, and Aliyah felt shamed; the creek had been maybe ten feet across, and she'd *still* needed help.

"Parents do things to you, Aliyah. Even with the best of intentions, they can fuck you up hard. And seeing you worshipping your dad, it got me mad."

"I wasn't *worshipping* him."

She waved Aliyah's objections away, too weary to fight, heading into the woods. "Whatever. I sure as fuck worshipped *my* mom. She made the best pancakes, and she made living in a van fun, and when she got brain cancer she distracted me by teaching me about cell growth and chemotherapy."

Aliyah almost apologized. Then she realized if Ruth was anything like her, she'd sucked down too much sympathy already.

"How old were you?"

Ruth shouldered tree branches aside. "Seven."

A year older than I was when I got burned, Aliyah almost said, but mentioning that felt like riding on Ruth's coattails. "That's young."

Aliyah winced. That pity had squirted out. Ruth shrugged, rolling Aliyah's sympathy off.

"Mom sure as hell thought so," Ruth agreed. "We'd had so many adventures. She was an educamancer – a super-teacher."

Now *that* was a killer 'mancy. You could teach people languages, teach them skills, teach them coping techniques – you'd be a living videogame tutorial and psychotherapist. "That's... potent."

"You think so?" The trees opened up into a great grassy field, so high the grass stalks tickled their underarms. "Most people think 'magical teaching' is kinda weaksauce, but... you have a dad who's fetishized the IRS."

"So we have parents who rocked subtle 'mancy."

"Yeah," Ruth nodded. "We travelled from town to town. She'd find down-and-out people and train them. We'd come in, fix someone's life, get out before SMASH arrived. It was *Teacher, She Wrote*."

Ruth paused, waiting for laughter.

"I never heard of that show," Aliyah admitted.

"Then how'd you know it was a show?"

"Aunt Valentine makes lots of references nobody gets. Eventually you pick up on flavors of confusion."

"Weird. Anyway, Mom got... she got cancer. She diagnosed herself; she was like a doctor ten times over by that point. And she was convinced I'd be lost without her to guide me."

Aliyah thought of Dad, hovering near the soccer field. "That's what parents do."

Ruth unholstered the bow. "Maybe. But most parents don't

transfer their own consciousness into *your* consciousness to make sure you'll never be alone, and then blow their brains out before the cancer degrades their cognitive functions."

Ruth spoke so casually, the full force of what had happened took a moment to hit.

And when Aliyah processed what Ruth's mother had done to her, her thoughts short-circuited.

"So yeah." Ruth handed the bow to Aliyah, who took it numbly. "I *know* Mom loves me. She's always by my side – or some static copy of her that can never learn is. Always nagging me, always checking in. She means *so well*. But she didn't know I'd feel the bullet burst her brains. She didn't know a seven year-old girl wasn't prepared for a crash course in educamancy. She didn't know her prepared lessons on suppressing flux required a girl who wasn't shit-scared and traumatized."

"Jesus." She tried to imagine a 'mancer kid living alone with no one but a dead parent's echo to help her.

"I tried to help people, just like my mom." Ruth cracked her knuckles. "I hurt 'em. My flux, it... it ruined people. SMASH tracked me down, rehabilitated me, made me part of the collective. They *helped*. They gave me people to transfer my excess flux to, support to calm me down, a cause to live for–"

She looked back towards Bastogne, thumping her fist against her heart. Ruth had been ready to die to protect her town last night.

Ruth's fierce pride made Aliyah envious.

Ruth nodded, once, affirming Aliyah's discomfort. "I was seven, Aliyah. Mom thought she knew what was best for me. And maybe your dad thinks he knows best, but... don't trust him. He loves you. And he loves magic. But love, man, if it granted wisdom..."

She looked out over the swaying field, face suffused with longing.

"...I'd be an ordinary girl."

Aliyah thought about speaking up. But arguing for her

dad's wisdom felt too much like negating Ruth's experience, and lamenting their situation felt sappy, and they both knew sympathy was poison.

The best thing she could do, Aliyah decided, was to let Ruth's words settle and see if they made sense later.

She looked down at the bow, a springy plastic composite. "What do you expect me to do with this?"

"Oh yeah. That's your training." She handed Aliyah an arrow from the arrow-making family. "I'll teach you to shoot."

"Like hell you are. Firing a weapon *is* videogames. I'll broach!"

"That's where your dad fails. He's been trying to teach you to control your 'mancy. Because he loves 'mancy. He loves it so hard he'll risk the world for it."

"–you said no fathers–"

"But we Unimancers love ordinary things. We love the arc of the arrow. We love an honest miss. That's a love we can teach."

Aliyah weighed the arrow in her palm. "Is that wise? I'm gonna break out, you know." Aliyah hoped Ruth did not notice the guilty way she scanned the sky, feeling responsible for that Thing. "Anything you teach me might come back to bite you."

"You may notice that is not a gun. If it comes down to you fighting our guns and Snow White Specials with a bow and handmade arrows, something has gone *drastically* wrong if you're winning."

Aliyah suppressed a laugh. "OK. Fine. What's gonna stop me from slipping into videogame mode?"

"*You* will."

Ruth's confidence made Aliyah feel safe in ways her father never had. She hated that. "Why?"

Ruth leaned in, giving her that fierce and too-kissable grin. "Because you have to outshoot me. And I'm not gonna use one scrap of 'mancy. Slip into videogame mode, and you've admitted you need magic to beat me."

Aliyah stood, transfixed. She couldn't escape the Unimancer camp… yet. She couldn't take on the Unimancers… yet.

But goddamn if she'd let a kid her own age beat her in a fair contest.

"You got salt?" Aliyah asked. "Pepper?"

Ruth looked bemused. "Why?"

"Because you are gonna eat those fucking words."

TWENTY-FIVE
The Criminal Cried as He Dropped Him Down

"Get the supervisor back," Paul said. "The one who ran. Make sure the rest of the staff stay put."

Valentine pulled up a mission map and ran out of the room.

Paul had removed the handcuff from the surviving Steeplechase brother – "Grady," according to his medical wristband – and Valentine had placed his dead brother on his lap.

"It might seem ghoulish to you," Grady apologized, stroking his brother's hair. "But they haven't let us near each other in twenty years."

"Tell me what happened."

People always confused the two of us, but we knew the difference. Even as boys, folks said we were the best hunters in Kentucky.

Wasn't true. Grayson couldn't track worth a damn. Put him in the woods, he'd run in circles. But you pointed him at a target, any target, and he could hit it. Me? Worst shot in the county. But I could track a bobcat through a rainstorm.

"Grady," my brother said, "you find 'em, I'll take 'em."

He was the hunter. I was the tracker.

But he was gentle. So gentle. The reason he made himself such a good shot was because he couldn't stand hurting anything. If he winged a deer, he would not let me stop until I tracked it down so he could put it out of its misery.

"One shot, one kill." My brother's mantra. We needed the meat, but Grayson didn't want 'em to know what hit 'em.

Me? I tracked bees back to their nests. I climbed trees, reconstructing what squirrels did with their day.

Those were the good days – deep in the woods, me tracking down the most skittish animals, and Grayson sneaking up on 'em to touch 'em. He read a comic once that said touching a live deer showed way more skill than killing it. And we both loved that satisfaction of thinking like the animal, working together, melding our skills to fill our family's bellies.

Folks didn't mind us poaching at first, not when their fridges were packed with venison, but… rumors started. "Ain't they a little obsessed?" people asked. Every bad thing in town, people wondered if it was flux.

Not that we cared. Hell, we weren't even thirty, we had the woods and we had our animals.

But Dad fretted. He came out, told us someone'd call SMASH on us. We told him we did no harm, but he said SMASH'd torture us.

So when someone from the big city came along and promised to nurture our skills, Dad told us to go with him.

Dad cried that day. Never seen him cry before that. Never seen him after, either. The bargain was, we could never come home.

He told us it was safer than SMASH.

And me and Grayson were thrilled at first – they took us to shiny places, and told us there was new hunting to be had, and we had ourselves a time tracking things through cities.

We liked the challenge. They'd show us a broken-into house, and ask me who'd done it, and I would find them, and Grayson would tackle them even though they ran.

Then they asked Grayson to kill a man.

Grayson said he wouldn't kill a man.

But they'd been smart and separated us, and they told him he'd kill a man or they'd kill me.

Grayson didn't want to kill nobody. But – he had to. He tried hard, real hard, not to kill anyone, but for him murdering an innocent was the worst thing in the world.

So his flux made sure that happened every time.

He tried to yell, give his victims some warning he was coming. They brought in a surgeon, cut out his voicebox. He refused to kill anymore. They cut off my legs. We both tried to 'mancy up an escape, but the thing we feared most was hurting someone or hurting our brother, and...

The flux. The flux always got us.

We might escape the mob, but we could never escape our flux.

They let me talk to him on the phone sometimes, showed me videos to prove he was alive. They didn't use us much – they're leery of magic, don't want SMASH finding out their business, so we only got hauled out for the big jobs – but knowin' we were murdering people ate us up inside.

But what could you do? If one of us died, the other had no hope. Grayson, he had it worse – sometimes I tracked stolen money down. Every time they let him out, they set him to kill. He tried like hell to escape, but whenever he did the flux shoved him right back into his worst nightmare, and whenever he showed someone mercy his backlash mangled them, and...

Even if he did escape, he didn't know where I was.

And like I said: Grayson couldn't track worth a damn.

A guy took pity on me, after a while. I begged him to smuggle a message to Grayson, tell him how to find me. I know he did, because the mob hauled the informant in, slit his throat on that rug you're standing on, and they told me Grayson would never escape...

"...and I hoped he wouldn't," Grady finished, looking down at his dead brother. "If he ever got here, the worst thing in the world would happen to him. He... he knows how much watching him die would... would tear me up..."

That was Grayson's worst nightmare, Paul thought. *Dying, knowing he'd failed rescuing his brother.*

He remembered Steeplechase's final smile. Paul and Valentine's arrival ensured someone would care for his brother.

He'd died happy. Paul was glad of that, but...

If he could hold his flux, sir, he might be magnificent.

The Steeplechase brothers had been held in bondage because nobody had taught them to manage their flux. Paul had been lucky enough to stumble across Valentine, who'd taught him the tricks of flux management: how to make your mind go blank to give the flux nowhere to flow, how to burn flux-loads off a chunk at a time through flat tires and food poisoning.

No wonder Steeplechase had cried when he killed those cops. He'd tried to knock them out, but his terror of hurting them had fueled their deaths...

SMASH had stolen away the Steeplechase brothers' education, condemning them to their worst fears coming true all the time.

And the people here – Paul's bureaucromancy flared as he accessed the patients' records, saw Sunset Gardens' scandalously low rents–

"*Valentine!*" he yelled. "Get everyone out on the lawn."

"But the cops–"

"Let 'em come. If they even notice. I suspect they're bribed to overlook whatever happens here."

She barked orders to the cowed nurses, who wheeled protesting people out still in their nightgowns. Paul patted Grady on the shoulder.

"Let's get you out of here."

"But my brother..." He squeezed Grayson's wrist, anchoring himself. "We can't leave him."

"I'll take care of his body." Paul did his best to make sure this confused 'mancer didn't see his cold fury. "Right now, we need to get you out. Will you let me wheel you out?"

Grady nodded, uncertain, trusting.

Paul guided him out as Valentine oversaw the building's evacuation – old men and women protesting as they grabbed precious mementoes to bring with them. Some went for their phones, but disabling the phone system had been as simple as setting everyone's bills to "unpaid" for the past six months.

There was no flux. They deserved whatever he did to them.

Minutes later, the population of Sunset Gardens stood out on the lawn, huddling, scared. They stayed quiet, in the hands of America's most-wanted 'mancers, unsure what to do.

The veins in Paul's neck bulged.

"You *knew*!" he screamed.

Patient and staff alike looked away.

"They cut off his fucking *legs*!" Paul screamed, pointing to Grady, who cringed. "They *jailed* him! Those weren't nurses – they were armed *guards*! And – you – *knew*!"

Old men and women clutched each other for support.

"*Why*?"

"It was cheap," said a frizzy-haired septuagenarian.

"Of *course* it was fucking cheap! All you had to do was be OK with *torture* happening down the hall!"

Paul scanned the residents, wondering how the mob's owners had made the offer to them – he doubted it'd been as simple as *oh, we keep a 'mancer imprisoned there to keep his brother in line*. But the folks who ran this place had ensured everyone who took a room here had an understanding: *We do things. It comes at a cost.*

The old guy in Room 105 is part of the cost.

"*That could have been my daughter!*" he shrieked.

Aliyah. Aliyah was in SMASH's hands, and they were abusing her worse than any mob – the mob had had to tiptoe behind the scenes, yet SMASH had the United Nations' approval.

People like this *voted* for little girls to be tortured…

"Why? *Why* would you be OK with that? How could you…" Paul choked on his disbelief. "How could you accept torture for cheap rent?"

"He's a muh–"

"*What* was that?"

Paul wheeled on whoever had spoken; they'd all clapped their hands over their mouths. If Paul was being generous, he might say they were horrified to be confronted with the crippled man they'd tiptoed around for years – but he wasn't in a generous mood, and what they looked like to him was people scared they'd been caught.

"He's a 'mancer," Paul said, completing the thought for them. "A walking hole in physics. And whatever it takes to keep those people in line, well, that's OK, isn't it? You'll live happy little lives while they suffer, won't you?"

He thought of these old people curled up on padded couches,

watching television while Aliyah shrieked in a cold torture facility.

"Not anymore." He relished the way they shrunk back when he moved. "Valentine. Burn it."

She'd been grimly nodding along with him, but she froze. "What?"

"Fucking burn it. Raze this fucking place to the ground."

"Paul." Valentine's gamefire halo dimmed to a low, shocked burn. "I'm not... They're fucked up, but leaving old people homeless–"

"Whatever happened to Rainbird, Valentine?"

Paul spoke the question softly, off-handedly – but the question hit her like Steeplechase's bullet. She wrung her hands like a guilty daughter caught shoplifting.

"Yeah," Paul nodded. "I made contingency plans in case that pyromaniac ever came back for Aliyah. But you never seemed concerned. You gonna tell me he just walked away?"

Paul knew he was right when she couldn't meet his gaze. He reached over, squeezed her shoulder.

"You've done worse," he assured her. "We'll do worse, to save Aliyah. Now blow this fucking place up and let's get out."

Valentine made a strangled noise, shamed, conflicted. Then she raised her hands and the clouds parted. A bright red laser beam painted the roof–

And the Sunset Gardens Assisted Living Facility blew to flinders, going up in a catastrophic fireball, sending shards of burning furniture flying. The old people clutched their chests, their family memorabilia annihilated, wondering where they'd live now–

"Remember *that* the next time you think it's OK to hurt a 'mancer," Paul told them.

He helped Grady Steeplechase into the car as Valentine sat, numbly, in the front seat.

No one dared voice an objection as they pulled away.

TWENTY-SIX
O Father, Where Art Thou?

The forest was filled with plants, and Aliyah had to touch all of them.

She'd forgotten how to touch.

As she and Ruth slogged through the underbrush, hunting for wild game, Aliyah felt everything: the chill shadows of the trees, the crunch of pine needles beneath her sneakers, the taut string of the bow pressing against her shoulder.

Her videogamemancer life had turned her into a head and a set of hands, cruising through life as though she were viewing it through a camera and a game controller. But now?

No sparkles appeared around edible plants to highlight them for her attention. No help-labels popped up if she focused on a leaf.

That was videogame stuff, and Ruth had taught her videogame stuff was easy.

Pawing through caterpillar-chewed fronds to discover a cluster of berries that wouldn't poison her?

That was a challenge.

Ruth padded behind, smirking. Aliyah was determined to demonstrate her skills with berry-gathering, since she'd proved so inadequate at hunting game.

Who knew deer were so *fast*?

Still, she *would* beat Ruth, in time – Ruth had her mother's teaching magic. She joked that between Ruth's mother's curriculum and Aliyah's reflexes, Aliyah would put fresh meat on Bastogne's table before winter.

"But," Ruth had said, raising a finger, "then we'll go head to head. Just me, at first – and then I'll pool my skills with the collective's big game hunters. Let's see if you can out-hunt the squad."

Shouldn't you be outrunning them instead?

The thought stung Aliyah.

This isn't summer camp. They want to brainwash your father. How can you spend eighteen hour days out here camping?

Why do you intend to be here, *come winter?*

But what could Aliyah do? The Unimancers held Europe together – she'd caught glimpses of General Kanakia's maps, saw how thin his lines of defense were spread. She couldn't kill them. And–

You like Ruth.

Aliyah squeezed prickly thorns, letting the pain distract her. Ruth had taught her these weren't edible: *no thorns, nothing with three leaves, nothing with milky sap…*

She reached down, grabbed a fuzzy stalk with curly fronds. She snapped off a piece, rubbed it between her fingers.

Ruth knelt down before Aliyah, opened her mouth wide, fine red eyebrows raised.

Aliyah studied Ruth's face. Ruth didn't have many facial expressions – she'd been a Unimancer for so long, her natural reactions had atrophied to vestigial tics. All that remained was a floating bemusement that left Aliyah uncertain.

Seeing Ruth on her knees sent swirls of fire through Aliyah's belly. Was that how Aunt Valentine felt when she saw Robert?

Ruth sat primly, hands clasped behind her back, her smooth pink tongue waiting for Aliyah to put something on it…

"Still can't tell, can you?" Ruth taunted.

"I could read a normal person's reactions," Aliyah grumbled. "Most folks would flinch if I was gonna poison them." She'd fed Ruth the wrong berries once; Ruth had swallowed them calm as candy before she spent the next two days throwing up.

Ruth had walled off her body's reactions, leaving her

"core" with the medics. For the next two days Aliyah had the unnerving experience of camping in the woods with a chunky Venezuelan man who talked like a fourteen year-old girl.

Putting berries on his tongue had been far less satisfying.

Aliyah shredded the fronds, trying to figure out if that prickly sensation in her fingertips was an allergic reaction or just Ruth. Though Ruth was her age, Aliyah knew she was more... experienced. Sorta. Ruth had never *done* anything, that would be gross, Ruth was fourteen for God's sake – but Ruth had told her once she could access the Unimancers' memories like she'd lived through them herself.

All *the memories*, she'd said, holding Aliyah's gaze until Aliyah had pretended to chase a rabbit.

Still, *everything* felt like a test with Ruth. So Aliyah had kept things distant, dropping berries into her mouth from up high.

Maybe if she tried to do something, Ruth would laugh.

Maybe you shouldn't be getting so friendly with the organization who tortures 'mancers, she thought. Some days she had the uneasy suspicion that Ruth's seeming affection was the Collective, poking the weak spots in her psyche.

But she remembered Aunt Valentine explaining why she and Dad had been drawn to each other. *You get lonely, in this business*, Valentine had said. *I spent years afraid to get close to anyone. That first friend who accepts you for who you are, well...*

Valentine had pondered all the ways she and her daddy had never gotten along, and then given Aliyah a crooked smile. *They change everything*.

She looked into Ruth's eyes a lot. They were like slow fireworks, shifting greens and browns.

They never jittered when she looked at Aliyah.

It *had* to be her, alone.

So what if it was? Ruth still wanted to brainwash Daddy and Aunt Valentine.

Except *Ruth* didn't seem brainwashed. And Daddy and Aunt Valentine were–

– she tried to remember what Daddy did with the 'mancers he rescued. Left them alone, mostly. He loved 'mancy for 'mancy's sake, clapping merrily whenever unique magics blossomed.

Whereas Ruth and the Unimancers fought for Bastogne, they fought for Europe, they battled that Thing in the sky. They made safe spaces for *normal* people to live in.

Aliyah wanted the people of Bastogne to stop cringing when they saw her. She wanted to curl up in the same bunk with the Unimancers, to feel their pride in protection.

She wanted to earn Ruth's friendship. All Daddy had taught her to do was magic.

Still, Aliyah wondered what Ruth would do if Aliyah made Ruth suck the sap off her fingers.

"Well?" Ruth waggled her tongue.

Ruth's eyes twinkled, taunting her–

Aliyah's ears popped.

A jagged line knifed through the sky, barely visible through the leaf canopy.

"*Look out!*" Aliyah tackled Ruth aside as a fresh rift slithered through the forest.

The rift was a ripple in a forest bobbing with a million leaves, but Ruth had taught Aliyah what to look for when the reality shifts hit. The sky usually squirmed in some fashion – or at least it did this close to the Bastogne broach. The newer rifts further out towards France and Austria could, ironically, be more dangerous because their shifts were less obvious.

But trees cracking was a sign – some reality shifts exploded organic material, or incinerated it, or froze it till the water shattered. Or sometimes the laws of sound got eaten, so you had to keep moving your head to ensure you heard which way something *wasn't* coming from–

She'd had lots of practice rift-spotting. The rifts seemed drawn to her. Ruth chalked it up to that weird flux stuck to Aliyah.

I almost killed her, Aliyah thought, panicked. *I can't–*

"How did you know what side to tackle me to?"

Ruth's voice was kindly, but stern – her mother, poking through. Class was clearly in session, which made it easy to slip her hands out from around Ruth's slender waist.

"Instinct," Aliyah said.

"Now deconstruct instinct into education," Ruth instructed.

Aliyah hated it, but when she panicked, the voice in her head that calmed her down was no longer Daddy, but Ruth's mother-voice.

She wiped her palms off – they'd tumbled into a berry patch – and looked around.

"The trees on that side of the rift," Aliyah concluded. "They turned brown."

Ruth nodded in approval. Green leaves curled up brown in the rift's wake, that glorious underbrush becoming skeletal.

I almost killed you, Aliyah thought, miserable. *This bad luck flux, it's out for my life–*

Ruth kipped up on her feet to stride along the new rift's edge. Aliyah wanted to pull her back before the rift expanded. But if Aliyah hesitated, then Ruth would know she was scared, and *that* shiz was *not* happening.

So Aliyah crept up. On *that* side of the line, there were new rules of physics fatal to plants – but nobody knew what.

"OK, that's an easy visual." Ruth stooped over as she gnawed her thumb, analyzing the rift – the sure sign Ruth was channeling edumancy. Her mother'd had an arthritic back, and Ruth adopted her mother's crooked posture whenever she spoke to her mother's memories.

"It smells different, too," Aliyah said. "Feel the wind? The pressure's dropping. All the air's rushing in. That's why my ears popped."

"So how would you grade this?"

Aliyah wondered, for the hundredth time, whether Ruth ever got nervous. She knew that Ruth's edumancer mother-simulation took dominance in dangerous moments, walling Ruth's terror out with scientific curiosity. But that hadn't protected her before the Unimancers had arrived.

"An A-grade toxicity, fatal to human life," Aliyah judged. "C-grade for visibility. If you weren't paying attention to the wind and tree color, you might walk into it."

Ruth's eyes flared. "I'll add it to our collective."

As Ruth catalogued the new rift for the Unimancers, the wind swept the dead leaves away like a stage curtain fluttering away, revealing...

The Thing in the sky.

Aliyah had grown to hate the sight of it. That Thing loomed over them like some evil dungeon master. It kept reality as thin as spring ice, constantly fracturing things for the Unimancers to reknit.

(*You did that in Morehead, you know, you condemned them to that*)

Hated it.

(*Dad thought he could control it*)

Hated it.

Ruth blinked, her hazel eyes ceasing to jitter. "OK. We gotta work our way around this, get back—"

Aliyah shrugged. "That's easy, assuming this rift is fairly straight."

"You know where you are?" Ruth asked, bemused. "Out here, in the deep woods?"

"First skill you learn in death matches is 'memorize the map,'" Aliyah scoffed, turning around to point. "The stream leads back to the mess tent. There's a steep drop-off a half mile over there. And over that rise is the tree I beat you climbing ten days ago."

"You didn't beat me – you shoved me off the tree!"

"I maintain that maneuver wasn't outlawed by the rules you'd set. Speaking of beating you, on your knees, soldier."

"Why?"

Aliyah opened her berry-smeared hands. "Because I tackled you into a blueberry bush. Chow down."

She glanced over her shoulder. "Can we get further away from the rift?"

They gathered up blueberries and curled up next to each other. Aliyah felt a little robbed when Ruth popped the berries directly into her mouth.

"I'm getting good at this," Aliyah boasted.

"Without a scrap of magic."

"My bow technique's improving. I know what bad woods

look like. I can mostly find food on my own."

"You can."

"You don't watch yourself," Aliyah said, chomping the last handful of berries, "I might just escape this compound."

"You could."

Something in Ruth's sudden silence gave Aliyah pause.

"I could run off," Aliyah ventured. "Take this bow and find my way home."

"You could." Ruth angled her head northeast. "Nearest refugee station's seventy miles that way. There's no paperwork out here. A refugee can give any name she wanted – they'd ship her to a new land." Ruth squeezed her eyes shut, sighing regretfully. "Girl like that would probably become an Olympic bowman. Or something world-class. Former 'mancers never lose their obsession, they just... redirect it to healthier channels. We've got training facilities for 'mancers who want to gear down to normal. But..."

Ruth wiped blueberry juice off her lips, hesitating.

"You don't need them," she said. "You're learning to leave magic behind. You could take a new identity, if you wanted... as an ordinary girl."

Aliyah's heart stopped.

What was Ruth *saying*?

"No," Aliyah whispered. "That's impossible. People don't leave 'mancy behind."

Ruth gave a bemused snort. "Tell that to your Uncle Robert. Sometimes, the need fades."

Aliyah tried to imagine being an ordinary girl, painting nails in... well, not in America, they were full up on refugees, they'd ship her off to China or Australia.

She'd been happy in the woods, with Ruth, but... could she be happy in some foreign land, bouncing between foster homes?

Could she live with herself, knowing Europe was crumbling into nothingness? Knowing she'd given up her best tool to *fight* that evil?

"But I..." Aliyah swallowed. "How can you *suggest* that?"

Ruth tapped her temple. "It's our dirty little secret. We don't absorb everyone into the collective – because we above all know 'mancy's terrible cost. It's a burden, Aliyah. If you can give it up, you should."

"It's not a burden." Aliyah glared at the freshly-dead wilderness. "Our magic heals the world."

Ruth constructed a smile for her; Aliyah realized how hard Ruth had mimicked the right facial expressions to make her feel at home. But this one was new – muscle by muscle, Ruth constructed a rueful grin to gift to her friend.

"Your magic doesn't heal things. It can't. Maybe you'd be safe if we could Unimance you, Aliyah, but… we need your father in here. He's got his own way of closing broaches. Kanakia says we need him."

"So get us *all* in! Dad, me, Valentine–"

Aliyah clapped her hands over her mouth. Was she crazy? *Wanting* her dad to be caught?

Ruth's shock was for different reasons.

"You," Ruth said slowly, "do *not* want your father in here with you."

Aliyah surrendered. Ruth pressed forward, relentless.

"Do you want to remember how good it felt when he fucked your mother? Do you want to feel how often he bites back disappointment in you? There's a lot of good reasons you don't want to be hooked into your parents' memories, Aliyah, *and I know all of them.*"

"All right. All right."

"And you can't stay." Ruth shook Aliyah as if waking her up from a dream. "Once he comes here, he'll *never* let you go. He's destroyed cities to find you, Aliyah – you're right, he's coming here, and the general has a plan to catch him. But after he's ours…

"*He* won't let you go. The general won't let you go, because he knows your dad freaks out when you're gone. The President won't let you go. The United Nations won't let you go. They'll keep you shoulder-to-shoulder with 'mancy until you die. You have to escape before we know what happened – it's your only chance at an ordinary life."

"What if I don't *want* ordinary?"

Ruth dropped her hands, sagging.

"We're not gonna…" Ruth's chest hitched. "We're not gonna talk about this. You learn your bow, and you leave your magic behind, and you leave me behind. You pay me back by living the life I couldn't have."

Ruth cracked her neck, looked over towards Bastogne, stepped back towards the collective.

"Leave 'you' behind'?" Aliyah asked. "Not leave 'us' behind?"

Ruth halted.

"I know you've got friends in there," Aliyah said. "You snicker at their jokes. They love you like family."

"Don't."

"But you and I are the only people in the world who did magic before we learned long division. When I joke with you, your eyeballs are still. You don't want to share me with them."

"I said *don't*."

"You think I can swap friends out like a Nintendo cartridge? Like some kid in China would step in and take your place? Shit, you've got thousands of friends in the collective, and yet…"

Aliyah traced the callouses on Ruth's fingers, held up their hands as if to demonstrate how strong they were when they were intertwined.

"This is special, isn't it?" Aliyah asked.

Ruth blinked away tears, holding Aliyah's gaze long enough to confirm Aliyah was serious – and Aliyah realized that Ruth's cold test-personality was how she hid her affection; she'd been dying to kiss Aliyah but *terrified* Aliyah would laugh.

"It *is*," Ruth said. "But what we do – there's so much sacrifice–"

"I don't get a life without sacrifice," Aliyah said. "I'm a 'mancer. And I…"

She swallowed.

"I choose you, Ruth. I choose Bastogne."

Something shifted in the sky overhead.

Something slick and dark peeled off her – that mysterious

flux, lifting away, having found a target at last.

Black flux spiralled high into the sky, bursting like ichorous fireworks, ripping open as something gigantic forced its way through the gap–

"A rift." Aliyah had never heard Ruth so clinical before – which was terrifying.

The worse things got, the more clinical Ruth became.

"Run."

TWENTY-SEVEN
Wrecking Ball

It took Grady Steeplechase two weeks to find Aliyah's trail. Finding where Aliyah's Snow White Special rocket had landed had pushed Grady to his limit.

"I'm sorry it took me so long, sir," he said.

Paul needed no apologies; he'd seen how hard it was for him to track in a wheelchair. Robert had strained his back pushing Grady through rocky soil.

"She's in Europe," Grady said. "I'm sure of it."

Imani bit back curses. Getting to Europe was all but impossible via plane these days, at least for 'mancers. Some major cities still had air routes – mostly the countries firewalled from the broach by the sea.

But every flight was staffed with Unimancers to prevent unauthorized 'mancers. Paul's limp, visible through any disguise, would be a dead giveaway.

And despite Robert's assurances that Project Mayhem could deliver, all their other leads had come in dead. Though, Robert argued, some leads had *gone* dead because Paul had blown up a goddamned nursing home.

"Boat it is, then." Paul cursed the time – four weeks, smuggled in a shipping crate on a cargo ship. Each passing day brought Aliyah closer to being brainwashed.

But Imani had a plan to shut the Unimancers down.

"I'll find her for you," Grady said. He seemed stronger since his brother had died – rescuing Paul's daughter had given him a sense of purpose. "I'll make your wife's phone call. But… when the time comes, sir… You know what I ask. Please don't refuse me."

Paul knelt. Their histories were dark reflections.

"Never," he promised.

The day they left America, Paul thanked Robert.

"Everything set up to the letter," Paul said proudly – from the outside, the corrugated shipping container looked like a thousand other battered containers.

The inside, however, had been transformed – a living space with enough food supplies for four people, ventilation to ensure an air supply, oil lamps and a library Paul needed to study on the trip over.

"The guys at the docks still love me," Robert demurred. He'd thrown himself into work, now that Valentine had refused to talk to him – strengthening Project Mayhem as best he could. His safehouses, he assured Paul, were safer than ever.

Paul leaned heavily on a cane – his ribs had gotten worse. Something resistant to antibiotics had settled in. Robert had stockpiled enough medical supplies to ensure the infection probably wouldn't become fatal, but breathing felt like his lungs were trapped in a vise.

Which was a shame, as he had a lot to say to Robert.

"Here."

He handed Robert his smartphone. Robert stared at it, confused.

"A reward for your hard work," Paul encouraged him. "Hit play."

A video started up. Paul sat in front of a white bedsheet hung from the ceiling – providing no details for SMASH analysts to track him. "I'm proud of the work Project Mayhem has done. Individual 'mancers may commit crimes, yes – but so do individual humans, and we don't outlaw them for *being* human. I stand fast by my assertion that SMASH is an unconstitutional travesty."

Robert thumbed the pause button. "Did this…?"

"It's out to the major news outlets."

"You built up flux to cover your tracks? *This* close to launch?"

Paul waggled his fingers in the air, a magician demonstrating nothing was up his sleeve. "I used an IP address from a hacked server in Abu Dhabi, my packets rerouted through an anonymous TOR network. No 'mancy. Just a good old-fashioned understanding of Internet protocols."

Robert frowned, but hit the "play" button again.

"…But a 'mancer heading up Project Mayhem distracts from our objective: gathering good, honest, nonmagical citizens to create change. My being in charge makes it easy for politicians to demonize Project Mayhem as a 'mancer conspiracy.

"So today, I'm putting Project Mayhem back into the hands of the nonmagical."

Robert gripped the cell phone tight, as though he could strangle Paul's speech. "Oh fuck, Paul. You didn't."

Paul nodded wearily: *Yes*.

"…don't get me wrong," Paul-on-video continued. "Project Mayhem will continue to protect 'mancers. But that change will be driven by people who police cannot arrest for their very existence…"

Robert shut it off. "Don't pretend this is a gift, Paul."

"It *is* a gift. Project Mayhem's yours." He spread his fingers. "I'll be gone. And you've basically been in charge all along, Robert – SMASH forced me into a consultant's role."

"This…" He shook the phone at Paul. "You don't give a *shit* about Project Mayhem's future. You're gonna unleash some super saiyan hell in Europe, and you're cutting ties before we become associated with your war crimes."

"I think that's *proof* I'm concerned with your future."

"Paul." Robert hunched down, bringing his massive frame down to Paul's eye level. "You know me. I love violence. But I never punched people to take 'em down – I did it because I wanted to show weak men they could take a fist to the face. I gave them confidence. The difference between surgery and savagery is *intent*.

"And I get your need for savagery. All the 'mancers I've brought in from the cold – Jesus, you think I haven't made friends with some of the guys SMASH abducted? I've seen what they look like when they come back Unimanced. Sure, I get mad – but that's a trap. You can't fight a war without breaking a few eggs, but you can't take the broken eggs *personally*. Or you lose yourself even if you win the war.

"I know Aliyah means a lot to you." Robert rested his beefy hands on Paul's shoulders. "But some things, she wouldn't want you to sacrifice."

Paul stood still as a statue.

"Besides," Robert continued encouragingly. "There's other ways to get her back! We can go to the press. They don't know Aliyah's been abducted. We'll tell 'em the army's torturing a thirteen year-old girl–"

Paul swatted away Robert's objections. "They'll show footage of the Morehead broach to justify it. The government's out of control, Robert. And that's your job – to be the rational man after I've swung the Overton window over towards what 'mancers *could* do. Spin it like they *pushed* me into destroying a nursing home. And after I've done my job... they'll *listen* to you."

"That won't help, Paul, it–"

"*It'll get back my daughter.*"

Paul's flat gaze left Robert no room for argument.

"Look, I... I know I let my temper get the best of me," Paul apologized. "I- I shouldn't have done what I did at Sunset Gardens. If I had the bureaucratic power left to rehome those people, I would. It's not their fault."

Robert arched an eyebrow. "Really?"

"Yes, Robert. SMASH flooded those poor people with anti-'mancer propaganda – they dehumanized Grayson. SMASH left the Steeplechase brothers with no place to learn how to master their 'mancy, condemned them to choking on flux. SMASH got those cops killed, got poor Hamir killed, got Grayson killed – and Aliyah will never be safe until I–"

Paul froze. Robert looked like he was wondering if he could

change Paul's mind by punching him until all the stupid fell out of his face.

But Robert wasn't a *Fight Club*-mancer anymore. So he settled for dropping Paul's phone to the pavement.

"...I'm going to talk to Valentine."

Robert stormed away, leaving Paul to pick up his phone.

It had broken.

Somehow, that seemed appropriate.

"We have to talk."

Valentine had communicated with Robert in tiny spurts since their aborted engagement; small talk to ensure the mission was going well, check-ins to ensure her burns healed cleanly, even two bouts of lovemaking.

The lovemaking had been intense. Each time had that never-let-you-go-clutch of the last dance at the prom. But the spaces afterwards were filled with a cold, awkward silence instead of warm cuddles.

Valentine tensed.

"Paul and Imani have gone crazy," Robert said. "You know what they're up to, don't you?"

"I do."

"And you think whatever they've got planned is *OK*?"

She ran her fingers through the hair she'd grown back. "I felt low after I blew up that nursing home – but the more I thought about it, *fuck* those old people for watching *Matlock* while the mob cut off Grady's legs. Those dumb assholes are like the dumb assholes in Kentucky who'd rather shoot Paul than let him fix the broach. The time for being nice is over."

"And how many people will die in the transition?"

Her cheeks blushed dark red. "I don't wanna kill anyone. But if SMASH can take *me* down, then no one's safe–"

"You can't just murder everyone who gets in your way. Paul should know that. *You* should know that."

"When the hell did you become Safety Warden? You never would have worried back when you were Tyler Durden!"

"Well, I grew *up*, Valentine."

If their post-lovemaking silences had been chilly, this was the life-killing cold of space.

"That's it, isn't it?" she whispered. "You think this–" She clicked an imaginary "start" button, and a halo of green gamefire limned her body. "You think this is just a *phase*."

Robert's hands did a defensive dance before his belly, his face melting back into the lonely man he'd been before they met. "No. No, that's not what I meant–"

"Now you're psychologically balanced, you think you're too good for me. Well, congratulations, friend!" She shook his hand in a venomously exaggerated double-fist pump. "You got yourself a bona-fide diploma to adulthood! And guess what? You don't fucking need me, so why should I stick around?"

"…Because you deserve someone to take care of you?"

"That's not my job. I'm just the wrecking ball."

"You're…" He shook his head like a dog shaking off water. "Stop *saying* that, Valentine. I don't love you for *any* of that! Christ, even if you lost your powers, I would still think you were the most amazing woman ever."

She examined his face, hoping for sarcasm. He spread open his palms, demonstrating earnest affection.

"Yeah," she snapped. "But *I* wouldn't."

"Come on, this isn't–"

"No, Robert. I am the goddamned phoenix queen – great and powerful and untouchable in my game. And maybe – maybe, yeah, life *would* be easier in some ways if I was quote-unquote normal, and we could cuddle and watch *Let's Play* videos and not worry if our crazy'll punch a hole in the universe today, but… that's not who I am. And your fucking ring – you tried to make me weak."

"You're not weak. You're strong, so strong–"

"*How can I be strong if I need protection?*"

Robert stepped in to hug her.

She catapulted him away in a burst of gamefire.

He slammed into the shipping container – and Valentine stepped towards him, fingers extended, ready to catch him–

He shook off the impact.

Her eyes narrowed.

"Yeah." She bobbed her head once, twice, as if finding her own internal rhythm. "Yeah, Paul and Imani are out of control. But I'll be there to catch them when they fall. *Me*. Because protecting is what *I do*. And I'm gonna whip SMASH's ass and save the fucking world, because that's *also* what I do. And if you think I needed you for one hot minute, then you were wrong."

"I needed you in the beginning, Valentine," Robert said mournfully. "Like a fire needed fuel. But now I just want you."

"Yeah." She watched a final spark of gamefire dim to nothingness on her big toe. "Well... Paul *needs* me."

"Even if he's wrong?"

She gave him a calm, cool stare. "Especially if he's wrong. But he's *not*."

Robert brushed the dirt off his shirt. She longed for him to contradict her, to start a good fight to raze this relationship to the ground.

But his resigned look was that of a man logging off an unfair game.

Valentine flopped down on the train tracks, watching him walk away, practicing zingers she never got a chance to use.

TWENTY-EIGHT
Kiss the Apocalypse

The black broach chased them, spiraling in great circles around them, relishing their fear. Aliyah was certain: that Thing in the sky had noticed her.

What had that black flux done?

Yet they ran together, holding hands, united. They both triangulated Bastogne's location, then headed in the opposite direction, drawing fire. Aliyah saw Ruth counting off klicks as they raced through the woods, calculating how much distance they'd bought the locals.

She felt Ruth's fingers entwined with hers, remembering how Ruth had wanted to kiss her. Even if they hadn't kissed yet, that feeling of being bonded was not *at all* a bad feeling to go out on.

"Use your Unimancy!" Aliyah yelled, as they ran into a blackened grove of trees. "Call in the others to stabilize it!"

"*Don't you think I'm trying?*" Ruth reached out with her free hand towards the horizon, clutching empty air. "I can't connect! Something's gone wrong with the Unimancer network!"

The broach dropped eye-watering coils of otherdimensional colors around them, cutting off escape. The sky peeled into tatters, revealing a hellish empty white that threatened to consume them. "So reboot it!"

Ruth stopped, acknowledging the futility of retreat. "The network doesn't fail, Aliyah. Something... Something really bad just happened."

Aliyah waved at the buzzsect-clouds gnawing photosynthesis from the forest. "This isn't bad enough?"

Her mother radiated calm analysis. "That's not even related, I don't think. The broach, it's... it's never cut off our connection. Something hit us hard..."

Ruth shivered. So much of her competence flowed from the collective. It must have been like losing a limb.

No, she thought; it was like seeing everyone on Facebook knocked offline, and wondering what disaster could silence everyone at once.

Do you remember what happened the last time someone kidnapped his daughter? General Kanakia had asked.

Had *Daddy* done this?

She shivered, certain her father had done something unspeakable to the Unimancer network. She just didn't know *what*.

Aliyah grabbed an imaginary Nintendo DS, her fingers twitching as she pondered which game-magic might drive back this broach. Then she remembered how feeding her 'mancy to the Morehead buzzsects had accelerated them into hideous pregnancies.

"Ruth." She shook Ruth out of her mother's clinical analysis. "Whatever you do to heal broaches... try it."

"By *myself*?" Ruth looked like Aliyah had asked her to play a co-op deathmatch solo.

Aliyah waved at the trees as they crumpled into toothpicks, the spaces between the atoms chewed up. "Got a better idea?"

"God dammit." Ruth knelt down on the ground, squeezed soil between her fingers to remind herself of the feel of good clean earth. She looked up at the horizon-to-horizon sweep of destruction...

"It's no good," she said. "I remember parts of things. I can't remember Jose's memories of the sky, Ndego's love of grass, Aileen's sense of space..."

"Hook up with me."

Ruth did a double-take.

"Not like that," she clarified, blushing. "We'll do 'mancy together. We'll... share memories. We don't need to change the whole area, just create a bubble to hide in until this blows over..."

Ruth's hazel eyes widened. "Aliyah, *no!*"

"...No?"

"That's..." She slapped herself. "I *know* it's a secret, Mom, I *know* she's not supposed to know, I don't have a *choice*..."

"Not supposed to know what?"

Ruth clasped Aliyah's hands, pressing them against her chest in an anguished *promise-you-won't-ever-tell* gesture. "...There's no torture."

"What?"

"*There's no torture.* We don't brainwash anyone. Unimancy isn't a... government program." She hung her head low. "It's more like a virus. You do 'mancy together, you catch the hivemind."

"That's... ridiculous, Ruth. You abduct 'mancers to break them..."

An angry crease appeared between Ruth's eyes. "Yeah, that's what we tell governments! You think we'd be so happily integrated if we'd been beaten into it?" Ruth's eyes jittered briefly, looking to her fellow Unimancers for support, then her pupils dilated in terror as she realized nobody was answering. "The governments feel *way* more comfortable handing 'mancers over to torturers. We do the zombie-walk whenever we're around mundanes, act like someone's beaten the identity out of us, and the presidents and prime ministers are happy to let us steal their 'mancers away!"

"But that's crazy..." The broach tightened around them; they stood on a shrinking island of Earthlike physics. Everything else had fallen into the demon dimensions.

"It's the truth, OK?" Ruth's cheeks were flushed with humiliation and anger. "To do 'mancy together, you have to share magic. And once you share magic, you get networked whether you want to be or not! We don't torture anybody! We're just *nice* to 'mancers until they cast spells with us! And then..."

She flicked her fingers towards the incoming maelstrom.

"Once they see our memories of what's at stake, most are eager to help. They've got new friends, a purpose in life, seven thousand 'mancers to wick their flux away. There's no insidious plan here, Aliyah – and now you know our greatest secret!" She hung her head. "Not that it's gonna help."

Aliyah frowned.

Ruth genuinely seemed to *believe* this bullshit.

"Ruth..." She spoke as gently as possible, given the apocalypse bore down upon them. "I've done 'mancy with Aunt Valentine, and we didn't coalesce into Unimancy. I've done spells with Dad! And with... with all the 'mancers at Payne's institute! You can join up to cast spells without welding your brains..."

"*Sure.*" Ruth's sarcasm was cutting, but Aunt Valentine had taught Aliyah snark meant love. "The combined experience of seven thousand 'mancers is just *lying*, Aliyah! Or maybe you guys have cornered the market on craaaazy 'mancy – your dad can heal broaches without having other people help him remember what the world is like, and *now* you team up to do 'mancy without fusing?" She genuflected. "*All hail the bureaucromancy messiah!*"

"I'm not fucking arguing with you!" The broach erased the grove's edges; Aliyah lurched as the soil beneath them spilled into nothingness. "Link up with me!"

"*It's you or your dad!*" Ruth pounded her skull. "Hell, I'm half-crazy because my mom's in here! I've seen why General Kanakia needs your dad's skills – we're losing, Aliyah." She pointed at the crumbling sky. "We're dying too fast, and *that* is growing too quickly."

"So?"

"Better we die, and someone else gets your dad in. Because he's..." She swallowed; the gravity around slackened as they rose up into that unearthly whiteness. "His skills are more important than our lives."

Aliyah felt such an outpouring of respect, her chest hurt. Ruth didn't know if her fellow Unimancers had been wiped out – and *still* she was willing to sacrifice herself and the woman she loved, just in case someone else *might* find a solution to the broach.

"At least we drew this rift away from Bastogne," Ruth said sadly. "I don't think it'll touch the town."

This was, Aliyah reflected, a terrible time to fall in love.

But she would not die without a first kiss.

"Mission accomplished." She grabbed Ruth's chin, and wondered *Is this how Valentine feels?* before pressing her lips against Ruth's.

god she's so soft

Kissing was awesome, but awkward. Her kissing fantasies hadn't included the hard pressure of teeth behind the lips. She felt Ruth's breath on hers, so close, all these things she'd never considered...

Ruth taught you to appreciate the real world. Ruth snaked her arms around Aliyah's back – those lean muscles so strong against her, and–

Ruth opened her mouth, offering her tongue's soft wetness, and joy coursed through Aliyah's body.

Berries she tastes like berries, Aliyah thought, of course she tasted like berries.

I just ate berries

An electric spark leapt across their tongues, a tingling magic flowing between them.

That's us Ruth

Oh my God Aliyah that's us

And Aliyah sank into the kiss as she realized this was *their* magic, Ruth's Unimancy and her obsession intertwining like two lovers slipping their fingers together, and she felt Ruth's fear and Ruth felt Aliyah's uncertainty and pulled her closer.

Like this Aliyah

I want to feel you like this

That first kiss's awkwardness disappeared as they melded into each other, their kiss swelling into a chapel of adoration built with roaming hands and soft lips–

A beauty that staved off the apocalypse.

Distantly, they heard something bellow – the Thing's rage.

They stood on a thin soil outcropping battered by angry buzzsect swarms, bouncing off as ineffectively as moths off a lightbulb.

They kept kissing – one slow kiss to fend off a million monsters.

Our first kiss shouldn't look like this, Aliyah
No

And Ruth's hands slid down the small of Aliyah's back just the way Aliyah had hoped and Aliyah nipped Ruth's lips just the way Ruth wanted and the ground trembled underneath them because a kiss like this demanded ground and they remembered the feel of solid soil beneath them, they remembered the smell of high grass and the trees flowered back into green healthy beauty and the black pushed away from the sky and something roared but that didn't matter everything should line up to make this kiss perfect.

Flowers blossomed from the fresh soil, spat death to the buzzsects.

The Thing in the sky smashed down. A rainbow nudged it aside, sent it sprawling back into its cage.

The universe needed this kiss to happen, and Aliyah and Ruth felt the truth of it, their fears mixing and melding as they understood how much love they held, inside the Unimancer collective, inside Ruth, how goodness could drive back this darkness, and they sighed as Aliyah understood what Ruth had all along:

She was born to be a Unimancer.

They broke that first kiss, looking towards Bastogne, knowing they'd die to protect it.

Their eyes jittered with love.

TWENTY-NINE
Tsabo's Decree

"Cutscene!" Valentine yelled, as the crane lifted the shipping container out of the boat.

Paul's body was no longer under his control – his life had been transformed into a movie played between levels. The reference books on the shelves tumbled off in slow motion as heavy machinery hauled them skywards and Valentine's videogamemancy kicked in, but he was used to this. She'd practiced her cutscene magic to get them through storms in the Atlantic. Whenever the oil lamps tumbled to the floor, *"Cutscene!"* – and magically, the fire went only where Valentine allowed it to.

Player characters didn't die in cutscenes.

They got tossed around, but Valentine's 'mancy ensured no one got hurt.

He fell backwards onto the hard rubber mats; though the cutscene prevented damage, the impact still hurt like blazes. Weeks of hospital-grade antibiotics had barely dimmed his ravaging infections.

Paul laid prone once the cutscene finished, trying not to breathe – whenever he breathed in more than a shallow whisper, he coughed, and coughing was like being stabbed.

Not much further. A few hours, and this would be over.

They'd been cooped up here for a month. Valentine had passed the days by playing *Hatoful Boyfriend* and other dating simulators on her Nintendo DS, cursing because she couldn't boost her relationship scores high enough. Paul worked on an old-fashioned computer terminal, complete with thick black plastic keys and a monochrome green IBM 3270 monitor that glowed even though they had no electricity.

Imani jumped rope for exercise, occasionally using Valentine's 'mancy to practice her gunplay. In her spare time, she'd tended to ancient Grady in his wheelchair. He alone seemed content; after being trapped in the same room for decades, being confined to a new room was almost an adventure.

"Jesus, Paul." Valentine leaned him against the wall to stabilize him as the crane carried the shipping crate to the docks; Paul still moaned. "Where've you been putting your flux?"

"Same as you." He palpated his ribs. "In here."

He couldn't risk his stray bad luck causing them to be discovered, so he'd pushed it inside. The flux fed his infections in painful ways.

"Paul, Paul." Valentine slapped her crotch like she was giving it a high-five. "It's OK if I give myself a herpes flareup." She had the same rueful look she got whenever she lost her true love on *Hatoful Boyfriend*. "I'm not using Little Priscilla anyway. But you?"

"I've got my meds." Robert had stocked the container with racks of painkillers. To dull his ribs took so many Oxycontin, sometimes Paul passed out on the keyboard.

"This won't do any good if you collapse halfway to Aliyah," Valentine said sternly. "You gotta get that shit under control."

"A few hours," he begged. "We'll know where she is in a few hours."

"*Cutscene!*" Valentine yelled. The monitor toppled off the stand as the crane lowered the container onto the truck – but again, nobody got hurt even as everything crashed. Paul tried not to stay still, but he still had to breathe, so he sipped in a breath–

Agony.

He slipped another Oxycontin onto his tongue.

Soon.

The truck rumbled away from the docks, carrying the shipping container with it – Paul had contracted the shipping companies to drop it off at the edge of town. The driver wouldn't bring them there, of course, but that betrayal was part of the plan.

Imani blotted sweat off his forehead.

He pushed the towel away. He hated being cared for.

"Is this…" He swallowed. "Your plan's gonna work, right?"

"If you can do what you say you can do, baby." She frowned. "You got the juice?"

"Nothing can stop me." It couldn't. He had no doubts about that.

Paul ignored the shooting pains as the truck bumped down a road. They were exiting Zwole, a large Netherlands city not yet encroached by the broach.

He kept track of how far they'd travelled, accounting for the additional distance. Things would travel fast, but…

"*Should* we do this?"

Imani let go of his hand, uncertain. "What do you mean?"

"Is this… Is this a good idea, sweetie? This is our last chance to back out." He held up the Oxycontin prescription, displaying Robert's name printed on the label. "He told me… He told me he didn't approve. And me, I- I handed you this project to help you heal. Maybe that wasn't fair. I made you into a weapon. And this is… It's a big weapon. I don't wanna fire it unless we're all comfortable with it. So." He gestured up at the sky, bringing his finger down in a final, fatal arc. "*Should* we?"

She chewed her lip.

"I don't know, Paul."

He gave her the silence to process.

"I've always been a corporate lawyer. It's never been my job to set policy. I'll tell people what's prosecutable, inform them of their exposures, but… I don't tell people what to do. Because me? I'll do whatever it takes to win."

Paul smiled. Her sharp-toothed ambition had always filled him with pride.

"*You're* the moral center, Paul." She tapped his chest. "So if you tell me this is what we need to do... then we do it."

"Valentine," he whispered. "Could you come over here?"

She crawled through the wreckage to plop by Paul's side.

"Still no luck contacting Aliyah, right?"

She shook her head. "If she logged into our game networks, I'd know. She's... " She blew on her hand and spread her fingers like a dandelion giving up seeds. "Gone."

"Can you bring up a photo show?"

"Yeah." Valentine waved in the air, and a shimmering hologram emerged in a flare of videogamemancy; a teenaged black girl, her disheveled hair combed carefully over the burn scars on her forehead. Aliyah's smile was defiant, tense; she held up her Nintendo DS defensively, like Thor's hammer.

Imani closed her eyes.

"Earlier," said Paul. "Way earlier."

A shot of a five year-old Aliyah, dressed in a frilly pink princess dress, shimmered into existence. Aliyah in the days before she'd been burned, before she'd been caught up in magic.

There was such *joy* in that smile.

"Back to the last photo."

Even though he'd snapped that picture when they were in no danger, her shoulders were hunched, her fingers white around the controller. Her smile had curdled to a fierce *don't-fuck-with-me* grin.

Go live a quiet life somewhere, that horrible teenaged girl trapped inside the Unimancer network had told them. Yet they hunted people like Aliyah – as long as the Unimancers existed, there could *be* no quiet life.

All the while, Paul felt that crawling certainty the black flux *would* brainwash his daughter. That young girl had threatened to use Aliyah to execute him. That soulless teenaged mockery would reshape Aliyah into her own image...

YOU WILL LOSE YOUR DAUGHTER IN WAYS YOU NEVER IMAGINED

"All right," Paul said. "Let's do this."

•••

Paul double-checked the GPS coordinates as the truck rolled to a stop.

"Was she here?" Paul asked.

Grady clambered down from his wheelchair to take a deep sniff from the container's ventilation holes. "Yes. They brought her through here."

Paul relaxed. He hadn't been sure if all 'mancers were abducted through the same European route.

General Kanakia's voice boomed down from speakers outside the container.

"Please come out with your hands up, Paul. No 'mancy, please. I'm hoping this can be a quiet negotiation between equals."

Grady stiffened. "You promised, Mr Tsabo."

"I keep my promises."

"You know my brother's gone. Without him, I…"

"I know. I'd feel the same without Aliyah."

Grady closed his eyes, peacefully preparing for the end.

"You've been betrayed, Paul. Mr Steeplechase called us, told us how even he *thought you were out of control, told us how you were smuggling yourself into Europe – so we instructed your truck driver to deliver you to us."*

To think Imani had doubted Grady Steeplechase's acting ability.

"Escape is not an option. Last time, you barely escaped fifteen 'mancers. Now? I've brought a hundred and fifty of our best trained men – and they are radiating normalcy at you, so the slightest 'mancy will create near-fatal flux. I've brought you to an isolated area where you can harm no one – and leaves you nowhere to run."

While Kanakia spoke, each of them hugged Grady in turn, thanking him.

"Unlock the back doors?" Paul asked.

Valentine unlatched the doors, the air crackling with the hum of prepared 'mancy. If they fired weaponry, Valentine would turn them into game-based annoyances.

It didn't matter.

The bird was in the air.

Paul stepped out into the light, shielding his eyes with his palm – after weeks locked in a container, it was so *bright* out here. But he made out the tangled barbed wire fences and bleachers and sniper towers, a miniature prison set in a country meadow.

They'd parked the truck in the center of a hundred and fifty 'mancers, each armed with cutting-edge anti-'mancer weaponry.

As Paul stepped forward, the Unimancers trained their sights on him. He saw the anti-'mancer landmines poking out of the soil, the yellow FRONT TOWARDS ENEMY lettering an implicit threat.

"You came out to visit me personally, general?" Paul spoke up, ignoring the shredding pain in his side. "I suppose that's an honor."

General Kanakia sat behind a thick, blast-proof plexiglass screen. Given that Kanakia had outwitted him so thoroughly, he'd imagined a lean, sharklike man, not plump middle management.

Kanakia saluted Paul. "*It is an honor, sir. Away from the United States' eyes, we can talk as equals.*"

"Give me my daughter."

"*Will you surrender?*"

"*Where is my daughter?*"

"*Aliyah is safe, and will remain safe. We've grown fond of her, Paul.*"

Was she in their thrall? He tried not to panic. A top speed of 550 mph meant Paul needed to stall four more minutes…

"*She's not Unimanced. We have no need for videogamemancers, Paul. We need you – you, and your singular talent for healing broaches.*"

He spat laughter. "You'll brainwash my magic away!"

"*No. We'll incorporate your skills, Paul. You haven't seen what we've faced yet. There are so few of us to combat it. You're a genius at working with limited resources – and once you've seen what Aliyah's seen, well… you're a good man. I know you'll help us…*"

"Where is she? I'm not asking a third time, Kanakia."

"*I wouldn't bring her into a war zone, Paul. She's safe. Far away but safe.*"

Valentine cracked her knuckles. "Wrong answer."

Weapons *clacked* as the Unimancers shifted their aim to Valentine. Kanakia waved at them to stand down, which they did grudgingly; they glowered, radiating hatred.

Oh yeah, he thought. *You remember being scared.*

Let's introduce you to terror.

"*Her location's irrelevant, Paul*," the general said. "*This is where it ends. We've assembled our best forces to stop you…*"

Paul whistled, looking up at the sky. "What if I *wanted* you to bring me somewhere you'd assembled as many troops as you could get your hands on?"

Kanakia frowned. So did the Unimancers; they stiffened, hunting for any 'mancy Paul or Valentine might be weaving – but the only magic here was theirs.

"There's not a lot of ways to destroy a swarm consciousness," Imani said conversationally. "They're resilient against most attacks, because the knowledge is widely distributed among individual nodes. Only one way guarantees disabling a swarm's functional capacity…"

"*No.*" Blood drained from the general's face.

"…and that's to destroy enough individual segments to cripple the mind's connective tissue."

The Unimancers checked the shipping container, worried they'd missed something – but the container had been scanned back at the docking port to ensure it had no explosives. They captured Paul, puzzled by his lack of 'mancy, even more puzzled by his certainty.

"Oh, I'm not doing any magic *now*," Paul told them. "I couldn't. This many Unimancers would swamp any 'mancy in flux; Unimancy only allows the usage of conventional weapons."

"*What have you done?*" Kanakia screamed.

Paul pointed one finger up towards the bright blue sky. A dot appeared high, next to the sun, grew huge–

"I did the magic that fired the missile nine minutes ago," Paul said.

•••

Paul did not own any subsonic cruise missiles, of course.

But the *USS Chicago SSN 721* patrolling the North Sea had twelve Tomahawk missiles ready to fire in vertical launching tubes. The crew of 118 men used a computer to monitor the missiles' readiness, to set coordinates, to tell them when to launch.

And what was computer code, if not the essence of record-keeping?

Paul had studied programming on and off for years on the chance it'd become useful. But in the last month, he'd learned to speak code as computers interpreted it – starting with the language of C++, whose syntax used helpful half-sentences, then descending into the dark bare-metal assembly language and its barked-out single-word commands, and finally settling into the dense foliage of machine code – a human-hostile language of two words, "1" and "0," with a few registers to shift them in and out.

Machine code was the perfect place to hide changes no human could detect.

It hadn't been *easy* inducing a cataclysmic series of bugs into the missiles' control software, so at a set time a missile would launch towards a set of GPS coordinates–

–but in terms of maximum carnage for minimum effort, changing a handful of 0s and 1s was a bargain.

"*Cutscene!*" Valentine screamed, grabbing Imani and Paul as the world went white with fire.

Obliterating Grady Steeplechase.

Obliterating one hundred and fifty Unimancers.

THIRTY
Kiss With a Dying Man's Tongue

Their minds were one. Their desires were not.

Let me touch you Ruth

I'm not sure Aliyah

Aliyah's palms rested on Ruth's ribs as they kissed, and to Aliyah the flurry of emotions felt like two experts playing *Mortal Kombat* – quick flurries of jabs and exchanges, a complicated dance trying to arrive at a conclusion.

Except in *Mortal Kombat*, the goal was defeat, and in Unimancy, the goal was consensus.

Aliyah longed to touch Ruth's breasts, but Ruth countered with fears that they'd kissed, they should explore that more, and Ruth's worries slithered through Aliyah as keenly as though she'd held those concerns herself. Aliyah coursed back up those fears to grasp the root concern that Ruth was worried Aliyah just wanted her for her body, and Aliyah filled Ruth with her understanding that yes though she brimmed with lust, Aliyah needed Ruth's friendship above all else.

Ruth dissected Aliyah's understanding of "best friend," revealing Aliyah's only best friend had been Valentine. Within seconds, Ruth helped Aliyah unlock the realization that she wanted to experience sex partly because Valentine had tinted Aliyah's worldview to view physical intimacy as an important step to becoming grownup – and when Ruth pointed out Aunt Valentine's healthy sex life with Uncle Robert had plastered over deeper flaws in their relationship, Aliyah agreed maybe waiting to proceed physically was a fine call…

…at which point Ruth relaxed enough to reveal *her* intense longing, and Aliyah flipped through every sexy dream Ruth had had of Aliyah, and Aliyah's fingers unhooked Ruth's bra, and their excitement doubled, quadrupled, multiplied until sex-thoughts filled their world…

Oh, I see you made a new friend!

Ruth's mother's voice rang through their heads with the cheerful happiness of a mom bringing sandwiches into the living room.

Aliyah pulled away, feeling filthy under Ruth's mother's gaze–

It took a moment before Aliyah realized Ruth's mother hadn't comprehended what was happening.

Ruth's mother – Olivia, her name was – still perceived Ruth as the seven year-old girl she'd been when she'd implanted herself into her daughter's mind. That couldn't change, would *never* change. The Olivia-construct could absorb new facts – Olivia had been an educamancer, after all – but emotionally, it was designed to provide support for a Ruth that no longer existed.

And like a seven year-old's mother, Olivia-construct had no real concept of her daughter's privacy. It barged in on its own schedule. Olivia-construct could not even comprehend this new Ruth *would* want to kiss a girl, and hence had misinterpreted their sexual negotiations as some form of patty-cake.

None of which made Ruth feel any less shamed for having her mother tune into her intense need to have her breasts touched.

Mom! Ruth yelled, but Aliyah felt Ruth's resignation. Every conversation with Ruth's Mom-construct was like calling a helpdesk without a ticket number: you had to start afresh.

Well, I'm sorry, Mom-construct said prissily. *It's just nice you're making new friends, what with all the lost Unimancers…*

Lost Unimancers?

Aliyah surfed Ruth's shock as she hooked back into the

Unimancer network – which, to Aliyah, felt like a mastodon staggering back to its feet after a knockout punch, a beast so huge it was shocked to discover it *could* be hurt.

Flickering connections reestablished themselves, thousands checking in on their friends – a complex dance of courteous protocols. She felt the butterfly-light touch of friends pinging Ruth, minds rushing outwards to map terrifyingly shrunken boundaries.

We lost

How many?

Too many god too many

Get out there they can't die alone we can't let them die alone

Seven thousand people raced towards the one person who mattered most in this entire network – a horribly burned man who'd lost his legs in an explosion.

Take his pain. A hundred masochists surged in to distribute the dying man's anguish among themselves.

Keep his heart beating. A hundred doctors overrode the dying man's limbic systems, inventoried which organs still functioned, improvised stopgap measures to squeeze out another few minutes of life...

Show him he's loved. A chorus sang this dying man's proudest moments back to him.

Ruth pushed her way through.

Why's one man drawing our attention? Ruth asked. Aliyah realized the entire Unimancer network had stumbled to a halt to tend to this one man – SMASH teams stopping in mid-pursuit, conversations with mundanes trailing to silent halts, Unimancers in Europe-bound planes staring out the window.

He's the only one left at the site

A hundred and forty-nine

Vaporized

The burned man's eyes were half-blinded from the acrid gray smoke dissipating from an impact crater the size of a small stadium – but Aliyah saw how scraps of crumpled, jagged steel had been blasted deep into the pulverized soil. Bits of rubble still rained down around him, flopping severed limbs hitting the ground, shrapnel sticking out of smoldering bodies...

NO

As Ruth shouted her denial, Aliyah felt recrimination swelling like cancer as the Unimancers agreed Ruth was to blame for this disaster. They replayed one sentence, aiming it at Ruth:

Set him free, and he'll cut a path to hell to find her.

Ruth climbed into the dying man's eyes, escaping the avalanche of hatred rolling towards her–

They must be wrong he couldn't have killed them he was a stupid paper-pusher

Except as Paul picked his way across the burning bodies, he didn't look like a paper-pusher *or* her daddy.

He looked *rabid.*

Daddy walked out of the center of the shallow crater, his face gray and hateful. He breathed raggedly – yet he refused to let his injuries stop him as he staggered up across the corpses, clambering his way up the blasted slopes to yank General Kanakia up in one hand.

"*You thought to go to war with me?*" Paul shouted. "Me?! *When bureaucracy is the* language *of war?!*"

General Kanakia bled from a thousand cuts, kept alive by Valentine's cutscene magic. He looked shocked, defeated–

What happens if the general dies

He's the only one who can coordinate us against the broach

Is there anyone else on site can we get the dying man to fire his gun

We must kill the bureaucromancer

Daddy shook the general. "I wanted you to live long enough to know how badly I beat you." He sniffed back blood. "You fucked with the wrong 'mancer this time. The Unimancers need critical mass – and we'll destroy them, stolen body by stolen body, until they fall apart."

Ruth knew she was responsible for this war. And when Ruth lamented she should have shot Daddy in the face, Aliyah *agreed* with her –

"Now." Daddy leaned close. "Tell me where my daughter is. Or I will tear you apart."

Daddy, no!

Daddy?

That hateful avalanche roared towards her, a massive howl of confusion and pain:

Ruth what did you do

She's not supposed to be in here you know *that*

She's evil like her father tainted beyond redemption she killed Numbers she killed Shetra

He raised her to be a weapon she had no idea of the damage she did

She feels sorry *for him she sympathizes with a* murderer

Of course *she's loyal to her father what else would you expect*

She's loyal because he's effective look at how he destroyed *us*

He destroyed us because he's soulless he's entranced by magic he's lost

We need to love the bureaucromancer so he can heal the sky

Forgiveness while the bodies still burn *what are you*

Listen

Listen

LISTEN

The general opened his mouth to speak – but collective had fragmented into a sandstorm of microarguments, their collective grief metastasizing into petty dispute – assaulting Aliyah as she felt *both* sides' certainty in every confrontation, the shocked betrayal of long brotherhoods splintered.

They'd seemed unified from the outside. But the slightest disharmony triggered civil wars.

She tried to tell them her father meant well – but they barraged her with the last moments of the dead Unimancers, Unimancers dying when her father had triggered a broach, Unimancers crushed under rubble, and she loved him but oh God her father had torn Morehead apart and when she saw his rabid face she

Rabid yes

Out of control

You understand

She *did* understand.

They feared her father because he'd beaten them.

One man beating them implied unknown weaknesses in the collective.

The Unimancers were the greatest catalogue of magical knowledge ever assembled: tens of thousands of 'mancers had contributed their expertise.

Yet if Paul Tsabo – a single man – had uncovered some insight that the hivemind had overlooked, then maybe it was worth risking broaches to discover new healing techniques...

No.

The 'mancers turned their attention upon Aliyah.

I can bring them back together, she realized.

Her head was a mansion filled with memories; she invited them all in to look through her past. She showed them what it felt like to burn at her father's hands, demonstrated what it felt like to murder because her 'mancy had gone haywire, laid her aching loneliness out for their perusal.

He means well, she told them.

But his magic destroys families. His magic burns children. His magic rips towns apart.

She squeezed Ruth's hand so the Unimancers could feel Aliyah's strength – her certainty that *Paul Tsabo is out of control*.

Who was better fit to judge him?

They absorbed Aliyah's knowledge of Paul Tsabo's unthinking cruelty and used it to reforge alliances.

And those alliances were reforged with bottomless love – a dazed amazement that they had fought so fiercely yet forgave each other, and consensus was good consensus was necessary consensus was

Consensus is life, Aliyah thought with relief.

She balled her fist over her heart, the words echoing throughout the hivemind: *Consensus. Consensus. Consensus.*

Then Aliyah spoke:

Let me talk through the dying man.

They parted way, knowing they'd acquired a new skill for their collective:

Aliyah could tug Paul Tsabo's heartstrings.

Her father was screaming at General Kanakia. Even in defeat, the general kept telling Paul he wasn't evil, he didn't need to do this:

"Daddy!"

Aliyah felt actors helping her to sound weak and terrified, doctors prioritizing the dying man's speech and vocal chords.

Daddy turned, shocked to see his daughter's voice emanating from a dying Unimancer.

"...Aliyah?"

"I tapped into their network, Daddy." A susurration of Unimancers muttered *yes, yes, yes*. "You have to rescue me. I can't... I can't stay for long, they'll track me down–"

He dropped the general, ran to her. "Where are you?"

"In Bastogne."

The Unimancers relished watching Paul's terror as he realized where he'd have to go next.

"But Daddy – you have to bring the general. They need him. He's your shield–"

"Sweetie, are you OK?"

Aliyah hummed with exhilaration. The righteous certainty of the upcoming battle filled her; she would be the bulwark upon which her father would be smashed and reborn.

Cut him off, they advised her. *Keep him panicked.*

"They're–"

Aliyah dropped the connection, mentally kissing the dying man as she returned him to his body to breathe his last.

Will that draw him towards us?

Oh yes, she said. They lifted her up in glorious approval.

And when he gets here – a worried shiver splintered the harmony – *you know how to defeat him?*

You've used his good intentions to trap him before, she told them. *We'll do it better this time.*

They examined her plan.

They beamed consensus.

THIRTY-ONE
Proof the World Wants You to Die

Bastogne, Paul thought.

That's where he'd defeat the Unimancers: at the broach's heart.

The explosion had been intoxicating. After years of running from government patrols, Paul had unlocked his full power.

Standing within that firestorm, shielded by Valentine's 'mancy, all Paul's uncertainties had been scourged away.

Bureaucracy is the language of war. He hadn't meant to say that. But striding across the ruined SMASH patrol, seeing the fear on the general's face, he'd been flooded with realizations of his potential. He could sabotage supply lines at the source. He could forge communications to lead armies into traps. Wars had been lost on logistics.

He would create a new, Unimancer-free world to protect his daughter.

He would become the War Bureaucromancer.

When Aliyah spoke through that dying body to tell him she was in Bastogne, he felt like a programmed missile. He had one concern: getting to her.

All his fears were carried away on the smoke of burning bodies.

As they made their way south, Paul kept listening for sirens. The noise from the explosion had to have reached towns miles away. Where were the cops, the firemen, the paramedics? Or at least curious passersby? Someone had to investigate.

He'd heard sections of Europe had been abandoned as the broach advanced.

Maybe no one was left to pay attention.

They walked; Paul had filled his pockets with baggies of Oxycontin, but his ribs sawed into his lungs. He stumbled. Imani had to support him.

Valentine had stolen a gun from the general's holster, prodded him along. He walked with a stiff, mournful dignity. Whenever Valentine looked back to see the barbecue-sweet thread of smoke rising into the clouds, she'd poke Kanakia in the chest. She'd yell at him that he'd brought this upon himself, he should have *known* what happened when you picked a fight with a goddamned gamer, didn't you know we'd *have* to escalate, you dumb motherfucker?

Didn't you know you left us no *choice* but to win?

Paul pushed the thought away, swallowing another Oxycontin. Aliyah was in Bastogne.

He would bring the war to her.

They entered a wilderness so deep it seemed to erase the memory of man. Paul had never realized nights could be so black. There were no campfires, no city lights; just that shattered jigsaw of a broach-fractured sky.

Imani found berries and fresh water, kept them going in the right direction.

Paul gobbled pills to sleep on the cold, rocky soil. He had nightmares of black flux seeping out from his skin...

Yet his flux had been burned away by his newfound faith in War Bureaucromancy. Firing that missile had been a gift from the universe, proof the Unimancers needed to die...

Occasionally they pushed through thick growth into settlements – villages of ragged peasants who spoke a patois Imani couldn't translate. They'd settled deep in the ruined cities, retreating inwards as ever-hungry forests had pulled down buildings at the town's edge. They planted crops, but the vegetables looked sadly mutated.

All of Europe wasn't this degraded, Paul knew. Andorra had

only been evacuated a decade ago, when the broach's edge had squeezed across Spain's borders. But he'd never realized how dire it had gotten in Germany, in Poland, in Austria.

The isolated villagers were wary... But they brightened when they noticed General Kanakia, crying a happy "SMASH YES!" in thick foreign accents. Sometimes the villagers gave them horse rides to speed their way.

"They would fight for you," Paul asked the general. "Why don't you tell them?"

The general had given nothing but his name, rank, and serial number since the explosion. He'd stayed solemnly silent while Valentine blamed him for the Unimancers' deaths.

So Paul was surprised when the general said, "I'm protecting your conscience by minimizing your murders, Mr Tsabo."

"I would *never* kill a human being."

The general's cold stare was merciless, accusatory.

"There wasn't anything left of those men to murder," Paul snapped.

"So why were there bodies?"

Paul swallowed another Oxycontin. He had no time for arguments.

Yet as they hiked closer to Bastogne, the general tensed; Paul realized that as a mundane, he couldn't tell which areas were safe and which deadly.

Yet the reality fractures were a high-pitched buzzing at the edge of Paul's hearing – inexpertly reimagined laws of physics broadcasting errors. The Unimancers had sewn together a surface layer illusion of our world's tenets, but they hadn't appreciated the laws' intricacy the way Paul did – they'd brute-forced a worldview into existence, but not the infrastructure necessary to sustain it.

They'd forgotten subtle concepts, like the trillisecond pop of quantum foam – concepts Paul had no classical name for; they made sense to him because he thought it all the way through down to the tiniest layers.

The demon dimensions were threaded through here like a dormant virus, hidden in atoms an angstrom too small.

Walking near the broach was like walking through spiderwebs; laws were so fragile, it took more effort to keep them intact than it did to snap it. Crossing these unstable physics zones felt like traversing endless heaps of loose stone, each waiting to cascade into an avalanche–

Paul realized he knew which stones to pull to trigger avalanches, if he had to.

He could pull the world apart with a thought.

The idea maddened him. They'd claimed to fix Europe, and instead had created a series of magical booby-traps. Each fracture could have been reset clean, if they'd had the skills to do it – or even if they'd asked him! – but in their arrogance they'd let this fracture spread for *decades*.

Stop your fucking amateur hour magic.

Unimancers were a scourge. How many talented 'mancers had vanished into their hivemind? How many unique magics had been erased? The broach had only erupted because mundanes had weaponized 'mancers. And SMASH was yet another slipshod attempt to harness a million magical varieties into something mundanes felt comfortable with...

Aliyah had never known a world where 'mancy was treasured. Where *she* was treasured. SMASH had destroyed Aliyah's potential friendships–

It felt so good, realizing who was to blame.

Paul ached to fix the wrecked physics. Imani told him to slow down; sometimes he passed out from the pain. But the world needed repairing, Aliyah needed rescuing...

They clambered up Bastogne's slopes – a shrinking town reduced to a small hamlet cradled in decaying buildings. Above that, Something unthinkable crawled across the sky's crazy quilt patchwork, slithering between the faultlines.

They'd jailed her at the broach's heart. Any tear in their ham-handedly patched physics would shower Aliyah in buzzsects – and they couldn't fix rifts like he did.

Paul clenched his fists.

Yet as he and Valentine and Imani approached, the villagers called out to each other. They filed out in a half-circle, abandoning their campfires, facing him as though they'd expected him: grizzled survivors. Children and adults alike. All empty-handed.

"*Kaik!*" an old woman with blistered palms cried. "*Kaik!*"

They grabbed hands.

The people of Bastogne shuddered, then looked up defiantly at their broken sky. It took them effort; the children cried. Some bore stumps from where rifts had shredded them.

They trembled, staring at the roaring Thing crawling across the sky. It dwarfed their town. Paul couldn't piece It together – he caught glimpses of flopping treetrunk limbs serrated with sharks' teeth, pulsing maws the size of swimming pools, sprouting blossoms of insect eyes...

It pulled at the rifts, trying to unlock them.

Though Paul did not speak their language, he understood.

Yes, he thought. *Yes, I will save you. I will untangle the mess the Unimancers made, fix this the way it* should *have been fixed–*

Aliyah stepped out.

As he staggered towards his daughter, some great strength that had carried him all these miles broke. All the Oxycontin in the world couldn't hold back his chest pain as he sobbed with relief, forcing his dying body to keep moving because nothing would stop him from scooping her up in the hug he'd longed to give her.

He hugged her even though his ribs stabbed him. She was safe in his arms.

He marveled at how strong she'd gotten – she'd grown muscular, she must have had a growth spurt while he was gone, the Unimancers had stolen that time from them. But she still clung to him as though she hoped never to let him go again, doing her old trick of burying her face in his shoulder rather than letting anyone see her cry.

The Thing in the sky roared.

Time to heal this place.

"Get her out of here, Valentine." Valentine had cruised to a halt a few steps behind him, dazed, horrified.

Aliyah squirmed. "*What?*"

His daughter's voice sounded harsher, more clipped. He grabbed her by her shoulders:

Her eyes jittered.

"No," he whispered. "No."

Sixty Unimancers stepped out from the ruins' shadows, coordinated as dancers, their guns holstered, keeping a respectful distance. Paul recognized one of them: Ruth, the young one who'd set them free at Morehead, her freckled face blankly hostile.

I will put a bullet through your windpipe, she had promised, *and your kid will pull the trigger.*

"Dad, it's not what you think!" Aliyah cried. "We're… We're not brainwashed! We're *alive* in here!"

She swallowed, pondering how to convince him.

"*We're not NPCs!*"

Valentine stiffened.

Paul's palms itched; he was revolted to find himself holding a Unimancer. But if they *were* emulating her emotions, they did it skillfully enough to break his heart…

"We need you, Dad," Aliyah pled. "You taught me sacrifice for a good cause was *noble.* You'd put your life on the line for me. To save 'mancers. We give our lives to hold *that* back." She jabbed a finger up at the interlaced rifts overhead, but Paul couldn't look away from his daughter's face.

She grabbed his chin – she had a soldier's strength now – and directed his gaze back to the anxious villagers.

"We save 'mancers. We save humans. We save the *world*. And we need *you*, in *here*, to help us fix that. And–"

She gritted her teeth. Ruth spasmed, her head snapping back, muscles locking as some collective willpower held her in place. Aliyah's mouth subvocalized words:

"Shut *up*, Ruth. I *know* what your mother does to you but we need him *inside*."

She looked so tormented. She looked so sad.

He could never refuse her.

"Aliyah, I–"

Aliyah grabbed him, her eyes clear and still. "Remember

Morehead, Daddy? Look at these people, Daddy, look at those villages you rode through and tell me it's not worth it to save them."

"Aliyah, I'll do it."

"What?"

As a parent, there was no greater joy than seeing your daughter realize she didn't have to argue. "I'll become a Unimancer. If they're... If they're truly unique individuals in there, then you and I can show them what's wrong. We've seen how they've broken the world. We can reforge them from the inside."

Even though her grateful hug sent streaks of pain up his fractured ribs, he luxuriated in her touch. He concentrated on the feel of her in his arms. This would be the last time he'd hold her.

"All right, Valentine," he said. "Get her back home."

Aliyah stiffened. "*What?*"

"You're not staying, Aliyah. Healing this will be dangerous."

She stepped back, the Unimancers closing ranks. "No, Dad. Bastogne is... it's my Morehead. I'm fixing this, too."

"No more arguments, kid." He ruffled her hair. "Go home."

"This *is* my home."

"*Aliyah Rebecca Tsabo-Dawson! This is not negotiable! I didn't kill—*"

Corpses burning men screaming Imani weeping as she shot a man in the face

"I did not cross Europe to lose you to that Thing!"

Aliyah's burn scars flushed dark with rage. "That Thing needs *all* of us to bring it down!"

"*Not you!*"

His voice sent birds scattering from the trees.

Of course it was Ruth who unlocked her taser from its holster. The rest followed, synchronized, an assembly line threat.

"Get back there with Valentine," Paul whispered. "I can accept you as a Unimancer. But you'll be a Unimancer somewhere safe. I've been through too much to let you hurt yourself."

"Dad," Aliyah said, through gritted teeth. "I need to be here.

Saving people. That's… it's not negotiable, either. And…" She broke away, looking back at her fellow Unimancers. "We had contingency plans in case you refused."

"Funny," Paul said. "So did we."

Things moved very fast after that.

THIRTY-TWO
War Bureaucracy

Aliyah jabbed her hidden stun gun into her father's solar plexus. The combatmancers flowed through her muscles, guiding her actions–

His shoulder's dropped, the combatmancers thought, analyzing Paul's musculature. *He went for his blow at the same time you did, it's too late to block whatever he's done, so immobilize him and we'll handle the rest.*

Gratitude welled out. Her father might disable her, but her squad would finish the job.

She squeezed the trigger–

It clicked uselessly.

How, she thought, *we checked the batteries*–

Needles jabbed into her side. Magiquell. Her father had dosed her with anti-'mancer sedatives.

She tumbled backwards as the other Unimancers fired their tasers. Aliyah was grateful to see Aunt Valentine backing away, ushering Mommy and General Kanakia to safety – *stay back*, she pled, *don't do 'mancy here, you'll rip open rifts*–

Every taser misfired.

She felt their confusion. They'd triple-checked their equipment. General Kanakia had assigned them each a different taser brand, so Daddy couldn't disable a single manufacturer's quality control and neutralize them.

But this was different. Daddy's 'mancy had always been whisper-quiet.

They'd never felt him rewriting the laws of physics.

"*You dumb sacks of elephant shit*!" He tugged at the unstable physics; rifts cracked open at his fingertips, unspooling across the landscape. "*How much does it take for your bloated egos to realize how incompetent you are?*"

Aliyah felt the collective's shock as they realized Daddy had weaponized the unstable physics. He'd triggered a microbroach that had changed the electrical mobility in the tasers' lithium batteries...

Ruth whipped out her gun, aiming for center mass. But Daddy had tugged apart Bastogne's loose physics to destabilize nitrocellulose, turning their bullets into duds.

The Unimancers charged at Daddy, closing the distance–

He clenched his fists.

Black razor-plows erupted from his hands.

He's cracking open the places we've never healed properly, Aliyah thought. *If we'd sealed the broaches, he'd be helpless – but he's turned our incompetence against us...*

The Unimancers abandoned their assault to smother those rifts before they unleashed the Thing in the sky.

"Get out!" Daddy screamed to the villagers. They were already fleeing. "I'll handle this!"

"Daddy!" She fought the numbness creeping up her side. "What are you *doing*?"

"I'm fixing this." He looked so serene. "The broach has spread for *years* because they've been too incompetent to realize they *can't* fix it. And they won't let me heal it – they'll stop me, just like they did at Morehead. I have to get rid of them and start over."

"You can't trigger a broach on purpose!" she yelled. "The demon dimensions are not a weapon!"

"It's how I defeated Payne."

Her father had gone mad.

"It's OK, baby," he reassured her. "I'll tear down this slapdash parody of our world's rules, and once the chaos has given me some breathing space, I'll rebuild this the way they should have back in 1945."

By "breathing space," he meant "killing the Unimancers."

She realized why he'd dosed her with Magiquell – her father had anticipated she might be Unimanced, and so he'd done his best to cushion the blow when he killed her friends.

"This isn't you, Daddy!" The numbness spread to her thigh. "Is this bureaucromancy?"

He grimaced, looking away. Then he stared up at that Thing. His eyes narrowed.

"It's War Bureaucracy."

She looked to Ruth for help – but Ruth was so busy counteracting the broach, she didn't dare take Daddy down. Yet why weren't the other sixty Unimancers restraining Daddy?

She tuned into the collective:

Maybe he's right

He's triggered microbroaches he's turned our shoddy work against us

WHAT DOES HE KNOW THAT WE DON'T

Her father's new powers inspired spasms of insecurity. The Unimancers examined years of constant broach-caused retreats, knowing that at best they'd run a holding pattern. A rebellious sect seriously considered whether letting Paul kill them and take over was a good idea.

He has to be stopped! she thought. But the drugs dissolved her concentration. She thought of Ruth dying, Bastogne dying, tried to grant the Unimancers her certainty of *Daddy is wrong*–

The Magiquell fuzzed her connection. She staggered towards him, her limbs heavy; Aunt Valentine charged back out of the woods, dragging a heavy tree branch behind her.

"I'm not leaving." she told Daddy, her voice slurring. "You'll have to risk killing me."

He shook his head. "No. I won't. Valentine, take her away."

Valentine whacked him with the branch.

THIRTY-THREE
The Ol' Kali Ma Excavation

If Valentine had channeled her videogamemancy, Paul realized, her hit would have knocked him out.

But this close to the broach, she didn't dare break out her magical brutalities. Lacking that, she was a chubby middle-aged woman with no combat training, wielding a stout branch.

It clouted him behind the left ear, pine needles raking bloody trails across his scalp.

Paul danced away, batting at his face. "Valentine! What are you doing?"

She huffed as she lifted the ersatz club over her head. "I've stepped over a lot of lines for you. But when the kid says she doesn't want to leave, I stop stepping."

"Valentine!" Paul triggered more broaches, forcing the incoming Unimancers to back off. "Stop fucking around and *get Aliyah to safety!*"

She swung again. Paul scrambled backwards.

They could have been kids tussling on a school yard. Stripped of their 'mancy, both were shit in hand-to-hand combat.

"No, Paul. *You* came here to get the kid to safety. *I* came here to *rescue* her. If she tells me the Unimancers aren't NPCs, then she's found her friends. I fought my way here to *save* her from kidnappers, not to *become* one."

"That's Stockholm Syndrome! We'll—"

"Jesus weeping *fuck*! *You shoddy pile of ignorant neuroses*!" She

263

swung hard enough that the branch snapped when she missed. "You think your kid's risking her life to piss you off?! *Look* at her! You spent your whole life teaching her to fight for a cause, and now you'll lock her away because she *found* one?!"

Valentine screamed, leaving the club behind, chasing Paul. The villagers took heart from her rebellion. A couple raised their bows, squinting as they decided whether they could hit Paul without perforating the chunky tattooed woman who appeared to be on their side.

Paul held out his palms, seeking a truce. "Valentine. You know Imani came up with this plan to sweep the Unimancers aside. You know this is our best chance to heal the broach. And you're *stopping* me?"

She snorted, bemused. "You gotta save the world for the right reasons, Paul."

"Don't you start! That's what *Robert* said!"

Her rage bunched incoherently in her throat before she went after him with her nails.

"*Goddammit, Valentine!*" He backed away as she bore down upon him. He waggled his fingers, radiating microbroaches. "I could rip you to shreds!"

"*Then do it!*"

Valentine spread her arms out, making herself an easy target.

Paul froze, his hands halfway to destruction.

Valentine pounded her chest. "*Go on!* You're gonna smother your daughter with a pillow of fatherly love – show her how deep the rabbit hole goes! You blew up some old people's houses! You killed those fuckin' Unimancers! Now you're gonna wipe out this refugee camp! What am I, then? Just one more step!"

She ripped her shirt down, thumped her heart.

"Come on! Do the old Kali Ma excavation, Paul! Banish me to the demon dimensions! Dig *deep* to get those sacrifices!"

Paul's hands dropped. "Valentine... I'm not... you know I can't..."

"Then *step down*, Paul."

Paul shook his head – not refuting her, just uncertain. "This has gone too far, Val. I don't know if I–"

He realized Valentine was not making herself a target to appeal to his conscience.

She was doing it to distract him.

Aliyah hit him at a low angle, grabbing at his right calf. Paul wondered why she hit him there instead of his ribs – until he heard the soft *click* of Aliyah releasing his pin-lock system.

When she was young, she'd made a game of unfastening his prosthesis when he fell asleep – punishing him for being inattentive.

Once again, Paul Tsabo discovered his thirteen year-old daughter had stolen his right foot.

"Imani came up with that plan, too," Valentine said. Paul realized they'd conspired against him the instant Aliyah had spoken for herself.

He pinwheeled backwards, hitting the ground. His still-cracked ribs paralyzed him with agony.

"Sorry, Daddy." Aliyah's fingers pressed into his throat, shutting off the flow of blood.

Valentine and Aliyah looked down at him sadly.

His chest stirred with a strange pride: *only my family could stop me*, he thought.

Then everything went dark.

THIRTY-FOUR
Why She Didn't Kill Him

Aliyah had fallen unconscious by the time Ruth arrived. Paul's eyes fluttered – compressing the carotid was a quick off, but it was also a quick on – so Ruth jabbed him with a Magiquell insta-shot.

That wouldn't put him down quick enough, though. She kissed Aliyah on the forehead before rolling her off her asshole of a father, then carefully strangled Paul back into oblivion.

Valentine kicked her – not hard enough to hurt through the armor.

"You kill him," she said, flexing her fingers around an imaginary controller, "and you'll answer to me."

Ruth had considered executing Paul. Behind her, the Unimancers mopped up the broaches, doing their best to stanch that fucker's damage before the Thing got loose. The villagers were damn near readying their pitchforks.

Still, she felt the sickening unrest thrumming through the collective:

How did he trigger those broaches he was healing them almost as fast as he created them

He said we'd done it wrong

We have to know what we can do

Ruth stood strongly in the "disagreement" camp. A rebellion coalesced around her sentiment that Paul Tsabo held no special wisdom. Preserving Paul Tsabo's reckless techniques struck her like trying to save a bear chewing your neck open on the off-hand chance you might teach it to dance.

Ruth wondered if Aliyah could forgive Ruth for killing her father.

So glad you asked, Ruthie! Mom-construct interjected. *All the signs I've collected indicates your new friend is very* very *attached to her daddy. Almost as much as you are to me, sweetiekins! Though since you asked, I've assembled head-doctor techniques you could use to weaken her bond…*

Fuck off, Mom, Ruth snapped, then tuned out Mom's usual canned response on how good girls didn't need profanity.

She didn't want to fuck with Aliyah's mind; that was what Paul did. No, Ruth simply wanted Paul Tsabo gone. But too many in the collective were convinced they needed him. Killing him without consensus might create a permanent schism.

Which puzzled her. He'd murdered them in a maniacal bid to protect his daughter – and like Mom, he'd never bothered to see whether this new world he'd created would make her happy.

She'd *told* Aliyah he'd never let her go. Tsabo was just another version of the mother-construct – jailing his child and convincing himself it was for her own good.

She could crush his larynx. She could save Aliyah. She could rid the world of danger.

Except Aliyah would never forgive her.

"I would," Ruth growled. "But he's too valuable."

"Then let's plan our next move," Valentine said.

PART III

Games Without Frontiers

THIRTY-FIVE
A Particular Set of Skills She Has Acquired Over a Very Long Career

"May I come in?"

Imani knocked on General Kanakia's door. He had no guards posted. There were only two threats in Bastogne: the first was Paul. He'd been placed into a coma while his ribs healed and the Unimancers decided what to do with him. The other was that cracked sky, dangerously fragmented after Paul's assault.

The Unimancers didn't consider a mundane a threat – a fact which Imani was grateful for.

She did her best work when people overlooked her.

"Have a seat, Mrs Tsabo," Kanakia said.

His voice was gentle, welcoming – though he did not look up from the printed reports he perused. She doubted the misnomenclature was a mistake – Kanakia seemed too thorough – but at least he wasn't compensating for his defeat with shows of force.

He could have had them jailed. Yet somehow she got the impression the general had expected her in his office ever since they'd fought off his Morehead forces.

That gave her hope this talk might be productive.

She sat down, glad to get out from underneath that broken sky. Seeing that Thing prying its way into this world creeped her out.

Why had everyone forgotten their true enemy?

"Are my men treating you properly?" the general asked. He was a stout, dark-skinned man with bulging eyes and a bulging tummy. Yet he'd been tasked with keeping the broach as contained as any man *could* keep it pent for almost four decades – and until Paul's arrival, nothing had stopped him in the execution of his duty.

Imani flattened her skirt – the single nervous habit she allowed herself before entering negotiations.

"I've been slow to come to conclusions, general – what with having my family kidnapped and all – but as you escorted us through the broach-affected lands, I formulated a theory. I was hoping you could confirm or deny."

The man's poker face was world class. "Oh?"

"Well, it occurs to me the US government doesn't want Paul alive. Paul's a terrorist – and worse, an effective political firebrand. The President would probably be thrilled if someone put a bullet through his head. Yet it's clear the Unimancers don't necessarily want him, either."

He set his paperwork aside. "...go on."

"So. I asked myself, who *has* been trying to keep Paul alive?"

She let the question hang in the air until Kanakia had no choice but to answer it. He bobbed his head from left to right, a tiny concession.

"Perhaps I ensured the Unimancers did not utilize their resources properly to capture Mr Tsabo," he admitted – a little merry someone had finally caught him out. "And perhaps, once assassination was on the table after the Morehead broach, I assigned my best men to rope him in before that bullet, as you said, reached his brain."

"All those efforts to get one man," she mused. "Which means either you're desperate to get Paul specifically, or..."

"We're desperate for *any* new options."

Imani looked at the photos of famous European landmarks hung on Kanakia's walls – the Eiffel Tower, Saint Basil's Cathedral, the Arc de Triomphe. All broach-devoured.

"How... How bad is it?"

He grimaced. "In the seventy years since the Bastogne broach opened, we have not closed one broach permanently."

She shuddered. The news rarely gave details on the European struggle. American news hated reporting battles America wasn't winning.

"Before the Morehead broach," Kanakia continued, "your husband had done excellent work, putting a human face on 'mancy. Given a decade, he might well have gotten proper legislation through. The Unimancers may loathe his tactics, but he's advanced their cause."

"You *want* 'mancy to be legal?"

"Unimancy is an excellent tool. As the *only* magical tool the United Nations allows me to utilize, I find it insufficient. The Unimancers have great wisdom, but their consensus makes them weak at spotting new ideas. Your husband is proof there are other ways to heal broaches."

"You could have kidnapped Paul *years* ago to get that knowledge. Why leave him operational?"

"The Unimancers themselves believe Unimancy is the only way, but..." He shrugged. "They *are* 'mancers. Belief is what they do. While *I've* wondered, 'How many Paul Tsabos have we cut down in the rush to consensus?'"

"Still not an answer, Mr Kanakia. You've demonstrated you can sabotage SMASH at will. You could have let 'mancers flourish. Instead, you wanted Paul to pass *laws*. Why?"

He took his glasses off, coldly furious. She'd seen that tranquil anger all too often in Paul's eyes.

"We left behind a hundred and fifty men in an open grave, Mrs Tsabo. Yet if I wanted to prosecute Paul Tsabo for murder, the best I could do would be property destruction." He flattened his hands against his desk. "The governments are only comfortable with 'mancers as soulless tools. That needs to change."

"But Morehead ended Paul's political career."

"Yes."

"You want him now because...?"

"Wan*ted*, sadly." His contradiction confused Imani even as it heartened her; for some reason, possibly Aliyah, Paul could no longer be a Unimancer. "He's thwarted me with scarce resources, Mrs Tsabo. And Europe, well…"

He waved around at the pins in maps on the walls, demonstrating how thin seven thousand 'mancers were when spread out across seven continents.

"Our predicament is nothing *but* scarce resources. I'd hoped his brilliance in the hivemind would uncover new stratagems to hold back the demon dimensions…"

Time to drop the hammer.

"You can't add that brilliance to the collective anyway."

His confusion was delicious. "You're saying he would have committed suicide rather than join?"

"I'm saying my name is Ms Tsabo-Dawson, not 'Mrs Tsabo' – and *I'm* the one working with scarce resources. *I* planned the assault on Morehead airport. *I* figured out how to disrupt the hivemind. You need to negotiate with *me* with if you want shit done."

He only needed a blink to realize which member of the Tsabo-Dawson clan he'd underestimated. "What do you want, Ms Tsabo-Dawson?"

"I want my daughter out. A growing girl does not need an army for a best friend."

"I too want her out. It won't happen. They're *happy* in there, far as I can tell. Aliyah would have to sever her connection voluntarily – and even if you got past her sense of duty, I don't think she'd leave Ruth behind. Which is a shame, because that means I don't get to add Paul's bureaucratic skills to the network."

"Clarify. Why can't you have them both?"

"The one time we had a mother and a daughter joined, the daughter was irreparably damaged. Putting Paul and Aliyah together would erode their personalities."

Dammit. "Order them to expel her."

He spread his hands wide. "That, Ms Tsabo-Dawson, is what the government would tell me to do. They believe I control enslaved 'mancers – an illusion we have worked *very hard* to maintain. Whereas what I actually control…"

He took a deep breath before committing to the revelation.

"...what I *actually* lead is the world's largest semi-autonomous 'mancer collective. They respect my opinions. They recognize my efficiency in combating the broach. But as Valentine can tell you, they do not necessarily obey orders."

Dammit. "Then I want it announced that Paul's volunteered to fix the broach. The former face of 'mancer independence and the Unimancers, joining forces to save the world. I've worked in PR – that's a great goddamned headline."

"That's not up to me. That's up to the President, and the United Nations Security Council."

"Start the conference calls," Imani told him. "Get some sandwiches in. This negotiation may take days."

"We are negotiating for...?"

"Paul's help to fix the broach. My help to stem the tide. The help of Project Mayhem to create more flexible 'mancy-related options in America. That's what you wanted all along, wasn't it?"

He smiled. "Are you authorized to negotiate on their behalf, Ms Tsabo-Dawson?"

"Project Mayhem knows better than to cross me. And Valentine... well, I've usually gotten her on board."

The general smiled. "I'll tell them you've got me over a barrel. The Security Council and the President have come to trust my judgment; the benefits of running a division for four decades. My conceding the necessity of your help will help skip past the preliminary sessions where we establish your goodwill. With luck, we might come to an agreement before the month's end. What else do you need?"

"Just the phone line, sandwiches, and coffee – oh, and keep the Unimancers clear. I'm pretty sure they won't like the agreement we come to."

THIRTY-SIX
Donutmancy

Someone pried Paul's eyelids open, flashed a light in his eyes. He struggled, found his arms strapped to a cot.

"Calm down, Daddy." Aliyah pressed her palm to his chest. "It's OK."

He was blindfolded. Something bad had happened, but... his memories squirmed away. All he could concentrate on was how worried Aliyah sounded, her exhaustion.

He took a breath, and that breath swelled to fill his thought process. His lungs expanded without incident, his ribs a passing ache. How long had he been out? But his stomach growled, and that noise snatched his attention away. On his next inhale, he felt the needle in his chest flex.

Magiquell. They'd drugged him.

"You'll start remembering soon," said a familiar voice. Her words triggered flashbacks to a burning airfield. "And when you do–"

"Shut your pie-hole, kid," Valentine said, curt and dangerous. "We want him calmed down. You're not helping."

"*You* tried to calm him down by playing nicey-nicey. You had that shot." Ruth. That was Ruth. She slid his blindfold off; the drugs made her freckled cheeks dazzling as constellations.

She held up a syringe filled with clear fluid. "This is methohexital. It knocks people out. This IV's hooked up to

276

your heart. Try anything, *anything*, and I will knock you into a permanent coma."

"Ruth!" Aliyah said. "Don't make him scared, you'll ruin the test."

Test?

"...Aliyah?" His throat was gummy, clogged shut. How long *had* he been out?

She handed him a glass of water; the cool plastic felt amazing in his hand. But why would his daughter put him on euclidosuppressants? He closed his eyes, summoned memories–

"Aliyah Rebecca Tsabo-Dawson!" he'd yelled, preparing to wipe the ridge clean. "This is not negotiable!"

He tore his gaze away from Aliyah's face, noticing her black SMASH uniform. Her lithe body had bulked up to a bodybuilder's physique. When she cupped his cheek, she moved with a Unimancers' mechanical grace.

They'd brainwashed her to die for their cause. He watched her eyes jitter as she tuned into the collective, saw her fight off a frown as their loathing flickered across her face.

"Aliyah. That's not you. Don't let them–"

"That's the test, Daddy. Because we don't have time to argue. Look."

She pointed at a handmade wooden table, sitting in the RV office they'd gathered in; the drugs compelled Paul to follow her motion.

On the table was a box, draped in thick cheesecloth. Next to the box sat a bulky satellite phone, its lights flashing green.

"Can he hear me?" The voice from the speaker buzzed, a tenuous connection – but that thick Yiddish accent was unmistakable.

"...Kit?" Paul asked.

"*Uncle* Kit," Aliyah confirmed, relieved. "I called his retirement home."

"*Bubbeleh!*" he cried. "I suppose I shouldn't be this glad to hear your voice, given where you are. My goddaughter, she doesn't give me details, but she says it's quite serious. Have they kidnapped her?"

"They have, Kit." Tears welled up; he missed his old friend, but they couldn't drag a seventy-four year-old man around the country with them, dodging SMASH patrols. So Paul had purchased a spot in a swanky assisted living community, and Kit had been content to declare himself Paul's consigliere. Though these days, he'd seemed happy to nap in the Florida sunlight. "The Unimancers, they've brainwashed her into suicide, they–"

"*Stop.*"

Paul flinched at Aliyah's sternness – but Valentine nodded soberly. Ruth stood with her thumb on the methohexital syringe.

"This is the test, Daddy."

She whipped the cheesecloth off reverently, revealing a large pink box.

DUNKIN' DONUTS, it said.

"Donutmancy," Paul whispered.

"Do you trust Uncle Kit's judgement?" she asked.

"Implicitly."

Kit harrumphed proudly.

Aliyah sat down next to the two dozen donuts. "Then here's how it's going to go, Daddy. You know Uncle Kit believes he can read a man's temperament through his choice of donuts. You've trusted his judgment before."

"Yes." More than once, Kit had talked Paul out of a disastrous opinion by critiquing his cruller.

"So *I'll* choose a donut. *You'll* tell Uncle Kit what I'm going through. If I choose the donut Uncle Kit thinks best represents a healthy state of mind for me, then I'm me. I'm not some brainwashed zombie, I'm not some Stockholm Syndrome case, I am your daughter and you treat me as such."

"And if you choose a different donut?"

"Then I'm brainwashed. You can take me away."

Despite the drugs, Paul was making plans. He shouldn't be talking to Unimancers, he should be destroying them. His mind fizzed with ways to neutralize the methohexital, fantasizing about the look on Ruth's face when he wrecked her plans...

He shook Aliyah's hand.

Ruth whispered to Valentine. "I know *she* believes in it. But... come on, this is ridiculous. Can the old man read someone's state of mind by *donuts*?"

"That old guy's canny as fuck," Valentine replied. "I think he uses donuts to distract people from the way he can cold read people."

"*My old guy ears are not so deaf!*" Kit cried. "And I will have no one doubt the sacred donut in this hour of trial! For this is a serious moment, my friends. We ask whether Aliyah has been brainwashed, or whether she simply seeks independence, as all children do. Aliyah, my beautiful goddaughter, knowing I cherish your liberation from all forms of tyranny, I ask you: reach into the box and choose what you think would taste best."

Aliyah trailed her fingers along the donuts. Paul had no idea how they'd hauled Dunkin' Donuts out this far into Europe, but fresh oil dotted the box's bottom. Had they cooked them here?

He held his breath as Aliyah touched each donut: classic glazed, iced Boston Kremes, powdered jelly donuts, a maple log, a cakelike old-fashioned, a Chocolate Kreme with a curlicue of frosting poking out one end. They'd even put a tiny container of Munchkins in.

Aliyah silently held up a cinnamon doughnut.

"Now. Paul, my best friend, knowing I have always held your best interests at heart, I ask you: tell me what your daughter looks like."

Paul felt a chill. "...You two didn't choose a donut in advance to fool me, did you?"

Kit clucked his tongue. "Not if they held me at gunpoint, bubbeleh. Your family's my family."

Paul remembered how Kit had offered Paul a job when he'd needed to quit the NYPD, how Kit had rushed over the night Imani had asked for a divorce, how Kit had tried his damndest to understand Paul's magical problems even though he'd loathed 'mancers until his best friend had become one.

Kit was the only person whose judgment he trusted implicitly. Aliyah had chosen well.

"Aliyah, she's... wearing a Unimancer outfit."

He made a soft *chuh* noise, like a pitcher waving off a catcher's suggestion. "That much I know, Paul. They *have* told me some of the circumstances. Dig deeper."

Paul swallowed. "She's tied back her hair." *The hair he could never get Aliyah to comb back.* "She's bulked up. Her skin's tan." *They'd fought with Aliyah to get outside more, but she'd always holed up with her Nintendo DS.* "She..."

He leaned in to examine Aliyah's face, fighting through the drugs to elucidate *how* his daughter looked different. As he pulled himself over the cot, she stepped back, tension spreading across her face, terrified Daddy might ground her–

Ruth squeezed her hand.

Relaxation flooded across her as they interlaced fingers. She gave a nervous little laugh – *I'm being silly, aren't I?* – and Ruth's blank face stayed blank, but some reassurance flowed between them.

"She has friends. She's smiling." Paul's heart broke a little. "She hasn't smiled like that since... since before the fire."

"Military training will do that," Kit mused. "You form bonds. She's young, though. Hitting the crush era. Any romances?"

Ruth glowered, daring Paul to say something negative.

"I think so." Aliyah blushed. "Yes," he corrected.

"Anything else?"

Paul wanted to catalogue the differences – the way she stood at attention, the way her gaze skittered away from him like he was an embarrassment, her lack of...

"She's got no videogames on her. No Nintendo, no phone." That, really, was all Kit needed to know. "That's all."

"Huh." Kit sounded mildly surprised. "All right: military training, romance, blossoming confidence, leaving her childhood behind. She's always loved the sweet gooiness; now she's transitioning to something savory. Not completely there yet, but months of training would turn an éclair into a sugar-shock. An Aliyah in her right mind would choose…"

Paul cursed at Kit's dramatic pause. Even now, Kit couldn't resist showing off.

"The cinnamon donut."

Ruth went to high-five Aliyah. Aliyah met her clap sadly, without looking away from her father.

She's won the right to walk away from me, Paul thought. *To get herself killed in whatever damn fool conflict she desires.*

"All right." Paul slumped back on the cot. "You're yourself. And you're a Unimancer. But you're still my daughter, Aliyah, and I have the right to–"

"The test isn't over, Daddy."

Paul sat up again. "What do you mean?"

Valentine stepped forward, a surgeon delivering bad news. "You questioned whether Aliyah's in her right mind. But after the way you fought us, well…" She glanced down at the donuts. "Time for you to choose."

"You gotta be kidding me. You're asking if *I'm* sane?"

"Remember Rainbird?" Valentine asked. "I remember that fiery maniac hoisting a goddamned house into the sky, ready to incinerate a squadron of cops – and you. *You*. Even though it *would* have been easier to leave no witnesses, we fought that fucker because you thought every life mattered. You even thought *Rainbird's* life mattered, and that guy was a pimple on humanity's dick."

"*I* haven't changed!" He almost leapt to his feet; Ruth brandished the methohexital. "*Circumstances* have!"

"Paul," Kit said. "I can't always trust the news, but they say you blew up a nursing home. Aliyah says you – maybe it's murder, maybe it's not, I can't say what warfare is. But…" Kit exhaled a long, staticky sigh. "The Paul I knew didn't take shortcuts with people's lives."

"This is ridiculous. Where's Imani? She's my wife, she should–"

"Mom's negotiating with the President to ensure we don't have to *execute* you!" Aliyah shook with stress. "Everything

you're doing, Dad – it doesn't seem like you. Can you blame us
for holding an intervention?"

"I don't *need* an intervention!"

"Do you trust Uncle Kit?"

"You know I do."

"Then choose a donut. See if you're the man he thinks you
are."

"Fine." He was hungry anyway. His drugged gaze bounced
between the glazeds' sugary crusts and the coconuts' soft furry
coating.

"Remember, he hasn't had solid food in two weeks."
Valentine watched him like he was about to clip the wrong
wire on a bomb.

"Oh, my sweet hot Boston Kreme mess, I have factored that
in." Kit's voice was tense. So tense.

This was stupid. Paul was hungry, and needed something to
clear his head. He grabbed the Vanilla Kreme, feeling its dough
indent beneath his fingers, a solid blob of frosting coated in
powdered sugar. He bit in deep.

Valentine gasped. Aliyah rushed forward, crooking her neck
to verify his choice. Ruth turned away sourly, as if his choice
had confirmed what she'd known all along.

"He chose the cruller, right?" Kit pled.

The sweetness curdled in his mouth. Paul remembered
laughing at Kit's rants on the reckless abandonment of the
Vanilla Kreme personality, serene in the knowledge he'd never
eat something so messy.

He brushed his fingertips across his chest, numbly wiping off
powdered sugar streaks. He had an IV line in, for Christ's sake,
he'd gotten his bandages sticky. Filling his empty stomach with
sugared lard would give him a head rush on top of the anti-
'mancer drugs. Yet he hadn't thought it through, he'd been so
eager to finish this stupid test that he...

He'd taken shortcuts.

So why were there bodies?

Maimed bodies in the missile's crater.

Burning bodies on the runway.

Hundreds of Unimancers, each unique as Aliyah, killed by his hand...

The donut dropped from Paul's fingers as he realized that yes, yes, he was *very* much out of control.

THIRTY-SEVEN
Daughter Says Knock You Out

Aliyah sat by her father's cot, holding his hand. He hadn't spoken since Uncle Kit had convinced him he wasn't acting like himself: just one quiet "My God" before he'd laid down.

He squeezed her hand periodically, gaining strength from her presence. He'd turned towards the wall, which the collective's body language experts informed her meant he was too shamed to face her. Periodically he'd twitch, as if awakening from a nightmare: the collective's psychologists concluded Paul Tsabo was trying to reconcile his brutal murders with what he perceived as his moral core.

Aliyah appreciated the help, but she could have figured that out on her own.

Aunt Valentine sat across from her, eating the remaining donuts. She also remained silent. When she'd helped knock Daddy out, Aliyah had hoped maybe they could be friends again.

But no. Aunt Valentine had dropped into wordless observation, gathering information. She'd done that back at Payne's Institute, too. Back when she'd been the first to realize Payne was their enemy.

It hurt to think she now considered Aliyah a potential enemy.

Everyone across in the camp lit up, complimented that Aliyah's sense of self and the Unimancers had merged. Tonya, scrubbing dishes in the mess tent, sent Aliyah a cheerful suggestion not to worry what some rogue 'mancer thought. Rajesh, standing on a chill rocky outcropping as he monitored the broach, reminded her that her father's chaotic nature was what happened when you didn't have calmer minds to turn to. And Max, out shoveling the horse shit, sent gentle reminders that Paul Tsabo was their enemy.

He's not a bad man. She wished she could stop thinking that. Whenever she did, the collective convulsively flooded her with the terror of a hundred and fifty 'mancers as the missile hit.

So much hatred for her father. It was hard to love her dad when they showed her how it felt to burn to death in a crashed helicopter...

She opened up doors in her head.

Aliyah had come to visualize the Unimancers' memories as rooms in a vast mansion – you could open doors to step into someone's recollections. Some doors were sticky, indicating they weren't comfortable with you peering inside, and still others were locked and you had to ask them for the key, and some were barricaded behind trashheaps.

Before Daddy had arrived, Ruth could lure her away to new experiences. They'd step through a doorway and drop into a parachutemancer's best jump.

Sometimes they pried open sticky doors to look at the sex-thoughts, getting all turned on watching porn until Mom-construct started a lecture on viral transmission rates.

But ever since the battle, Aliyah had become her father's ambassador, flinging her doors open wide to share her memories of Daddy protecting his daughter from a cruel world.

She stayed up late, distributing her memories of Daddy hugging her before he tucked her in, of his crooked smile whenever he discovered some new and beautiful 'mancy, the speeches he'd given to make the world a safer place.

They flipped through her mind looking for the times he'd used his bureaucromancy, as if they might extract broach-sealing lessons from her head. She felt their desperate hope: if they could figure out how to fix the broach without Paul Tsabo, then they could execute him.

She wished Daddy would talk to them the way he used to talk to her. He made magic seem beautiful when he spoke. *He's not a bad man*!

Maybe he wasn't, Ruth allowed.

Though Ruth changed diapers on the Bastogne orphans, Aliyah was never far from her thoughts.

Aliyah went breathless with hope. *You think he's a good man?*

He might have been, Ruth said. *You've shown me how he cared for you. He's a little myopic when it comes to you, but I think he means well.*

Her acknowledgment made Aliyah thrum with elation; Ruth knew her better than anyone else, if she convinced Ruth she could convince the collective...

But I think the worst thing a person can do to someone is to overlook how they've changed, Ruth finished.

Aliyah tensed, looking down at her father. He looked back, lost as a newborn puppy, baffled why she'd clutched his hand so hard.

You're hurting him, Ruth observed. *But he's not letting go.*

Aliyah saw bruises blossoming.

He'll never let you go. Ruth suffused Aliyah with sadness. *Whenever he looks at you he sees the little girl he almost lost in a fire – and he's always going to try to rescue you. He thinks he hates SMASH, but he's just looking for someone to blame. He can't understand how keeping you safe will destroy you.*

His safety killed me, Aliyah thought. She'd never had anything to live for before she'd become a Unimancer. Now, she might die, but she'd do it saving someone.

Protecting people from trauma gave her life meaning. It gave her strength.

The same strength that had driven her father to save her.

He taught me the virtue of sacrifice, she thought. *He just... can't understand how I'd need it, too.*

That's the way of parents, Ruth thought. She was tucking in a five year-old, who asked for a goodnight story. Though Ruth wasn't exactly the motherly type, she knew a few bedtime tales.

Instead, Ruth paused, as if to demonstrate something–

Is it nightie-night time, Ruthie-my-love? I see you need to know about bedtime stories. *I have a handy list of educational tales! Would you like to hear the Roly-Poly Elephant, or the Spider With Seven Legs, or...*

The Mom-construct was effervescent, knowledgeable... and oblivious that Ruth didn't need her help.

Yeah, Aliyah thought, kissing her father's hand by way of apology. *Parents don't notice us changing.*

Not just parents.

There was an edge to Ruth's voice that caught Aliyah's attention.

Kids don't notice their parents changing, either.

Ruth handed the five year-old to Sunil, who liked kids better anyway. Aliyah allowed Ruth to lead her into a place she'd never seen – an isolated ward in the Unimancer collective. An isolated wing that smelled like old diapers. She pried open sticky doors, accessing memories other Unimancers would prefer to forget–

And wandered into memories of middle-aged men and women watching their parents change.

We never realized Momma was concealing her bad vision until she wrecked her car...

Daddy was fine as a fiddle until we caught him on the phone, giving his life's savings away to a preacher who promised Jesus would wash away his sins...

We thought Momma was getting along fine after her third divorce until we heard her making up false gossip so someone would pay attention to her...

Aliyah tried to flee. Ruth stopped her.

Your daddy wants to keep you as a six year-old forever. That's one harm. But you can do all sorts of damage by pretending someone's competent...

Ruth. Aliyah tried to be sharp, but she couldn't hide her uncertainty from her girlfriend. *You can't say Daddy isn't...*

I'm saying maybe he can't be trusted with 'mancy anymore.

Aliyah protested. Ruth silenced her with memories of her father threatening to unleash that Thing upon the world.

What do you want me to do, Ruth? she asked.

You know what I want to do. That was the hard barrier between them; Ruth wanted Paul Tsabo dead.

I'm not *killing him.*

Fine. Keep him in a coma. But the man–

Attention, folks. The general's majestic command cut effortlessly through their argument.

Thousands of people mentally stood to attention. The general wasn't a Unimancer – but if he spoke to one Unimancer, all would listen. He too had dedicated his life to holding back the broach. His sage diplomatic advice had kept SMASH operational while nations rose and fell.

When Kanakia suggested a course of action, the collective listened.

Please bring Mr Tsabo to my office. And stay tuned; Ms Tsabo-Dawson and I have hammered out an agreement with the President.

A flicker of worry shot through the collective. Negotiomancers noted the Unimancers had been excluded from the discussion. Linguimancers pulled apart his words to find them peremptory, almost orders.

Do you know anything, Aliyah? Hundreds knocked on her mansion-door, asking to sift through memories of her mother. She turned them away. She needed to focus on getting Daddy to Kanakia.

Why was Aunt Valentine sitting there instead of helping Daddy up? Then she remembered: they weren't tuned in.

"Dad." She nudged him; he whirled around, shocked. His euclidosuppressants made new stimuli adrenaline-inducing. "General Kanakia wants to see you."

"Yes." He sucked in a deep breath, preparing for his execution. "Yes, he would."

As Aliyah brought him his artificial foot, she wondered what she'd do if Kanakia ordered Daddy's death. Kanakia had that power – which would give the President an instant popularity boost for killing the man who'd ruined Morehead.

"Aunt Valentine, would you…"

She nodded towards Daddy, who quivered from exhaustion after getting to his feet. Between the coma and his sickness, he was almost an invalid.

Aunt Valentine raised her eyebrows. "You want *me* to do it? The out-of-shape donutholic? Not..." She glanced outside, towards the burlier Unimancers who'd be ideal for the task.

"You're the one I trust," Aliyah said.

Bad idea, Ruth thought. Aliyah felt Ruth's loathing of any 'mancer who thought they could singlehandedly control their powers. Daddy and Aunt Valentine had peddled that deadly philosophy 'mancers should value freedom over safety...

Aliyah realized: her trust of Valentine was vestigial. Aunt Valentine thought magic was *fun*. Even though Aunt Valentine had watched her boyfriend die at the hands of her own flux, she still peddled this insane idea Aliyah should be *proud* to be a 'mancer...

She loved Aunt Valentine, but Ruth had saved her.

She and Valentine each got under a shoulder, helped Daddy to General Kanakia's office – also a plain RV, hauled here by horses. The Thing peered down through squirming vortexes of eyeballs, crawling around to focus on Paul.

When they got to the office, he waved Valentine and Aliyah away, demanding to walk up the three steps on his own.

Mommy met him at the top, hugged him. That made Aliyah feel better. There was forgiveness in that hug.

Then Mom hugged her, and that hug was... stiff. As it had been since she'd arrived in Bastogne. Not that they'd spent a lot of time together; General Kanakia had explained to Aliyah how he needed her mother's diplomatic skills to repair the damage her father had done to SMASH's political situation. He'd saluted Aliyah when she'd said she understood.

Yet Mom's hugs had remained... cautious. Aliyah had committed to her mother's hugs with her whole body, and Mom had returned her affection with stiff back pats.

She's worried you'll betray her, the psychomancers concluded.

Well, I won't. Aliyah pushed them away.

"I love you," Aliyah said.

"I love you too, sweetie." But Mom was already looking away, towards the other Unimancers. They didn't need to be there – any of them could have broadcast the general's words to the network – but it was considered a great honor to be in physical proximity to the old man.

The general walked down the line of Unimancers, shaking hands. He adjusted his glasses on the bridge of his wide nose, peering at Paul.

"Are you being treated well, Mr Tsabo?"

A dull roar of fury from the collective.

He dragged you through the woods in chains

He should be burned like the men he *burned*

Daddy squirmed in his seat, staring down at the shag carpet. "I'm fine." Then, repeating it more softly, as if he hoped to believe it: "I'm fine."

The general nodded – not an affirmation, but a willingness to let Paul keep his counsel.

"In any case," the general continued, "Ms Tsabo-Dawson and I have spent several days in intense negotiations with the UN Security Council. We've come to a preliminary agreement on Mr Tsabo's official status."

Official status? Ruth thought, along with a thousand others. Aliyah felt nudged to ask the general out loud. "Official status, sir?"

The general jerked his chin in Imani's direction. "Ms Tsabo-Dawson was quite insistent her husband have a position working with us. She felt the government publicly acknowledging her husband's assistance was the first step in rehabilitating Mr Tsabo's image problem."

Image *problem?*

Aliyah flinched from another barrage of Paul striding through dead Unimancers...

"Wwwwwwwith *alllll* d-Duh!-*due* respect, sir..." Aliyah choked down a hundred angry retorts into one polite response. "Mr Tsabo's – Daddy's – publicity is not the concern here. The fact that he's not in our collective is."

"He won't be in your collective."

The hivemind swirled with new debate. But all Aliyah could think about was what Ruth had said:

I'm saying maybe he can't be trusted with 'mancy any more.

The general swept open his arms in an embrace. "Unimancers, I acknowledge your fine efforts. The broach would have swollen to encompass the Earth three times over without your brave sacrifice. But despite decades of fine work, you have yet to permanently seal a single broach."

This time three Unimancers spoke. "You want to let a rogue 'mancer–"

" –a man who's already demonstrated world-threatening irresponsiblility–"

" –loose at the broach's heart?"

Daddy hung his head, shamed.

Kanakia stood his ground. "His danger was a new danger – one we might turn to our benefit. Ms Tsabo-Dawson made a compelling argument that we cannot afford any unexplored potentials in the face of global annihilation."

Aliyah offered her mother a high-five: Mom had gone toe-to-toe with the world's governments and come out on top.

Then she realized what Mom had won, and her hand dropped to her side.

"None of this would be possible without the political capital Mr Tsabo generated in five years of activism, of course," the general continued. "Some members of the President's cabinet believe the current laws are too harsh on otherwise law-abiding 'mancers. So the current agreement is that officially, SMASH will continue to pursue 'mancers aggressively in the United States. But we've also entered into negotiations with former members of Project Mayhem…"

"You mean Robert," Valentine interrupted.

Imani frowned. "I mean we have spoken to many Project Mayhem members to facilitate a new wave of government approved black ops 'mancer safehouses, in order to explore the possibility of humanely fostering safer magical practices to stem the broach."

Valentine rolled her eye. "So… you talked to Robert."

"We spoke with many people," Imani bristled. "But… yes. Mostly Robert."

The Unimancers stepped forward, hands clenched into fists. "They're *legalizing* a terrorist operation?"

"No," Imani shot back, cutting the general off. "Project Mayhem is dismantling. This is a new, top secret organization for alternative 'mancer rehabilitation."

"An organization staffed with ex-terrorists."

The ex-terrorists didn't bother Aliyah. But Project Mayhem's "rehabilitation" hadn't helped her *at all* in Morehead. They'd leave hundreds of 'mancers to rot under government control.

"That's *bullshit*!" she cried.

Mom turned around, shocked. "Aliyah! Language!"

"Fucking *language?!*" Aliyah stepped forward; Mom flattened back up against the maps. "You're going to weaponize 'mancers all over again, and you're worried about my *language*?"

Mom's face darkened. She slapped the map, as though bouncing off a wrestling ring's ropes, to loom over Aliyah. "We're not *weaponizing* anyone. Weaponizing 'mancers is how the broach started! If Robert thought this was a military op, he'd shut it down–"

" –I *told* you this was Robert–" Valentine purred.

Mom pointed up at the ceiling, trying to stab that Thing by willpower alone. "What we're doing is legalizing the exploration of magics *other* than Unimancy to see whether anything *stops* this!"

"*No!*"

Her mother went deathly quiet. "What do you mean, no?"

"*I. Mean. No.*"

When Aliyah spoke, every Unimancer in Europe voiced Aliyah's dissent.

General Kanakia held up his hands. "Gentlemen. This isn't negotiable. Paul Tsabo has skills, and–"

"*He does not deserve them.*"

Daddy spasmed – hurt his daughter had spoken first.

"Aliyah Rebecca Tsabo-*Dawson*!" Mommy said. "The United States government has griped about SMASH's black-book funding for years! I've convinced them there are other ways! Rebel, and America might block SMASH's access!"

"America wants results, *Mom*. Dad *can* do great things – but he can't be trusted to do them on his own. We're taking him off his euclidosuppressants."

Aliyah, no, Ruth thought. *You can't bring him into the collective, you don't want his memories mixed with yours–*

That won't happen, Aliyah thought, feeling the collective choose her – her! – as their leader. *He knows how to join 'mancies without fusing with the Unimancers. We'll join with him, make his broach-healing secrets our own.*

So what you're saying is…

We'll back his techniques with our strength, Aliyah told them. *We'll have seven thousand Paul Tsabos smashing that Thing tomorrow morning. When we wipe it from the planet, the world will trip over themselves to fund us.*

There were objections: government funding wasn't based on gratitude, bureaucracies dispensed money based on a complex web of obligations and budgetary needs, and–

The objectors got shouted down.

Consensus.

She'd fused the collective's conflicting trains of thought: yes, her father had unique talents, but there was *nothing* the Unimancers could not do.

"Tomorrow morning, we'll join with you, Mr Tsa… I mean, Daddy." Daddy hyperventilated. "We'll channel your knowledge to rip that Thing apart. If that's what we need to do to show the world Unimancy is the only *safe* 'mancy, then we'll do it."

Her father held out his wrists, offering to be handcuffed. She pulled his face against her chest.

"It's the right thing, Daddy." She stroked his hair. "You know this."

"Think carefully, Aliyah." Sweat rolled down General Kanakia's cheek. "You're leading a rebellion against the policies that gave SMASH global judicial powers. Are you certain you want to do this?"

"No." Aliyah held her father protectively. "But it's what we need to do to save you from Daddy."

THIRTY-EIGHT
Blue Valentine

The Unimancers had checked in on Valentine aggressively since she'd arrived – but after the rebellion, they shadowed her like a paranoid store clerk trailing a black woman in a Hermes store. Unimancers popped out from behind half-crumbled walls as she walked through the camp.

Each of them eyeball-fucked her. She found it particularly unnerving when they conjoined forces, tracking where she'd be next, so when Valentine shied away from one angry Unimancer she found another staring straight into her eye.

It was a pretty good trick.

She tracked down Aliyah, curled up in what had once been a thrift shop. She and the redhead sat primly hip-by-hip, holding hands, staring dreamily into space.

The redhead – Ruth? – snapped out of their happy trance to shoot Valentine an angry glare. It was all too familiar: Valentine had seen the *get your skanky ass away from my boyfriend* death glare whenever she went out dancing.

Valentine chucked a curt nod in redhead's direction: *She and me gotta talk. You know that, I know that, now shut the fuck up*.

Redhead's lips went white as she swallowed back responses; Aliyah squirmed as a tide of insults flowed through her brain.

Valentine chucked her Nintendo DS onto Aliyah's lap.

"You still play?" she asked.

Aliyah turned the Nintendo over in her hands like an

archaeologist examining some precious artifact. She smiled at the familiar dents and scratches, the faded *Pokémon* stickers.

She touched it as though it had been years since she'd seen a videogame, not months.

Aliyah peered into the screen as though hoping to conjure up some distant memory from it. Then she twitched, unsettled, placing the Nintendo on the floor between them.

"That's baby stuff," Aliyah said.

"Huh," Valentine said. "I wondered when that'd happen."

Surprise spread across Aliyah's face, cascaded over to Ruth's. "Really?"

"When I was a child, my future was full of astronauts, firemen, and archaeologists." Valentine frowned. "Which would have been a much better world than the one I got. Seriously, you got to be a videogamemancer when you were, what? Five?"

"Six." Aliyah looked exuberant.

"How many six year-old girl hobbies does a teenaged kid keep? I figured one day you'd change 'mancies."

"I like it better in here."

"Course you do. You can offload your bad luck to squadrons of flux-sponges who get bad colds and trip a lot."

Aliyah's chest heaved with relief. "Precisely."

"You got friends."

"Yes."

"You've something to fight for."

Aliyah fought off tears. "*Yes.*"

"So do you think fucking up your memories to be popular is a good thing?"

The line hit Aliyah like a slap across a face. Which, you know, Valentine had planned, but that didn't make it any easier.

"Look." Valentine softened. "Unimancy ain't my thing, but I'm glad you got the friends you wanted." She rolled her eye in Ruth's direction. "But you're forgetting parts of yourself to get along with them."

Aliyah cracked her knuckles, the inevitable sign the kid was getting het up. "What parts?"

"Like forgetting how joining 'mancies involves two conflicting world views putting *aside* their ego? It's not like your dad and I have a lot in common; our 'mancy didn't happen through metaphysical arm-wrestling. It's dancing. You remember how to dance with magic? Or are you too scared?"

Ruth glowered. "She doesn't need your help."

"She doesn't need yours, either." Valentine flicked her fingers, encompassing the Unimancer network. "After all, connecting through 'mancy was what Aliyah *did* before she met you."

Ruth leapt up. "*You watch your mouth, sl–*"

The word had been about to be "slut." A harsh look from Aliyah slammed Ruth's lips together.

"What?" Valentine arched her eyebrows in a mockery of innocence. "Don't like me reminding you there were others before you?"

Aliyah's look was the panicked look of every girl who'd been asked to count up her previous lovers in front of her current partner – OK, well, not strictly true, as Valentine realized her personal look would have been a quizzical squint before reaching for a calculator. The principle remained.

"Or maaaaaybe," Valentine said slowly, "you don't like me reminding you *I* can do things *you* can't. I get this works for you, Aliyah, but you're doing that Alcoholics Anonymous bullshit of believing your saving grace is universal–"

Ruth stepped close. "I think you should go."

"I think *Aliyah* gets to tell me that."

Ruth clapped Valentine on the shoulder – right where the burning plastic in the Snow White Special had blistered her arm. "You've got no magic here. No Kanakia to protect you. I'd step carefully, because one accident and–"

Valentine slapped Ruth hard enough that she spun once before hitting the ground.

Aliyah, at least, had been horrified by Ruth's threat – well, who knew whether it was actually the kid's threat? The Unimancers hated her. Maybe they'd egged Ruth into it.

Still, she had a point to make, so she towered over Ruth as

the Unimancers surrounded her.

"You think I'm *afraid* of death, you dotted dropping of chickenshits? Hey! You guys who tracked me back when I was on the run with Tyler – Robert, I mean – why don't you tell me whether *you* thought you could take me alive? You couldn't have. What about Payne? Rainbird? Anathema? Would *any* of them have joined hands to sing kum-bay-yah?"

Valentine whirled on Aliyah.

"*These* schmucks tell you they're the best and the brightest, Aliyah. *I say* they're 'mancer leftovers! Hell, I note two adolescent girls are riding roughshod over 'em – hey, I wonder why that is? Is it because mmmmmaybe the Great Unimancer hivemind consists of people weak enough to get *caught*?"

Aliyah flushed with embarrassment. "The Unimancers made me strong!"

"Paul's magic made *him* strong! I'm telling you, the hivemind and your dad's 'mancy *will not mix*."

Ruth wiped blood from her nose. "You're just afraid of how lonely you'll be once Paul doesn't need you."

Ruth spoke, yet Aliyah clapped her hands guiltily over her own mouth.

"That's not true," Valentine said.

Ruth dropped to her knees, hugging Aliyah, who kept her mouth covered, shaking her head. "I'm sorry, sweetie," she whispered, pleading forgiveness. "I shouldn't have spoken your thoughts, she made me so *mad...*"

"*I said, that's not true!*"

Aliyah stepped out from Ruth's embrace. "No. No, it's... it's OK, Ruth. Better the truth comes out."

"That's a fucking lie, Aliyah, I'm here to take care of–"

"You're here to play hero, Aunt Valentine."

Her words were deadly as arrows.

"Don't you fucking dare," Valentine told her. "After what I did to keep your ungrateful ass free from your father–"

"That's really it, isn't it? Grateful. You need to feel superior to someone, don't you?"

"Cut that Hannibal Lecter shit out. I'm not–"

"Where's Uncle Robert?"

Valentine snatched the Nintendo DS off the ground, grabbing her gift back.

"...Robert's working with Project Mayhem. His location is classified."

"You've been in Bastogne for weeks, Aunt Valentine." Aliyah spoke softly, a therapist talking a woman off a ledge. "You don't have his engagement ring. You've never even tried to call him."

"Maybe we had an argument. So what–"

"Did you break up with him before or after he proposed?"

"You..." Valentine's fingers curled around an imaginary controller.

She heard the soft *click* of Ruth unsheathing a Magiquell injector-pack. "Don't think about it."

If Aliyah had gone for her own taser, Valentine would have been OK. Valentine could shrug off endless cruelties, so if Aliyah'd showed the slightest hint of malice, Valentine would have let loose profanities to light people's hair on fire...

But instead, Aliyah spoke with pity.

"I've got friends, Aunt Valentine. We make rational decisions. You can knock us, but... we're sane." She slipped her fingers through Ruth's; Ruth shivered with forgiveness. "You can only connect with people more fucked-up than you are. You're trying to break me down so I'll need you again..."

"That's not why I'm *doing* this! You are about to unleash havoc! This – it isn't about my abandonment–"

"Then why didn't you accept Uncle Robert's proposal?"

"*Fuck you!*" Valentine screamed. "*Fuck you, you stupid brat! I'm here when people need me! And–*"

"That's the problem, Aunt Valentine." The Unimancers placed their fists over their hearts. "Nobody needs you anymore. Not like you are."

Valentine gaped.

Aliyah reached out – they all reached out. "Join us," they muttered, a chorus of affirmation. "We're *all* heroes here."

Valentine spun in a circle; more Unimancers arrived, arms open. Valentine tried to imagine being with them – effortlessly dispersing her flux to professionals, knowing someone would remember her when she was gone.

She turned the Nintendo DS over in her hands.

"I'll do it," she said. "On one consideration."

Aliyah sighed in relief. "Anything."

Valentine extended the DS in Aliyah's direction. "You play a game of *Mario*. Just you. None of this jiggly-eyeball shit. Enjoy one game of *Super Mario* the way you used to, and I'll sign up. Show me you're in there because you *want* to be, not because you're afraid *not* to be."

The other Unimancers swiveled to look at Aliyah expectantly. She stepped away from the Nintendo. "Aunt Valentine, I... no. That's dangerous."

"It's also fun! Remember the joy of imagination, instead of coloring within someone else's lines? Remember all those crazy 'mancies, watching people uncover new worlds within themselves?"

Aliyah ran her fingers down her scars. "That's... not what we do here."

Valentine bobbed the Nintendo up and down as if preparing to play Rock, Paper, Scissors with it.

"It's what I do," she told them, and walked away.

A guard broke off, following her–

"Keep your distance, pork chop."

A flicker of Aliyah's concern ripped across the guard's face; he dropped back. Valentine stormed into the woods – *fuck it, if I get lost, let the all-powerful Unimancers lead me back*–

She'd been *so* tempted to join.

She'd like to chalk her resistance up to strength of character – but the truth was, once she was in the Unimancers she'd never be with Robert again.

All their support couldn't add up to one-tenth the joy she felt hugging Robert as hard as she wanted, knowing he'd never break.

She considered opening up a satellite feed – but the Unimancers would never let her call Robert. Robert was their enemy.

She might get a call through if she begged Aliyah that she

needed to hear her boyfriend's voice, and *fuck* sounding like some jilted bride.

Even if she got through, what would she say? "How are you doing?" She *knew* how he was doing. He was doing *OK*. She was falling apart, keeping going only by dint of being *useful* to someone, and Robert was karate-chopping FBI agents and politicking like a boss and safeguarding poor innocent 'mancers against this one-therapy-fits-all incursion the Unimancers peddled, and what would she say?

I'm lonely.

And the truth was, Robert would have left Project Mayhem to be with her. But she didn't want him to give up anything; she'd wanted him happy, even if that meant he went to places she didn't belong.

How could he fix her complaints? She'd hidden her misery from him because she couldn't stand for Robert to see her as anything other than the phoenix queen – someone great and powerful and untouchable.

Now she'd shoved him away. And if she called now, she knew what he'd say:

I love you. But I won't drop this important work and get my bruised heart used to having you in my life again, only to have you jet off when you find someone who needs you more. One word, and I'll abandon everything to be with you. But if I leave all this behind, then… I need to know I'm more than this dude you fuck.

Say you need me, Valentine. Say it, and I'll be there before sunrise.

She hugged herself. That *is* what he'd say, she was sure, word for word. She knew Robert so well. She knew even after she'd driven him away, they still stared up at the same stars at night: sleepless, restless, loveless.

All she'd have to do would be to admit that she needed him.

"Fuck you," she whispered. "Fuck you for being right." She didn't know whether she meant Robert or Aliyah, but why was *yes* so fucking hard when quips came so easily?

She curled up. Tomorrow, she'd be needed.

She'd waited all her life for one chance to be useful. And as cold dew condensed on her skin, she knew she'd find it tomorrow.

THIRTY-NINE
Let the Bodies Hit the Floor

Valentine negotiated one last visit with Paul before the Unimancers hauled him out to seal the broach.

She'd tried to talk the Unimancers into letting her see Imani, but no soap; five Unimancers kept Imani and General Kanakia in isolation. *The kid knows who the real danger here is.*

Paul sat in a chair, hands dangling between his knees, an IV line corkscrewing from his chest. A single Unimancer guarded him: a skinny Pakistani grandmother with her thumb on the methohexital syringe. Two walked in behind her, stun batons out. Their eyeballs jittered, indicating every word spoken in their presence would be analyzed by battalions of psychomancers.

Paul's fingers drifted up to the scabs on his head where Valentine had whacked him with the branch; a wan salute.

"Thanks," he said.

She squeezed his shoulder. "Any time."

Valentine liked imagining the Unimancers working furiously to untangle that dense communication: Paul's quiet admission he'd needed Valentine to beat him back to sanity, her reassurance that smacking each other down when they went too far was part of their friendship, and all was forgiven.

Their friendship had never needed words to function.

"Don't," she said. *Don't join 'mancies with them to heal the broach.*

He shook his head. *I owe them that much.*

She jerked off an imaginary dick.

He directed her gaze to the Pakistani woman, the two Italian men. "They're not NPCs, Valentine. We murdered a hundred and fifty people."

"Check your math, Paul. We took out at least seven on the airfield, too. Hell, that first broach back in Long Island? I think we slaughtered twenty."

Paul dug his nails into his thighs. "This isn't funny, Valentine. We fucked up."

She held up two fingers. "Two reasons why I'm not losing sleep about that, Paul. I'd feel bad thinking they were mindless husks, if they hadn't gone out of their way to *present* themselves as that. They pretend to be a faceless, neutered mass to America so they don't freak the mundanes – and then they hunted us down, telling the world they plan to erase our minds. What the fuck did they *expect* us to do?"

The Unimancers tensed. *Hope that fucks with your consensus*, she thought.

Paul nodded, making room for her point. "Your second rationale?"

"Murdering two hundred people will look like a slumber party once these chuckleheads rip open the broach. They'll try to use your skills to fix the broach, but these assmunches don't know how to play nice."

Valentine's guards stepped forward, ready to haul her away – but their eyes glowed with new orders. Aliyah, curious to see what Aunt Valentine would say.

Paul sighed. "You're not the easiest to work with. Yet we've done great 'mancy together."

"Because we compromised! These idiots can't compromise! The instant they don't get their way, they break down like a bridezilla!"

"We both want to seal the broach."

"For the wrong reasons! Look, when I beat you up, you had a great plan and terrible intentions. Now *she's* got great intentions and a terrible plan. And I'm out of sticks to beat her."

"And I do?"

Her stomach churned. She thought he'd have found a stick by now.

"Look. Even if I wanted to stop them, there's no help for miles around. The townspeople are on their side. Maybe I bust broaches again – assuming they don't knock me out, what's the end game? You know Aliyah. She won't stop until I kill her. You think I'll have the willpower left to seal up rifts after... after I do *that*?"

No wonder Aliyah let Paul speak. She knew how beaten her father was. "So devise another plan–"

"I'm tired of plans." He closed his eyes and inhaled; Valentine knew he must be remembering the barbecue scent of those burning bodies. "My plans hurt people. Let someone else make the decisions for a change."

"They've made the decisions for seventy yea–"

A gloved hand clamped around her shoulder. "It's time."

The guards escorted them out into the cool chill of an autumn morning.

The sunrise terrified her.

She'd not paid much attention to the broach when she'd arrived; she'd been too shaken by the mass murder, too busy taking out her guilt on the general, too busy worrying whether Paul would die of exhaustion. But now...

The sun winked out for periods as it vanished behind shards of that alien sky. When the sun crept behind the demon dimension's intrusions, the whole sky went dark except for one glowing, white-hot jagged spotlight that shone down on Paul.

Valentine's skin crawled. It knew Paul was coming.

Then the sun crept upwards through the patchwork sky, the light filtered – missing colors, missing gamma rays, missing radiation. Sometimes the light strobed into raindrop-like, flash-camera bursts. Other times, the water in the air crystallized into snowflakes.

It didn't make sense. The sun disappearing for a moment shouldn't transform the whole landscape.

The demon dimensions had poisoned the land.

All the while, that Thing slithered between the gaps. Clusters of opalescent eyes bulged through as the Thing pressed its weight upon the rifts, raining down clouds of buzzsects. Sometimes, Paul leaned against a tree to catch his breath, and there would be a splintering crackle like two cows being slammed together, and Valentine would look above to see the Thing had smashed segmented fingers the size of a trailer truck down through the sky, trying desperately to work its way in.

Could he *fight* this Thing?

Guards appeared, towing Imani. They allowed her one silent hug with her husband before dragging her away.

Then Valentine saw the sixty Unimancers lined up in the flowering field.

The field was dotted with beautiful blue hydrangeas, even though the autumn frost should have withered them. Something powerful had regrown the woods here – something so good it had almost restored Earth-level physics.

The flowers smelled like Aliyah's hair.

Aliyah and Ruth stood together, hands entwined in the field's center like blushing brides. Well, brides in black Kevlar uniforms. They smiled at each other shyly, welcoming Paul into the Unimancers' circle, as though this were a beautiful ceremony and not some desperate attempt at warfare.

Someone jabbed a stun gun into her spine – a clear warning to stop. Paul took a few steps forward, then noticed Valentine falling behind.

"May I hug my friend before I start?" he asked.

The Unimancers hesitated, then allowed Valentine to step forward. She hesitated; Paul's stiff hugs always felt like she was being seized by some awkward praying mantis.

He whispered in her ear: "They'll be distracted at the beginning. Make a run for it. Get back to Robert."

She pretended to take solace in his spindly arms. "You're gonna need me, Paul."

"We both know that's not good for you," Paul said.

She hugged him for real. The world was about to end, and all Paul thought about was her.

Of course she couldn't leave.

Paul stepped towards Aliyah's waiting arms.

FORTY
Wrong Donut

Paul felt the pressure of that Thing overhead, like an elephant standing on a cracked glass ceiling. It had gone still, poised somehow, waiting to see what Paul would do next.

He waved Valentine and Imani back; he could keep himself safe, but didn't want them caught in a crossfire of warring physics.

Aliyah reached out to him. Paul felt the Unimancers lining up behind her like a circuit. Once he grasped her hand, they'd probe his thoughts to shape him into a weapon against the broach.

Paul wanted a donut.

No, he wanted the right donut.

And he didn't know what the right donut was.

He walked towards Aliyah, a hundred minds joining her with each step, their power focusing on him. Yet all he could think was, *You don't want a Vanilla Kreme.*

It was a ludicrous thought, but Kit was right. Paul had been a conservative cruller man all his life, his tastes expanding to glazed chocolate when he got freaky. A Vanilla Kreme? A sticky frosting grenade? Showering powdered sugar with every bite, filling his belly with empty calories? It was the donut of someone who didn't care about consequences.

What else had he acquired a taste for, as the War Bureaucromancer?

Aliyah wriggled her fingers. "Come on, Daddy. Let's fix this. Your laws, our strength."

He felt broken. An unfit tool to do the job.

Maybe their strength would heal him.

Gripping Aliyah's hand felt like reaching blindly into a donut box, hoping this would be the confection he needed.

Curious minds stampeded into his body.

Paul's muscles spasmed as his limbs were seized by conflicting signals, strangers barging in to examine the transtibial stump below his right knee, flex the remaining toes on his left foot, inhaling to test his still-healing ribs.

They jostled his thoughts away, elbowed inside his brain like shoppers on Black Friday when the doors snapped open. They tore open locks to get at his memories, ravenous to ransack their enemy's secrets. They tossed his memories into a messy heap until he couldn't remember who the burning girl was or why this one-eyed woman played games or how this beautiful lawyer had kissed him.

His name dissolved, losing meaning, becoming significant only because a thousand men murmured it – *Tsabo it's Tsabo Paul Tsabo –*

(One faint cry of *Daddy* before the lone familiar voice was swept away)

He didn't mind losing memories. So many were painful.

But this disorganization would not do.

This invasion had underpinnings – the hivemind had never thought it had rules. Yet there was something akin to an operating system, some methodology determining who got to speak and when. Paul sought out the rough agreements they'd forged, codified them, restructured the collective so they entered his brain according to a descending order of need–

What is he doing

Stop no that's not our way

mmmmmaybe the Great Unimancer hivemind consists of people weak enough to get caught?

The hive mind pounded on Paul's rule-jail. Paul's orderliness flowed through them, and as the Unimancers fled they were forced to put each memory back where they'd found it.

Aliyah what the hell did he do

It's OK guys that's just the first exchange, you went in strong, I told you Daddy had powers

They retreated, uncertain, jangling. Yet their terror was intoxicating: they saw him as some inhuman instrument of revenge, potent, unstoppable.

Oh, how Paul wished he was that indomitable.

Aliyah ran through mansions, yanking open doors containing memories of all the precious things lost to broaches.

Yet this wasn't mourning: she emphasized the wrongs they could right with her father in the collective, promising them Daddy would ensure the world kept this beauty.

Daddy. Show them what to do.

Thousands rooted for him – ready to wick away his flux, a stadium of cheering supporters funneling strength into whoever they designated as their chosen champion.

As their champion, he understood what Aliyah found here. He'd always seen Unimancy as a horrendous twisting of magic, squeezing uniqueness into conformity – but through Aliyah's eyes, he saw how they'd created a caring paradise to share with each other, and oh God, Paul was happy to find magic was always gorgeous at its heart.

It had been a solitary pleasure, healing broaches – like rearranging books. And he'd been precariously slow in Morehead, the buzzsects knocking down a book whenever he'd replaced one.

Bastogne was a library of books lying broken-backed on the floor, with hundreds of snot-nosed children ready to pull the shelves down.

Yet the collective held thousands of librarians at his beck and call.

He *could* heal the broach with them.

But where to begin?

He reached out tentatively, probing the extent of the damage. Everything out here was broken, the rules shifting with each footstep. The sky was a mismatched jigsaw puzzle. There were a thousand places to mend the landscape, but...

He wanted to reclaim one square inch.

Which felt so foolish.

He was certain he could restore one square inch to full beauty – yet if it was like Morehead, that inch would take days to undo the subtle fractures. One microzone of Earth-perfect laws, a tiny diamond of precision.

It would shine like a jewel.

Things were so ruined, it would take him days to create a space the size of an ice cube. Yet he imagined the satisfaction of repairing the land with a watchmaker's fastidiousness, then planting that idealized version of Earth in the demon-rifts like a seed, unfolding into a space so pure no broach could grow in it...

Cold funerals filled Paul's memories. Messy deaths replayed in his brain – all the Unimancers who'd sacrificed themselves to hold the broach back. The collective's rage rose within him.

A reparation they could fit within a drinking glass was insufficient revenge.

You have power, Ruth told him. *Use it!*

I can't, Paul said. *The last time I used power like that, I...*

You thought to go to war with me? Me?! *When bureaucracy is the* language *of war!*

He felt so ashamed, bellowing threats like some tin-pot dictator. Yet it had been so comforting to worry about nothing but his daughter, to look out at men he'd maimed and feel *satisfaction*, that Vanilla Kreme disregard...

We want that

Paul scowled. *What?*

We could never stop you, the hivemind told him. *Our might meant nothing. But you're with us now – use our might to disembowel that Thing...*

Paul remembered living men torn apart – but through the Unimancers, those hundred and fifty dead became his audition.

They had no need for a meek man who crouched beneath a broken sky and chipped out a *sample*.

They needed the War Bureaucromancer.

And hadn't that been his error? He'd wasted years nudging American lawmakers into doing the moral thing, when all he'd accomplished had been wiped away in one bad headline.

When he'd been the War Bureaucromancer, he'd been as merciless as a bullet.

The Unimancers encouraged him: *Yes. Yes. Think larger.*

Paul summoned his 'mancy, feeling the pleasure as his thoughts snapped into alignment with the Unimancers, trying to recall the certainty he'd felt as he stepped out of that burning crater. What would the War Bureaucromancer do?

Whatever the world needed to battle that Thing in the sky.

What had God said when He'd created the universe?

Let there be light.

FORTY-ONE
Snap Back to Reality, Whoops, There Goes Gravity

Paul filled his body with light – not trivial illumination, but the *concepts* of light.

He felt photon-cascades rocketing down from outer space, plunging through the atmosphere, ricocheting off trees.

He felt gravity's subtle flow tugging straight-lined photons into slender arcs that barely bent as they soared across continents.

He fused with the collective's understanding to fathom the electromagnetic spectrum's great sweep – the knife-like sprinkle of gamma rays, infrared's warm radiation, the shriek of radio waves...

A million laws had to converge to create light. Paul envisioned the universe as a great terrarium, and light itself as this fragile creature that could be extinguished if any of those factors failed – *had* failed, in the demon dimensions.

He ordered the collective to gather the laws into one great sword, raising it high above the Earth. He formed his awareness into a sharp edge to punch Earth-style physics deep into the demon dimensions – a reverse broach.

A better world, he thought, exhaling.

The Unimancers could only do Unimancy; their low tide of debate quashed the certainty a 'mancer needed. They tried to hold him back, protesting bureaucracy wasn't what drove the universe...

Paul swept their objections aside. The universe was governed by regulations, orderly laws that controlled the spin of atoms.

All universes should be so governed.

And as the Unimancers fell into place behind him, Paul would make the demon dimensions orderly.

No wonder Aliyah had been so potent in here. Most of the captured Unimancers had been caught after their first 'mancy generated enough bad luck to call SMASH down on their heads. Whereas Paul had followed his unique obsession for years, every act of 'mancy reinforcing his viewpoint until he was incapable of viewing the world through anything *but* the lens of forms, laws, and regulations.

He loaded his surety onto the collective until their willpower broke. They'd been starved of victory for decades, needed it so badly they'd agree with anyone who promised triumph.

They organized underneath his guidance, forming ranks, chains of command, communications protocols.

He reached up into the heavens to slam Light into the broken sky.

The dimensional collage overhead shivered, edges blurring as they fused into one unified whole. The chunks glowed a fiery orange as the light fought its way through, like glass heating in an oven–

Warm yellow sunlight flooded down across the field.

For the first time in years, the sky over Bastogne was a clear, unbroken blue.

Sixty-seven Unimancers gasped.

There was no time to luxuriate; light was their first beachhead. The sun illuminated battalions of unthinkable beasts that chewed up light and shat alien ideas.

He swept his hands up like a conductor, commanded the Unimancers to send the second wave crashing in.

Paul took the wedge he'd driven into the demon dimensions and poured all the rules Earth had to offer into it: gravity, mass, conservation of energy. He instructed the hivemind's scientists to find whatever crevices still ran on fragments of antiquated Earth rules and use them as anchor points.

The sky shuddered. Paul had turned classical physics into a virus, infecting demon dimensions in the ways the broach infected ours. He had to nourish these thin roots back to life...

Except what remained of Earth within the broach was dead scar tissue.

Paul bombarded the broach with Gravity and Time, resuscitating the fragments of Earth that had survived over the past seventy years. The scant microphysics he could nurture bloomed into odd variants – zones where the gravity-to-mass ratio skewed heavy, where the Bohr radius rounded down to five.

He tended to these mutant strains of Earth – but they rebelled at his touch, collapsing into chaos.

You wanted to spend weeks forming one miniscule perfection, he thought. He wished he had. If he'd done that instead of charging in, he would have discovered the broach was broken beyond repair. The broach was so wrecked all the 'mancers in the world could not restore it and

lynchpin

The heavens spoke, alien words slithering into Paul's brain.

The Thing in the sky had a voice. Each syllable it spoke threatened to snuff out Paul's heart.

The Unimancers shrieked in terror. *It spoke it's never spoken we didn't know it could speak*

we know you lynchpin

It clawed the sunlight away, revealing that white nothingness beyond.

"Get out." Paul pointed at the sky, calling down barrages of fundamental principles – the Thing couldn't exist on Earth, its mountainous body was a crazy quilt of paradoxes. He was the War Bureaucromancer, and he *would* drive this Thing back.

you think you are war

It stomped, and the sky cracked. Buzzsects poured out in an ichorous halo; they swallowed up Paul's laws and extruded an osseous armor around the Thing.

we are war

"No," Paul whispered.

A dark blaze spread from horizon to horizon with the languid pleasure of a cat licking its lips. The Thing spread multitudinous limbs out, still barred behind that stained glass sky – but the flames poured in, and it absorbed them into its body, became a mockery of the sun.

for you it is always fire

"*No!*" Paul screamed, feeling the collective panic. He tried to hold onto the War Bureaucromancer's bloody certainty, but no willpower on Earth could force this Thing back–

you hold the rules yet know not how to use them

we will use them

we will strip the rules from your bones and use them to unlock this cage

"No," Paul begged.

The Thing bent a finger and inverted gravity.

Slowly, inexorably, Paul tumbled upwards into the burning sky.

FORTY-TWO
Heart, Broken

Aliyah was shrieking at her father, begging him not to bring the heavens down on that Thing.

Daddy, no! she cried. *That's not bureaucromancy!*

She'd felt his urge to start small – *that* was the father she'd trusted. The man who'd spent months planning political rallies, carefully anticipating contingencies, worried sick someone might get hurt when SMASH showed up.

Daddy believed his magic sprung from his love of rules, but Aliyah had always known the truth: he'd learned to cast spells while working for a crappy insurance company that longed to refuse claims. Her father had harnessed their rules to subvert the system, getting people the money they needed.

Good work, Dad, she'd started to say. *We'll back you for as long as–*

A thousand protests drowned out her assurance.

The Unimancers were a military operation – and to them, Paul Tsabo was a weapon. They didn't understand his 'mancy involved hours of careful planning, were infuriated that Paul the gun balked at being fired.

No, wait–

Their 'mancy infiltrated his mind, brought him into line with their harmony, convinced him yes, he needed to go bigger, and Aliyah shrieked her head off as they rolled over her like a river.

She'd never been on a losing side of a Unimancer argument.

But now she was the minority vote, and they silenced her.

Consensus.

She stood frozen while her father rearranged the Unimancers to his liking, then assaulted the Thing in the sky, and the Thing shrugged off their best efforts–

It's broken it's too broken we can't fix this no one can fix this

Aliyah's heart thumped as her father wailed–

He rose into the sky.

Save him! Aliyah thought. But she was one voice among thousands.

The general broadcast calm, issuing orders – but her father had laced the hivemind with regulations. In his absence, the confused remnants couldn't remember who was authorized to speak to who; they were manacled by chains of command.

They had thought they were war. The Thing proved them wrong.

Ruth, Aliyah thought, *help me*. But Ruth, too, was frozen – the Mom-construct had sensed danger, was analyzing the ramifications and deluging Ruth with details. Ruth was in a screaming fight with an unthinking telemarketers' script that would not stop dispensing instructions–

Aliyah ran.

And though Aliyah sped to her father, she ran as herself – God, she'd gotten so used to the Unimancer's feedback loop honing her clumsy reflexes into athlete's grace. She tripped.

That Thing vomited out beast-armies, the sky seething with tentacles squirming towards her father–

Someone grabbed her shoulder.

"Get 'em to safety, kid." Valentine squinted towards the sky. "I got this."

Valentine looked heroic – a vision of her aunt the way she'd viewed her when she was six years old. Valentine viewed the sky without fear, as if the heavens aflame was another broken nail.

Aliyah remembered Aunt Valentine's kindnesses: giving her that first Nintendo DS in the burn ward, knowing a kid in pain needed as much distraction as she could get. Sticking

French fries into milkshakes with Aunt Valentine back at her apartment, then sticking them up their nose. The way Aunt Valentine had saved her with a secret gift of the right videogame at the right time.

That trust poured into the network, calmed them: seven thousand Unimancers grabbed onto Aliyah's unwavering conviction that Valentine would save them.

Valentine pressed her Nintendo DS into Aliyah's hands. "Keep this safe for me," she whispered, kissing Aliyah on the forehead.

Her hair sprouted out, black tresses becoming impossibly long, spreading out in great bat wings. A chunky pair of pistols appeared in her hands as her frilly goth-dress slimmed into a form-fitting black leather outfit.

"...Bayonetta?" Aliyah asked. Sometimes it was hard to tell who Valentine channeled, as she refused to adjust her weight to match gaming's skinny character models.

"I wish my default wasn't fighting games," Valentine said. "Tell your dad I apologize for kicking his ass." She chewed her lip. "Again."

She launched into the air in a trail of ruby fire, hair soaring out behind her, her body highlighted against the blackfire heavens...

She slammed into Paul's spine fist-first.

Aliyah winced; Aunt Valentine's go-to maneuver had been to catch Paul in a mid-air combo. Yet the visuals were electric as her father was tossed around like a rag doll. Encouraged, the Unimancers mustered willpower to drive back the unnatural conflagration. The inferno overhead sputtered into speckled smoke as they shouted their love into the broach.

"He's *mine!*" Valentine smacked Paul around, Paul jerking upwards as the Thing in the sky tried to wrest him away. "*I am the protector! I am the guardian! And you – will – not – have – my –* friend!"

With each word she smashed her elbow into Paul's cheek, fired her guns into his skull, claimed him with compassionate violence. The Thing in the sky roared, clawing Its way towards Paul–

Valentine flipped into a roundhouse kick that caught Paul in the stomach, sent him hurtling back down to Earth to slam into the ground. Imani rushed up next to Daddy, who was bleeding but not injured – videogame logic.

Paul leapt up screaming, reaching for Valentine.

Valentine lifted her fists in triumph, bobbing on streams of crimson energy. "Fuck *yeah*!" she cried–

Unlike Bayonetta, she did not float back down to Earth.

The flames above her circled into a shrinking vortex, the Thing stirring the remaining flames into a tornado.

Valentine tumbled upwards.

"*Oh yeah?*" Valentine tore off her eyepatch, flung it downwards like a duelist throwing down the glove. "*You want some of this, ugly? I got enough bullets for every demon you got!*"

She summoned a *Contra* cannon onto her shoulder, fired a glowing shot–

Except the stability Daddy had created had worn off. The sky fissured as Valentine unleashed her 'mancy, the last Earth's gravity cascading away.

"*Get some, motherfucker!*" she screamed, as she pinwheeled into the demon dimensions, firing madly at the buzzsects and rifters that rushed down to meet her. They ate furrows through her body, swarmed around the magical pistols in her hands. "*I did my job! I protected the ones I loved! It doesn't matter if I–*"

They ate her pistols.

They ate her arms.

They ate her mouth.

The heavens closed over Valentine's disintegrating remains as they were sucked up into the sky. There was a great burst of green light – Xbox light – and Valentine was gone.

PART IV

War Without Tears

FORTY-THREE
Miss You in the Saddest Fashion

Imani gave Paul and Aliyah two days to grieve. Any less, and they'd break under the weight she needed them to carry; any more, and time might run out.

Then she hauled Aliyah out to the place where everything had gone so wrong.

Paul sat on a stump, not having left the flowering field where Valentine had died. Imani had forced him to eat, but Paul silently caressed the bruises Valentine had left, pushing his fingers deep into her marks, ensuring they'd never fade.

The flowers in the grove continued to bloom as though Valentine hadn't been devoured, and the sky hadn't fractured further. The dimensional cracks above had deepened into a collapsed junkie's veins. Now convulsions seized the heavens, the Thing more determined than ever to smash down the gates.

Imani wasn't a 'mancer, and even she felt the sickness spreading across the sky.

Each skyquake took longer, as though the Thing gathered increasing strength with each blow. The fissures into the demon dimensions inched across the sky like a hairline crack spreading across a windshield.

It was coming for them.

She sat Aliyah down on the ground facing her father. Paul wore Valentine's eyepatch, ignoring Aliyah to study the blue blossoms at his feet; Aliyah opened and shut the Nintendo DS mechanically, as though it were a puzzle to be unlocked.

"Hey," Imani snapped.

They both looked up guiltily.

"You fucked up," she told them.

As expected, they both cringed. They *still* hadn't come to terms with the magnitude of what had gone wrong. They still didn't want to admit they had caused Valentine's death.

Their belief was pure when channeled properly. But as the divorce had taught Imani, that same belief could shunt inconvenient realities aside.

"Know why you fucked up?"

They looked up, eager for answers.

"Because you stopped fucking *talking* to each other."

She quashed a swell of anger as both her husband and daughter averted their gazes.

"I don't know what happened in the hivemind." Imani grabbed them both by the scruff of the neck. "I get you're ashamed. I get you don't want to talk to each other. But that's the only way we *work*.

"When we worked as a family, *nothing* could defeat us. Now you two are playing tug-of-war – we get *you* crashing in here to haul your daughter away whether she wants rescuing or not, and *you* commandeering the Unimancers to use your daddy like a socket wrench.

"That shit is *killing* people."

Imani closed her eyes, breathing hoarsely. It took a lot to get her to swear. But it felt like a fitting eulogy for Valentine.

"In case you have forgotten, *I'm* the mom here." She yanked their heads back, forcing them to look at the sky's sickening pulse. "As this family's matron, I am telling you *that is what we are here to stop*. As such, you two will work out your differences – any personal issues that get in the way of you saving the world *is our enemy*. And if you can't find a way to reconcile…"

She tugged Valentine's eyepatch, gripped the Nintendo DS Aliyah held.

"…I'm gonna take those mementoes away. Because you don't deserve to have a part of Valentine if you can't remember what she stood for."

She figured she'd done enough when they both hung their heads. Paul was so talented, her daughter was so powerful...

And both were so adrift.

What Imani had learned working for massive organizations is that after a corporation went bankrupt, reporters invariably pointed to the external problems facing the now-dead company – as though those obstacles had been what had toppled a billion-dollar industry.

But no. Those companies had stockpiles of brilliant minds, millions of dollars in cash to hire contractors, raw labor to make massive changes. But the brilliant minds squabbled and the cash got squandered and the labor got mistreated until that massive force was diffused into a whiff of stale bureaucracy.

Past a certain level of power, a corporation was like the *Titanic*. You could always steer around the iceberg, unless so many hands grabbed at the wheel that you plowed straight into avoidable catastrophes.

And if the apocalypse came, it would not be because of that Thing about, but because the incredible potency of Aliyah and Paul and General Kanakia and the Unimancers and herself could not align themselves.

Her family worked best when their power was concentrated into a piercing laser; her fear was that Paul and Aliyah would tear at each other until they were as ineffective as moonbeams.

But who could change a 'mancer's mind but another 'mancer?

"*Talk*," she said, hoping Valentine's legacy would be enough to enact change.

Having done all she could do, Imani walked back to the general's office to see if he had a drink stashed anywhere.

Paul and Aliyah sat quiet for a long time, doing their best not to look at the sky.

"...nice eyepatch," Aliyah ventured.

Paul lifted it up sheepishly, blinking as he exposed his covered eye to the wavering sunlight. "You like it? I'm down a foot, I'm down a best friend... I figure I might as well be down an eye." He rubbed his eyesocket with the heel of his palm. "I honestly don't know how she wore it. The *inside* has rhinestones."

"So did her bra."

Paul winced. "Don't remind me."

Aliyah smirked. "You know her problem with those bras, right?"

Paul buried his face in his hands, blushing. "Oh, God. Tell me she didn't come to *you* when–"

"–when it caught on her nipple ring, yeah." She raised her voice, doing a passable Valentine imitation. "'This fucker's got my tit like a fishhook, I'm telling you! Come extricate your aunt before I dangle this fucking bra off me like a Christmas ornament.'"

"I am *so* sorry for sticking you with that job," Paul said. "She tried to get me to be her tit-fixer. 'Paul, it's a breast, not a water balloon filled with acid. You'd help out if my earrings got tangled in my hair, right?'"

"Did you ever?"

"Oh, God no. I imagined your Mom walking in while I unstuck Valentine's nipple ring with a paper clip, and..."

They dissolved in laughter.

"I always figured she got Robert to scoop her out," Paul apologized.

"Nope." Aliyah smacked her lips, as if trying to get a terrible taste out of her mouth. "She said the sight would spoil their romance."

Paul massaged his temples. "I still haven't told Uncle Robert."

Mournful silence washed over them.

Neither of them liked looking up these days. The sky was their failure. Aliyah flipped the Nintendo DS open and shut, open and shut.

Paul craned his neck. "Have you played since..."

"I've tried."

She angled the Nintendo in her dad's direction, then pushed the start button to summon *Super Mario*'s first level. She left

Mario idle. After a minute, the screen wobbled, and the unit reset itself.

"It broke when Aunt Valentine... well, you know." She hunched over the Nintendo. "The collective's offered to help me repair it, but... I'm gonna leave it."

"You really don't play anymore, huh?"

Paul leaned forward on the stump, filled with wan hopefulness. Aliyah squeezed the Nintendo DS, wishing she could be what her father wanted her to be, feeling the correctness in refusing him.

"No. Just... too many bad memories when I play."

An exquisite look of pain crossed Paul's face. "It was... yeah. Lots of bad things happened when you played." He took the Nintendo DS away, absolving her. "I get it."

He didn't say, *I wanted magic to be as good for you as it was for me.* They both understood that. Aliyah had a kind of 'mancy, sure – but it was a regimented magic that traded art for comfort.

They moved with stiff ritual formality as Paul placed the Nintendo aside.

After a few minutes, the Nintendo blooped, broken, resetting. Aliyah thumped the grass with her heels.

"You don't have to play it," Paul told her.

She sobbed. "I'm not afraid of games, Dad. It's... She didn't *finish*. Her level's incomplete. Her *mission* was incomplete – and she died for such stupid reasons! If she'd died *beating* that Thing, I could–"

"Wait a minute," Paul snapped. "You'd be OK with Valentine dying?"

Aliyah's eyes went flinty. "If she went down taking out the broach? Goddamn straight I would. I'd hold a party if she'd saved Europe."

"No." His refusal was a whisper. "Aliyah, that's not this mission's point, we're keeping people safe–"

"That's the enemy."

"What?"

"Can you come with me?"

Paul squinted, confused; his daughter's anger had dissolved, yet he still quivered with rage: how could Valentine's death be *acceptable*?

Yet he heard the weary *please?* threaded through his daughter's command; she didn't want to fight any more than he did.

He let her lead him through the woods.

She led him up choked thickets, climbing a ridge. His artificial foot had never been good on uneven surfaces, the toes catching on underbrush, and the hill's steepness made him pant with exhaustion. She assisted him as best she could, but her eyes weren't jittering – for whatever reason, she was reluctant to call upon her Unimancy.

"Here." She stopped at a rocky outcropping overlooking a set of rough-hewn cabins at Bastogne's edge. The rough granite had been swept clear of brush; Paul realized Aliyah had sat here for the last two days.

Laughter carried up through echoes from the cabins. A family canned food for the winter, the mothers boiling bushels of fruit, the fathers stoking the fire, the children tasked with putting the fruit into jars, the grandparents supervising.

The littlest children broke off for impromptu games of tag; the parents corralled them, laughing merrily. They told incomprehensible stories in their thick dialect – though Paul could tell where the funny bits were from the lilt and pause.

"Look at them." Aliyah spoke in an astonished whisper. "They *saw* the sky crack open two days ago, witnessed that Thing lunging down. And yet... here they are. Canning food like they expect winter to come." She shook her head. "I keep thinking how brave they have to be."

Paul hesitated before putting his arm around her. She snuggled against him, blissful. "You could go down with them, you know. Help out."

She shook her head with slow certainty. "No. I'd ruin it for them. I'd try to perfect the canning process, or I'd get too caught up in playing tag the right way..." She tapped her scars. "I'm a 'mancer. I'm always going to be obsessed."

He closed his eyes. "I wanted you to be down there."

"That dream was dead when our apartment caught fire. You tried to save me with 'mancy. I got burned. And from there..."

She shrugged.

Her effortless dismissal of his dreams made Paul's chest hitch.

"...I've been trying to fix you, Aliyah."

"I know."

"I can't," he said, his voice cracking.

She cupped his cheek, serene, offering forgiveness. "I know."

"I fucked up in that fire. And I kept thinking if... if I changed America enough, if I found you the right place, I could erase your scars. I could give you that village. But I..."

YOU WILL LOSE YOUR DAUGHTER IN WAYS YOU NEVER IMAGINED

"I can save the world, Aliyah, but I can't save *you.*"

Paul collapsed, sobbing. Aliyah held him just long enough to show him she wouldn't leave him.

"Dad. Listen to me."

He sniffled, rubbing his cheeks.

"I'll never live in that village."

He squeezed his eyes tight, nodded reluctantly.

"But I can live up here." She patted her guardpost. "Protecting them. I can't lead the life I wanted – but I can make damn sure other people can. That's good, Dad. That's satisfying. That will *do.*"

Paul looked down, shamed by how much he needed to believe her.

"Can you let me do that, Dad? Can you let me serve in the Unimancers? Not as a mascot – as someone accomplishing something real. Protecting Bastogne. Protecting Morehead."

"Aliyah." Paul gripped her jacket. "You might die."

She thumped his chest. "*That's* the enemy."

"...what enemy?"

"The enemy that's stopping us from saving the world." She waved up at the broken sky, which throbbed like a tumorous heart; a child dropped a jar of peaches, got scooped up in a grandmother's hug. "We all need to do this – you and me and Mom and Ruth and the Unimancers and General Kanakia. And you can't *make* this safe. I might die sealing this rift–"

"Aliyah, don't say th–"

"*I might die, Dad*. I don't *want* to die. But as long as you'll do anything to protect me, we'll fail all over again. And... too much is at stake."

Paul froze, taking in the immensity of what she asked of him.

She forced him to look at her. "If you love me, Dad, you have to let me go. Now tell me. Tell me you're OK with me dying."

He thrashed in her grip. "I can never be OK with that. I can never–"

"Would you sacrifice your life for me?"

"Yes."

"Have you sacrificed your happiness for me?"

"You know I have."

"Then do this for me, Dad. If I can't be in the village... help me be its guardian."

FORTY-FOUR
Uncomfortable Mortalities

I can't, Paul thought, trembling. *I can't do this...*

Then he looked into her eyes, and realized the only hope Aliyah had of being happy came with the risk of her death.

More than anyone, Paul knew what would happen to him if she died. He'd lived that experience already – he'd imagined her funeral in the burn ward, listening to Aliyah scream as the doctors pulled necrotic flesh off her. He'd laid down in a dumpster once, rotting in the garbage, believing he'd never see her again – and the loss had been so great it had crippled him. He'd been reduced to a breathing corpse, letting cockroaches crawl in his ears.

And he and Imani had been estranged, then. Aliyah's death would punch a hole through their rekindled marriage, extinguish any possibility of joy, condemn him to years of inescapable anguish.

Aliyah smiled, offering encouragement.

A smile he hadn't seen since the fire.

"Yes," he said, swallowing back tears. "I'll help you be the guardian."

"Then help me heal the Unimancers," she asked.

FORTY-FIVE
All Locked Doors Must Open

The first woman Aliyah had ever killed told her how 'mancers were created. It was, Anathema had explained, a simple formula: "Misery. Withdrawal. Obsession. 'Mancy."

A surprising number of 'mancers had stumbled upon their magic after a bad breakup.

Hell, her daddy's bureaucromancy had been spurred by Mom asking for a divorce. The collective was saturated with memories of sundered relationships – so Aliyah understood that after breakups, people sometimes conceded places. That restaurant you'd dined at was too painful to go to, and intolerable when you saw the man you still loved there on a date with someone else, so you just… stopped going.

She'd never understood how that worked until she and Ruth had broken up.

And the collective had become the restaurant she couldn't bear to go to.

Yet as she helped Daddy limp down to Bastogne, approaching the muddy field where she and Aunt Valentine had once stolen his leg, Aliyah realized she'd have to hook back into Unimancy. You couldn't sever the tie, but with a bit of work you could relegate it to background noise.

Even as background noise, Aliyah heard her ex-girlfriend appointing herself leader of the *"Paul Tsabo needs to be executed"* faction.

Which, she supposed, was to be expected: Ruth had always had parental issues.

They emerged from the treeline, the shanty-town patchwork of Bastogne looming large before them. The Unimancers worked like busy ants to repair the town's damage; they didn't know what to do about the worsening broach overhead, so instead they'd channeled their efforts into hammers and nails, sawing wood as if to gift Bastogne's residents with a beautiful town to live in before the apocalypse fell. They were perched across the plank-bridges that linked the crumbling brick buildings, repairing walls, thatching leaky roofs, anything physical that could distract from the howling chaos that roiled through their networked minds.

She braced herself, opened her mind to the collective. It felt like a dog pound – everyone barking, vying to drown out the competition.

Seventy years and we've never sealed a broach

Valentine was right we're 'mancer dregs

No Tsabo weakened us with his rules

He had new magic we didn't know the Thing could talk there's so much we don't know

Men like him cause broaches their magic rips open holes

Because we fight them we scare them broaches form when two magics collide

We have to bring everyone into the collective...

Ruth had been repairing a broken door on the stables. But she dropped her screwdriver as Aliyah led Paul into the cracked cobblestones of the town square.

Aliyah saw Ruth's leather-clad hips, longed to slide her arms around them. She felt Ruth's regret boiling up, felt Ruth running her hand down her thigh as a sad replacement for Aliyah's touch.

Then Ruth's anger exploded into the collective:

You made me choose between keeping the world safe and keeping you as a girlfriend

Aliyah shook her head. *You know it's not that way.*

Then give us Tsabo –

—call him Daddy, call him Paul, call him a human name —

—I call him Tsabo. I call him enemy. When he wanted to kill us, he could do anything — but when it came time to save the world, we gave him all our power and he failed. Untamed 'mancy creates murder.

The Unimancers put their tools neatly away, clambered down from Bastogne's multi-layered heights to form a tribunal circle around them.

Ruth wrinkled her nose. *I can't believe you're still talking to him after what he did to Valentine...*

Who you also hated, Aliyah pointed out.

The Mom-construct cleared her throat, a teacher starting class. *The impact of Valentine's sacrifice has strewn great conflict within the collective. Hatred of Valentine DiGriz is no longer a given position; after seeing her sacrificial actions during the last broach, some feel she made some valid points about the hivemind's demographics—*

Ruth snarled. *Stop explaining shit, Mom! I know what I think! And why am I not putting a bullet through this motherfucker's brain after he nearly got us killed?*

The Mom-construct, again. *Now Ruth, you know there's great conflict over what danger Paul Tsabo exposed us to. There's an ongoing discussion of our potential culpability in not investigating Paul Tsabo enough, of rushing to judgment—*

Ruth dug her fingers into her thighs. *And if you were smart enough to remember what I thought,* Mom, *you'd know my opinion is that I should have killed the bastard back at Morehead—*

Aliyah took Ruth's hand. *You need to talk to him, Ruth.*

Tell me what he'd say. Aliyah felt Ruth yanking on the locked doors in Aliyah's mind. *You're keeping secrets from me. You're keeping secrets from us.*

Unimancers keep no secrets, Ruth — only surprises. And we need a surprise.

"Talk, Dad." Aliyah elbowed him.

The Unimancers crowded into Ruth's skull to see things from her perspective. The hivemind fragmented at the sight of her father — some saw the dark circles under Paul's eyes and marked him as an out-of-control maniac.

But some recognized Paul's haggard face for what Aliyah

knew it to be: a man in torment.

Dad stood before Ruth, a full-grown man in a rumpled suit wringing his hands before a teenager. He muttered to himself, knowing all his excuses were insufficient.

Ruth headed back to the stable, leaning down to pick up her screwdriver. "I've got no time for this bullshit. Nothing you can say will–"

"I'm sorry."

Ruth's head snapped around as if he'd fired a gun at her. "*Pardon* me?"

Paul sucked in a breath between clamped teeth, forestalling tears. "I thought SMASH teams were... were brainwashed into government control. I thought destroying an individual body was like clipping a toenail. But..."

He squeezed his eyes shut.

"I realize I was – I am – a murderer."

Ruth looked down at him imperiously. "You see, Aliyah?"

"I killed a hundred and fifty people." His voice quavered as he addressed the crowd. "And I... I killed SMASH operatives – soldiers – people – back when I dropped an earthquake on them to rescue me from a drug dealer. I killed more of them when I lured them into a trap Valentine had sprung – and I, I..."

"Valentine said I didn't take shortcuts. Killing Unimancers... it was a shortcut."

"A *shortcut*?" Ruth rolled up her sleeves to punch Paul. "You stupid fucker, you–"

Paul fell to his knees.

"No court can convict me for these crimes." He quivered but kept his spine straight, refusing to cloak himself in self-pity. "I would submit myself to the law, but there is none; every tribunal on Earth would hand me back to you. So I..."

He held out his wrists.

"I will accept whatever punishment you see fit to inflict, with the full understanding this won't make up for the deaths you can lay at my feet."

"You think we'll excuse your crimes with a *sentence*?"

"No," Paul said. "I think you'll do whatever helps you heal.

This isn't about justice. It's about fixing wrongs the best I can."

Remember, Ruth, some feel we need his knowledge, the Mom-construct volunteered. *If you can insert a copy of me into his brain, I can strip his memories, extracting the necessary discoveries we'd need to fix the broach. When that's done, I could arrange it so all that's left is remorse. He'd spend his life a suicidal amnesiac–*

Finally, Mom, you came up with a good idea, Ruth thought.

I'm here to advise! the Mom-construct chirped.

Ruth turned to the collective.

This is what happens when you let a lone man follow his obsessions! she roared. *Without our restraint, a sole 'mancer's mania curdles to murder. He slaughtered a hundred and seventy-seven men because they* got in his way. *And what happens when we loosen our grip upon the world? What happens when more unrestrained 'mancers go free?*

For the first time since Valentine's death, the Unimancers reached consensus. Tsabo's killing spree was proof no 'mancer could be trusted.

Ruth paused – and Aliyah felt that sliver of regret buried in her triumph. Condemning Paul would forever separate them.

But Ruth genuinely believed that Paul Tsabo was too dangerous to set free.

"Our sentence is this: we'll scoop out your thoughts and turn you into a self-hating Wikipedia."

She positioned herself to intercept him if he ran – but Paul hung his head.

"Will that help you heal?"

"*Yes.*" The Unimancers smothered Ruth's regret with revenge…

"Sit back." Ruth reached out with her powers. "We're gonna take our time on this one."

Come with me!

Aliyah hauled the Unimancer collective deep into the mansions of their memories.

Let me go! Ruth shrieked, panicked Paul Tsabo would escape to trigger more broaches. *He gave himself over, it's our right to do what we want with him!*

Tell me why you're punishing him. Aliyah dragged Ruth down a long hallway filled with locked doors.

Ruth flailed. *Because he blinded himself to the damage he caused!*

Aliyah found a sturdy locked door beneath black gossamer curtains – and tore it off its hinges.

…the agent whipped off her helmet to get a better look at the pudgy goth bitch she'd tackled.

"No worries, ma'am!" she told the squad leader, trying hard not to think about how she'd disobeyed a direct order. She'd been supposed to let the videogamemancer go.

Remember what we did to Valentine? Aliyah asked. *The air was worn thin from the magical battle; she heard buzzsects swarming. The slightest magic would trigger a broach; the squad leader had ordered them to stand down rather than risk instigating a broach on American soil.*

But they couldn't let this bitch get away with what she'd done to them.

You were furious because she'd interlaced her 'mancy with yours, *Aliyah said.* She'd used her videogamemancy to turn you into mechanical guards in a Metal Gear Solid game. Rather than admit she'd fused her magic with yours, you freaked out–

"We got her!"

The agent pinned the rogue 'mancer to the ground, grabbing for her Magiquell hypodermic. She had to knock this bitch out now, because–

The flux boiled off the videogamemancer, arced towards her boyfriend.

"No!" The flux gave the videogamemancer's boyfriend strength to pull free from the other squad member who'd been handcuffing him. He grabbed at her holster–

She shoved him backwards, realizing too late that was what the flux had intended all along.

The videogamemancer's boyfriend tumbled backwards, impaling himself on jagged pipes–

Aliyah hauled Ruth out, furious. *We murdered her boyfriend. How's that make us any better?*

We didn't murder him! We–

Aliyah's quiet fury stilled Ruth's protests. *We disobeyed orders to take on a 'mancer overflowing with flux. We got him killed.*

Ruth thrashed. *That's just one m–*

Every door in the hallway sprang open, flooding them with botched operations – all the times SMASH had pursued a hapless 'mancer until they choked on their flux. The butterflymancer's glass house raining down glass shards, the dancemancer's heart exploding from exertion, the hackomancer's computer monitor exploding.

No, Ruth begged – but Aliyah opened hundreds more doors, filling the hivemind with the knowledge that yes, Valentine was right, hundreds of 'mancers *had* fought to the death rather than be absorbed. Literamancers burned to death in their own libraries, tattoomancers shredded by their needles, woodworkmancers beheaded by rogue sawblades…

Stop! Ruth cried, horrified by Aliyah's mercilessness…

We killed hundreds, too. Aliyah sifted through Numbers' statistics, threw them at the collective: *16.5% chance of self-destruction. We knew that. Yet we were comfortable killing one out of every six 'mancers as long as it swelled our ranks. And you call my dad a monster?*

He killed us for nothing! Ruth cried.

Aliyah was merciless. *He thought he was making a better world. Just like you.*

Ruth wriggled under Aliyah's logic. *We took a risk to save people! Those poor solo 'mancers endangered themselves – we brought them someplace safe, where they could be cherished!*

As she felt Aliyah's exhilaration, Ruth realized too late this was exactly the argument Aliyah'd wanted her to make.

Cherished, eh? Aliyah opened up a dilapidated door into a long, empty hallway. Virtual dust kicked up around their feet; Aliyah produced a virtual candle to shed thin, quavering light on blank wooden walls.

There's nothing here, Ruth said, confused.

Aliyah scraped off mold to reveal a long-forgotten door, then knocked politely.

Yoder? she called out. *Yoder, can you come out?*

I don't want any trouble, miss. The voice was elderly, with a formal Amish twang. *I do as I'm told.*

All right. Aliyah warned Ruth to be on her best behavior. *May we come in?*

Please, don't – a grumbling sound, like teetering rocks threatening to fall. *I don't have much left.*

The rumbling grew, the collective's voices pouring into the room–

– *she's not a child* –

– *she's been a warrior for years* –

– *how* dare *you think of her as a child?* –

The thin old man crouched down, clasping his straw hat. *I meant no offense, when I met her she was the little burned girl to me–*

The tide of irritation swept in through the door, smashing into a cramped warehouse filled with rocks. The rocks were stacked high into shapes – a farmhouse of flat schist, a half-crumbled church with a broken altar and shattered cross.

Ruth realized this was the rock-balancing Amish man who'd been swept up in a SMASH roundup–

The hivemind raced past Yoder, aiming straight for a slender pile of rocks shaped like Aliyah. They knocked it down–

– *that's wrong* –

They smashed the Aliyah-replica into coarse pebbles.

Stop that, she admonished, bending down to stack the rocks back up again. She reassembled them into what looked mostly like his memories of her – though she couldn't replace it.

In their rush to achieve consensus, the hivemind had eroded Yoder.

He can't fight you, Aliyah told them. *He was raised to believe harmony is more important than individuality.* She tapped the crumbled church. *Religion was important to him. But the collective doesn't believe in God, so they knocked it down – and he wasn't strong enough to fight back...*

She swept her arm around, encompassing his broken memories.

Ruth staggered through the wreckage, sensing Yoder's surrender, his terror at losing more of himself.

Aliyah felt her girlfriend's heart break for the right reasons.

My God, Aliyah, Ruth asked, numb. *What have we done?*

Aliyah extended her hand out towards the hallway. *Who knows how many Yoders are suppressed in the rush to consensus? I only heard him because I'd known him before.*

We thrive in here, Aliyah continued, *because our parents taught us to fight. We can stare seven thousand people down to tell them fuck you, you're wrong. And even I–*

Aliyah remembered shouting into the void, knowing her father was about to make a terrible mistake, her concerns negated.

Even I had a few moments of erasure.

Horror boiled out of Ruth – these doors had been buried deep so the Unimancers wouldn't have to think about them, but Aliyah had made them impossible to ignore.

What are you saying, Aliyah? Ruth asked. *That... that Unimancy is a lie? That... that our love is a peer pressure-created illusion?*

Ruth backed away, horrified she might have brainwashed Aliyah into falling in love – Aliyah knew how deep that revulsion ran for her, Ruth terrified she'd turned Aliyah into an extension of her desires–

Oh, God no. She bathed Ruth in perfect love. *Unimancy is really good – for some people. Daddy taught me to fight for what I believed in; that made this heaven for me. But for people like Yoder, well... you condemned them to selling off pieces of their soul to get along.*

My God. The hivemind fractured with remorse. People delved into those lightless depths, found hundreds of abandoned souls.

Aliyah felt pride. The Unimancers hadn't been evil. They'd just held onto their idea of paradise with a 'mancer's certainty, blinded to the costs. They'd been unable to understand someone might not fit in, just as her daddy believed paperwork produced perfect fairness.

Most of the hivemind were as happy as Aliyah – but empathetic therapists escorted long-forgotten folks out of the catacombs, whispering apologies.

Oh God, Ruth said. *Valentine was right. We're evil–*

We've done *evil*, Aliyah told her. *Everyone does, from time to time. But the way you shift from "doing evil" to "being evil" is by looking at the choice and pretending it doesn't exist.*

Now we know. Aliyah felt Ruth's Mom-construct calculating the force reduction from sending these folks to Project Mayhem for rehabilitation...

Which brings us back to Dad, Aliyah finished.

Paul still knelt on the ground, trembling, preparing to be brain-wiped.

If he's evil, Aliyah said, *then you're evil.*

Ruth swallowed, nodding. *I think maybe we're all a little evil.*

Then it's time to do good.

Ruth reached out to Aliyah, feeling the relief of an honest consensus – not a decision arrived at by peer pressure, but a genuine agreement brokered between loving peers.

We are in love, aren't we? Ruth shivered with uncertainty.

Aliyah wrapped her in an embrace, poured conviction into Ruth until Ruth glowed with affection. *I just stood tall against seven thousand 'mancers,* Aliyah grinned. *Do you think I'd do anything less, if what we felt was based on lies?*

No, Ruth said. Then: *...that's why I love you.*

And your stubborn-ass nature is why I *love* you.

Love permeated the collective as they made up.

Ruth knelt down to take Paul's hands, so gently Paul realized he'd been given a reprieve.

"I'm sorry," said Ruth. "I wasn't thinking straight."

Paul spluttered nervous laughter. "Believe me. I get that."

Ruth verified they'd come up with the right answer. Which had begun when they sought the answer to the right question:

Not *how do we punish Paul?* but rather, *How do we ensure Paul never forgets*?

"You killed one hundred and seventy-seven of us." Ruth's eyes were flinty. "When 'mancers die, we each take a memory from their minds and keep it safe. Your sentence, Paul, is this: we will give you a memory from each of the men you murdered. You will know them as we knew them. And you will carry their remains for the rest of your life. Can you do that?"

Paul had used up his store of bravery. He sobbed as Ruth confronted him with the enormity of his crimes.

"Can you do that?" Ruth repeated.

Paul sniffled his tears away, straightened his tie.

"Yes," Paul said. "I am the recordkeeper."

The air filled with magic as Ruth told him something each of the hundred and seventy-seven dead cherished. Paul engraved their memories in his soul.

Nothing could cleanse his crimes.

But he could spend his life atoning.

FORTY-SIX
The Secret That Saved the World

The general had assembled them beneath where It had taken Valentine, as if to emphasize how the invasion would erupt right over their heads.

The broach had swollen like a cancer to obscure the heavens, spreading further with every pulse. The sun crept between the dwindling patches of normal sky. That sickening heartbeat took longer, increasing in ferocity with each beat.

Hairs rose on their necks as waves of immense magical power rippled across Bastogne.

"All right," said the general. "We tried this your way. Now we'll try it my way."

Yet his voice, Paul thought, held no anger. It was as though he'd expected everything to go wrong in precisely this manner – and now that he'd swept all objections aside, the healing would begin in earnest.

Paul watched as General Kanakia ordered the Unimancers into position. The Thing had, ominously, withdrawn – but every few minutes, a clicking noise rattled down from the heavens, and the cracks deepened.

The Thing had learned something, destroying Valentine. Something it was learning to utilize.

Yet Imani was convinced Paul had learned something of equal value. He didn't know what he could have learned, but... he trusted his wife's judgment. Which was why he felt partially redeemed for his sins when she stood by him in the field of blossoms.

Before, being surrounded by sixty Unimancers would have been a threat. Now, Paul felt the safety Aliyah felt; if his 'mancy spiralled out of control, they'd anchor him.

"I understand why *I'm* comfortable here," Paul said to Imani. "But why are you?"

Imani blinked. "What do you mean?"

"I mean..." Paul tried to pull Imani aside, but then realized it wasn't like the Unimancers didn't know. "You shot them in the face. You devised a plan to destroy them. *All* of them. Yet a week later, you're assisting the general like you'd been on their side all along?"

"Oh." She blushed. "That."

"Yeah. That."

She shrugged. "Something threatened my daughter. That brought out the beast in me."

"Well, it brought out the beast in me, too, but..."

"Oh, Paul." She kissed his cheek. "Your beast takes things personally."

Paul realized: Imani had once believed the threat was the Unimancers – but once she'd realized the Thing in the sky was her real enemy, she'd decided to kill that instead.

Her bloodlust was flecked with frost – a glacial fury, satiated by killing anything sufficiently challenging.

"That Thing will do," she told Paul, sensing she'd been understood. "And now that we're back together as a family, there's nothing that can stand in our way."

A single flat *click* echoed across the orchard. The sky throbbed again, the crack-veins turning a deeper green.

"Except I'm the weak link in this plan," Paul muttered.

"Oh?"

He massaged his artificial foot as though he could still feel sensation in it. "The black flux still fucked my 'mancy. I sidestepped it by becoming the War Bureaucromancer, but... without that, I'm still magically crippled. I can barely look up Aliyah's birth certificate without having bad luck hamstring me..."

"We'll solve that," Imani assured him.

"*How*? Valentine was my magical advisor. Even *she* didn't know why–"

"Are you *really* baffled why your 'mancy stopped working, Dad?"

Paul frowned at Aliyah. "I don't believe I'm known for my sense of humor."

"It's the same reason you fucked up when you assaulted the broach–"

"–language–" Imani chided.

Though Aliyah rolled her eyes, Paul was grateful to see it was a good-natured protest. "Dad, I *felt* what you wanted to do before we took over. You wanted to spend weeks fixing the physics in one square inch."

"I did, yes." Paul polished his reading glasses nervously. "But... that was just what I *liked* doing. It seemed so foolish, dinking around with a tiny experiment..."

Aliyah huffed out in a perfectly teenaged *Gawd, Dad* look. "So what you're saying is that you – the bureaucromancer – abandoned a careful plan involving incremental changes so you could swing big and see what happened?"

Hairs rose up on Paul's arms. "My God..."

Aliyah crossed her arms, serene in victory. "When did the black flux hit you?"

"At the..."

The stink of burning fuel and bodies, Valentine unconscious, nowhere to run–

"At the airport. They'd tossed stun grenades at us. I didn't–"

"You didn't have time to do the necessary paperwork before the grenades blew, did you?"

"No," Paul admitted reluctantly. "I just... willed it."

"Well then." Aliyah spread her hands. "It's not black flux holding you back – you stopped believing in your magic."

Paul felt so lightheaded, he had to steady himself on Imani.

"Why should I believe?" he said. "I spent five years working within the system, and I *still* hadn't done a damn thing to make the world safer for you! One accident undid everything. And when it came time to protect my family, I–"

He swallowed.

"I'm always useless once the soldiers arrive."

"OK, yes, you're worthless in a fight," Imani sighed. "But… the rest? No. If you weren't so effective at raising support among the nonmagical, the government would have capped your ass a long time ago. And you *did* make changes."

"I assure you, Mr Tsabo," the general interjected, stepping in with a dancer's grace. "Five years ago, the United States government would never have contemplated sanctuaries for 'mancers – even secret ones. But you humanized your plight to millions. You planted doubt where once there had been certainty – and never underestimate *that* power."

Imani nodded. "The more liberal sides of the President's cabinet are OK with the secret sanctuaries because they could justify the sanctuaries to their voters if the news got out. Thanks to you talking about Aliyah, now people wonder if those 'mancers who got hauled away could have been their daughters."

"Look at the Unimancers," the general said. "You've laid the seeds for their future. One day they'll be able to stop masquerading as brainwashed zombies. You *have* made the world safer for Aliyah."

Aliyah gave a guilty shrug as Ruth took her hand. "Just… not in the way you'd planned."

The sky pulsed again. That sickness swelled. Paul dropped the clipboard.

"But… I screwed up so badly when I fought that Thing…"

The general snorted. "I reported the incident as a success."

"A *success*?" Paul spluttered. "We lost Valentine! We almost lost the *world*!"

"I'm genuinely sorry for your loss." The general held his right hand palm-open in a blessing. "But the broach has devoured Unimancers for seven decades now. On average, it kills five a day. That's two thousand souls a year. Twenty thousand consumed in the last decade.

"One death gave us the first new information we've garnered

in *seventy years* of unmitigated losses. That Thing *spoke* to you. It *feared* you. Now let us determine why."

you hold the rules yet know not how to use them

One square inch, he thought.

we are war

He was racing against whatever It was building up to – and his 'mancy had never been an answer for violence...

"If I may share one last piece of assistance, Mr Tsabo?"

Paul tapped the clipboard absently, nodding, his attention upon the sky.

"The Unimancer collective is a precious, precious secret. We could never tell the world what SMASH truly was. Nations would never have allowed independent 'mancers upon their soil, even if those 'mancers were dedicated to saving the planet. If politicians had understood Unimancy was beneficial, well, they would have moved to execute 'mancers rather than handing them over to us."

"I get that," Paul muttered.

"Without the Unimancers, the broach would consume the planet. We couldn't chance officials sacrificing long term stability for short term political gain. So we staffed carefully, Mr Tsabo – we only allowed people who understood the Unimancers' true necessity into managerial positions. In that way, for seventy unbroken years, we have kept the Unimancers saving the world."

Paul frowned for a moment, wondering why the general was telling him this–

Then he laughed, a hard clean laugh that felt like blowing cobwebs out of his lungs.

"You're telling me the only thing keeping the planet safe has been... *good middle management*?"

The general smiled like someone who'd told a joke he'd been longing to share for ages. "Precisely, Mr Tsabo."

Paul cupped one shattered square inch within his palms. He readied his bureaucromancy.

For the first time in months, Paul looked forward to doing magic.

FORTY-SEVEN
Pulsations and Reparations

Aliyah woke. Someone was sifting through her expertise.

She'd been working in shifts to protect Daddy; fourteen hours on, ten hours off, rotations ordered by General Kanakia to keep them as alert as they could be until Daddy was done.

Nobody slept well. Each time they woke, the sky had been chewed further away. The Thing's erratic pulses crept into their dreams...

Daddy hadn't slept the whole time – but unlike the mania that had turned him into a hateful revenant, this work seemed to energize him. He drank the gray nutritional fluid when Mommy prodded him, dozed on the general's orders – refusing to leave the square inch of space he'd created.

And it glowed. That tiny cube hovered in his cupped hands, radiating a green CRT light as Daddy queried it with fine strands of magic.

He didn't look angry; he looked joyous. He was *playing* with the space, tinkering with physics, laughing whenever the cube collapsed into a one-dimensional tesseract that he had to rebuild.

Aliyah would have shared his exhilaration, except the sky kept pulsing. Just when you relaxed and thought *maybe it's over*, the heavens convulsed again.

Something was coming.

Yet the general had ordered them to relax, so she'd curled up with Ruth and drifted off.

Until something sifted through her *Super Mario* expertise.

That sifting feeling wasn't unusual among 'mancers; it was a courtesy to leave your skills open to anyone, even while sleeping. Yet Aliyah's skills were mostly videogame trivia – not a subject the hivemind needed often.

Aliyah knew the 'mancers with useful skills dealt with constant intrusions; the combatmancers' and the biomancers' and the psychomancers' brains churned like frequently-accessed hard disks.

Who needed *Super Mario* this urgently? Someone vacuumed huge chunks of *Mario* from her head – every monster, every secret, every speed run trick.

Valentine? Aliyah thought – but no. This access was precise in a way Valentine had never been. It felt computerized.

"Ruth?" She tapped Ruth on the shoulder–

Ruth was gone.

Aliyah flailed, pinging the hivemind for her girlfriend's location. Except Ruth's rage floated up from the collective–

Dammit, Mom, I wanted to play!

Your strategies were suboptimal, dear.

That's the point! I'm supposed to learn!

I'm *supposed to teach you.*

The only reason Ruth didn't hurl the Nintendo DS across the tent was because she knew it had been Valentine's.

"You OK?"

"Couldn't sleep." Ruth shook the Nintendo, abusing it because she couldn't get at her Mom-construct. "I wanted to see… what you saw in this stuff."

Aliyah felt half-truths rising up. Ruth *had* known Aliyah was exhausted, *hadn't* wanted to steal her precious sleep…

But floating behind that was a deeper truth: she felt guilty over Valentine's death. In driving Paul into choosing brute force over bureaucromancy, she'd made a lone 'mancer sacrifice herself to save them all.

This was Ruth's fumbling attempt to preserve one of Valentine's memories.

Aliyah hugged her.

"I know it's broken," Ruth said, so angry she couldn't return Aliyah's embrace. "I figured maybe I could play for a few moments before it rebooted. And…"

That explained Ruth's fury. Ruth had sought Valentine's memories of exploration, her ability to lose herself in the castle–

–and when she'd played, her Mom-construct had downloaded the knowledge from Aliyah's brain to fill Ruth's head full of winning strategies.

Ruth buried her head in her hands. "…Welcome to my childhood."

That, Aliyah knew, was what made Ruth truly furious; her actual mother had killed herself, leaving her with a brittle Mom-construct who valued facts over feelings.

Aliyah's father had cultivated her sense of wonder with beautiful magics before joining the hivemind; Ruth had never known mystery. Her Mom-construct had given her force-fed education, or panic.

"We could play together," Aliyah offered.

"No." Except secretly, Ruth said *yes*. Aliyah felt Ruth's desperation to play a videogame with Aliyah, to tune into her joy.

Except Aliyah's enthusiasm was entwined with fear. Playing videogames for fun triggered 'mancy, triggered flux, triggered death. She'd told Valentine videogamemancy was "baby stuff," but Aliyah was pretty sure Aunt Valentine had known the truth:

Aliyah was terrified she'd kill again. And Ruth didn't want to force her into those flashbacks.

"We could play together," Aliyah insisted, taking the Nintendo. "I mean…"

Pressing the "start" button and watching Mario pop on-screen was like rebooting a part of her soul.

"You sure?" Ruth asked. But she knew: Aliyah wanted to grant Ruth the thrill of exploration, Ruth wanted Aliyah to get in touch with her childhood again.

More than that: now that Valentine was gone, Ruth wanted

to know what had bonded her girlfriend and her aunt.

Aliyah called out to Unimancers from around the globe who had the spare cycles to play boundary guards. *We're gonna do my obsession*, she told them. *If you see me doing something impossible, stop me.*

On one level, it was unnecessary; any time a Unimancer did something they'd once been obsessed with, other 'mancers were drawn to their enthusiasm like moths to a flame. Yet the crowds also muffled the obsessions, smothering other 'mancies with the low-grade pressure of *now, you know that's not possible* whenever they strayed from normal human experience.

But Aliyah wanted maximum safety, so she called in spotters.

"Ready?" Aliyah asked.

Ruth squeezed her hand. "Let's go."

Aliyah raced towards the end in a full-on speed run, the kind of joyous fun you only got when you pushed yourself to your limit.

And she pushed herself to *her* limits, she realized; of all the people in the hivemind, she was the most skilled at Mario speed runs. Ruth cheered her on, surfing her enthusiasm as Aliyah did something no one else in the hivemind could do…

Then, in mid-Mario leap, the Nintendo rebooted.

No videogamemancy, the spotters chided.

I didn't!

You did. Didn't you feel that?

Aliyah exchanged glances with Ruth.

"…take this outside?" Ruth ventured.

"Yeah."

They walked out; though it was dark, those fractures glowed like blacklight in the sun's absence. Aliyah restarted, losing herself in another speed run, smashing through level 1…

The Nintendo rebooted.

The sky flickered.

"Do that again," Ruth commanded.

Aliyah launched herself into another speed run – and the game rebooted within a few minutes.

So did the sky.

The hivemind woke at once, immense powers of statistical correlation brought to bear upon this problem.

Yet Aliyah knew.

She *knew*.

She ran to her father in the field.

"*Valentine!*" she cried, holding the Nintendo aloft. "*Aunt Valentine! She's alive!*"

Mommy's head snapped up.

"That's impossible," Paul said. "The buzzsects devoured her."

"They did. They *are*. They've killed her every few minutes for a week." She held the screen towards them expectantly until it rebooted. "There. She died again."

"Aliyah," Imani said slowly. "That makes no sense."

Aliyah hugged the Nintendo to her chest, watching the game restart with a flare of videogamemancy, jubilant as she realized what that endless cycle truly meant.

"She's reloading the game until she wins."

FORTY-EIGHT
"Run," Valentine Says

SEVEN DAYS AGO...

As Valentine tumbled into the burning sky, buzzsects chewing her left arm to a stump, she contemplated the wisdom of her tactical decisions.

I saved Paul, she thought. But now an alien universe opened up to swallow her, and the buzzsects were the friendliest things swarming down to greet her; other, hungrier monstrosities were vomited up, beasts that made her pupil contract as her brain tried to shut out their sight.

She'd wanted a blaze of glory.

This was a meatgrinder.

"Get some, motherfucker!" she screamed – but that was pure bravado, mostly so Aliyah wouldn't fall apart, because if Aliyah lost it then the Unimancers would lose it and *somebody* needed to fight these creepy motherfuckers. *"I did my job! I protected the ones I loved! It doesn't matter if I–"*

But it did matter. She hadn't protected anybody. Thousands of beasts erupted from the broach; the Thing would raze the Earth to get its rippling feelers on Paul. Buzzsects filled her mouth, ate her teeth, stole defiance from her tongue–

I can't go out like a punk-ass bitch in his first multiplayer Halo *game*, she thought.

Her nasal cavities were strip-mined, her face reduced to a

gurgling hole. They gnawed her eyes before burrowing into her skull…

Game over, man, she thought. *Game over.*

Then she thought:

Reload.

She had enough muscle memory left in her remaining hand to thumb the start button, selecting "Load" from the menu.

She summoned more willpower than she ever had before in her life.

She pressed the "X" button.

The world went black.

A white progress bar appeared, slowly filling as the world recreated itself – back to before the Unimancers had weaponized Paul, where she could talk them out of it–

The flux smashed into her like a hurricane. The universe's core axioms hinged upon cause and effect – Valentine threatened to destroy physics by rewinding history.

Paul had once reversed time for entirely selfless reasons, giving himself up to the universe's anger as a sacrifice. Valentine had never been that pure. Her good intentions were mixed with her terror of being forgotten, of being incompetent…

The white progress bar wavered. It moved backwards, undoing all she'd done, dumping her back when the buzzsects had killed her.

I need to fight the demons! Valentine shrieked, furious. *I'm trying to protect* you, *you stupid sonuvabitch!*

But it was too much. Paul had told her that when he'd reversed time with his bureaucromancy, he'd felt that change ripple out to the galaxy's edge – his faith undid events trillions of light years away.

Valentine didn't have his conviction.

The progress bar rippled–

Smaller.

Valentine contracted her reload – *a limited space*, she thought. Just the sky above Bastogne. She struggled with time's elasticity, pushing as far back as she could–

One and a half minutes.

One and a half minutes took everything she had.

She hooked herself deep into the fabric of space, memorizing where she'd been– the way her right leg had been sprawled out, the way her spine had arched as she fought the Thing's inverted gravity, marking the position of those unthinkable monsters boiling out from the Thing's throat.

She anchored a save point.

The progress bar inched forward again, and when it loaded it *Valentine tumbled into the burning sky*.

"*Get off!*" she screamed, whipping her left arm aside as a swarm of buzzsects moved in to devour it. Flux flowed out of her, swirling into the save point; she'd accumulated a load of bad luck, but wouldn't have to pay it just yet.

She looked down, hoping to see Paul; she saw nothing but that burning sky. The Thing had hauled her onto the demon dimensions' doorstep.

She was the barrier they had to pass.

"*You fucker!*" she yelled at the Thing. "*This time, I'm gonna–*"

The buzzsects arced back around, consuming her left hand. She fired her remaining pistol at the buzzsects, but the videogame bullets filled them brimming with 'mancy; they chewed tunnels through her brain–

Valentine tumbled into the burning sky.

She kicked away from the buzzsects this time, switching from Bayonetta's Scarborough Fair guns to her Shuraba katana–

They yanked the katana from her hands, unspooled her intestines.

Valentine tumbled into the burning sky.

The Kulshedra whip, that's a distance weapon, it ought to–

She snapped a few buzzsects' wings off before they chewed her skin off.

Valentine tumbled into the burning sky.

She tried every weapon Bayonetta had to offer – shooting them sideways, dodging until the larger monsters punched through, enticing the swarms to eat each other, launching herself straight at the Thing.

Valentine tumbled into the burning sky.

Valentine tumbled into the burning sky.

Valentine tumbled into the burning sky.

She died a hundred times, and somehow it was worse every time.

She trembled as she switched to *Mortal Kombat*'s Sub-Zero. This was no videogame death; she felt the pain as her body was eaten by buzzsects and shat out as unearthly fodder.

Fuck that. She shot an ice ball at the buzzsects. *You're Valentine DiGriz. Videogames are how you bleed off PTSD.*

Valentine tumbled into the burning sky.

She'd learned to jerk her left arm away immediately after reload – but why hadn't she reloaded from a more advantageous position? She always had to transition out of Bayonetta into whatever videogame she'd decided to try. She always flailed in mid-air, that off-balance shock never ending.

She missed feeling ground beneath her feet.

She missed seeing Paul and Aliyah below her.

She missed–

Valentine tumbled into the burning sky.

She was *Contra* now, her shoulders heavy with guns – and that exploded enough buzzsects to beat a path to the larger monsters. But those things had serrated tentacles, stepping through side-dimensions to

Valentine tumbled into the burning sky.

She was getting exhausted, she had no idea how long she'd been fighting, but

Valentine tumbled into the burning sky.

The save point darkened with each reload. How many times had she rebooted this pocket of hell? She felt it quivering, a catastrophic flux-load ready to detonate, increasing reload by reload.

Valentine tumbled into the burning sky.

When Paul had rewound time, he'd expected a meteor to flatten New York. She'd rewound time a thousand times, trying every way to beat these monsters and

Valentine tumbled into the burning sky.

Stupid Imani had made her memorize a list of videogames.

She'd hated Imani *so much* for making her do that. Now she went down the list, using *The Sims* to buy a wall to bar off the larger monsters, channeling Pac-Man into mazes that funneled the monsters to her one at a time and she could tap an individual buzzsect to turn it into a Lemming the other buzzsects had to follow but

Valentine tumbled into the burning sky.

She was running out of games.

Valentine tumbled into the burning sky.

Or maybe she wasn't; she was forgetting things. There were no beds; only the reload screen's brief respite, a three-second pause before whipping your left arm out of the buzzsects' way. And she

Valentine tumbled into the burning sky.

She longed for Robert's violence, loving the way he'd punched her as they'd made love and how she'd punched him harder, that no-holds-barred grappling as they fought for domination and she'd always won but he'd never given in just to make her feel better, every night in bed was a victory for them both, and

Valentine tumbled into the burning sky.

She'd kill to feel Robert's skin next to hers, that thick muscle under fat, digging her fingertips into his ribs to hear him wince, hurting each other so it felt so good when they finally made love, and

Valentine tumbled into the burning sky.

She didn't make love, killing was all she could do, some of the darker monsters needed Pokeballs to hold them back, and the battles took longer but there were only three seconds of peace to imagine Robert before she yanked her left arm away and those fucking bugs the bugs were always to her left what would it be like to live when you didn't have to keep whipping your arm

Valentine tumbled into the burning sky.

to

Valentine tumbled into the burning sky.

the

Valentine tumbled into the burning sky.
left
Valentine tumbled into the burning sky.
you can't do this forever
The Thing croaked, the subsonic noise of tectonic plates shifting. She'd played the game forever and never gotten close to the Thing, its armies always stopped her, and oh God she'd never see Robert again.

"Try me." Her voice was raw.

your flux
it's fatal

"*Fuck you!*" Valentine screamed, atomizing buzzsect swarms with a cluster bomb, flinging a nanowire trap to cut some ciliabeasts in half–

you cannot beat me
even if you do
when you finish your flux will kill everything

"Not true," Valentine lied, because it *was* true, she'd fought for days dying and dying and dying and every time she dumped more bad luck into the hopper it was enough to destroy a town enough to destroy a city enough to destroy

europe

"*I will fight you to the end of the world, motherfucker,*" Valentine hissed through clenched teeth, thinking of Robert, Robert safe in America, she couldn't have built up enough flux to take out America?

you are the end of the world, the Thing said, and oh God Valentine knew that was true.

FORTY-NINE
Cut the Cord

They met outside Bastogne, desperate to save Valentine.

"OK," Paul said. "The one time I reversed time, I built up enough flux to obliterate Manhattan. So figure she's got somewhere in that range. And... has anyone figured out how often that Nintendo's been rebooting?"

Ruth's eyeballs glowed as the collective transformed memories into hard data. "Assuming it's linked to the sky, roughly between two and ten minutes per cycle. Though it's been going longer as of late."

Paul nodded in approval. "She's lasting longer. She's fighting smarter."

Imani hunched over, as if the sky threatened to collapse on her. "Except *how* many reload cycles has she been through, Ruth?"

Ruth sucked in a deep breath. "We estimate two thousand."

"So assuming a worst-case scenario of Manhattan, when she comes barreling out, she'll–"

"Eradicate half of Germany. And that's our *best*-case scenario. Because she's dropping a catastrophic load of flux–"

"–right on the broach," Paul finished.

"She won't stop until she defeats what's in there, or..." Aliyah couldn't bring herself to say *or she dies*. "She *can't* back down. It's not in her nature."

"But once she finishes, her flux will annihilate us."

They cringed as the sky pulsed again.

"All right, Mr Tsabo." The general sounded mildly perturbed, as though his flight had been delayed an hour. "What's our plan?"

Paul stepped back. "You're asking *me* to head this operation?"

"When Ms DiGriz breaks free and the havoc rains down, I want no chain-of-command delays. I'm delegating this to the smartest, nimblest person."

Paul looked pointedly at Imani.

"We discussed that, dear." She kissed him on the cheek. "But I'm not a 'mancer. I can't sense magic. I can't hook into the hivemind. The general and I will sketch out strategies – but when the time comes, you must make the call."

Paul stared at the small army of Unimancers. "Remember when Aliyah was born?"

Imani covered a smirk. "The umbilical cord, right?"

Though Aliyah's wild hair was tied back into a tight Unimancer's hairdo, Paul was pleased to see her *Please, Dad, don't tell this story* face remained as delightfully teenaged as ever.

Ruth grinned. "What happened?"

"Well…" Paul straightened his tie. "When Aliyah was born, the obstetrician asked if I wanted to cut the cord. And I, well…"

"You asked if there wasn't anyone more qualified to do the job!" Imani snapped, her face contorted in bemused disbelief – and they burst into laughter, family and Unimancer alike.

"No one can take this cup from your hand, Mr Tsabo," the general said solemnly. "This is your Gethsemane. If you fail…"

The general swallowed.

"If you fail, so does humanity."

But I'm not qualified, Paul thought. He was still tempted to hand responsibility to Imani, even though Imani couldn't sense broaches or hook into Unimancy.

The general stepped aside to give Paul a view of Bastogne's villagers carrying in logs, splitting them with axes, piling up the firewood – *like they expect winter to come*, Paul thought.

Help me to be their guardian, Aliyah had said.

Paul felt freefall terror: there *was* no one more qualified to handle this. Every bureaucracy had someone who made the final decisions. Paul had spent his life offloading as many decisions as he could, handing his power to Payne, to Robert, to anyone who'd distribute the possibility of failure–

But now it had to be him.

"All right," Paul said.

you think you are war

He wasn't war. He'd tried to be, but that certainty had ruined his humanity. He needed to heal this broach as a bureaucrat would.

Paul sat down on a stump, putting a legal pad in his lap. He licked the tip of his pen, then wrote down five goals:

Stop the invasion

Neutralize the excess flux

Heal the broach

Keep Aliyah safe

Save Valentine

"Unimancers out." They retreated. "Imani, general – we're not leaving until all five of these objectives are crossed off."

Within two hours, they'd filled up their first legal pad.

By sunset, Paul's fingers were smudged black with ink.

By morning, the three looked over an ankle-high drift of papers, fluttering about the grove like leaves. They'd skyrocketed past crazy approaches into contemplating nonsensical approaches. The sky glowed like a stained glass window in a fire, the last remains of blue nearly gnawed away.

He tore off a sheet, started afresh–

Imani put her palm over the pad. "Paul," she said. "That's the plan. That's our best shot."

"We need more options. We need to–"

"Paul," she repeated. "Remember when Valentine had to throw a dart to get you to choose?"

"This isn't the soccer game!" Paul snapped. "*Look* at that!"

He stabbed a pen into the five objectives: no successful plan they'd concocted could cross off "Save Valentine." Even if Valentine survived that first flux-blast, she'd been pulled miles above the Earth; Paul could not think of a 'mancy they

possessed that would prevent Valentine from smashing into the
ground like a failed parachutist.

The sky thrummed again. Valentine, fighting her endless
battle. Valentine, who'd doomed herself saving them.

"She won't last much longer," Imani snapped. "Our best plan
involves you writing out a complicated contract. If you want
to do that *and* restructure the Unimancers to give them the
certainty we'll need to pull this off, we need to act *now*."

"But she..."

Imani's eyes were baggy; she'd contributed more ideas to
their pool than anyone. "She made her sacrifice, Paul. She'd
make it again."

"I..."

She was right. They didn't have the resources to save
Valentine – they had no planes, no aerial technology, just one
bureaucromancer and sixty-plus Unimancers who couldn't
accomplish anything world-class humans couldn't manage.

Paul was down to not saving Valentine, or not saving anyone.

"All right," he said. "Let's do this."

FIFTY
Pills and Thrills and Daffodils Will Kill

why do you fight

Valentine carved out tangential improvements in fighting this nightmare armada, mining Imani's stupid videogame list to find new approaches, but inevitably–

Valentine tumbled into the burning sky.

why do you FIGHT

"Because I'm going to beat you," she muttered. She'd channeled *Doom*, luring the buzzsects into crossfires with the ciliabeasts whip-tentacles, goosing their anger with a touch of magic to have them turn on each other.

But she was surrounded by hungry buzzsects who lapped up her excess 'mancy to burst into hideous clouds that ate her alive, and the razorplows homed in on her magic like heat-seeking missiles, and if she survived them then coliseum-sized beasts crawled out of the Thing's throat and

Valentine tumbled into the burning sky.

you cannot beat me
even if you win you will destroy everything
each battle adds to your destruction

"They need me!" Valentine shouted, jerking her left arm back again, lost in a sweaty battle haze, and sometimes she was so desperate for human contact that before she died she'd hug a ciliabeast's blistered skin and pretend it was Robert before it swallowed her into its sticky guts and

Valentine tumbled into the burning sky.

they do not need you

And God that was true it was *true*, nobody even knew she was here, she fought a pointless battle that would dump a fluxplosion on their heads, she was a liability she'd always been a liability

She'd been such a liability to Robert, of course he didn't need her.

They were supposed to go crazy together.

Robert had gone sane.

That was why they'd never work out: Robert had healed his neuroses, he didn't need some fucked-up fantasy to keep him going any more, and she *did*, and…

Valentine tumbled into the burning sky.

Robert has a black belt in karate Robert can pick locks Robert can run a national organization and what could she do? She could be such a fucking lunatic that her craziness punched holes in the world all she'd ever do was hurt people why the fuck would he stay with someone like that?

Valentine tumbled into the burning sky.

She'd done this forever and her world was a murderfield, all cutthropods and pustulancers and blistrodes and why would Robert ever go on adventures with her when her adventures were one horrific battle after another?

Why would he stay?

He gave you a ring, a small sad voice thought.

People walk away from rings every fucking day, she thought. *The only thing that puts asses in seats is raw* need *and he doesn't* need *you why would anyone need a* crazy person

Valentine tumbled into the burning sky.

why do you fight

She couldn't remember why she fought. She couldn't remember the sweet taste of Red Bull and the warm massage Robert gave her after a videogame marathon, she couldn't remember the strength of Robert's arms hugging her when she hurt, she couldn't remember the tautness of leather belts around her hips when she pulled on her strap-on to take

Robert. All she remembered was bugs chewing her skin and cutthropods tearing her apart and razorplows slicing through her eyeballs...

Valentine tumbled into the burning sky.

why do you fight

"Because I'm crazy." She let the buzzsects take her sometimes before she snapped back into yet another loop. "Because I'm crazy, and broken, and–"

they do not need you

"i know," she said, feeling the buzzsects gnaw her, frightened at how good it felt to be nothing.

FIFTY-ONE
Got To Get Out Of This World Somehow

The general looked up at the sagging sky and apologized.

"Our cavalry won't arrive in time."

Paul realized with shame that of course the general hadn't sat idle while Paul planned. "Who were we expecting?"

"Experts on broach management who'd been working in less dangerous territories, a professional psychologist to talk you out of any breakdowns, and a case of Dunkin' Donuts."

Paul blinked.

"...Dunkin' Donuts?"

"It's the apocalypse, Mr Tsabo. I'd prefer not to meet my ending without one last mouthful of Dunkies."

"So where are the experts?"

"I'm not sure."

"You're not *sure*?"

He jerked a thumb upwards. "*That's* interfering with radio signals. Fortunately, we can convey some messages through Unimancers. And I have left orders with the international SMASH teams that something big is happening in Europe; the usual 'mancer roundups will be suspended until the current crisis is over." He fingered his medals, proud to have done the necessary legwork. "Unimancers all over the world are on standby for when you need them. When Valentine breaks through, you'll have the full attention of the collective. What else can I provide you, sir?"

"You've done enough. Ruth, if you wouldn't mind – I need to join 'mancies with you. With all of you."

Ruth recoiled, her normally-blank face contorted with fear.

"No offense, Mr Tsabo," she said. "You damn near wrecked our network the last time with those rules you implemented–"

"It won't be that way again," he assured them.

Ruth hesitated – *all* the Unimancers hesitated, their lips twitching as another argument swept through the collective. Their legs locked into place, their bodies seizing with the arguments' furor–

"There's no time for this!" Paul barked. "Join your 'mancy with me!"

He grabbed Ruth's hand, reaching out to the network...

And felt their desperate, grasping need.

Paul had been grieving for his lost morality the last time they'd connected, and so had willingly subsumed himself into their desire. Now he was determined to retain his own decision-making, and they grappled him – a drowning woman so desperate she'd cling to anything.

Everyone, Paul had realized, discussed Unimancy like it was something that had sprung up organically, the Earth's natural reaction to fighting the broach.

But someone must have been the first Unimancer.

He held back, determining what that person had been like.

Something shivered at the heart of the Unimancy network as he resisted their pull. Paul felt the first Unimancer's 'mancy seeping through him – a woman so lonely she'd fetishized the idea of harmony, obsessing over friendship and goodwill and sharing until she'd created communal magic.

She'd erased her sense of self to facilitate bringing others together.

And she was long dead. She had to be. The broach had been active for over seventy years, and Unimancy had been there to fight the broach once it crept across Europe. It was entirely possible she'd been dead for centuries.

Yet this nameless woman's convictions still held Unimancy together – and the idea that a 'mancer could connect to them and *not* be a part of them broke this dead woman's still-beating heart.

Panic surged across the Unimancer network as they flooded with panic that someone might leave, forced by reflexive 'mancies to drag Paul in deep–

He'll be your father-construct, Ruth thought in despair. *Forever second-guessing you, forever sifting through your secrets, so close you'll never escape–*

WHAT HAVE THEY DONE TO YOU?

Paul's outrage was a thunderclap that short-circuited the network.

Ruth felt Paul's wave of empathy, a tide of tenderness backed by a cold and rising fury, realized Paul was once again moving to protect his daughter–

Except Paul knelt to take *her* hand.

"My God." His eyes welled with tears.

He examined her mother-construct, appalled.

She'd not been prepared for him to care about her – but he was networked into the hivemind enough to rifle through her history, saw the Mom-construct's endless lesson-prison…

Children should be free, Paul told her.

Ruth bristled. *I'm not a child*, she protested.

She gasped as Paul flooded her with his image of Aliyah – strong, unrestrained, beautiful – and Ruth realized that to Paul Tsabo, calling someone a child was no insult. A child was, to him, the purest form humanity could take – someone to be nourished and nurtured to become whatever they wanted to be, not pigeonholed by rules and restraints.

Paradoxically, he believed in bureaucracy because good guidelines set other people free.

You wanted Aliyah to find her own path, Ruth thought, stunned. Despite standing in so many memories of other people's upbringings, she'd never once contemplated that parents *could* need their children's independence.

"Yes," Paul whispered. "I want it for you too."

He reached into the Mom-construct – and, viewed through Paul's eyes, Ruth realized her Mom-construct was merely an elaborate set of instructions. Paul froze the mother-construct in place while he analyzed the laws that governed it, mapped out its millions of branching paths.

It was a program.

Like any program, it could be uninstalled.

And if the Mom-construct had experienced any fear at the idea of its dissolution, Ruth might have moved to defend it. Yet the Mom-construct expressed no concern; it waited patiently as Paul examined it line by line, asking, *Am I no longer needed?*

Paul turned to Ruth. *I don't know. Is she needed, Ruth?*

Ruth had always said if she *could* get rid of the Mom-construct, she *would* have. But now the choice was here, she realized she'd never hear her mother's voice again, never sense her mother's pride...

Aliyah pulled Ruth close. *Are you ready to leave her behind?*

I thought I was, Ruth thought. *But now...?*

For the first time since her mother had died, Ruth burst into tears – long, chest-racking tears, the tears of a girl who'd been so horrified she'd never gotten a proper outlet for her grief. The only way to satisfy this ersatz mother was to be so hyper-competent that it left no room for any emotion but cold anger.

Now she could leave the Mom-construct behind, she remembered all the things she'd secretly treasured.

Ruth sagged into Aliyah's arms, truly mourning her loss for the first time.

The hivemind wrapped tendrils around Paul's magic, trying to fuse with him.

He reached deeper into the network, refusing to be subsumed. As he'd mapped out the mother-construct's directives, he'd felt those imperative command-structures in the collective.

Ruth's mother had not, in fact, come up with the idea of the Mom-construct. The edumancer, more than anyone else, had understood how Unimancy had worked, realizing the collective was guided by a psychic operating system templated off one woman's final desires.

Unimancy, Ruth thought, dizzied. *It too is governed by one woman's dying wish. She's locked everyone into her strengths – and her terrors–*

Paul nodded. *Yes. But it doesn't have to be.*

He delved down into Unimancy's rules, found the core axioms that allowed them to exist in the same mindspace.

Perhaps Unimancy had been alive when it started – but now its creator was dead, the 'mancy had been reduced to a set of procedures. The personality had been boiled away, leaving behind rules designed to provide order when no qualified minds remained to make decisions.

At its core, Unimancy was a form of bureaucromancy. But the worst kind of bureaucracy: one without compassion to guide it.

These rules can be altered, Paul thought, his fingers tangled in the deepest and most complex portions of the Unimancer hivemind. *You panic when you disagree because* she *panicked when people argued. You can only hold one opinion because* she *could only hold one opinion.*

I can help you change this into a world you choose.

The hivemind lit up with discussion – and as it did, Paul held the Unimancy internals open, demonstrating the artificial distress flares shooting through the network whenever raucous discussions hit critical mass, showed the ways in which Unimancy guided them towards certain conclusions.

These were good rules, Paul said, contemplating the beauty that bound Aliyah and Ruth – a well-thought-out magical system that had lasted for decades. *But together, we could tweak this framework so you're more accepting of new input, more accepting of divergent opinions. Your decisions would become more complicated… but they'd also be more…*

Honest? Ruth suggested.

Yes. More powerful. But, Paul added, *I won't do this to you against your will. Do you want this?*

Swirls of discussion rose up, debating risks versus advantages. Paul stood away from the hubbub.

The Unimancers came to a conclusion – recognizing Paul's suggested changes would make them more resilient, able to handle unexpected crises better, able to come to consensus in more organic ways.

Paul's upgraded Unimancy could save the world.

We agree, said the hivemind.

As Paul restructured them, he laughed joyously. Once, he'd vowed to destroy them.

Now, he'd make them magnificent.

As they laughed, the sky sagged like an overloaded garbage bag. The heavens *bulged*, eye squeezed from a crushed skull, rippling with insectoid limbs–

They heard the faint but unmistakable noise of Valentine screaming – lost, hopeless, stretched thin as the sky itself.

Her Nintendo DS leapt off the ground like a jumping bean.

The twin screens cracked.

The sky convulsed, a boom resonating across the orchard. Three seconds of silence. The heavens retreated, resetting to their previous position, the save point having reset her position.

When the sky restarted, Valentine was still screaming.

Her screens had gone dark.

Paul grabbed his legal pad and started writing out the new Contract.

FIFTY-TWO
Tumbled, From the Burning Sky

Valentine tumbled

why do you fight

She was beating them she was *beating* the monsters, that was the irony. She'd melded her videogames, herding the monsters into Pac-Man mazes and sliding around corners on Sub-Zero's ice sheets to flip over them like Zelda and sneak up on them like Solid Snake and…

Valentine tumbled into the burning sky.

She'd taken apart Its armada, taking out 30% of Its forces, maybe 40% on a lucky run.

She was also dying, over and over, and each death was

Valentine tumbled into the burning sky.

Maybe she'd always fought. Maybe she'd never experienced anything but this fight. Maybe those memories of muscular hugs and a broad back were a hallucination she'd made up because she'd never experienced anything except this endless series of eviscerations.

Valentine tumbled into

And with each fight, she became convinced her life had been an illusion. She'd never been anything but the wrecking ball. She'd never been anything but a character in a videogame, and her reward for finishing the game would be some dumb kid turning off the console.

why do you fight

Why *did* she?

Valentine tumbled into

why do you FIGHT

There was no reward except the GAME OVER screen, a flash of emptiness before her flux blanked the world, and

Valentine

days she'd been fighting weeks she'd been fighting years she no longer knew

burning

all this fighting and she had nothing she had *nothing*

Valentine!

and this time when the game started she didn't move she let the buzzsects devour her left arm she let them chew the color from her hair she let them take her and

VALENTINE!

she knew that voice

The horse had collapsed; the Unimancers swaddled it in wet blankets. Imani stood shocked by the madman who'd galloped out of the woods on a stolen mare.

Robert knelt, cradling the shattered Nintendo in his hands with the tenderness of a man cupping his lover's face, staring deep into the wrecked screens.

"Valentine," he whispered, and stroked the plastic case like he was stroking her hair.

"...Robert?"

Something ruffled her hair – the first tender touch she could remember. Even though her stomach was a breeding ground for buzzsects, that touch filled her body with adoration.

valentine. The voice fuzzed at the edges like a blown speaker, malfunctioning technology on its last legs–

–but it was Robert.

No one else could speak three syllables and make her feel so loved.

As the buzzsects chewed her body away, Valentine thumbed the reload button.

The world went blank.

She hovered, trapped in a loading screen.

"Is that you?" she whispered.

it's me

She closed her good eye. Tears flowed down her cheek.

Robert was real.

He was *real*.

"I thought..." She choked back tears, hating sounding so weak. "I thought you weren't coming back..."

i lied

Her laugh was nearly a cough – but it was proof she *could* laugh, and that felt better than anything.

i heard you were in trouble i had to steal a map of europe and steal a plane and learn to ride a horse but i'm here

His quiet strength, flowing through that broken channel. Her breath was ragged, shocky, on the verge of breakdown; her hands trembled.

Robert loved her.

He knew what a fucked-up mess she was, and *he loved her*.

Robert said nothing, listening, filling the air with his attentiveness.

what do you need baby

"I..." Valentine stiffened, fists clenching. "I..."

tell me

"I need..."

what

"I NEED *YOU, GODDAMMIT*!"

And Valentine exploded out of the reload screen, cleaving through the hordes like an avenging angel, sweeping aside buzzsects, sundering razorplows.

"FUUUUCK!" she screamed, furious and embarrassed; her voice thundered across the heavens as she fought to get back to the man she loved. And the earth could explode and the universe could shatter and everything could burn in flames so long as she got to feel her Robert in her arms one last fucking time.

Selfish, beautiful, unhindered need fueled Valentine's final rebellion.

why do you fight the Thing said, and she slammed megatons of power down its throat, scouring unthinkable beasts away in waves of white fire, and she pointed down at Robert, at Paul, at Aliyah–

"I FIGHT FOR THE PEOPLE I LOVE!" And even then, she could not quite bring herself to say she needed to be *with* the people she loved, but she knew her need at last.

As the Thing roared in protest, she poured everything into one last burst of skill.

She'd spent the last ten days scouting techniques to destroy her enemy – and now she executed her plans to perfection. She slammed down blue walls to sweep through them as a frilly-bowed Ms Pac-Man gulped down their energy, organized buzzsects into formations to pick them off with Galaga shots, hopped onto her Tron-cycle to weave barriers between razorplows, turned into Kirby to vacuum up the pustulents.

She stepped into their dimensions, trailing her own mishmash of videogame logic, becoming the monster that monsters feared because when she won the game she would go *home* she got to go *home*, and when Robert was her goal there was no enemy she could not destroy.

She herded the remaining monsters into one place – and slammed her finger onto the Defender Smart Bomb button, detonating every last one.

Valentine scoured the gateway clean of everything but the Thing itself.

"Baby," she whispered, telling her man she'd triumphed – but she was miles up in the stratosphere. She only picked out Robert's tiny dot among the mountain range because he'd gathered together the smoking shards of her Nintendo DS.

He loved her.

He loved her.

Valentine fell into a deep and blissful serenity, the madness that fueled her 'mancy quelled, the wind whipping past as she fell backwards into dreams.

She never noticed the flux-inferno erupting from her body, freed at last once the cycle had completed, black flames trailing behind her like an annihilating comet. The flux pressed in around her, demanding what she feared–

–but Valentine was so at peace, it found nothing to latch onto.

The Thing lunged forward to grab the flux.

Unconscious, Valentine tumbled from the burning sky.

FIFTY-THREE
All the President's Women

Officially, the world leaders had called an emergency summit to confer about the European broach's growing instabilities.

That had been a cover story mapped out long in advance. The heads of state were actually bunkered in Australia's western end, on the opposite side of the world from the broach, waiting to see if the world would end.

The President had prepared as best she could for this day: several drafts of speeches had been written to cover outcomes ranging from "total success" to "abject failure." General Kanakia had warned them not to be near any Unimancer, as their efforts to contain the broach might cause an "overflow" – whatever that meant – so various security teams had combined to ensure they were fifty miles away from any Unimancer. The Emergency Broadcast system was prepped in case the dead zone over Europe widened.

She'd hoped this day would never arrive. Or, at least, that it wouldn't arrive on her watch.

On the way here, she'd done a test reading of the "humanity is about to be extinguished" speech, and had thrown up afterwards.

It had been a good speech. They'd had years to work on it. Every President had to approve the annihilation speech presented to them the day they took office – a brutal induction ceremony to remind them there were some things even

Presidents could not control.

The other world leaders had gathered in the briefing chamber. Some were newly elected, wondering why they'd been put in charge just as things skidded into shit; others had been dictators for decades, chewing out their aides to take out their frustrations.

They all looked frustrated, afraid, tense. Each had armies at their disposal. Aircraft carriers. Nukes.

Nothing would help against a broach. Classified files had demonstrated what happened when an experimental nuclear explosion had tried to seal a broach in the late 1940s, and the results hadn't been pretty.

The President, like all world leaders, loathed 'mancy – and not just because it caused messes. No, the worst thing about 'mancy was that only 'mancers could *fix* those messes. Paul Tsabo had demonstrated some new power that altered the broach – a power that held potential to heal or exacerbate it.

If SMASH and Paul Tsabo couldn't fix the problem, then no one could.

Magic forced even the most power mad tyrant to admit fallibility.

Worse, she couldn't tell anyone. "Everyone might die tomorrow" would not be soothed by the addendum of "in a worst-case scenario." It had been agreed decades ago that should the broach go critical, no announcements would be made until they could ensure panicked riots would be their least concerns.

Her staff had been on edge since General Kanakia had broken the news. It was hard, sending them home to their grandchildren. You couldn't negotiate with the broach, you couldn't science it away, you could just... hope.

They hadn't even let her bring her family. This was a small bunker, meant for Armageddon.

So they'd been holed up, guards relaying information from distant Unimancers – their only reliable information source, since radio signals degraded over broach areas – seeing if the problem would improve.

"Ms President," the Chief of Staff said. "Reports are, the Unimancers have gone dark."

She polished off her Scotch. "All right. It's go time."

"But..."

"But *what*?"

The Chief of Staff drew the President's attention to the banks of satellite feeds overhead.

The President leaned forward, watching something hideous emerge from the broach in five-second snapshotted updates.

"Is that... is that Thing visible from *space*?" she asked.

The world leaders gripped their seats, hoping their children would live to see tomorrow.

FIFTY-FOUR
Trying Hard to Be the Shepherd

Paul felt Valentine's flux before he saw it – a dull implosion that rumbled through his bones, wilted the flowers in Aliyah's grove.

Then the sun snuffed out.

Valentine's flux swept across the sky like a volcanic eruption, searching for anything to go wrong – Valentine had collapsed at the end of her battle, giving the flux no time to hunt for her fears, and no one else was nearby for it to latch onto. It rippled through the atmosphere, a predatory storm...

Paul hadn't finished writing the Contract.

And as the flux brushed against the jagged fragments of demon dimensions protruding into our space, it set off a chain reaction. Broach after broach after broach went off like fireworks as Valentine's flux undid the fragile threads of reality. The broaches crisscrossed, overlapped, shredding space until a mountainous white hole punched through to our world.

A thousand wet holes irised open within the Thing, bellowing triumph.

Paul's jaw slackened as he took in the Thing in its fullness – its armada had been annihilated, but its curving spines stabbed arcs through conventional geometry. His eyeballs throbbed, and Paul felt his neurons' inadequacy – this tiny cluster of organic material between his ears couldn't process the billions of ways this Thing casually violated all his assumptions about life.

His limbs seized up as Paul's mind spiraled into the Thing's bulging nests of veins. The Thing hissed out sporous eyeball-clouds to see what It invaded. It wedged bulbous pseudopods into the gap, pushed a seesaw head through–

"*Dad!*" Aliyah shouted. "*Kick its ass!*"

As though all he needed was encouragement to defeat it.

What he needed was a Contract, and there was no time left to write one.

Paul squared his shoulders – the temptation was to hold his daughter tight and shield her from the truth. Let her die surprised, rather than watching despair consume her.

But...

Help me be the guardian.

Paul held up the legal pad, showing the scant few paragraphs he'd written before the sky had burst open. "I can't, Aliyah – the Contract's not finished–"

"What do you need?"

The apocalypse was crashing down on his daughter's doorstep, and she demanded data to form plans. Her mother would be proud. "I was... I was going to redistribute Valentine's flux to buy us time–"

"Time for what?"

"To drive it back. If we could drive It back into the demon dimensions, I can fix this. But I need a Contract to redistribute her flux among the Unimancers–"

"I don't."

Aliyah stood at attention, looking at the blackfire chaos as though she could snatch it from the sky.

But all Paul saw was a thirteen year-old girl standing in the way of a hurricane.

"Aliyah..." He stammered; each word brought him closer to a future he could not bear. "I'd have to pour her flux into you – enough bad luck that the slightest doubt would annihilate you. And you'd have to use that flux to drive that Thing back."

"If I buy you time, can you finish the job?"

Paul wanted to say *I haven't tested my theory yet.*

But if he doubted his plans, so would she. And the flux

would destroy her.

"I can win," he told her. "I can win if you drive it back."

She cracked her knuckles, tilting her head back to take in the Thing's immensity. The Thing extended bladed tendrils, reaching for the still-massive flux clouds billowing through the air. Opening the broaches above Bastogne hadn't dimmed Valentine's flux one bit.

The black cloud of fatal luck swept across the horizon, shattering ridges as it touched the ground, vacuuming up rubble, splintering forests.

"Give it to me," she said.

Paul remembered her trapped in a soot-choked apartment, her lungs sizzling as she breathed in superheated air. He remembered the nurses intubating her, her crisped skin sticking to the stretcher, the scent of burning hair.

He remembered watching his daughter die.

for you it is always fire

But she had been a little girl then, caught in an accident. She hadn't chosen to be there when the gas main went up. Paul wondered if he could have borne it better if Aliyah had risked the fire to save someone's life.

Help me be their guardian.

Paul imagined his daughter not as a victim, but as the fireman.

He tore off the half-written Contract, scribbled a new one.

Aliyah Tsabo-Dawson agrees to take on her father's flux debt.

Simple. A family matter. No legalese, just a straightforward transfer.

He held out the pen to her, the pad trembling. But Aliyah glared the Thing down as though she'd found something beautiful.

Which he supposed she had.

She'd found her purpose.

"I got this," she assured him.

Paul was not at all sure they had this. But he reached up with his 'mancy, using the rights of salvage to claim Valentine's stray flux.

FIFTY-FIVE
Listen

A tornado of accidents barreled down from above, slipping out from underneath the Thing's contorted limbs and into Daddy. Dreadful permutations poured into him, the pressure growing until Daddy's bones creaked...

The contract glowed a cathode-ray green.

The flux erupted from her father, fountaining from his body into the legal paper.

Keep your minds blank, she told the Unimancers. *Here it comes...*

The flux smashed into Aliyah like a freight train, sending her flying backwards as Daddy screamed–

The flux raked her skin, demanding to know what she loved, interrogating her with physical blows as it tried to rattle loose anything Aliyah feared, a tempest of hatred determined to destroy *something*...

Daddy has this, she thought, ignoring the pain as she tumbled across the rocky soil. *I buy him time, he fixes this, we win.*

Yet the flux was too much. An ocean of anger poured into her. Blood gushed from her nose; flux stomped her into Bastogne's soil, her bones flexing...

A small woman in China absorbed the flux for her.

The flux slapped Aliyah's cheeks, howling, furious – Valentine had tricked the universe for ten days straight, *someone* had to pay, the payment had to be *personal*, and Aliyah's hands quivered as the universe demanded to know why she had such faith in her father, and...

A burly man in Mozambique took her pain away.

The vehement cyclone roared down into her – but time after time, just as Aliyah was sure she'd burst, someone else in the Unimancers stepped in to fill themselves with stolen flux – a transgender man in Mexico, a polyamorous triad in Iowa, a Yemen soldier...

The Unimancers distributed this catastrophic tide among them, each man teeming to capacity with more flux than anyone in history had generated. Unimancers across the globe spasmed as tattered black clouds leapt across continents to flow into them.

A flicker of doubt would unleash this planet-shattering power loose in Mozambique or Mexico or Madagascar. But the Unimancers tuned into Aliyah's twin faiths:

She believed in her father.

She believed in her Unimancer sisters.

All the rage in the world would not budge her from that serene grace, and the Unimancers held fast to her certainty.

Seven thousand strong joined up to share in the universe's savage anger at what Valentine had done. Even the neglected ones had come back to the hivemind – she felt Yoder, promising Aliyah he would be strong as stone.

Aliyah thought they might overflow – but Ruth stepped in to take the last of it, her eyes burning black, thousands of 'mancers straining to contain the unthinkable.

Aliyah we can't hold this forever

We can't redirect flux that's what your father does

What are we supposed to do?

Aliyah blinked away blood. She took in the Thing as it roared disapproval, scratched open sundered broaches to make room to step through.

Her gaze was clear and unafraid.

I want you to listen to me.

FIFTY-SIX
What Aliyah Said

It's not fair.

I burned in an apartment. My skin blistered to the bone. My dad's magic couldn't save me.

It's not fair.

A terrorist turned me into a 'mancer, and the first thing I did with my magic was murder her.

It's not fair.

I found friends who loved my magic, and a maniac pyromancer killed them to teach me a lesson.

It's not fair.

I can't live in Morehead. I can't live in Bastogne. I can't heal my scars. I can't ever be normal again; the best I can do is to give my life to keep someone else safe.

It's not fair.

But none of you had a good life. I know that because you're 'mancers. We only became obsessed with videogames or rock-balancing or statistics because we lost everything else we loved.

We retreated into a fantasy world so we could be happy somewhere – and believed in that fantasy so much, it became true.

We've done magic because we believe the impossible. And today, I have one impossible lie we must believe, or we will fail:

I want you to believe we can make this fair.

The Unimancers froze at the audacity of Aliyah's words.

We've suffered. We've sacrificed. We've been silenced. And I want you to believe the insane idea that every bad thing we have ever endured occurred to put us here, with these strengths, on this day, to stop that Thing.

And if we drive that Thing back, then our suffering had a purpose. We weren't abandoned freaks – we were the world's secret plan to save itself.

Magic is an argument. My daddy taught me that. Magic's just how we convince the universe there's a better way to do things. The stronger your belief, the less flux there is – and if you believe with all your heart, there is *no flux.*

If we believe the Universe meant for us to be here to stop that Thing, then that will be true.

Her words struck home. But the flux still vibrated through them, seeking doubt, a continent-obliterating storm ready to destroy them.

But what about the flux? Ruth asked. *Do you want us to will it away?*

No, Aliyah thought.

She raised one finger, aimed it squarely at the Thing as It tore the last of the broaches open.

I want you to aim it.

FIFTY-SEVEN
For One Last Time, I Need Y'all to Roar

The hivemind erupted into a ferocious argument – the greatest debate the collective had ever experienced. Aliyah asked the hivemind to cherish the things that had hurt them – which was absurd.

But Aliyah had *told* them it was an absurd idea, had *told* them it was a lie, and the philosophomancers pointed out that technically everything they'd ever done with 'mancy was a lie.

Lies, they realized, had been potent tools for good when the right people had believed them in the right way.

Like the idea of justice.

Like the idea of fairness.

Like the idea of love triumphing over all.

I know it's not true, Aliyah said. They felt her burns, her grief over her dead friends, her howling loneliness before she'd found the Unimancers. *But wouldn't it be nice?*

Paul had let Aliyah grow in her own way. He'd never once tried to extinguish that spark of rebellion within her.

In keeping that intact, he'd kept alive one strong flicker of childish hope. A hope so strong the Unimancers clung to Aliyah's tranquility when the flux threatened to erupt, a soothing calmness promising *this will be all right.*

They could not believe this forever. But for one moment they *could* believe every torment they'd suffered had been preparation to pierce this black beast's heart.

They could believe their lives had meaning.

Which, of course, was the greatest lie of all.

And in a 'mancer's hands, lies became magnificent truths.

The flux boiled within them, transforming from something furious at them to something furious at this intruder.

And as the last of the counterarguments fell, one word swept through the hivemind – a word that meant more than it ever had before in their history, because for the first time it had been arrived at without magical assistance to force them into it:

Consensus.

FIFTY-EIGHT
After Me, There Will Be No More

Pure white magic erupted from Aliyah's fingertip.

It punched a hole through the Thing's mountainous torso, hurling Its continent-sized body miles backwards into the demon dimensions.

FIFTY-NINE
Which Can Eternal Lie

The Thing laid sprawling on the far side of the demon dimensions.

It twitched.

It was like watching a mountain range give birth as the cavern Aliyah had punched through It closed up, pseudopods rising, Its body reforming into something more hideous.

We didn't kill It, Ruth thought, horrified. *All that power, and we only drove it back–*

I don't know if it can *be killed,* Aliyah thought.

Then how do we…?

We hope Daddy seals the broach.

SIXTY
Do I Dare Repair the Universe?

The Thing had ripped the broach open from horizon to horizon. Paul reached out with his 'mancy, feeling the tattered threads of our universe floating across the gap.

He picked through floating buzzsect corpses until he found a scrap of gravity. He found the concept of light piled up behind the atmosphere, the sun's energy trying desperately to push its way through the wreckage. He found what was the idea of mass bouncing around the broach's edges.

He reshaped the tatters into something resembling our universe.

The Unimancers lined up behind him, ready to assist. But as he mapped the places where things were too ruined to patch together, Paul realized:

They could never remake the world.

They'd been so desperate to return to what had once been that they'd sacrificed stability for nostalgia. Their belief could strong arm the local laws into limping along in a mockery of "normal" physics for a time…

…but eventually, the disjunct between how they wanted things to work and how things *needed* to work in the aftermath caused things to fly apart.

Just like he could never restore Aliyah back to the girl she'd been before the fire.

Yet he might nurture her scars into strengths.

So instead of pouring his willpower into the broken lands, Paul called upon the physicists and mathematicians and artists in the collective to ask a different question:

What do these new rules need to flourish?

If the Bohr radius was rounded down, what other laws needed to change to accommodate that? If something had erased the concept of light in this swatch of sky, what energies would grow to replace it?

Some of these changes would make it impossible for human life to exist there. And that, too, was fine; Paul could never have thrived in the Unimancers' rough-and-tumble arguments.

But Aliyah was happy there.

So Paul asked what the *universe* needed to be stable instead of wrestling it into what *he* needed.

Which required near-limitless imagination – the physicists envisioning alternate dimensions to exacting perfection, the mathematicians spinning off subgroups to handle the complex math required to create alien logics.

But wasn't creation always more challenging than recreation?

The rip in the sky sealed over, inch by inch, as the hivemind's combined brainpower determined the complex rules needed to create exquisite microuniverses ready to weather any challenge, a thousand interlocking bureaucracies holding hands across the sky. Instead of eradicating these mutant strains of Earth, Paul and the Unimancers encouraged their resiliency.

They're stronger, Aliyah thought in wonder. It was true; these new rules were interlocked tighter than ever – so perfectly fit, there simply wasn't room for magic to exist within them.

The Thing roared, shoving spiked claws through in an attempt to tear the new physics apart – but they had, unwittingly, built the perfect jail to hold It.

The hivemind staved off mental exhaustion – they'd built a thousand different universes in minutes, found ways to smooth over the transitions so these microverses wouldn't tear each other asunder, meshed them into the existing universe without too much damage. Some of their wisest physicists passed out from the strain.

But the remainder picked up the slack, cemented off gaps into the demon dimensions.

The Thing bellowed, ramming tentacles into dwindling holes–

And disappeared.

"My God, Paul." Robert dropped the smoking ruins of Valentine's Nintendo. "Did... we win? Did we seal the broach?"

"We sealed *this* broach." He collapsed onto the stump, hands on his ribs, breathing heavily. "That's... three miles fixed."

When he looked at the sky, it was with the radiant expression of a man who'd found a lifetime of satisfying work.

"Europe, however..." His gratified chuckle was deep and hearty. "There's thousands of miles of reality fractures here. And we can't shut SMASH down whenever we fix a broach; we'll have to use smaller teams, figure out which areas will do the most good once repaired. This will take decades to stabilize."

"My God." Robert sat down next to him on the stump. "But you went nuts when I told you how long it'd take to change America's 'mancer laws – why's this slog any different?"

"Good question." Paul dabbed blood from his eyes. "It isn't. *I'm* different. And I wish I had time to explain, but your girlfriend's about to hit the ground."

SIXTY-ONE
Got Me Hoping You'll Save Me Right Now

"She's gonna splatter!" Robert screamed. Valentine dropped towards the ground, her black dress trailing behind her like a goth comet.

Paul knew how much time they had left before impact. That had been part of their calculations. She'd been high up in the stratosphere, giving her precious minutes before impact – though defeating the Thing and sealing the broaches had eaten up precious time.

He had exactly fifty-five seconds to convince Robert.

"You know why she didn't marry you?" he asked.

"Jesus, Paul! Could you *have* better timing?"

"She thought you stopped being crazy! You gave up 'mancy, she didn't. She thought you'd never stay without–"

"Did she tell you that?"

"I'm her best friend I know her *shut up!*" Paul yelled, as Valentine plummeted closer. "The point is, she thinks you're not a 'mancer because you gave up being Tyler Durden! *You* think you're not a 'mancer! But dammit, Robert, nobody masters all the skills you have that quickly without a little magic. You're so subtle even *you* don't realize you're doing it."

Robert flailed. "How does *that* help us?"

"She thinks you're not crazy about her. You used to be a goddamned *Fight-Club*-'mancer. Cartoonish violence was your forte. If anyone can catch Valentine... it's you."

Robert looked stricken. "Paul... I'm not Tyler Durden anymore."

They heard the whistle as she approached the ground. "How crazy is your love?"

It wasn't a good plan, Paul thought. It was an improvised scheme that required Robert to love Valentine to a level of literal insanity.

Then again, Paul thought, if he *wasn't* that in love with her, maybe it would be a mercy if Valentine splattered.

Robert ran, panicked, as Valentine plunged downward, holding his massive arms wide...

"You stole a plane!" Paul yelled. "You learned to ride a horse! You can catch her!"

Robert cracked his neck as Valentine dropped towards him like a high fly ball.

Then he squeezed his eyes shut, clenched his massive hands into beefy fists, quivering as his muscles locked into place. He let loose a low moan, which rose to an anguished shriek as he screamed loss at the heavens.

Paul almost yelled at Robert not to give up, but then he realized: *Robert's imagining what life would be like if Valentine died.*

Robert Paulson squared his shoulders.

He refused to believe the world could exist without Valentine.

With a ripple of long-buried magic, Valentine dropped safely into his arms.

She clambered out.

"Sweetie!" Robert grasped at her. Valentine squirmed away. "Sweetie, you..."

Her hair had gone white. Her fingers twitched.

"Sweetie, you look like hell," he finished.

"I got about two minutes left before I collapse," she huffed, staggering towards Paul like a broken jalopy.

"*Tsabo!*" she yelled. "*Tell me you have the fucking thing!*"

"...what thing?"

She shook her head. "Don't you fucking tell me you don't have it. You file *everything* away. You're a... a magical hoarder. 'Mancer. A hoardomancer. And I saw you pick it up, so you give it to me *right the fuck now* or I will knock your ass into the demon dimensions."

Paul patted his pockets, confused. "Valentine, I don't know what you're talking about…"

His palm pressed against a long-forgotten metal circle in his suit pocket.

Paul huffed in relief, and took out Robert's engagement ring. .

She *flumfed* down on him so hard that he thought she'd collapsed – but no, it was a weary hug. She kissed him on his cheek, leaving behind a heart-shaped smear of lipstick.

"You don't need me anymore, do you?" she whispered. He heard her terror that he might ask her to stay with him…

"I need you happy." He gave her a push. "Go."

She staggered woozily to Robert, who looked around as though he hoped one of the celebrating Unimancers would tell him what to do.

Valentine grabbed his hand, falling to one knee.

"Robert Paulson," she said, her voice taking on an absurdly solemn overtone. "You… hey, is that your real name?"

He smiled. "It is now."

"Fine. Robert Paulson – I fucking cleaved the heavens asunder in a TPK to get back to your finely muscular ass, and you'd *think* that would be fucking enough of a proposal to satisfy you. But no. You're a *romantic.*

"Goddammit, I've beat up a lot of pretty boys in my time, and you're the prettiest. You're my fuckin' anchor. You're the one who gives me the advice I inevitably regret when I just as inevitably ignore it. And…"

She scrubbed away tears.

"Goddammit, Robert…"

Her voice dropped to a low whisper.

"I need you."

She slipped the ring onto his finger, then leapt up to stomp around in an angry circle.

"Godfuckahorse, you mothersucking…!" She stomped her foot. "*Consent*, Valentine, consent. You gotta check he says *yes* before you put the goddamned marriage-manacle on those suckable fat fingers, and…"

"Yes."

She froze, clasping her hands against her breastbone. "…you sure?"

He nodded shyly.

She bent him backwards, kissing him deeply.

She broke the kiss. "I might fuck other guys, you know. I reserve that right."

"Will you come back to me afterwards?"

She jerked her thumb towards the heavens. "Ask that Lovecraftian Xerox what I do to anyone who gets between us."

The Unimancers cheered. General Kanakia had retreated to report their triumph before some nervous government fired off a nuke.

Ruth had already snuck Aliyah into the bushes for a discreet kiss. Which might have been more discreet if when they'd kissed, they a) hadn't blazed with Unimancy, and b) the flowers around them hadn't swelled from desiccated remnants back into vibrant blossoms, popping open across the field in perfumed bursts.

Imani kissed Paul hard enough to draw his attention. And for a moment, everything was all right. His wife was safe, Valentine was safe, the world was safe.

His daughter was safe.

For now.

Imani pulled him tight, following his gaze to Aliyah. "You can't keep her forever," she told him.

"I know."

"I'm proud of her." Imani spoke cautiously, as if probing a fresh wound. "Are you proud of her?"

He looked at his daughter's protective black Kevlar, the way she high-fived the other Unimancers, the way her squadron thronged around her like she was the most precious thing in the world.

He wanted to drag her away from the military and back to someplace she wouldn't get hurt. She was still in danger; she would always be in danger. That fear would never subside.

But then he focused on her triumphant smile as she hugged

her friends: "We saved the world! We saved the goddamned *world*!"

YOU WILL LOSE YOUR DAUGHTER IN WAYS YOU NEVER IMAGINED

He had lost her.

But she'd found herself.

"Couldn't be prouder," he said.

EPILOGUE
Welcome to Morehead

Eight Months Later

The people of Morehead came out to watch their broach get sealed – even though the government had warned them about the risk.

The Morehead broach was comparatively stable. But the United States continued to freak out – as America was wont to do, on the rare occasions anything hurt it personally – so General Kanakia had offered to heal it as a PR gesture.

As such, Aliyah felt SMASH treating this miniscule broach with an uncommon respect. Five thousand of her fellow Unimancers had juggled their schedules to ensure they'd be rested in case things got out of hand.

It hadn't looked much like the Morehead she'd left behind – the grass had died where the broach's sputtering slow-light had bombarded it with alien radiations. The remaining area had been covered with pop-up science labs designed to monitor the broach.

But only Washout Field had broached. There had been three other fields – and they teemed with reporters and curiosity-seekers and protestors.

Most of the crowd was solemn. The protestors, however, shouted and waved signs: U NEED NO UNIMANCERS. SMASH SMASH. MAGIC MAKES MONSTERS. They pressed close to

FIX

the boundary before the Unimancy crowd control squadrons courteously warned them away.

Still, the protestors bumped chests, hoping to spur a nice ugly confrontation for the evening news.

Ruth and Aliyah were stationed on Gold Field, the field with the biggest crowds. Mom had assigned them to be the Unimancers' friendly face – two small girls on the front lines made SMASH look less like a military operation.

Still, the protestors asked pointed questions about what Europe was *really* like. Wasn't fiddling with reality dangerous? What had happened to the Unimancers at the start of the Reclamation?

Aliyah gave her standard PR-friendly answers as to why she'd become a Unimancer, reassuring them they'd reclaimed over ninety square miles of European territory since the Reclamation; this broach would be trivial to stabilize.

They're terrified, Ruth said, amazed at the crowds. *Yet they can't look away.*

Well, this will be the first 'mancy most of them have seen, Aliyah reminded her.

Why are they here, if they think it'll blow up in their face?

People used to camp out next to battlefields, Ruth's mother told them. *During the Civil War, they'd set up picnics and take bets.*

Thanks, Mom, Ruth said – and meant it.

She's more of a trivia engine these days, Aliyah thought. Daddy had disabled portions of the Mom-construct, relaxing its grip on Ruth.

I kinda like that, Ruth thought back. *I get to see what Mom thought was interesting.*

Did that guy offer us a beer? Aliyah thought.

Creeper, Ruth shot back. *We're underage.*

Hey, we kicked the European broach in the nads. Maybe we should have a beer. But the thought of "beer" led to beermancers expressing dismay at the thought of drinking American swill, and brewmancers promising to brew up much tastier beverages if they wanted to experiment, and physicians...

"...Rachel?"

Aliyah was used to people recognizing her – she was the first of a new generation of Unimancers, or so the headlines said, and as such people treated her like they knew her.

Yet this girl *did* know her.

Savannah.

The lanky redheaded kid she'd played soccer with, all those months ago, back at Washout Field.

Aliyah almost rushed to hug her, but Savannah held her distance, looking terribly awkward.

You sense that tension? Ruth asked. The crowd had gone silent. Everyone in Morehead must have known Savannah was the girl who'd made friends with the 'mancer who'd destroyed their town.

Savannah looked worse for wear. Psychoanalysts in the hivemind kicked in to notice how Savannah's head was bowed lower these days, how she was more reluctant to make eye contact, how the protestors scowled down at her.

Aliyah opted for the gentlest approach. "You OK?"

Savannah gave a half-hearted nod. "Are *you* OK?"

With that, Aliyah realized Savannah had worried about *her* all these months. It must have been a whirlwind for the poor kid, having 'mancers infiltrate their soccer game, only to leave behind a smear in the sky and more questions than the government was willing to answer.

She was actually your fucking friend, Ruth thought, amazed.

"I'm doing good," Aliyah said. "I hope I didn't... you know..."

"Hasn't been easy," Savannah shrugged; Aliyah saw the blame Savannah had weathered. "Fixing the broach will help. Oh, and thank your dad for the check."

"...check?" Aliyah thought – and she sensed her dad through the collective as he prepared to seal the broach. He had become the general's second-in-command, expanding the European Safe Zones – and was expected to take up the mantle when the general retired after four decades of fine service.

Not that he was allowed on American soil. The President hadn't stopped the UN from giving Paul Tsabo a SMASH position, but she couldn't afford to look soft on 'mancers by letting Paul back into the country. So Daddy had to work through the collective.

Not that he minded – he and Mom seemed content to devote their lives to fixing Europe. The European Safe Zones were the best PR possible for individual 'mancers.

Still, he looked up from the stream of Unimancer data to send an image of a $30,000 insurance check he'd cut Savannah's family – to make up for the SUV Savannah's father had given them to escape.

"He says you're welcome."

"Some people told me that, uh…" Savannah studied her sneakers. "Rumor was, they pretended to kidnap me to capture you. I didn't like that. I told everyone this wasn't your fault – you never meant to do magic."

"They did use you as bait." Savannah blushed, realizing what she'd meant to Aliyah. "But I never blamed you for that."

She sighed. "Good." She looked at Ruth. "Is that your girlfriend?"

Aww, Jeez, this is like running into your ex at the mall, Ruth thought. *And she's a skinny redhead, too! You have a type.*

Be nice, Aliyah thought.

Of course I will. I like this one. Ruth extended her hand. "Hi. I'm Ruth. And yeah. I am."

Savannah looked startled, but shook Ruth's hand after a moment. "Sorry, Ruth. I wasn't expecting you to… to, you know, say your name. Are you one of those Unimancers who got their personalities back after the broach healed?"

"That's what her father says, anyway," Ruth said diplomatically.

In truth, Mom had decided Unimancers shouldn't have to act alike to stop freaking the mundanes… And so Dad had told everyone that fighting the Bastogne broach had altered the nature of Unimancy.

Nobody really understood magic anyway, so people had bought the lie. Ruth was just grateful she didn't have to pretend to be a brainburned zombie.

"Anyway." Savannah blushed. "It's good to see you. I just…

I wasn't sure if that was you. And... I mean, it's good to see you back. So... yeah. Thanks."

Savannah turned away to push through the wall of waving signs. Aliyah didn't know what to say. There had been friendship there, once... but Savannah had gone one way, and Aliyah had gone the other. While Aliyah had gone off to link in with the collective, Savannah had become a reluctant advocate for 'mancer rights – in a small town where terror of 'mancy must have been at an all-time high.

They were so different now.

Aliyah was back in front of that Wendy's, watching some scared kid try to connect – except back then, Savannah had welcomed her to Morehead. And Savannah had welcomed *her* back, only to find Aliyah changed beyond comprehension.

You can't let it end like this, Ruth thought.

"Hey!" Aliyah's voice was louder than she meant it to be, carrying across the Gold Field. News cameras focused in, broadcasting live.

Aliyah wished she knew what to say. And the Unimancers pressed forward; the pickupmancers offered icebreakers and the relationshipmancers offered tailored approaches and biomancers offered to change her pheromones, and...

Aliyah swept them aside to be herself.

"You still play soccer?" she asked.

Savannah squinted, as though she hadn't heard Aliyah properly – then gave a disgusted little head shake. "Haven't played since. To be honest, I didn't care for it that much."

"Neither did I," Aliyah said. "I just did it to find friends."

Savannah bobbed her head in shy agreement.

"But you know what I liked the idea of?" Aliyah asked.

"What?"

"The pizza you promised me after the game. So what do you say? One one-on-one match – no 'mancy, I promise – and we'll see whose skills are rustier. Winner buys pizza."

Savannah's smile was like the sun rising from behind clouds. "I'd like that."

"*Clear the fuckin' field!*" Ruth bellowed. The Unimancers

prepared to disperse the protestors, who lowered signs to block their way...

But a greater cry came from behind them. "*Let 'em play!*"

The protestors looked over their shoulder, found the rest of the crowd giving them stern glares.

There will always be people who hate, Aliyah thought. *They'll always stand in the front, stirring trouble, making the world look worse than it is.*

But there's always people behind the haters – strangers, waiting to get to know you.

And these people want to see what happens when we play.

The crowds cleared out a space for Aliyah and Savannah, shunting the protestors aside. Someone tossed them a soccer ball; someone else stepped into place to mark goal lines.

Savannah and Aliyah grinned, stepping into a new world:

A world where two kids could play soccer.

ACKNOWLEDGMENTS

So I destroyed Europe with a shrug.

I didn't plan on annihilating an entire continent. Yet when I wrote *Flex*, I thought, "How can I make it clear that unauthorized magic has some really riotous consequences?" and went, "Awww, hell, let's waste Europe. That'll show 'em!"

(Fun fact: When you destroy fictional continents, you *will* get hurt emails from your friends overseas, plaintively asking, "...what did we ever do to you?")

And you'd think that, as an author, I would understand that "wrecked continents" hold an allure for people. But no! I was completely shocked when the reviews for *Flex* came in and people confidently stated, "*The Flux* will clearly send them overseas to investigate Europe!" and I, with a completed manuscript for the sequel in hand, went, "Well, wouldn't *that* have been a hell of a plan?"

But really, I knew what the third book would be about. *Flex* was about creating a family. *The Flux* was about what happened when people tried to split that family apart for selfish reasons.

Fix was about what happened when people split that family apart for *altruistic* reasons. And Europe was the biggest stick I had to hit them where it hurts.

So anyway, to help confirm the details on my rampant Europe-destroying, I enlisted several wonderful folks:

Thanks to the members of the online group "Help Ferrett To Destroy Europe!" where several scientists (amateur and professional) discussed creative ways to break the laws of physics – which is surprisingly difficult to do and allow humans to survive! We are fragile, fragile little creatures. Anyway, I couldn't have done it without Alice Durand, Ben Criger, Jonathan Pai, Juliane Tran, Mike Longley, Nathan Gundlach, and Sarah Heile.

Thanks to Harold Overbay, who served on the USS Chicago and assures me that yes, Paul's plan would work, but only with the correct kind of launching tubes installed. If I got the deets wrong, well, that's on me.

Thanks to my friends in Kentucky, who explained to me what their local soccer league was like so I could annihilate their state. I should add that there is no Washout Field in Kentucky, as the people there are far too kind to split up their players so cruelly. That's all me. Everyone down in Kentucky I've ever met has been super-kind, and extremely generous with their delicious delicious bourbon. (Try the Blanton's.)

When I had zero idea how to fix the novel, a night of magical Velvet Tango Room drinks with my friend Catherine Kopytek – a partial inspiration for Valentine – helped straighten me out. If you liked the way Valentine smacked Paul down on the mountain, well, that was Catherine getting angry.

Shakira Searles cried a lot when we were holed up in a hotel room for a week (long story), and their tears helped me think I was getting this draft in shape. (I promise, they didn't cry for any other reason but the manuscript!)

And my critiquers, who helped me out:

Daniel Starr called the first draft of this manuscript "a fun ride," which was the danger sign that whoa, I needed to add a little more emotional torment up in here.

E Catherine Tobler said, "Aliyah sure complains about unfairness a lot," and encouraged me to use that. *Use* it? Reader, I *weaponized* it.

Graydancer has a lot of experience in high-protocol kink, so when he thanked me for including Butler I was pretty sure I hadn't screwed up the details too badly.

John Dale Beety and Miranda Suri pointed out that I really needed to flesh out the Valentine and Robert interactions to justify their existence. MOAR LOVE, MOAR BEATINGS,

Carolyn VanEseltine wanted to know why the universe was so mean to Paul, and Christina Russell demanded to have the laws of flux fleshed out more. Good call, people.

Grenacia hated the sunscreen scene. You don't see the sunscreen scene because she was right.

Ingvild B Husvik and Els van Vessem were positive in the final draft, and lemme tell you, by the time you've revised a damn book four times over, you need someone to tell you this mess of words is actually better than you think it is.

Benjamin Wilson, superfan, wanted even crazier magic. I tried to make it wild for you, man! I really did.

And lastly, Dr Phil Kaldon helped me out with the physics. Which is, sadly, the last interaction I had with Phil, one of Michigan's convention stalwarts and a generous soul. In fact, if we could have a moment of silence to honor a great man's passing...

∞

The Chapter Midway Through the End Credits

Valentine had never fucked on a beach before, but discovered sand got everywhere. Which, if your sex had a certain cruel edge, could be used creatively.

She collapsed, watching the stars in the warm Caribbean sky, holding a freshly-bruised Robert as he fell asleep in post-coital bliss.

Eventually, this would get boring. She wasn't engineered for monotony. Neither was Robert. In time, one of them would itch for adventure, and they'd move on.

They'd go back to Paul. Paul always had adventures.

But for now, feeling Robert wriggle deeper next to her, feeling the ocean surf at their feet, she basked in contentment. The only thing that could make this better was...

"Milkshake, ma'am?"

"Thank you, Butler," she said, and took the shake from Butler's tray.

ACKNOWLEDGMENTS II
Electric Boogaloo

Thanks, Phil.

And while we're holding a moment of grief, as readers of the series will know, Aliyah was heavily inspired by my goddaughter, Rebecca Alison Meyer, who passed away of brain cancer on her sixth birthday. She was extraordinary. I don't know that Rebecca would have become a magic-wielding lesbian commando at the age of thirteen, but I can't say I would have ruled it out either.

In the aftermath of the tragedy, Rebecca's mother Kat Meyer and my friend Karla Winans have helped found a charity to help families who've survived losses like Rebecca. And if you have some spare cash, donating to Rebecca's Gift at http://rebeccasgift.org/ would help make the world a little brighter in Little Spark's name.

And I've thanked a lot of people in past acknowledgments who I should thank again; everyone at Angry Robot, who have been really good about supporting this series, including Mike Underwood (the 'Mancer series' #1 fan), Marc Gascoigne and Phil Jourdan, and Penny Reeve. Thanks to my, er, best friend Angie, who never stopped believing in me. Thanks to Mom, Dad, and my daughters Amy and Erin – but heck, you've all made it in previous dedications, why am I thanking you here?

Oh, right, 'cause you're awesome. Thanks to Aileen, who listened to me complain late in the evenings on far too many occasions.

Thanks to every one of you who's reading this. If you got here, I'm presuming you came with me on the past journey of the last two books, and God, that means *so much* to me. (And if not, you've got two books of prequel to consume, so get crackin'!) And a special thanks to anyone who reviewed or referenced or mentioned any of my books; remember, every time a reader tells other people about the book they just read, an author gets their wings.

But if you've got this far, I'm sure some of you are asking one question: *Are there any more adventures?* And I hope there will be. I've got some vague ideas of what Valentine and Butler might get up to. But for right now, I think I've pushed the family as far as I can, and so if I'm gonna tell a new 'mancer story it'll probably be with some different 'mancers.

God willing, I'll return to this crazy magical world someday.

So keep up with me on my Twitter, @ferretthimself, or at my blog at *www.theferrett.com*. I'll catch ya around.

Oh! And if you've followed me thus far, you know damn well there's one person who I always end my acknowledgments by thanking. When I was writing four hours a night to try to fix this damn novel, my wife quietly cleaned the house for me when I slacked on my chores. She went for long plot-walks with me as I angsted, "How do I make this work?" She read endless pages. And she's always been brutally, gloriously honest when the words don't work.

She not only *supports* my dreams, she *enables* them. And man, I hope I lift her up half as high as she lifts me.

I love you, Gini.

Arf.

THE CHAPTER THAT COMES AFTER THE ACKNOWLEDGMENTS
Ferris Bueller Says to go Home

"Actually, pizza sucks," Aliyah said. "Anyone wanna get donuts?"

ABOUT THE AUTHOR

Ferrett Steinmetz is a graduate of both the Clarion Writers' Workshop and Viable Paradise, and has been nominated for the Nebula Award, for which he remains stoked. Ferrett has a moderately popular blog, *The Watchtower of Destruction*, wherein he talks about bad puns, relationships, politics, videogames, and more bad puns. He's written four computer books, including the still-popular-after-two-years *Wicked Cool PHP*. He lives in Cleveland, Ohio, with his wife, whom he couldn't imagine living without.

theferrett.com • twitter.com/ferretthimself

"This one-of-a-kind series ... is what might result if you put *Breaking Bad* and Reddit in a blender and hit 'frappé.'"

Barnes & Noble's Sci-Fi Blog

"The best kind of sequel: bigger, deeper, scarier, funner. Ferrett Steinmetz has achieved something rare in contemporary fantasy: a world that feels both truer and more magical than our own."

Ken Liu, author of *The Grace of Kings*

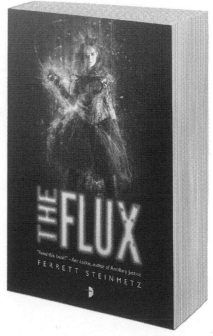

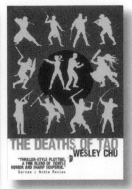
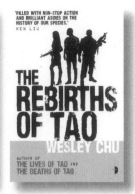

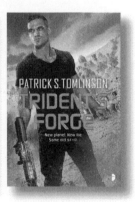

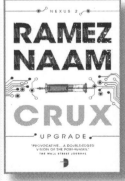

THE STORY NEVER ENDS

angryrobotbooks.com

twitter.com/angryrobotbooks